Diary of a Simple Girl

ENJOY!
Adriana

Diary of a Simple Girl

Adriana Caruso-Toncic

iUniverse, Inc.
Bloomington

Diary of a Simple Girl

This is a work of fiction. All of the characters, names, incidents, organizations, and dialogue in this novel are either the products of the author's imagination or are used fictitiously.

iUniverse books may be ordered through booksellers or by contacting:

iUniverse
1663 Liberty Drive
Bloomington, IN 47403
www.iuniverse.com
1-800-Authors (1-800-288-4677)

ISBN: 978-1-4620-2066-9 (sc)
ISBN: 978-1-4620-2067-6 (ebook)
ISBN: 978-1-4620-2068-3 (dj)

Library of Congress Control Number: 2011908507

Printed in the United States of America

iUniverse rev. date: 09/12/2011

To Lino, Stephen, Victoria and Vanessa—for always believing in their simple girl

Chapter One

❧

"Mom! Mommy! Mama!" Ella is shouting from what sounds like the bottom of the stairs. "Mama, where are you? I need you *N-O-W!*"

Oh, dear God, couldn't you have named me Louise, Susan, even Martha—anything but Mommy? How is it that not so long ago I longed to hear her call out "Mommy," while today I think I might jump from my fucking bathroom window if I hear it one more time? I look down at the delicate pink daisies on my La Perla bra and panties. *I might as well look pretty if I jump.*

Gee, I wonder what the neighbours might think though. Now *that* would give them something to talk about! "There goes Kat, all dolled up again" ... well, sort of, anyways. On second thought, who am I kidding? Knowing me, I'd probably get my bra strap caught on the lantern on the way down and only succeed at completely embarrassing myself—sprawled out on the grass stark naked instead of lying there like some heroine pining to get rescued by Prince Charming ... and then we cut to music, a crescendo of staccato piano notes à la Alicia Keys.

"Ella, sweetheart, Mama is upstairs in the bathroom," I yell, *trying to get ready for work.* "What's wrong, my angel?" I say in the sweetest, most loving voice I can muster up. Too late for an answer. I can hear Ella marching up the stairs, one by one, thrusting all of the mighty weight her tiny six-year-old frame can pack into each step she takes.

Princess Ella appears in the bathroom doorway, hands securely clinched on her small hips, her usually pouty lips pierced together in frustration, or is that anger? Actually, it appears to be both.

"I've been calling you!" Ella announces.

"I know you have, sweetheart, but as you can see, I'm in the bathroom trying to get ready for work. And besides, what do I always tell you? If you need me, come and find me, but please do not shout from the bottom of the stairs. Mommy does not like that." If that isn't the understatement of the year, I don't know what is.

Did I mention that I was having this tête-à-tête with Ella all the while still staring into the bathroom mirror? My Dior mascara wand, still held firmly between my right thumb and index finger, is taunting me the entire time—*apply me, twice if you can handle it, and you too will have long, sexy eyelashes just like all the gorgeous runway models have.* "I'm trying," I want to shriek back to the mirror. I bet those runway models don't have to deal with childish temper tantrums while some five-hundred-dollar-an-hour makeup artiste is applying their eyelash plumper. I insert the wand back into the tube; my lashes will have to wait for now. I feel it only appropriate to finally turn and face my precocious six-year-old at this point, especially since I am the one who is always trying to instil proper speaking etiquette in my kids. It seems only fair that I do the same. As I bend down to put my arms around Ella's firm round body and embrace her solid stance, I am met with what appears to be some *very* early preteen-age daughter attitude and the palm of a pudgy, cherubic hand in my face.

"You never listen to me!" Ella cries out from behind what appears to be a chocolate-streaked palm. *Yuck! Watch the lingerie, please!*

I sigh, heavily. Oh God, is this just the beginning of an argument that I am not going to win? I gently lower Ella's hand, moving it down to her side, and attempt for the second time this morning to envelop her body in my arms.

"Honey," I begin, using the sweetest "Mama" voice I can find, "first of all, I do listen to you; and second of all, it is extremely rude for a young lady to put her hand up to someone's face when she is speaking—or otherwise," I add. "Now just tell me what the problem is and why in heaven's name you are so upset."

I can see Ella is attempting to gather up all the courage a six-year-old can possibly find when preparing to have a royal meltdown. I know that with tears welling up in her eyes, a tsunami is about to erupt, and I, *Mama, Mommy, Mother,* am going to be the sole victim caught up in this storm. *Sucks to be me!*

"Michael says I'm stupid and have a pea-brain-mush-ball-dummy-head between my ears, and *I do not!*" Ella explodes into an ocean of tears.

I'm not sure whether to laugh or cry. Laugh at the fact that Ella is able to recite what her brother has said verbatim (and I'm sure it is), or cry that my baby girl has become trapped in a sea of hurtful emotions. Fast-forward twenty years, and I may be having this similar type of conversation with Ella, only then it might be some overeducated university jock that she will be going head-to-head with on a job interview. For now, I am happy (sort of happy) to be dealing with the juvenile emotions that are running rampant in my house. I continue to hold Ella between my bare arms in an attempt to quiet her shaking figure and try to soothe her with comforting and soft words as best as I can.

"Ella, honey, you are not a dummy-head. You are a beautiful, smart, and sweet little girl. Why do you allow Michael to upset you so much?" I ask rhetorically, since truth must be told, I don't care all that much about the answer at this very moment. I need to get ready! I know that engaging Ella in conversation right now will make me *really* late for work this morning. Yes, work! That thing we mommies try to do when we're not breaking up fights, wiping snotty noses, and trying to wrestle our offspring into clothing they clearly aren't interested in wearing. All the while, we are praying to God that they won't be late for the school bus, because then we will be stuck driving them to school and making ourselves late for work since we will get stuck behind the school bus they didn't seem able to get on!

I admit it! Work seems like play to me most days in comparison to what I do when I'm not at work and just being a mother to my three children. Yeah, right, *just* being a mom. Like who's *just* a mom?

I can see that today is, simply put, going to be *just* one of those days, exactly like *just* being a mom. It is only 7:28 a.m. and the day is not off to a very good start—not the start I had anticipated in any event—for the first day of school. See, that was my first mistake, thinking that today should or would be any different than any other day.

"Ella, honey, how would you like it if Mommy uses her magic wand and magic kisses to make all of your tears disappear? Would that make you feel better?" I ask, praying this might do the trick. "Then Mommy can finish getting ready for work, and you will go and finish your breakfast; I promise you I will deal with Michael later." As I smooth my hands over Ella's sandy brown hair, I can sense by her soldier-like stance that she isn't going to let me off the hook that easily. I am dreaming if I think that I am going to recoup any lost time this morning. *Shit!*

With her tear-streaked face and lips pouted just so, Ella's shrill voice bellows out, "No, Mommy, go and deal with Michael *now!*"

I look up to my milky white-coloured ceiling. *Uh, hello, God. God, are you up there? Are you listening to me at all? 'Cause if you are, I could really use your help right about now. Remember how I prayed to you last night that if you let me get out of the house this morning unscathed and untattered and on time so I could go to what is probably the most important meeting of my interior design career, that I would do anything in return? Remember, God, remember I promised no more spending, no more designer purses? Remember I said no more online Bergdorf's or Neiman Marcus while working? I meant it, really I did. I still do mean it, so please, please, please, will you help me right now? I did tell you how important today was, remember I did, so why are you doing this to me? … I want to cry.* I believe in God, honestly I do, and I believe that everything in life happens for a reason (blah, blah, blah …), but right now there is no humanly good reason that I can think of for my six-year-old to be acting like the child she in fact is. No good reason at all!

Oh my gosh! He heard me, he really heard me! God must have heard me this time because he sent me an angel, just now, in my time of need! The angel he sent me appears without an obvious halo and without fluttery wings, but she has the most beautiful golden hair and sky-blue eyes I have ever seen. My angel answers to the name of Nikki.

"Mommy, do you want me to help you with Ella?" my daughter Nikki asks in the most angelic eight-year-old voice I have ever heard.

Thank you, man upstairs, for patient, sweet Nikki, always there when I need her. The mere fact that I have come to rely on my eight-year-old as much as I have makes me feel like I am somehow a flawed and incompetent mother. Maybe I am—flawed at times, not incompetent. But I do not have time to deal with my insecurities right now. I need Nikki's assistance ASAP!

"Sure, honey." I let out a huge sigh. "That would be really great." Another gigantic sigh escapes. "Ella, will you please go with Nikki, and I promise, promise, promise that I will deal with Michael later. Promise!"

Reluctantly Ella turns on her heels and marches out of what is supposed to be my space of sanctuary (at least that's what they tell you on all those DIY TV decorating programs). Nikki follows her quickly behind. Looking back at me, she smirks. "Thank you," I mouth.

Who am I kidding? This isn't over by a long shot, but for now at least I will be able to finish getting ready and still try to make up for some lost time. With any luck, and with no more excitement, I might still be able to get to my meeting on time. If I ever needed a miracle, now might really be the time. Really!

Excuse me, I hate to be rude but I really must shut the door and get myself ready now!

~

A little bio about moi might help you understand my crazy existence in this otherwise chaotic world. I'm Katarina Bancari, the mother species of the family, as Ella so eloquently refers to me. I'm thirty-five years old and have my own interior design business. My husband, Jack, a.k.a. the father species, is a stockbroker by day, taxi driver, hockey coach, bicycle mechanic, and truly a jack-of-all-trades (no pun intended) by night. Jack and I met in high school. High school sweethearts—they really do still exist, but that seems like so long ago now, mostly because it was.

It was never a question for us. Jack and I agreed right from the beginning of our marriage that we were going to have children, a whole bunch of them actually. We also agreed that once our kids came along, one of us would try and stay home to raise them, the old-fashioned June Cleaver kind of way. The other person would attempt to climb the corporate ladder. Since there is no resemblance between my husband Jack and June Cleaver, not to mention that he's a much faster climber than I am, mostly due to the fact that his legs are much longer than mine, it made sense then that he would do the climbing. Given how non-sports oriented I am, I thought I was completely okay with this. Key phrase here, though: *thought I was okay*, because one baby, two babies, three babies later, I realized that maybe I wasn't so okay with it after all. It didn't take me long to figure out that I needed to get out and be a *someone* too, and fast, or this mama bird was going to turn into one ugly crow! No matter how cute the baby birds were—and trust me, they were adorable—and I'm not just saying that 'cause they're mine, I'm saying it 'cause it's true (just ask anybody who saw my little bundles of joy, and they'll tell you too). But let's face it, there had to be more to life than filling my days making homemade baby food, folding cute GAP onesies, and buying *more* Burberry anything than three little kids could ever possibly wear, no matter how gorgeous they looked in those outfits, spit-up and all.

So after a ton of restless days and sleepless nights, I finally made the decision to fly the proverbial coop and start my own business.

So now, years later, the year 2010 later, here I am, and things seem to be going pretty smoothly, most of the time, that is.

Perhaps now might be a good time to introduce the children. Baby number one is Michael. Also known as Mike, Mikey, or just the ten-year-old brother who loves to torture his younger sisters. Michael is a boy's boy in every sense of the word. Skateboarder, hockey player, and don't-kiss-me-in-public-Ma-or-I'll-just-die type of boy. Though on the outside Michael appears to be the macho, rugged boy type, on the inside he is a warm and cuddly mama's boy, much to Jack's dismay.

Then there's Nikki. I often refer to Nikki, blonde-haired and blue-eyed, as mini-me, except for the minor fact that I'm a brown-eyed brunette (merely minor details in the grand scheme of it all). Nikki is far wiser than most thirty-year-olds I've come across, which is kind of scary. Highly motivated, Nikki loves all things beautiful, material, nature-inspired, or otherwise. Nikki's vocabulary would not be complete without her three favourite words: *wow, like,* and *really.* And *wow, like* they've *really* become my favourite words too … *really*!

And last, but certainly not least, there's Ella, my rambunctious, vibrant, freckle-faced, spunky, and not-so girly-girl little girl (did I leave anything out here?). My six-year-old might be tiny, but she packs a whole lot of punch in her little form. And boy oh boy, does she have a set of lungs on her!

Like I said before, I really do need to get a move on things this morning. So, man upstairs, if you can still hear me, could you please lend me a helping hand? I promise one day I will sit down and write to you, maybe with a cup of tea by my side. I'll pour out my feelings more often, like in the way of a journal or a diary, but with so much going on here these days I just don't have time to write much of anything anymore. So if you really are everywhere all of the time, could you just do me a little favour for now and be a mind reader? Now that would really help to expedite things around here. Really, it would!

Dear Diary,

Please give me the wisdom, patience, and strength to get through this morning and my oh-so-important meeting today without any more hiccups. Could you make sure, too, that none of the kids' breakfasts should fly onto my new Diane Von Furstenberg wrap dress because really there is no more time to change once this goes on. And please, please, please could you let this new client love me? Let this finally be the "it" job I've been waiting for. You know the one—the one that's going to make me scream from the rooftops "I did it!"—that one! I know I've asked for it enough times, but maybe, just maybe, could this time be the right time for it? Anyways, I gotta go now. Gotta get the kids to school; it's the first day, you know, so I'd like to be on time at least for today ...

Later!
Me, Your Simple Girl

"Mom," the door swings open slightly, revealing a somewhat embarrassed Nikki. "Sorry, Mommy, I know I'm supposed to knock first, but Ella says she is not eating breakfast and I can't make her." Nikki wrinkles up her face in query. "You're not dressed yet? But don't you have some big meeting today, Mommy?"

Tell me something I don't already know. "Yes, I do." I try to sound upbeat, fully aware that I am failing miserably; instead, I sound defeated.

At this rate, I'm not going to get to my meeting until, I don't know, like tomorrow! As I continue to race around the bathroom putting on the last of my makeup, I can still hear the craziness of what is going on one floor below me. It figures that today of all days, both Jack and I would have early meetings to get to. And to top it all off, it is the first day back to school for the kids. It's Ella's first day of grade one! All-day school! I don't know who is more anxious about it, Ella or me, though my bet is on me. Since Jack has already left for the day, I can't even ask him to cover for me this time. I still have to get myself and these kids out the door. Things are not looking favourable for me right about now. On the radio behind me, I can hear the music intro announcing the eight o'clock news about to begin. *Whew*, one final morning ritual to complete before donning my new power dress, and at least I will finally be ready to face the world. As I spray my power fragrance, Bond no. 9, Bleecker Street, onto my pulse points, I notice Nikki watching. I know she loves it as much as I do—or at least that's what she said when she sat perched on a pristine white leather stool at the department store where the salesgirl, in her valiant effort to make a sale to me, doted over my young prodigy in tow.

"Hold out your arms, my love." I spray her delicate wrists. Nikki is a pro at this drill, requiring little prompting from me. "Come see Mommy's new dress." I take Nikki's small hand into my own and lead her to my closet, one of her favourite places in our home. I ease my new floral-print wrap dress from the rack, careful to not let it catch on anything.

"Oh, Mommy, that's so pretti-ful!" Nikki exclaims, using one petite hand to swathe her agape mouth.

Whether her emotions are exaggerated for the benefit of colouring over my previous foul mood, Nikki knows exactly how to help make the best out of any eventful morning. I wrap the dress around my body while Nikki bolts for my closet. She is a girl on a mission. Moments later, she emerges with a solid grin and a pair of snakeskin slingbacks.

"I think these will look pretty with your new dress, Mommy!" she exclaims, proud of her selection.

"Then Prada slingbacks it is!" I chime in. Taking the shoes from her, I am quick to not get carried away with our mother-daughter fashion show. "We'd better get downstairs quickly, honey. Michael and Ella need your help too. Could you go and find their shoes and put them by the front door while I finish making your lunches?"

"Sure, Mommy. I love helping you!" Nikki's reply is exactly what I need to hear. And with that said, off we march downstairs with some trepidation on my part since I have no idea what surprise may lay ahead for me in the kitchen. *Please let it be a little mess. I don't think I can handle a really big mess right now.*

"Wow, guys, awesome breakfast." I muster up the most excited voice I can find inside of me, albeit it is laced with sarcasm. If the kids do take any notice of it, they sure don't seem to care all that much.

Any reasonable bystander observing this display would strike me off as one of the candidates for the much-coveted mother-of-the-year award. Michael and Ella have laid out quite a spread on the kitchen island. Frosted Flakes, a carton of chocolate milk, a bowl of whipped cream, and of course, because they are concerned with making selections from all of the major food groups, a less-than-ripe banana, though I'm quite positive that is only present for my benefit. This is the first day of school and I have already successfully managed to hinder my children by lack of a proper nutritional send-off. I'm sure in their minds this is a fantastic meal to begin their day.

"Look, Mommy, I'm eating my breakfast!" Ella announces, so proud of the spread set before her.

"Wow, you sure are eating, honey, and it looks delicious!" I can't be more sarcastic.

"Mom?" Nikki stops, firmly planting herself directly behind me. I am still standing in the doorway of the kitchen, unsure whether to continue further in or not since I fear what more I might see.

"Mom! That is the biggest lie I've ever heard! Just look at that mess. Look at what she is eating! That's disgusting!" That's what I love about my Nikki. She never wastes any time mincing her words. Truth is, until my veins are completely saturated with my daily morning ritual of three cups of coffee with a single splash of 5 percent cream, the thought of any kind of food looks rather unappealing to me. This is, without doubt, no exception. *God, are you still there? Could you or one of your archangels please inject me with some java right now? Please? Right here in my arm! I'll even settle for one cup ... no, make that two please; I'm feeling needy. A bold venti will work too if a trip to Starbucks is easier for you!* Why did Jack have to pick this morning of all mornings to leave so early and leave me alone to deal with these kids? *Our kids!*

"Okay, guys, time's ticking. Finish up while I pack your lunches. Michael, are you listening to me?" I ask, rather unsure if he has heard anything I've said. Evidently he has.

"School sucks! I don't get why we even have to go. Why can't you homeschool us? Now that would be cool. I saw it on a show where the mom ..."

"Stop right there, Michael!" *Shoot me first!* "School is fun. You get to play with your friends, learn new things, run around. I wish I could go back to school." *Sort of.*

Michael wrinkles up his face and looks at me with a perplexed expression. I guess he isn't buying what I'm trying to sell him. I begin to gather the kids' lunch bags, completely proud of my accomplishment at being organized at least in this area, if nothing else. I was wise enough to have left food items out on the counter last night, anticipating, I suppose, that in fact the morning might have taken this ill-fated turn. As I stuff snacks into lunch bags, I once again am reassured that I am not a likely contender for mother of the year. For the time being, I really don't care! *Huh?* Now that's actually an accomplishment, even if I do say so myself. Dunkaroos, rice cakes, and itty-bitty cupcakes (those are homemade at least). See? I'm not that negligent after all!

Dear Diary,

Okay, so maybe I didn't think everything through this time, but do you know what it's like to go to the grocery store with three kids? I mean, seriously do you have any idea how full my cart and my head are by the time I end up in the checkout line? Not to mention that I have to be extra careful because Ella's usually hanging off the front of the cart swinging her legs, so I have to be mindful to keep watch she doesn't get hurt. Like that time ... oh well, forget about that time; I can't think about that again because it makes the hair on my arms stand up. But then there's Michael who insists on running back to the cereal aisle for just "one more thing" so I'm trying to keep an eye on him too. Nikki is doing her best to review the quasi list I managed to scribble down with a crayon before running out the door—and freaking out because Michael keeps putting things in the cart that aren't on her list, which is totally messing up the organizational skills she prides herself on. So if you could just help me out a bit please and keep my children healthy, I promise I will make better and wiser snack choices the next time. I'll even sit down and write out a REAL list, like all the normal mothers do, instead of racing around the grocery store and throwing random stuff into my cart. I promise I will even hold my ground when Ella has a meltdown at the checkout because I'm taking all of the "good stuff" out ... I promise.

Later!
Me, Your Simple Girl

One look around the kitchen, and I know that I have my work cut out for me when I get home tonight. I swear it didn't look this bad last night before going to bed. Or was I too tired to even notice? Oh well, it doesn't really make much of a difference right now since I can't do anything about it.

Heading to the door I scroll down a mental checklist I have formulated to get through my morning meeting. Portfolio? Check. Client wish list? Check. Purse? Check. Keys? *Shit! Where are my keys?* Oh yes, I put them in my new purse.

I hear Nikki reprimanding her siblings. "Um, I didn't hear a 'thank-you' from you two for putting your shoes by the door."

"Who cares?" Michael snaps back at her.

"I care! Mom! Mommy! Michael is being ungrateful," Nikki hollers.

"Blah! Blah! Blah!" Michael adds in. He has to have the last word.

Heaving a deep sigh, I query in a faux-happy mommy voice, "Okay, gang, so are we all ready to go?" I think I sound convincing.

"Oh, Mommy," Nikki excitedly exclaims. "Is that a new Louis purse?"

Even I know what is incredibly wrong with this question. The mere fact that an eight-year-old can genuinely distinguish her Louis Vuitton's from her Gucci's from her no-names is disturbing. I really need some therapy where my designer handbag fetish is concerned. This one, however, had been too delicious to pass up and is a nonnegotiable topic for any therapy session.

"I guess it's sort of new," I say hesitantly, the sound of guilt looming in my voice.

Nikki looks like the disapproving mother and I the mischievous child caught in the act. "Did you buy that yesterday, Mommy?"

Actually, the stores were closed yesterday, I want to correct Nikki. Yesterday was Labour Day, but even my little bit of interjectory humour is not going to let me off the hook that easily with the shopping police underfoot. I decide it is probably best not to respond. You know the old cliché: if you don't have anything nice to say, say nothing at all. I figure it might be best to take this stance.

"Does Papa know you bought it, Mama?" Ella asks, concerned.

"Not yet." *But I'm sure one of you will tell him soon—sooner than I can come up with a good reason to have bought it.*

"Tell you what, guys, let's not worry about my purse. Instead, let's put all that energy into having a fantastic first day of school.

What do you think?" I usher my crew out the door, completely aware that all eyes are still on me. In particular one set of piercing blue eyes. I look down, but there is no escaping her. *Crap!*

"You do look really pretty today, Mommy," Nikki offers up.

I think I might melt. "Thank you, my angel. You look really pretty today too."

"Don't worry, Mommy. I won't tell Daddy about your new purse."

And with that, my little diva winks at me, turns on her heels, and saunters towards the car door, not once glancing back.

Question: So, by not responding to Nikki, does that mean I'm teaching my young prodigy to lie? On second thought, some things are just better left not discussed. This is most definitely one of those things.

Chapter Two

Though this day began in a frenzy of sorts, the beautiful weather outdoors is comforting given my current flustered state. The sun is shining a luminous golden yellow all around. The birds are out in hefty flocks singing so sweetly it's as though they have rehearsed a harmonious serenade welcoming all school-age children making their way to classes this morning. The sweet and fragrant scents of the last remaining days of summer linger smugly in the air. A wave of calm washes over my body and I feel as though I can suddenly breathe a little more easily.

"Okay, kids, stand over by the tree, Mommy wants to take a picture." *Quickly please.*

"Oh, come on, Mom." Michael's hand is firmly planted on the car door. "The guys are waiting for me."

"I hate pictures. I'm not going to smile for you if that's what you're thinking," Ella chimes in.

I cling onto my one last hope, Nikki. "Nikki, honey, you'll smile for the picture, won't you?" I ask.

True to form, Nikki complies. Making her way towards a towering maple tree that stands mighty in our front yard, she manages to bully her brother and sister into doing the same. Okay, so bullying is not allowed, a firm rule in our school system (even I know that), but when it's an eight-year-old coercing her siblings into posing for a picture for her mother's scrapbook, it's not actually bullying, is it?

"Say 'cheese'!" my voice rings out.

And with that, a melody from the most acrimonious to the most heartfelt "cheese" can be heard in front yards everywhere. My Kodak moment has been captured, forever to be cherished!

Dear Diary,

Not so bad ... I owe you one ... okay, maybe two!

Much later!
Me, Your Simple Girl

~

The school parking lot resembles an ocean swimming with multicoloured vehicles. As car doors fly open, vibrant-hued backpacks—newly purchased, from their obvious pristine appearance—come stumbling out, followed by their dutiful owners, most not taller than three feet.

I too had frantically made my way through the mall only last week to purchase the sturdiest knapsacks I could find for the kids—only the best would do for my babies. Too bad for those new bags, though, since I was all too aware that history has a funny way of repeating itself and those poor suckers don't stand a chance with their newfangled owners. They will hardly make it past the Christmas holidays, at which point they will be retired, only to be replaced by new ones *again*, only these will be without tears and broken zippers. Can't blame a girl for trying, I suppose.

Once my car is carefully parked, the kids and I make our way through the school yard, where in crooked row upon crooked row stand this year's fresh and perkiest grade school teachers eagerly awaiting their newest students. As I click my way through the playground holding firmly onto Ella's chubby petite hand, Nikki marches proudly alongside me while Michael purposely lags behind. From what appear to be smiling adult faces all around me, it is evident that I am definitely not the only relieved mummy in town today!

Hardly a minute has passed since we made our less-than-grand entrance when out of nowhere, a flailing arm waves excitedly in the air, evidently doing its fervent best to capture my attention.

"Kat-a-rina! KAT! Over here!"

Oh brother! Here we go. The arm and its bubbly owner hurriedly make their way over to where we are. As she stops close in front of me, I can hear her intense breathing from the marathon she has just sprinted in my direction, the apparent finish line. The arm, body, and nasally voice all belong to none other than Piper Hampton. Piper is the exasperating and snoopy mummy of one of Nikki's schoolmates, Skye. I know all too well what will follow next since I have heard this sonata played time and again. By now I have it completely memorized. Piper is such an easy read!

"Oh, my G-A-W-D! Let me have a closer look. I love it, Kat! All of it! Look at your purse! It's gorgeous! You are so-o-o-o lucky Jack lets you shop like that because Brady, well, he would never condone such triv …"

I attempt to tune out. I am guilty of owning an unconscionable and foul potty mouth that has a mind all of its own. Something I'm not terribly proud of, but claim ownership of nonetheless. If only I had a dollar for every time I had heard about Brady and what he will and will not allow, I'd own those new Jimmy Choo's I've been eyeing—the black patent leather ankle booties with the five-inch killer heels, so amazing with jeans! Come to think of it, if Piper had a dollar for every time she told someone her sob story, she might actually be the one wearing them instead, possibly toting a new handbag alongside. I sometimes wonder if Brady has any idea that his wife tells all to most everyone she encounters, whether they are interested in listening to her lamenting or not.

By now a small crowd of women and their offspring have gathered close by. The *Yummy Mummy Club* is what I had so eloquently named them a couple of years back. These are the mummies that barely put their vehicles into park to let their kids off at school, and then off to the gym they go for their morning toning, firming, and elongating of every part of their body.

And so the inquisition begins.

"I love your bag? Whose is it?" Rhonda asks.

"Was it expensive?" Carmen needs to know.

"Where did you buy it?" Lexie has to be in the know.

"What about your shoes? They must be designer too?" Carmen is not giving up.

"Of course they are. Have you ever known Kat to wear anything but designer clothes?" Piper answers.

"Of course, she does!"

"No, she doesn't!"

I feel as though I am witnessing the most exciting tennis match ever. My head turns quickly from left to right, and then back right to left, careful to not overlook any go-around or the ball might drop and I might have missed a fabulous shot.

Ella is not impressed at this show of attention my physical appearance is making. Turning to see if Michael is still with us, I watch as he rolls his eyes as if to say, "Mom, you've got to be kidding me!" Regrettably I am not. What do I do? I should keep moving along with the kids, given that I am in a hurry, but even I know that deep down these women do not mean any harm, and the idle chatter is par for the course. I should feel flattered by their obvious display of interest, but it makes me very uncomfortable since I never intend to intentionally seek this kind of attention. Piper is not letting up as the ringleader. She wants to know all, *now*, and it is clear that she isn't going to be setting me free from this circus ring without a twirl. I need to act fast. I can't waste another minute in it, or I might get sucked in for the long haul.

"Um ..." I take a moment to formulate what I am going to say, not wanting to provide too much information since I shy away from the discussion of clothing labels and their cost with people I scarcely even know. As long as it looks good and feels good, the label hardly matters. "I really don't remember where I purchased these shoes, and as for when, gosh, I've forgotten that too." My voice trails off.

Nikki comes to my rescue, *sort of,* her childish honesty charming all the while, though she's a little too forthright with accurate details. "Mommy?" she looks up at me innocently. "They're Prada. Remember, I was with you when you bought them." Nikki is so proud of herself for having remembered. "Mommy has a big important meeting today. Doesn't she look pretty? Mommy says I will have beautiful, fancy clothes just like her when I'm a grown-up." Nikki's confidence is spilling over.

"I don't know how you do it," Carmen continues. "You always look so put together first thing in the morning! Like, what time do you start getting ready?"

Like, not as early as you'd like to think, I want to say, but don't. See, I told you it isn't just ten-year-old girls who start their sentences with the word "like," though it doesn't sound nearly as endearing coming from a grown woman.

The truth is, these women don't want to hear the truth. *They can't handle the truth!* I did try, when we first met, to be more of an open book, so to speak, do the coffee thing, mummy dinners, you know, that kind of mommy-bonding stuff, only to realize in a relatively short period of time that my attempts at establishing a genuine friendship were essentially futile. As far as I can see, the biggest problem is that I am not nearly as self-engrossed with myself as some of them seem to be. No hunky personal trainer, no binge-purge, and no live-in chef—though I do fantasize about a live-in chef often. No, it's just moi, running—quite literally, from early morning till late night, when at last I simply collapse into bed. If there is a secret to staying fit, I suppose this is mine. It definitely isn't the juicy version any of them are quite interested in perking up their Spock ears to listen to. Still, this is my bona fide life story. *Pretty boring stuff.*

"Oh my gosh!" I cry, looking down at my watch. "I've got to get the kids into their lines, or we'll be really late. It was nice seeing you guys. I'm sure I'll see you all soon!" I wave to the mummies and dart off with the kids before any of them has an opportunity to interject more bothersome questions. Piper blows me an air-kiss as I dash off. I send one back in return. If it means a peaceful end to the ongoing inquisition, it is well worth it in my books.

"Let's do lunch soon!" Piper shouts *alta voce*, ensuring that I along with everyone else within earshot hears.

"For sure!" I shout back, despite the fact that I am all too aware that I will not allow that to happen.

And with that, the niceties are over, *at last*. I hurry myself and the kids along.

"Mom!" Michael tugs on my arm to get my attention. "There's Josh and Zach. Can I go and say hi to them?"

"Oh, honey, can you just wait until we find your teacher first?" If I let Michael go now, I might never find him again in this crowd, and time is really of the essence. He is put off but knows by my exasperated tone not to argue with me. As we make our way through the crowd of joyful parents and not-so-joyful children, camera flashes are going off all around us. The parent paparazzi are everywhere. Try as one might, getting away from it all seems next to impossible. Starlet heirs and heiresses raise trembling hands to their faces as if to say "stop, please, no more pictures!" Finally, I catch a glimpse of a familiar face nearby. It is Mrs. Worthwright—Michael's teacher from grade four.

"Hi there, Bancari family!" Mrs. Worthwright cries out. "Michael, look how much you've grown!"

Michael looks away, slightly embarrassed. He dislikes too much fuss being made over him, and reference to his height is definitely a sore point. Michael has in fact grown slightly taller over the summer months, but not nearly as much as Nikki has, and certainly not enough for there to be a noticeable difference. Still, Mrs. Worthwright is probably just being kind, knowing how hard it is for boys at this age to accept their slower growth progress in comparison to their female counterparts, who seem to sprout up overnight and tower over them from one school year to the next. The last thing I want for him today is to get off to a bad start, especially over an innocent comment from a kindhearted teacher.

Dear Diary,

Please don't let another teacher, parent, or student comment on the growth spurts or lack thereof over summer break. I know people mean well and are trying to be kind, but some things are just better left unsaid. Michael doesn't understand this just yet, no matter how many times I try to explain it to him. All he sees is that some of his friends are growing in leaps and bounds and he is not. I know that no matter how much I reassure him that he will shoot up soon, just like his friends have, he doesn't really believe me ... yet. I know he will one day—grow that is, and actually believe what I tell him, but for now could we just get through the first day back protocol without any more interruptions? PLEASE!

Later!
Me, Your Simple Girl

Now seems to be as good a time as any to acknowledge Mrs. Worthwright. If nothing else, her sweet demeanour is a much-needed presence in the wake of first day jitters.

"Hello, Mrs. Worthwright. Did you have a nice summer break?" I ask. My voice is sincere.

"I did, thank you, Mrs. Bancari, too short of course! I can't believe it is September again. But I'm looking forward to a fantastic school year." She approaches closely, inching in to whisper something into my ear. "In case you didn't know, I think Mrs. Carter will be teaching Michael this year. He'll love her. So will you. She's right over there." She winks at me.

I think I catch the innuendo.

Mrs. Worthwright has a genuine soft spot for Michael and evidently had a say in who would be his homeroom teacher this year. The word out there on the gossip circuit is that Mrs. Carter is the most patient and qualified grade-five teacher in the entire school district, making her the most-requested instructor among parents in the community.

"Thanks so much. Enjoy your first day back," I chime in graciously.

The kids and I make our way over to Michael's new teacher. *God, I hope he likes her. He just has to!*

"Are you excited to meet your new teacher, Michael?"

I figure now is as good a time as any to ask, not that it makes much of a difference, I suppose, but conversation is always good. Too bad for me, the expression on Michael's face tells me everything I need to know without him even uttering a single solitary word.

Michael shrugs his shoulders. "No, not really. Guess it doesn't really matter, does it?"

Am I supposed to answer that as the adult here? I think about it hastily. I'm not so sure how to respond, so I leave well enough alone, realizing that sometimes saying nothing is the best and most suitable way to handle a bumpy situation. This is one of those times. Why can't Michael be more enthusiastic about school, like Nikki is? For instance, show some high-spirited interest? I would even take some bogus interest at this point to see a smile form on his face.

As we wait patiently for Mrs. Carter to finish checking over her list and welcome the newest student in front of us, I attempt to put on a brave face, for Michael's sake, if nothing else. The first few weeks of school are always difficult for my son. Waking up early and shuffling through the morning rituals are not on his list of favourite things to do. Not to mention that no matter how hard I try to be organized in the mornings, it always seems that Jack and I are rushing around in a frantic attempt to get the kids and ourselves ready to get out the door on time and not appear like careless parents. I often wonder if other households are as chaotic as ours in the mornings. I hate the lack of peace in our domicile every morning.

Finally, it is our turn to introduce ourselves to Mrs. Carter.

"Good morning. Who do we have here?" the matriarchic voice rings out.

"Michael. Michael Bancari," I, the mother bird, answer overenthusiastically.

Mrs. Carter, with pointed pencil in hand, gazes down her list until she arrives at what must be Michael's name. "Here we are." She glances up. "Welcome to grade five, Michael!"

I do a quick once-over of Mrs. Carter. Are all teachers all across the world wearing their happy-teacher faces this morning, complete with their primary-coloured vests? I swear they all have them. Maybe there's a special shopping mall out there just for blissful teacher wear—and one single store that stocks primary-coloured clothes and another strictly for secondary- and tertiary-coloured items. Up until high school, primary-coloured clothing almost seems like mandatory attire, after which they seem to venture out a bit. As for the ear-to-ear grin, we know all too well that doesn't last very long either (though I heard that with Mrs. Carter, it is in fact authentic and does actually endure the entire school year—can you imagine?). As for the rest of them, who are we kidding? By day two, voices begin to elevate, an octave or so, especially once the class clown has been nominated for the year.

Michael still doesn't seem impressed in the slightest, offering a barely inaudible "thanks" to her salutation, all the while staring down at his new DC skater shoes—the ones all the cool boys are wearing this year. They too will lose their newness once week one is over. As we move out of the way for the next family to introduce themselves, I can't help but feel that Michael is pulling on my heartstrings. This is such a tough age for a young boy, wanting to appear cool to his friends but still wanting and needing his mommy to hold onto. I notice Michael looking around uncomfortably, probably looking to see if any of his friends are going to be in Mrs. Carter's class with him. I bet he is even wondering if his best friend,

Oliver, is hanging out with a new "best friend," since we were already told that Oliver is in Mr. O'Neil's grade-five class.

Carefully selecting my words, I ask, "Do you want to come and help me find Nikki's and Ella's teachers too? I could sure use the extra help."

Michael seems to be sizing up my question. Patiently I wait for his answer. As he shrugs his shoulders, I can sense that Michael is going to remain neutral and have me decide for him. "Come on, let's go then," I say, not giving him an opportunity to change his mind. Making our way, I see a small gathering of children that appear to be roughly Nikki's age. Out of the blue, a voice sings out towards us. For some strange reason, I am feeling like somewhat of a celebrity today.

"Hello there! Mrs. Bancari, over here! Nikki's in my class."

Thank goodness! Nikki is going to be spending third grade with Miss Pratchard, a rather young and pretty blonde girl, much like Nikki only twenty years her senior. Nikki is sure to get along with Miss Pratchard, who is trendy and fashionable (she definitely does not shop in the primary-colour store). We move in a little bit closer.

"Hi, Miss Pratchard, Nikki's in your class this year?" I ask, rhetorically since she has already given me confirmation that she is. I just want some reassurance. Nikki looks on adoringly. An entire school year with your *twin*, it couldn't get better than this for an eight-year-old.

"She sure is! This is going to be a great year, Nikki. We've got an awesome class, kiddo. You're going to love grade three!" Pretty, perky, and popular, Miss Pratchard is a huge hit with all of the little girls, and some of the bigger boys in the school. No doubt she is definitely eye candy for most of the dads too! Some men are so shallow, making their stares and snickers so apparent to those of us who know better. Too bad for them, though. You would think by now that they would realize that those perky young breasts will sag one day just like the rest of them out there and grow up to be mature, shapeless breasts. Oh well, I suppose you can't blame them for looking for now. Good thing for her, Miss Pratchard is much smarter than most of the old men gawking at her and pays very little attention to their stares, always maintaining the utmost professionalism.

I promptly bring myself back to the present moment. I haven't the slightest of free time available right now to let my mind wander to such mind-numbing matters, especially since I have a potential client of the year waiting to meet with me. I better get moving, or I can kiss this job ciao-ciao; after so many years of trying to prove myself, I am not prepared to let that happen.

As I kiss Nikki good-bye and wish her an *awesome day* (we cool moms have to stay present with the current lingo among the kids, or we will become extinct very quickly to them, just like the dinosaurs did), I scan the faces around me looking for the wet and teary mommy eyes. Those will be the faces I have to encounter next. They are sure to be the moms of the grade-one kiddies. Our once-chubby babies, cooing and full of stinky poopy diapers, are now among the big kids and going to school all day! For working moms, this day is bittersweet.

"Over there, Mama, look, I see Alexis and Mimi!" Ella is thrilled to notice some of her playmates standing over by a reasonably tall woman, chocolate-brown-coloured hair pushed behind her ears, sporting a bob-style haircut with pixie-type bangs.

Is this their grade-one teacher? As we make our way over, I feel as though all eyes are on me again! Honestly, I am not being paranoid or narcissistic. A person knows when she is being watched, and I most certainly am by this woman, man, he/she—whatever it is, it is staring me down! Oh boy, if this in fact is Ella's teacher for the year, I do not anticipate good things happening here. If there is such a thing as woman's intuition (and I am reasonably confident there is), my intuition is telling me that this might be a long school year for my Ella! Apprehensively we make our way over to Madame X. In my mind I am doing my best to come up with a witty opening sentence, a good icebreaker. A high-pitched, squeaky *"hi"* is all I manage to let out. Not the strong start I am looking for. I am careful not to make too much eye contact with her since Jack frequently reminds me I have this uncanny way of wearing my feelings on my face, particularly when they are feelings of repugnance or disgust. I am quite certain this time is no different.

"Hi there!" I try again, hoping that this time around I might sound more convincing and not so much like an awkward teenage girl attempting to make a new friend. "Could you check your list to see if there is an Ella Bancari on it?" There! That sounds better—I think. I sound sweet, polite, very succinct and to the point.

"And you are …?" Madame X asks, looking me up and down in what seems to be a very condescending fashion.

I am speechless. Ella is clinging onto my hand. Seriously, do I look like the fucking nanny? I am sure that my face is now expressing that look; it has to be. If my Louis Vuitton Alma bag wasn't so new I think I might whack her over the head with it. Stupid woman! *I'm standing in front of you with two miniature kids. Do I look like the babysitter dressed in my fucking power dress, power shoes, and drop-dead-gorgeous purse? Duh! I have two sweaty little palms hanging onto mine and speak perfect English, no accent—who else can I possibly be?* For Ella's sake and for Michael's, I know I have to contain my cool, but my Italian blood pressure is sure rising and I have no patience for this! What is worse is that I really have to pee now. *Shit!* This means a stop at Starbucks on my way! This is so not the way I had envisioned this morning to be.

I take a deep breath and put on the best, fakest smile I can fabricate on such short notice. "I'm Katarina Bancari, Ella Bancari's mother." I speak very slowly and calmly. Any calmer, and anyone hearing me might think I am in some sort of weird meditative state. "Is Ella in your class this year?" *Please say no, please say no,* I am praying. Madame X scans her list so slowly it looks as though she is examining cells in a petri dish. *Come on, lady. B! B! The letter B is at the top of the list—how difficult can this be? And why is your fucking pencil down at W?*

"Oh, here we go, E-L-L-A. Ella Bancari. Yes, you're in my class. Welcome." Madame X lowers her chin and stares down at Ella with dark, wrinkled-up eyes. That look is enough to scare even me away. Ella makes no eye contact with her, keeping her eyes fixed to the ground the entire time.

"I'm Ms. Tromini. Welcome to grade one." I am no longer sure who Ms. Tromini is talking to—Ella, me, or no one in particular, since now her beady eyes are no longer piercing through my child but clearly fixated on my handbag.

Ms. Tromini. A fellow Italian. I had better be careful not to say something profane in my ethnic tongue under my breath. I have a bad habit of doing that too. Okay, so I have a lot of bad habits, I admit it; and try as I might every year at Lent, I do promise to relinquish my foul mouth, if only for a short while, but even at this, I typically fall short. At the very least, I hope the big guy upstairs acknowledges my valiant attempt year after year. I even promised Jack I would try harder too, since my potty mouth earns me a raised eyebrow from him frequently. Jack often wonders how I can look so ladylike in my personal grooming and yet have a tainted mouth worse than a long-distance trucker's. "One of my many fine qualities," I typically joke. He fails to see the humour. I figure I just need to try harder—to have him see the humour, that is.

"Shall I wait here with Ella while the other children arrive?" I ask politely. I think this is a reasonable question given Ella's age and the fact that some newcomers may experience some separation anxiety. At least my kid will have a parent nearby in the event that other children do not. I think I am being helpful and at the very least trying to repair our relationship, which in my opinion has gotten off to a dreadful start. Ms. Tromini looks at me as though I am some sort of idiotic parent.

"Do you feel you need to stay, Mrs. Bancari? Your child looks just fine to me. Maybe you and your son could just say your good-byes and be on your way."

Uh, excuse me, are you shooing me away? I don't think so, lady! This is my kid, her first day of grade one, and you want to dash me off? Not fucking likely!

I admit, Ella has spotted some of her friends, and a small group of playmates have formed all around her. Giggles are being shared amongst them, a truly adorable juvenile sight. But this isn't easy—at least for me, it isn't. Ella is my baby, my little girl, and this is it! I mean, think about it. I will never get another chance at her first day of big school, and I want to experience it my way. Cherish it. I sure am not going to let Madame X ruin it for me. I look over to where Ella is now standing with her friends. With her angel-like cheeks and sparkling brown eyes, she too is all giggles. I lean over to her.

"Ella." I speak softly so as to not embarrass her in front of her friends. "Can Mommy just take one more picture of you before I go?"

Ella rolls her eyes at me. Kodak moments are not among her top five favourite things to participate in. Come to think of it, I'm sure it doesn't even make her top ten. Ella is a little shy, just as I had been at her age. Fortunately for me, I grew out of it. I hope she will too.

"Okay, Mommy, but just one more. Promise? Just one picture, and no more?"

I concede.

Ella immediately takes hold of Alexis's arm and the two embrace. Their smiles are enormous. With her free hand, Ella forms the peace symbol high in the air. "Now take the picture, Mommy!" Ella squeals.

And so once again, on one, two, three, and *click*, another Kodak moment is locked in forever.

Dear Diary,
  Don't ever let me forget this moment. Let it stay frozen in my mind forever and ever, just as I want Ella to be this happy forever and ever. How sweet and innocent she and her friends look today. Dear God, let them be this happy always! You know those little bumps and potholes along the road in life that we often stumble

upon? Well, even if they should cause her to fall down, could you help me to teach her the tricks to getting right back up? That would sure be a great big help.

Later!
Me, Your Simple Girl

As the tears well up in my eyes, I can't help but feel that my heart is playing tricks on me once again, just as it had with Michael only a few short moments ago. I am supposed to be thrilled, aren't I? Elated? Like the couple on the TV commercial pushing their shopping cart through the aisles at Business Depot, while music plays in the background reminding us that it is the most wonderful time of the year. I should be skipping and dancing too right now, so why am I not skipping and dancing? Why the hell am I crying like a first-time mother dropping off her young at day care for the very first time? Ella seems perfectly content, unscathed by the first of anything today. She is completely immersed with childish laughter and play. Another milestone has been crossed today, and she seems completely oblivious to it. So what gives here? Why am I the one about to walk away with the tear-stained face?

Dear Diary,

Please don't let Ella miss me too much once she realizes she is going to be here all day, every day. Most of all, please don't let ME miss her too much, since I think I'm the one about to have a meltdown right here right now, not her. Oh, and one more thing while I'm at it, would it be possible for her to like her teacher so she actually wants to come to school?

Later!
Me, Your Simple Girl

My mind is once again in full swing skipping down memory lane. The night Ella was born; Ella as a newborn baby as I rocked her back to sleep after her nightly feeding; Ella taking her first steps—a tug at my arm startles me, and my eyes open wide.

"Mom?" Michael asks gently. "You all right?"

Does he notice my apparent tears about to take shape? Even behind my oversize, black, Chanel, Jackie O sunglasses, I can't hide my emotions from Michael. How did this kid become so intuitive? *Oh right, he's my son, never mind.*

"Sure I am, honey!" I lie. I have to. I don't want my moment of nostalgia to put a damper on Michael's first day—he already has enough on his plate to deal with. He doesn't need to worry about his overly emotional mother too.

"You know, Mom, Ella will be fine. She's not a baby anymore."

Smart boy, my son, given that he is reading my mind; I haven't said a word about this, though it's exactly what I am thinking. Michael is far too wise for his age.

"Come on," I say, gently grabbing Michael's hand and holding onto it a little bit more firmly than I had before. "Let's get you back to your class."

Walking, I can't help but look over my shoulder a couple of times. Does Ella even notice that I have gone? It doesn't appear so, since I can see her giggling and bouncing around just like all the other six-year-olds in her group.

Back within sight of his peers, brightness returns to Michael's face. Cody, Miles, and Matthew, three of Michael's closest buddies, all seem to be encircled in the vicinity of where Mrs. Carter is standing, her clipboard still firmly attached to her breast. Secretly I am hoping that their presence there means that they are all in Mrs. Carter's class as well. That was sure to make this day a much better one for Michael, and I suppose for me as well.

"Hey, Michael, look over there." I point to the group of boys we had both already spotted amongst the crowd. "Want to go over and hang out with the guys?"

"Sure you'll be okay if I leave, Mom?" Michael asks sweetly. "I'm positive! Go on and hang out with your friends." I smile back at him. Michael makes a beeline over to his friends. Watching him run over sparks another episode of memory-lane reruns; this time Michael is playing the lead role. I can hear my inner voice loud and clear this time. *Knock it off, Kat, and get your ass in the car, or you can kiss your next project good-bye!* I do as told. I know better than to argue with that part of me: she is stronger, wiser, and almost always right. Come to think of it, I should listen to her more often.

Making my way to the car, I know better than to look either left or right. Doing so might catch the attention of another mummy, and I am fresh out of mummy small talk. Any energy I have left is reserved for my très important meeting. Not that I am antisocial or anything, but right now is not the time for idle chitchat, not when later this morning I could actually land my dream project, the one that designers like me wait forever for. I keep my head down, focusing on the dial of my Cartier watch. A ballon bleu, to be precise. A gift from Jack and the kids on my thirty-fifth birthday. Lavish, perhaps. But who can't use a little lux in their lives? I know I sure can. Do I really want to focus on the time right now and become even more anxious over how tardy I truly am? Damn, how could I have been so stupid and not set aside enough time to get to my meeting in the city?

How late do I have to be before I am considered officially late?

Oh shit, here goes; I'd better look closely. What? Oh, my God!

Are the dainty black hands telling me the truth? (*They better be for that price*). Could it really be 8:50 a.m.? I have forty minutes to get into the city and look as fresh as a daisy as I make my way to this client's front door. Is that even possible? Right about now, it doesn't feel promising, to say the least.

Shit! Shit! Shit! Why do I always do this? Why do I always think I can do it all, when clearly I cannot?

This is hardly the time for me to break out into song, but all I can think of in this moment is singing, *"because I am Superwoman, yes, I am ..."* Well, I've got news for you, girlfriend, you might be superwoman, but I clearly am *not*! Because if I were, I would spread out my superwoman cape right now and fly to my meeting. Hmm ... now that is an interesting thought. I wonder if Louis Vuitton makes a monogrammed superwoman cape—that would be quite something, wouldn't it? I'll have to check that out later tonight, online of course. For now I had better take my queue in the morning gridlock. Maybe now is not the time for humour, but what else is a simple girl to do?

Whoa! It is sweltering out here. I dive into my car, immediately switching on the AC. Could it be possible that I have only been dressed in this fabulous new outfit for what, an hour or so, and I already feel like I need a cold shower? Really, God, is it humanly possible that any one person should sweat this much—unless you've been running a marathon, of course, which I haven't? As I gently set down my Alma bag, I grab hold of the zipper, carefully pulling away at it. Chipped fingernails are a pet peeve of mine, particularly in my line of work, where I'm ceaselessly using my hands to show clients designs, layouts, and fabric samples. As I retrieve my cell phone and begin keying in the numbers, I take a long, deep breath, exhaling slowly (apparently this is supposed to benefit you by calming down your anxiety. Right now, I don't think anything short of a miracle will settle mine).

"Hello?" the female voice on the other end answers.

"Hello, Mrs. Saunders. This is Katarina Bancari. We have a meeting scheduled this morning for nine thirty. I apologize, but I am running a little behind this morning. (*If this isn't the story of my life, I don't know what is*). It might be closer to ten o'clock when I get to you. Is that going to pose a problem?" I ask. *Please say no. Please, please, please!*

After a slight pause, the voice replies, "Well, I suppose that will be fine. I'll see you then." *Click.*

Well, that was a great first impression I just made. Did she sound pissed? I can't really tell if it's pissed or just annoyed. I guess it doesn't really matter. I'm going to be late, end of story. I can't get there any faster. I know I did the right thing by calling at the very least, though her response—or lack thereof—isn't what I had hoped for.

So now I desperately have to pee on top of everything else. Sweet Jesus, what else could go wrong this morning? I suppose I could be sitting in the middle of traffic having to pee really badly. That would be worse—a whole lot worse. Imagine peeing all over my new DVF dress. That would make for some really expensive toilet paper.

Yes! Here finally. No need for my wallet. Another coffee is not at all what I need this morning. Keys only will suffice for this jaunt to the loo. As I quickly race into Starbucks, I am clearly a woman on a mission. I must appear this way to others too, since I can spot curious heads turning my way as I form an immediate straight line to the ladies room. *What?* Haven't they ever seen a woman who has to pee really badly?

~

Okay, baby, do your thing! I jump back into the car. No time to waste.

Driving, a million thoughts are floating in and out of my head.

Are the kids okay? Will they notice the little love notes I sweetly tucked away into their lunch bags? (I methodically had the good sense to at least write them out last night, thank goodness)!

Will my new prospective clients like me? Will they consider hiring me?

Did I unplug the curling iron?

Breathe, Kat, just breathe. I must say, I actually do give myself credit for my incredible talent (or is it just an irritating habit?) of breaking out into song when the going gets tough, which for yours truly happens all too frequently.

I lower the air-conditioning, again. Stinky armpits are completely out of the question this morning.

Jack is notorious for freaking out on me when he gets into my car. If I am unlucky enough to be sitting in the passenger seat, I am privy to an earful about how loud the music is or how cold the temperature is set at. I am a bit of an extremist—just a little bit—even I can admit this, but so what? It is my car after all. I can listen to my music loud if I want to. I am an adult, for God's sake!

"Holy shit, Kat, were you having a party in here?" Jack would ask. This, of course, was usually followed by a lecture on how I should turn the radio down before shutting the ignition off because it was bad for the speakers, and that the AC should only be set on automatic because it can't cool any faster by setting it as low as I do ... *blah, blah, blah. I'm not listening, Jack!* And so it would go. Jack obviously has no clue what perimenopause is and the very fact that it could go on for years—he is in for a surprise, all right!

Arriving at destination, on right. That is the voice of Gina, my GPS girl, talking.

Thank goodness. Checking my watch, I feel a slight smirk coming across my cheeks. I'm finally here. Not bad. I have a few minutes to spare.

Mentally I check the contents of my portfolio once again, hoping that I haven't forgotten anything. Running my fingers through my hair, I do the best I can to fluff myself up.

Showtime, Kat!

Dear Diary,

This is it, isn't it? I'm already exhausted, and it's not even 10:00 a.m. What the hell am I doing? How can I put on my best performance in front of these people when I'm already tired from the morning's events? The day has hardly even begun if you really think about it. Why do I do this to myself? Maybe I should just forget this career thing and stay home like the yummy mummies. They seem to enjoy it—why can't I?

Instead of running around like a lunatic trying to prove I can juggle everything and still stay on top. Who am I kidding, really? I could be at the gym right now with a hot trainer, or sitting in Starbucks reading the newspaper. Instead, I'm sweltering in front of a complete stranger's front door, about to convince her why I'm the person she and her husband want to hire to decorate their home. I don't even know if I would hire me right now—why should they?

Later ... I'm late!
Me, Your Tired Simple Girl

Chapter Three

I press down on the bell. *Ding-dong.* I am as ready as I am ever going to be. Hardly a minute passes before the oversize mahogany door swings open to a well-coiffed fifty-something-year-old woman standing opposite the threshold. I stretch out my arm, all the while wearing a friendly smile.

"Mrs. Saunders? I'm Katarina Bancari." I am cordial yet not overly zealous—better to be a bit reserved. I step inside. What a place! From my speedy once-over, I can see that no expense has been spared in the decoration of this house.

"How do you do, Katarina? Please call me Camilla."

As she ushers me into the living room, I once again apologize for my tardiness. Scanning the room quickly, I am slightly perplexed as to why Camilla has even called me here in the first place requesting my services. From what I can see so far, this house looks magnificent and doesn't require much more primping. Whoever she and her husband used to decorate their home was good—damn good, and even I have to admit that I don't think I can improve on this too much.

"I completely understand. I remember when my children were school age and how busy and full my life was then. Oh, how long ago that seems now. Things were so different then." Her voice trails off.

Now whose turn is it to take a trip down memory lane? Camilla continues to walk towards the back of the living area, where a set of grand double doors stand tall. She opens them, and I follow her into what appears to be an orangerie—an airy, sun-drenched room full of luminous golden sunlight on this spectacular morning. I bet it looks like this all the time. *Wow!* This room is a designer's dream. Rosewood klismos chairs encircle a white lacquer Saarinen breakfast table. A Missoni-style area rug in muted colours lies underfoot, grouping the entire seating arrangement together. And resting on the table proudly is a large, circular, Tiffany Atlas crystal bowl brimming over with an arrangement of yellow roses, burnt orange calla lilies, and pink phalaenopsis orchids. There is no question that this woman has a great sense of style. And though it is her home and not mine, and someone else has created this vision and not me, I feel as though I am the lucky one, standing smack-dab in the middle of paradise.

As I sit down at the deco table, it suddenly strikes me that in this moment I am a small tadpole swimming in a giant fish tank. *Why am I even here?*

"Camilla," I speak ever so softly, taking my vocal cues from her, "from what I have seen so far of your home, it all appears truly fantastic. I have to say that I am a little confused as to what you would like to hire me for, since I'm not sure that there's much I would actually change here."

Okay, so maybe it isn't the smartest business technique—my complete honesty, that is—but I am forever telling my children to speak the truth, so I at least need to do the same.

She smiles, chuckling moderately. "Actually, Katarina, my husband and I do love this house very much; we aren't looking to change anything here, not for now, anyways. However, you've come highly recommended as being very eclectic, really thinking outside of the box. We like that. And with that said, we are in the process of purchasing an apartment, a pied-à-terre, if you will, in New York City. I called you because I thought we could discuss the apartment with you and have you assist us in redesigning and decorating that space."

I am frozen. As in shocked frozen, not cold frozen. *Like seriously?* Did she just say what I think she just said? New York freakin' city? *Oh, my God!* Like I know I have been praying for this very thing to happen this morning—well, I actually pray for it every time my phone rings. In fact, I think I've been praying for it my entire life, even when I didn't realize I was praying for it—but I never expected that it might actually come true. Now that it might, now that it could come true, I'm stunned and speechless! My dream job in my dream city! Oh, by the way, did I forget to mention that New York City is my very favourite city on this entire planet? Jack mocks me, teasing me that my love of New York City consists of a six-block radius surrounding Fifth Avenue and Central Park, but that is so not true! And even if there is the slightest hint of truth to it, so be it. But all joking aside, I love the cultural diversity of the city, the people, the energy, the fashions, and the style! *Oh, the style!* Just walking along the streets aimlessly and people watching is my very favourite pastime while I'm there. (Okay, so it's actually my second-favourite pastime; my first favourite is shopping at Berdorf's)! I suppose I forgot to mention all of this because I was too busy trying to get it all together this morning. But it is my favourite place. So who cares that I live in a house in the suburbs of Toronto, totally north of New York City, have three kids, a husband, no dog, no station wagon or minivan (a station wagon— over my dead body!)? A girl can still dream, can't she?

Composure, Kat! I need to gain some composure right now and not freak out, or I will totally look like an amateur in front of this woman. I take a deep breath. "Well, Camilla," I ease in gently, "I don't know what to say. I'm very flattered by your offer. Of course, we'll need to discuss your thoughts on the pied-à-terre and what you and your husband are envisioning for it. What styles you like, if you are fond of any particular periods of furnishings, things like that." I feel as though I am starting to ramble. "I have to ask, though, I am a little curious why me and not a New York City decorator?" *The Big Apple does not lack in the brilliant decorator department, that's for sure.*

Camilla speaks openly. "I love what our last decorator did with this home. We wanted a regal space, and she helped us to create exactly that. We wanted an opulent and majestic feel, and that is precisely how this home feels. However, for this new apartment, we want something completely different. We want more chic and a lot more eclectic. We want something more dynamic that is representative of the city. We just don't believe she can deliver that. I want New York City glamour!"

(I admire her honesty and her added playfulness.)

And that wasn't all. Camilla went on to mention that the decorator she used was not receptive to working with what she considered to be a *smallish* apartment space. She had a particular look, and that look was only conducive for grandiose houses. *Thank you, Ms. Not-So-Interested Decorator! I'll be happy to take this one on.* She had considered calling Nate Berkus—Oprah's decorating boy wonder—but then stopped from doing so after being told about me from a friend of a friend. Camilla likes the idea of working with a designer from home, someone she can meet with regularly in town and not have to board an aircraft every time concepts need reviewing or fabric samples require viewing. The more Camilla speaks, the more I take a personal liking to her. We seem to have a lot in common—married young, three children, spouses committed to their careers, a passion for flowers and interior design, and most of all, an innate sense of style that we both admit we come by honestly. After a rather candid conversation, I get to know some of her likes and dislikes—invaluable information considering the venture I am about to embark on.

I know that there is no time like the present to have the "fee" conversation with Camilla. This is still a part of running my own business that I am not entirely comfortable with, but it is vital if Katarina Design Inc. is going to stay afloat. Even I have to admit that I am definitely a better designer than I am businessperson. For the past few years, I have been treading shallow waters, doing my best just to try and stay afloat. I would have been happy with a life preserver being tossed in my direction today. Never in my wildest dreams did I think a rescue boat was going to come my way and pull me from the torrid waters. Lucky for me, Camilla is perfectly comfortable with my hourly rate of one hundred and ninety-five dollars per hour. All she has to do now is get approval from her husband, which of course shouldn't be a problem, she reassures me.

"I was under the impression when we last spoke that your husband was going to be present at our meeting this morning. Was he detained elsewhere?" I ask.

"Actually, he's away on business at the moment," Camilla offers up. "He travels a great deal for his business. We'll probably meet without him most of the time. That's not a problem for you, is it, Katarina?" she asks blankly, never making eye contact with me, keeping her stare steadfastly locked gazing out the window and onto the Bahamian resort-style backyard this house is set in front of.

Something doesn't seem quite right to me, that much I can sense. Call it woman's intuition, but there is something very reserved about Camilla when she speaks of her husband that makes me wonder—a lot of things actually. I know better than to ask any questions—I hardly know her well enough to do so—but still I am a little curious. I also know when to leave well enough alone, and this feels like one of those times.

"Oh, my gosh, no, Camilla, it's not a problem at all. I just want to ensure that your husband is always aware of any decisions we make, so as to make him feel included, that's all." *Make him feel included and not get myself into trouble.* I had learned long ago that if a wife has to get the final approval from her husband, then ultimately he is the real decision maker and not her. Before I get myself into a predicament of assuming something is a *yes* when it is really a *maybe,* I want to ensure that the one signing the cheque is well informed.

~

For the most part, I love the fact that my job is a pleasurable one. Think about it: most of the time people are calling me during happy periods of their lives, when they are building homes or renovating existing ones, which in my books usually equates to happy days. I say *usually* because initially at least, the entire process seems like so much fun for people. How excited they are to be involved in the designing of their dream home, the thought of being able to have input in the selection of all things new—new finishes, new floor tiles, and new luxurious fabrics. Once in a while, though, you run into some brick walls—couples that simply don't and can't agree, contractors who call with unforeseeable delays in meeting deadlines, and product that for some reason essentially goes missing. While smack-dab in the midst of it all, it really sucks! (I suppose I could put it more eloquently, but really, what we're all thinking in that moment is "this really sucks," so why sugarcoat it)? In the end, though, my job is truly a satisfying one.

I take great pleasure in assisting people in making an intangible concept become a tangible reality. Most often after working with families for so long, they become friends, not just clients any longer. It's just one of those things. It just happens. It's not as though we intend for the working relationship to turn that way, but it often does just by happenstance. Half of my job is being able to understand design concepts and design principles, knowing what works with what, but the other half of my job—the more important half, if you ask me—is getting my clients to like me and to trust me. The best way I know to do this is to actually listen to what they really want and need for their space. Mix it together with what I essentially know, and voilà, I have a superb recipe for a fabulous client/designer relationship. So far, this appears to be a flavourful recipe in the making.

It seems that our preliminary meeting is coming to an eventful closure. Camilla informs me that Shane will be returning later on in the week. I recommend that perhaps a meeting amongst the three of us might be appropriate, so he can get to know me and I can get to know him. Could we meet again, say early next week if he is available? Camilla promises she will get back to me on that one and will check with Shane's assistant to see if and when he can find the time to get together.

Uh-oh! Check with Shane's assistant? Why not ask Shane himself? After all, she is married to the man. Don't they talk? Check in? You know, that kind of stuff we married people do. I smell something fishy here, and it definitely isn't my heavenly Bond No. 9 fragrance. I am all too aware of when to keep my big Italian mouth shut. This is unquestionably one of those times.

With a quick embrace, Camilla and I say our good-byes, and I dash off.

Dear Diary,

Thank you! Thank you! Thank you! Holy shit! I can't believe this! Does it get better than this? Okay, so I know it's not a complete for-sure thing yet and that she still has to run it by her husband, but it sounds like an almost-for-sure thing, so THANK YOU! But why now? Why send this one to me now? It's not like I haven't been asking forever 'cause you know I have, so what's different now? Okay, I know, I know, I ask way too many questions, right? Never mind, I suppose it doesn't really matter why now. Just please, please, please give me the strength to pull this off. I think I can do this, I know I can do this ... crap, I'm starting to sound like a little choo-choo train right now. But you know what I mean. You of all people have to know what I mean. But I really do believe that I can pull this one off! I mean, this is what I do for a living, this is what I'm good at. Please make Jack and the kids cooperate on this one for me, P-L-E-A-S-E! New York City! I can't believe it! The Plaza Hotel, here I come! Bergdorf's! Oh my God, please Bergdorf lady, could you hold that Milly dress for me? I'll be back soon to pick it up. You do remember which one, don't you?

Later!
Yeah Me! Your Over-The-Moon Simple Girl

Chapter Four

As I speed across the highway again, driving west this time, homeward bound, I figure I am deserving of a little *something-something* for a job well-landed. What could it hurt? Maybe a new fall jacket for those brisk New York City nights? Knee length might be nice for those cool evenings after a long day of work as I walk back to my hotel. A girl has to stay warm, doesn't she? Maybe a gorgeous merino wool scarf to go with it might be just the right accessory too. *Tee-hee!* Nothing could burst my proverbial bubble right about now!

After years of diapers, spit-up, mommy-and-me play groups, and endless nights of crying and sniffles *(not me, the kids ... okay, well, maybe me too ... just a little)*, I am now finally going to be joining the ranks of the really and truly employed! *I am* going to be making a difference in someone's life. Transform four barren walls into someone's home. Not just any home, but a splendid and brilliant home. Sure, I've been doing this for some time now, but this job, this house is different!

One quick stop at the mall, and then I will go home to share my incredible news.

~

Clunk!

This should do it for those nippy New York City nights. *This* being a Kelly-green bouclé Juicy Couture three-quarter-length coat, complete with oversize buttons comprised of tiny Kelly-green crystal clusters. *So stunning!* With my new purchase pristinely wrapped and carefully stowed in the trunk of my car, I am off to gather up the kids from school.

And just in the nick of time too! With late afternoon traffic beginning to take shape, I want to allow myself enough time to get to West Elm Public School before the end-of-day school bell rings.

Arriving with scarcely five minutes to spare, I circle the already-overflowing parking lot filled with other doting parents. I edge my car into one of the few remaining spaces. *In the future, I have really got to ensure that I get here in plenty of time to park in the lot; otherwise, I will be parking on a side street and sprinting my way across the playground in my stilettos, not a spectacle I'm too keen on demonstrating.*

Taking my place behind the fence, I scan the playground looking for a child of my own and hoping like hell that the kids have had a great first day back today.

Dill-l-ling-g-g-g!

The end-of-day bell starts to sound. And here they all emerge, coming into view and bolting out the doors like herds of wild animals being released from their pens. What a sight this is. Smiling faces bounce around the playground, indicating that day one hasn't been so bad after all. Bright eyes and giggles throughout mean we are off to a good start. Little boys and big boys are high-fiving each other as if to say, "Cool, man, day one is over. We made it!" The first to run over to greet me is Michael.

"Hi, honey!" I say enthusiastically, running my hand through his already-messed-up hair, "how was your first day?"

"Okay, I guess. Mrs. Carter seems pretty nice."

I'll gladly take "okay"!

Dear Diary,

Thank you for making Michael's day terrific! I know he didn't exactly say that it was a terrific day, but he did say that it was okay, which means it wasn't bad, so it had to have been great at the very least, right? It means so much to him to fit in with the other guys, and liking his teacher means he'll like coming to school. Please let the girls be equally as happy."

Later,
Me, Your Simple Girl

Within seconds of Michael's arrival, Nikki and Ella come bouncing over too.

"Hi-ya, Mama!" Nikki sings out.

"Hi-ya back, my baby dolls. Great day, I hope?"

"Yeah, awesome," Nikki responds.

"I hate my teacher! She's a meanie-head!" Ella announces, a little too loudly.

I should have known better than to think that Ella would have expressed anything but her innermost feelings. Straight to the point, that's my little girl! No beating around the bush with her. I have been trying to explain political correctness to Ella recently, preparing her for full days at school and the need for filtering out some thoughts before they become words. But who am I kidding? She isn't the least bit interested in what I have been trying to teach her, instead opting for "but you always tell me to say the truth, so I'm telling the truth."

She has me there. I am stumped!

Really, how am I supposed to respond to that? What is there left for me to say? Nothing, that's what! So I don't. Not yet anyways. I need some time to collect my thoughts, think of something firm and authoritative to say to Ella. Something a six-year-old precocious brain can comprehend. Now that I think about it, this is going to be tougher than I had initially thought.

~

Once at home, the kids armed with their exploding backpacks and me with my latest purchase (not to mention fantastic news) set about unloading our packages. I am dying to share my news with the kids, but figure I should wait until Jack gets home and tell them all at the same time.

In the meantime, my real job is about to commence. I have my work cut out for me. Out flow the thousands of forms that need filling in (at least it feels like thousands): medical forms, consent forms, parent volunteer forms, pizza forms, and the list goes on and on. Really, can West Elm not stagger these forms? Is this really necessary? Do they honestly have to bombard parents like this on day one? Like, why not start sending them mid-August so we have time to gently ease into filling all of them in?

And then it starts. I knew it had been too calm for too long. Let the war begin!

"That's mine, stupid!" Ella's voice pierces through the yelling.

"No, it's not, butt-face, it's mine!" Michael retorts back.

"*Mommy*! Michael is calling me a butt-face! I don't like being called a butt-face!"

Seriously? The key is barely out of the front door. My precious Alma bag is still slung over my shoulder, and all hell is already breaking loose? Why put it off any longer? The screaming is not going to be ending anytime soon. Any semiconscious parent with children knows this. The telephone call I had been trying to avoid all morning and all afternoon now has to be made.

"Hello?"

"Jack?" I am partially surprised that he has in fact answered his phone, but utterly elated that he has. It is refreshing to hear an adult voice after the shrilling I have been listening to. "Uh, Jack, I hate to bother you, but are you coming home anytime soon?"

Does my voice sound desperate? Probably, but I really don't care if it does. In fact, I hope it does, so Jack might call it quits for the day at the office and get home to the chaos (a.k.a. the children) we have created together. Unfortunately for Jack, he is all too familiar with my desperate tone of voice. But since he was the one who was so adamant that we didn't need a nanny or a cleaning lady, or even Alice from "The Brady Bunch," he has gotten used to my you'd-better-be-coming-home-soon tone of voice.

"I guess I could if you want me to. What's wrong?" Jack sounds puzzled.

"What's wrong?" I repeat. *Oh, I don't know, where should I start?* "The kids are beating the crap out of each other, school forms are all over the kitchen table, I need to get dinner started since clearly nobody enjoyed their lunch, made obvious from the barely eaten sandwiches bouncing around on the kitchen island … no, make that the floor too, but other than that everything is great, really! Just another ordinary day."

"I'm just asking, that's all."

I am doing my best to remain composed, though it is abundantly clear that I am failing miserably.

"If it's okay with you, I still need to do some work here, so if you can handle it on your own for a little bit longer, I promise I will be home by dinner."

Terrific! If I could handle it, I wouldn't have called, Jack! The truth is, I can tell by the tone of Jack's voice that he is in the middle of something important. I put the phone down. I am flying solo for the next couple of hours, like it or not.

"Hey, guys," my voice is strained, "could you please just try to get along for a few minutes, at least until I go and change out of my work clothes, and then I will get you a snack? Is it a deal?" I am begging more than I am asking. My meaningless pleading is falling upon deaf ears.

"E-L-L-A!" Nikki cries out. I spin around with arms outstretched (force of habit when I hear Ella's name being hollered out), but it is too late. A steady stream of orange juice is flowing like a rapid river right down the side of the walnut island. The brand-new, drop-dead-gorgeous, marble-topped walnut island recently installed in my kitchen.

Oh fuck! Fuck! Double fuck!

God, did I just say that in my head, or was it out loud? I'm not even sure anymore, and quite frankly, I don't really know that I care.

I bet this sort of thing never happened at Camilla's house. She appears far too polished and far too put together to have ever let such an episode occur in her home, even when her kids were small, like my monsters are. I bet she was too sophisticated even back then to blurt out profanities even when under pressure. Ironic, isn't it, since if truth be told, I believe a lot of people think the same about me. Many have even said so ... oh, if they only knew!

Since seeing Mommy in panic mode is an all-too-familiar scene around my house, Michael and Nikki get right on it. Nikki runs to get paper towels from under the kitchen sink; Michael, my Yves Delorme tea towels, the freshly pressed ones hanging from the oven doors, the only items that had been left unscathed from this morning's hurricane.

Ella stands unmoved.

Dear Diary,

> *Don't let me freak out, please, please, please ... don't let me freak out, please! Don't let me ... I gotta go, I don't have time for this ... CRAP!*

Later,
Me, Your Freaked-Out Simple Girl

What is happening before my very eyes really only happens on television shows, doesn't it? The only visible difference that I can see right now is that there is no director here waiting to yell "Cut!" and no set crew waiting in the wings ready to come on set and clean this disaster up.

Still in my new DVF power dress, I have no choice but to begin wiping it all up. One sticky wipe after another, I do my best to soak up the 100 percent pulp-free premium juice. The kids know better than to utter a sound. Ella, looking positively stoic, is standing resolutely still in a nearby corner. In what is her smallest voice yet today, she makes a valiant attempt at an apology.

"I'm really sorry, Mama. I didn't mean to."

I know that I have to acknowledge her apology, angry as I am. Red-faced, I reply, "It's okay, Ella."

I want to say more, reassure her that as much as I know she didn't mean to spill the juice, I am just so pissed at having to clean up yet another mess. But the words just won't come out. No matter how hard I try, they just won't. I am just that mad.

So I say nothing else. Nothing at all.

Dear Diary,

Please tell me who the women are who think I have it all together. Really, I want to know their names. Are they aliens? What planet do these women exist on? Do they have any clue what happens behind my front door? Or do they only see what they want to see. Me, when I am dropping the kids off on my way to see a client or when I am picking them up after I've been to a meeting and therefore still seem slightly intact. They see me at school picnics, basket in hand, looking like Goldilocks going to Grandma's house, but outside of that, I don't think they have a clue as to what I do when I'm just being a mom—just like them. I don't think they want to believe that I am just like them, dealing with the exact same things they are. But I AM!

Much later, I have more juice to clean up!
Me, Your Citrus-Smelling Simple Girl

Chapter Five

Click. Jack is finally home! I hear the door close softly behind him. This is so typical of Jack. He is so much gentler than me at everything he does.

"Hi, guys. Daddy's home!" Jack announces his arrival, setting down his portfolio, which no doubt is chock-full of work, tonight's entertainment. I often wonder if Jack's vocal proclamation of his arrival is, in fact, an open invitation for me to run and greet him at the door, dry vodka martini in hand, all the while being neatly coiffed and wearing my pearls (*of course*) especially saved for such occasions. *Huh! Not fucking likely in this house. Sorry, Jack!*

With the aftermath of juice still fresh in my mind and the scent of it still lingering on my hands (but at the very least cleaned up), the kids have finally each settled into their own quiet activities for the time being. I at last have had a chance to get dinner underway. With my back to the kitchen door, I don't even take notice of Jack as he enters into what was a war zone only a short couple of hours ago.

"Hi, hon," Jack says coyly, slipping his arms around my waist. The faint smell of his cologne still endures after what I am certain has been a long day at work for him too.

"Hey." My mannerism is still distant, cold by most standards, but given the events of the late afternoon, this is the best I can offer him.

"Is everything okay? You seemed kind of mad when you called. Sorry, it was a bad time. I was in with a client."

Of course you were, Jack. It's not like my cell phone has never rung when I've been in meetings with clients. But really, it was no biggy, just a river of OJ all over the kitchen and three squirrely kids, but nothing I couldn't handle by myself, really. Oh, and by the way, the new marble island we just paid a small fortune for, well, it's still a little sticky right now, you know, that juice thing and all. Oh, and while I'm at it, I forgot to mention, I think I might have landed my dream job today too, in case anyone around here is at all interested. Somehow I doubt that Jack will be as fascinated as me by the turn of events that has taken place today.

"Mommy, is dinner ready yet? My tummy is grumbly," Ella informs me in her sweetest voice. She sounds remorseful and tired, all in the same breath.

I can't stay mad, not at her. "It's almost ready, honey," I answer.

Jack bends down and scoops Ella up into his arms, planting a solid, sloppy kiss on her cherubic cheek. "How was your first day of school, Peanut?"

"My teacher is a meanie-head, Daddy."

"Really?" Jack pretends to be taken aback.

"Mama's gonna fix her though!" Ella proclaims.

Jack and I both burst into laughter at her submission.

"No, I'm not, sweetie. You're just going to have to figure out a way to get along with Ms. Tromini."

Our conversation is swiftly halted as the music intro to "The Suite Life of Zach and Cody" can be heard coming across the TV. Ella takes this as her cue to bolt out of Jack's arms and race towards the family room to take her seat.

It appears that Jack is finally tuning into the prospect that I have not had the best of days (which, in fact, is not completely true because most of my day has been great, fantastic in fact). It has only been in the last couple of hours that things have gone due south, rapidly. Jack stands in front of me, pointing to the full wine glass he holds out towards me, a peace offering of sorts.

"Cheers, honey." Jack smiles, clinking his glass with mine. After a quiet pause, he attempts to make conversation with me, I'm sure in the hopes that my mood might lift. "What a long day at work," he declares. "If dinner is still going to be a few minutes, I think I'll go up and change."

"Sure, go ahead. It's going to be a little while still." I don't bother looking up from my spot standing in front of the cutting board because, should I, my unpredictable mouth might say something insensitive. Is he at all interested in the fact that I have donned my power dress for a reason today? That I've been in this same dress since 7:30 this morning? That between eau du sweat and premium Florida orange juice still permeating my skin, coupled with the fragrant scent of sweet red onions and elephant clove garlic in preparation of this evening's fine meal, I too might have liked to freshen up a tad bit? Something more comfortable perhaps? How ironic, isn't it, how this phrase takes on a whole other meaning post-children than pre-?

Dear Diary,

Dinner's almost ready, the kids are watching TV, quietly, at least for now, and Jack is finally home! So I suppose that it really hasn't been such a bad day except for a few minor incidents. Okay, so at the time, they didn't seem so minor, but in the grand scheme of things, it's not the end of the world, even I know that. How does that saying go—you can't cry over spilled milk, well, juice in this case ... whatever. So if it wasn't such a bad day, why am I feeling so blue? Who cares that my new DVF dress went from making a fantastic sale to making mashed potatoes—what's wrong with that? In a weird kind of way, I suppose I am truly getting my money's worth out of it. So, then, what's wrong with me? I'm supposed to—oh shit, I forgot to make the salad!

Later!
Me, Your Simple Girl

"Okay, gang, wash up. Dinner's ready!"

~

The one thing Jack and I have always insisted on is that as much as possible, we will always try to have dinner together as a family. Since Jack works many late nights, this isn't always feasible. Fortunately, I'm at least home most evenings as a constant for the kids. How I dream about the day that he actually collects the kids from school, races home to unload their backpacks, half-eaten lunches complete with rotting food, and starts the chopping, slicing, and dicing. Just once I want to see what it feels like to be the one walking through the front door with my Louis Vuitton portfolio swinging from my hands, only to be confronted with a beautifully laid meal spread across the kitchen table. Yeah, okay! *Earth to Katarina—not likely going to happen in this lifetime!*

The kids take turns telling us about their first day at school, the new friends they have made, and how some of their old friends have returned with thrilling summer tales. There seems to be a little melancholy over the loss of old friends who didn't return today. With any luck, that sadness will soon be replaced with imminent friendships currently in the making. I wait for everyone to finish their turn. I don't want my news to be interrupted by the urgency of some other important piece of information that has been left out, like "Oh, and by the way, did I tell you that Maddie's hamster had babies?" That kind of important stuff.

I take a deep breath, hoping that they can all be still just long enough to listen to me for a change. "So," I start, "I had a really interesting meeting with a new client today."

"That's great, hon," Jack offers between bites of food.

"Will you be doing more work for them, Mommy?" Michael's voice sounds genuinely interested.

"Actually, I think I will," I offer, not raising my eyes up from my roasted chicken and salad, which have been sitting on my dinner plate barely touched. "The Saunders are in the midst of purchasing an apartment in New York City and want me to decorate it for them. Isn't that great?" I ask rhetorically. I am trying my best to contain my excitement and appear nonchalant about it even though the little kid inside of me wants to jump up and down and blurt out my news with juvenile exuberance. I resist the temptation.

All eyes are fixated on me. No matter how natural I am trying to be, inside I am bubbling over with excitement. Jack is staring at me with a perplexed look on his face. I can sense that there are questions beginning to formulate in his head.

He takes hold of his wine glass, pressing it to his lips, and takes a long drawn-out sip. Setting his glass down again and clearing his throat, he looks directly at me. "So, um, really, hon, that's terrific news, really it is. But why you? What about the kids?"

My back goes up like an angry cat ready to pounce on her prey. "Why not me, Jack?" Is he insinuating that I can't handle it?

"What I mean is, why not a designer from New York? God knows it's full of them."

So I go on to explain to Jack and the kids the nature of my meeting with Camilla and her reasons for selecting me. It all makes perfectly good sense to me, but then again, why wouldn't it? This is exactly what I have been working towards. This is what my dream has always been.

I've been enamoured with New York City ever since I can remember. As a little girl watching Audrey Hepburn in *Breakfast at Tiffany's*, I can recall the glint in my eyes as I carefully studied her every move, her every nuance. In the eyes of a young girl, she was the epitome of glamour, elegance, style, sophistication, and quirkiness, all rolled up into one person. It left me the impression that all of New York City was this exact way. And so I promised myself then that if I couldn't live there, then at the very least I would go and visit as frequently as I could. I too want to run across Fifth Avenue just like she did. And so I did once, on a visit there. Jack thought I was crazy! I felt exhilarated. The energy of the city is contagious. How could anyone not love it?

And now here is my opportunity to go and finally work there, intermittently, but that's good enough for me. Apprehension and all, I would be crazy to pass this opportunity up. I go on to recount to Jack and the kids the fine particulars of our meeting (the kids seem legitimately bored). I tell them that I still have to meet Camilla's husband, Shane, and that he still has to approve my working on this project, not to mention that the offer to purchase on their Park Avenue apartment still has to close—mere minor details. Of course, I will have to visit the site on several occasions (I secretly hope), but realistically maybe just a few. Much of our sourcing can be done locally at home if we are able to find what it is that we are looking for. For those things we can't find at home, there is no better place to source interior design materials and accessories than New York City itself. Jack listens attentively as I speak, though I am getting a funny feeling he isn't nearly as excited as I am about this, and not nearly as keen as I had hoped he might be. In fact, the kids seem to be displaying faintly more enthusiasm than he is.

"Mommy, can I come with you when you go to New York?" Nikki asks adoringly.

My eyes become moist with tears, but I refuse to let Nikki or the rest of my family see me cry. Trying to explain to my eight-year-old daughter who follows me most everywhere I go why she cannot come along this time is no easy feat. So I try in my best Mommy voice to make her understand that when travelling for work, her coming along with me would not be appropriate, to say the least, but we would go back together as a family, for a vacation, and that would be so much more fun. She seems satisfied with this explanation—for now, at any rate.

"Mommy, will you buy me an American Girl dolly when you go? Maddie's daddy goes to New York for work, and he always brings her back something from the American Girl store."

"Me too! Me too! I want a pretty dolly too!" Ella chimes in.

I sigh with relief. If lifelike dolls will put a smile back on their faces, it is a small price to pay. "Of course, I will buy you a dolly from American Girl Place." *I'll even buy you two.*

One lone tear manages to escape from the corner of my eye, trickling down onto my dinner plate. The peas I have been swirling around for quite some time cushion its fall. Good thing I have no appetite and am not especially interested in eating those tiny, green, tasteless balls anyways.

Dear Diary,

Do they really understand how important this new project is to me? How do I make them see that I'm not abandoning them, that this is a once-in-a-lifetime opportunity for most designers. For me, this is a dream come true in a city that I've longed to be a part of my entire life. Not to mention that a job like this can open up so many doors for me, jobs that I could have never imagined coming my way, and now there could be a potential of them becoming real. No matter how much I love my family, I just can't pass this opportunity up. Is there any chance that with time they might understand?

Later,
Me, Your Simple Girl

My news on the first day back to school certainly has a way of halting any further evening conversation outside of the customary pleasantries. The kids are right back to where they were before dinner: fighting over the TV remote, calling each other amusing names like stupid, dummy-head, and my all-time favourite, fart-face. Jack and I are being unusually quiet, tiptoeing around each other, something we only do when a massive pink elephant stands between us and we are both too afraid to disturb it for fear that it might go wild. I figure Jack still has a lot of questions to ask me, and I answers and obstacles to overcome. But in the meantime, New York, New York, if you're ready for me, then here I come!

~

Bedtime ritual frequently seems to be a production around this house. Too many kids and not enough of Mama to go around! Everyone calling me to go and attend to them first, including Jack wanting my undivided grown-up attention, leaves me longing to run out the front door and down the street many nights and wait for someone to tuck me in under a maple tree—anywhere would be just fine. Hermès blankie, anyone?

I think it might be best to say my good-nights to the girls first and save Michael for last. I don't want any interruptions with my son tonight. I have this feeling that he is full of questions after my groundbreaking news earlier this evening and that he needs some time to process the information and formulate his questions the best way a ten-year-old can.

With the girls snugly tucked into their beds, the soft scent of powder lingering on their innocent bodies, I gently make my way down the faintly lit corridor to Michael's room. He is sitting propped up against his pillows and seems to be deeply engrossed in the latest novel that has made its journey from amazon.ca to his cluttered night table.

"Hey, Buddy," I whisper barely audibly, "mind if I sit with you for a bit?" Michael looks forward to our nightly conversations sans the interruptions of his two overbearing younger sisters.

Setting his book down on his bed, Michael looks up directly at me. Stretching out his arms, he smiles, "Sure, I can read later."

I know full well that Michael has been waiting for me, his questions ready to launch. The last thing I want, though, is for the conversation to be solely around my new project, so I ease in carefully, picking up the hardcover book that lies on his comforter.

"How's the book?" I ask, glancing over the cover. "Is it good?"

"Yeah, it's pretty good, I guess. It's about the guy, and he sees ghosts and thinks he has special powers, but really it's not him that has the special power, it's this other kid, who is already dead and comes back to life—that kind of stuff. Not your kind of book, Mom." Michael snickers, making a deliberate attempt to ease the tension we are both feeling now.

I am all too aware that he isn't really interested in making small talk about his latest read. Michael knows me so well: sci-fi books are not at all my thing, and the blank look on my face each and every time he attempts to share what he is reading with me sends him and me into fits of hysterical laughter. Funny, though, how neither one of us is laughing this time. Dressed in blue-and-green-checked pyjamas and with his eyes staring down at the plaid print of his comforter, he is the epitome of a miniature man. His big brown eyes, usually dancing with excitement, seem pensive and slightly sad. It is apparent that something is bothering him, and I have a feeling I know exactly what it is.

"Feel like talking about anything?"

He glances up. "I'm really glad you got this new client, Mom, and I know you always talk about New York and wanting to go there, but does that mean you'll never be home now and we have to get a babysitter and stuff like that? 'Cause I'm bigger now and responsible, so I was thinking that maybe I could just watch the girls after school and make us snacks and help them with their homework and ..."

Oh my gosh! My sweet little man, who only a few short hours ago was referring to his sisters as butt-head and other endearing names like it, is suddenly taking it upon himself to be their caregiver. How's that for dependability?

"Michael, you are absolutely not going to be responsible for taking care of Nikki and Ella." My words are gentle. "Daddy and I will figure out who will watch you guys when I'm not home. Is that what's got you all worried?" I stop talking for a moment, just long enough to collect my thoughts. "Michael," I ease his chin up, looking directly into his eyes, "would you rather I not take on this new client?" Our relationship is such that I typically know by the look in Michael's eyes if he is telling me the truth or not. In fact, he and his sisters often wonder if I am the one with magic powers since I can *almost* always tell if they are telling a fib. Michael turns his face away from me, not wanting me to see his expression. The least I can do is to give him his space.

"It's not that I don't want you to take the job, Mom; it's just that I'm afraid you may love New York so much and not want to come back home. You know how sometimes when the girls and I are really bad, you say you feel like running away. I'm just afraid you might do it now!"

Oh no! I have really messed things up this time! This is so not how I envisioned all of this playing out. I continue, choosing my words carefully, so as to not cause any more damage than I already evidently have. "Michael, I could never, would never, love my job more than you and the girls! It's not possible because well … you guys are my babies, and all mommies everywhere love their kids more, they just have to! Work is just the stuff that a lot of us have to do. It's important to me, and I do enjoy my job, but it's definitely not more important than my family. Can you understand that?"

"Sure, Mommy, I understand." Michael hardly ever refers to me as *Mommy* anymore. "I just like it when you are here to tuck me into bed and stuff like that. But please, don't tell anyone I told you so."

I give up on allowing him any more space. I take Michael and wrap my arms around his body. His secret is safe with me.

Dear Diary,

    What have I done? Am I the worst mother in the world, or what? Michael thinks I want to run away, that I'm trying to run away, but that's not it at all! Sure, I say stupid things sometimes, things I don't mean, but who doesn't say something and then later regret it? We've all done that at one time or another. I'm just tired when I say some of those things, that's all. Am I not allowed to be tired? Am I not allowed to want a career too? Something that I love to do, something I can call my own? I swear I'm not trying to run away or even get away, but this job, this client, this is what I've always dreamed of as a designer. Please let Michael understand that I am not running away from him or the girls, or Jack, or for that matter, even this life. I'm running toward something bigger ... something that I've wanted for my life ... and that's okay, isn't it? Well, isn't it?

Later,
Me, Your Simple Girl

~

"Kat? Hey, Kat, you awake?"

"Huh? What? What's wrong? What time is it? Is it six already?" I attempt to turn. Oh, shit! My neck is stiff again. I must have fallen asleep putting Michael to bed, a scene that Jack is all too familiar with and not overly impressed by. Once again he is shaking me to rouse and make the daunting walk down the stairs to watch the late-night news with him. My arms feel limp and are still encircled around Michael's thin frame. Unlocking my arms, I gently place Michael's head down on his plaid pillowcase. Kissing his damp head, I make my exit as quietly as I made my entrance not that long ago. Rubbing my burning eyes, I pull my arms closer towards my face, hoping that the numbers of my watch might force me back from the lifeless. Damn! Is it really 10:45 p.m.? I still have laundry to face, and tomorrow's lunches ominously chanting my name. Never mind that I haven't checked my e-mails in a couple of days, and clients are waiting for responses to questions they have posed. I guess it is all going to have to wait until tomorrow because I can barely keep my eyes open any longer. My own bed seems like the perfect place for me right now.

Jack clues into the fact that I am not following him. In a hushed voice, or so he seems to think it is quiet, he calls out my name. Breaking the silence of the evening lull, it sounds weirdly annoying.

"Aren't you coming down?"

"No, Jack, I'm not." I am pretty irritated at the prospect of having to recoup the valuable domesticity hours I have just lost out on, succumbing to sleep instead.

Jack snickers, "Whatever, Kat. Good-night."

If I thought he was annoyed before, I am most certain of it now. Too tired to argue, I am not in the mood to defend my fatigue to Jack. Any conversation will just have to wait until tomorrow. Flicking the light switch on in my own bedroom, I take stock that I am still clad in my same power dress from early this morning. Thinking back over the course of the day, I realize that my DVF dress has played a lot of diverse but significant roles today.

Dear Diary,

I'm beat, I mean really beat. What a long day. Thank you for letting the kids have a really good first day of school, and thank you for helping me keep it together when I was sure I was going to fall apart. I am so thankful for my new clients and this wonderful opportunity. I know I can do a great job—thanks for the chance! As for Michael, I know that he is trying to be brave, but I'm not abandoning my family just because I want to work. Any chance he might understand that? I will always be their mommy first, but that doesn't mean I can't be a great designer too, does it? Does it have to be one or the other—can't it be both? Hmm-m-m, I'm really tired, I need to get some sleep. 'Night.

Later,
Me, Your Very Tired Simple Girl

Chapter Six

Day two of back-to-school, and I am praying that things run a little more smoothly this morning because, I swear to God, I don't think my Italian nerves can handle a repeat of yesterday morning's shenanigans. My BFF, Alessia, downtown attorney by day, world-class shopper by afternoon, and swanky lounge bar attendee by night, lives by the adage that what you resist persists. Should I interpret that as *bring on the craziness, kids, 'cause I won't crack*, and then it might not occur? Yeah, like that is so not going to happen! Ever since she started up with her new life coach, I get weekly updates on how I *should* be living my life. *Thanks, Lessia,* but for starters, a hot cup of coffee this morning would be awesome. And just because I value our friendship, maybe I'll even throw in a little prayer to the universe for less drama this morning since I have a full day ahead of me and have neither the time nor the patience for childish antics. Speaking of Alessia, I have got to call her this morning and fill her in on yesterday's turn of events. One thing is for certain, Miss Single-and-Carefree will be ecstatic to hear of my news.

Much as I tease her, I absolutely adore Alessia. I have from the day we first met as kids in elementary school. Alessia has chutzpah, plain and simple. She always seems to know what she wants and where she's going and doesn't let anyone or anything stand in her way of getting it—well, most of the time, that is.

See, there was this one minor incident last year ... okay, so maybe it was a major incident. Scratch that out 'cause who am I kidding here? It was one ginormous, colossal incident! Alessia had her heart majorly broken by a guy. Yeah sure, big whoop, so this happens all the time, right? But this wasn't just any guy, oh no, this was the man of her dreams! The one she was going to walk down the aisle with, quite literally, and have babies with. The one that she bought the Monique Lhullier wedding gown for! The positively stunning, crystal-beaded bodice and full ballerina skirt trimmed with lace and beads Monique Lhullier wedding gown. The one that could have paid for an entire university education for one kid for four years, but "totally worth the price because he is so-o-o worth it," Alessia defended. *Boy, was she ever wrong!*

The guy, Marcello, decided that he couldn't go through with it and called the wedding off two weeks before the big day! "I love you, but I'm just not *in* love with you," he blubbered to her. *Can you imagine? Bastard! Jerk!* But that's not the worst part, oh no, the worst part is that lo and behold, we found out from our sources (let's face it, every woman has her sources) that a mere six months later, Marcello walked down the aisle with some skanky (overgrown roots, *yuck*) ex-girlfriend of his.

What a D-A-W-G!

The aftermath of Marcello was a messy cleanup, to say the least. But if it was any consolation to Alessia (and it was), we did hear from our sources, again, that the bride wore some generic gown that day, probably a ho-hum Vera Wang or something like that. *So predictable!*

Anyways, I think that Marcello-mania may have had an effect in shaping who Alessia is today ... just a smidge!

Secretly I've always hoped that they would bump into each other on a street corner or something like that and Marcello could see again just exactly what he lost, because Alessia is definitely one live firecracker! But she's so much more than that. She's a fabulous lawyer and a wonderful person with a huge heart ... yes, I know this is such an oxymoron, but in Alessia's case, it is the complete and honest truth. I swear it! It's really too bad that most people can't understand this about her because all they seem to focus on is the glamorous life she boasts about at times—wild independence and a designer wardrobe that would make even Carrie Bradshaw jealous (well, sort of jealous). And the irony to all of this is that I think Alessia would trade it all in for a chance at true love again. Even with that dog Marcello! If he were to come grovelling back, that is. As much as she mocks the house and the kids and the white picket fence, I think that's exactly what she longs for, but she would never admit to that.

When my kids were little, just babies in fact, Auntie Lessia would pop in often and play up her role as the doting aunt with them. Outfitting Michael with every pint-size version of Ralph Lauren button-down shirts and chinos available was one of her favourite ways of spoiling my son. Bonpoint cashmere sweaters for Nikki and teeny-weeny Burberry everything else for Ella. I can barely count the number of times I would stand waiting impatiently behind the front door in anticipation of Alessia's arrival. At the time, she seemed like my only connection to the real world. On second thought, maybe I was the one living in the real world, and she wasn't. Sometimes I'm just not sure. All I know is that when I was elbow-deep in poopy Huggies and smashed-up carrots, Alessia would walk in with perfectly wrapped designer packages in hand and save the day. To me, she looked like she belonged somewhere on the Champs-Elysées instead of in my boring and baby-infested suburban kitchen. And to top all that off—as if that wasn't enough—my BFF would always manage to have the time to stop and pick up a piping-hot Starbucks for yours truly!

Repeatedly Alessia told me that I was crazy for putting my career on hold for "those little munchkins." Sure, they were cute, she would offer, but "just hire a nanny, Kat, like the rest of the fuckin' world does! What's wrong with you?" she often pleaded.

Of course, due to her blunt nature, her needling was always done in the most obvious of ways, but always with an edge of humour attached to it. She was wise enough to realize that the frail state of this young mother was questionable. Humour was therefore a must! Between sips of her latte and flipping through the latest edition of *In Style* magazine, which always lay sprawled across my coffee table (I wasn't totally out of the loop), just having her presence near comforted me more than she could have ever possibly imagined. Over and over, Alessia would ask me how I could bear staying home doing the same thing over and over again day after day. "What a monotonous and boring life," she would express to me. "You're insane!" I had heard it so many times before that I could recite the speech verbatim if I had wanted to—which I didn't, 'cause I was living it, remember?

I can vividly recall this one particular time when Michael was about six months old and Alessia had stopped by for one of her visits. My dishevelled appearance on that particular afternoon was more than she could bear. "For Christ's sake, Kat, are you going to get yourself some help or what? If not a nanny, then a cleaning lady? Or better yet, a shrink to check your brain? *Somebody?*"

"No, Less, I can do this on my own. It's not so bad." I was a good liar back then. "And besides, Jack doesn't feel comfortable with strangers helping out."

"Who cares what Jack says; what do you want?"

Rolling my eyes and with arms stretched out, I would pass off Michael to Alessia like a linebacker to his teammate. "Here, Less, burp the baby for me; I have to get dinner started."

Reminiscing about those days right now made me want to laugh and cry at the same time, if that is even possible. The laughter was due to my watching Alessia's squeamish expression every time I handed over my cherub-faced son for her to burp. I knew Alessia well enough to know that the only thing running through her mind in that instance was the outrageous cost of whatever designer garb she had on and that if Michael threw up on her, how on earth could she make it home and change before her dinner meeting? My tears? I wanted to be the one dressed in designer wear and going to a fabulous dinner that someone else had cooked!

With my back to the two of them pulling vegetables out of the refrigerator, I would typically use the same defensive line I always recited, the only one I had in fact. "Alessia, we've been through this how many times? Jack and I agreed that I would put my career plans on hold while we started a family. It made sense at the time. What do you not understand?"

Patiently patting Michael on the back, Alessia, not one to ever hold back, would blurt out her usual line, "You're fucked, kid! Seriously fucked, and so is your husband!"

"Besides, I have you to help me; why would I want anyone else?" I chided her often.

I couldn't help but giggle as I chopped up squash and carrots and occasionally glanced up and noticed how Alessia was holding Michael. Not a natural mommy at the time, that was for sure, but I had no doubt in my mind that when the time came for her to have a child of her own, she would know precisely what to do.

"And now what the hell are you doing?" Alessia asked, half-joking, half not.

"Making baby food?" I answered haphazardly. Was I doing something unquestionable?

Throwing her head back (at least she made sure to keep her hands securely on the baby), Alessia cried out in a high-pitched voice, "Oh fuck, are you Martha Stewart now? You can buy that shit in stores, Kat, even I know that! Why in God's name are you making baby food?"

I really couldn't fault Alessia for not being able to contain her explosive personality—that's just who she was, fiery and lovable all rolled into one beautiful best friend. But at last, my mundane life was far too much for my downtown chi-chi girlfriend to handle. I had managed to throw her over the suburban edge.

Alessia glanced down at her stainless steel Cartier and announced, "Well, golly gee, look at the time. I gotta go." We both laughed.

As much as I was well aware that Alessia really did have to leave, the tone in which she broadcast it sent us both into fits of schoolgirl laughter, something neither one of us could refrain from doing and something not very many people from the outside looking in would find very humorous. But that's the thing between BFFs: you're well aware of what the other person is thinking and feeling, and you know when they are being comical without them ever having to explain it to you. It just happens. I also understood that for now, my domestic way of life was worlds apart from the enchanting world she resided in. The truth was, it was even more than I could handle a lot of the times.

I took Michael from Alessia's arms and placed him in his baby swing, securing his seat belt and ensuring he was content. I walked Alessia to the front door, embracing her in our great big Italian-girl hug. Kiss, kiss on both checks. I plunged right into the sentimental fool I knew I had become.

"Hey you, why the tears?" Alessia's voice was sweet and comforting. My meltdowns were a common occurrence in those days.

"Thanks for coming by. I know how busy you are, and you always seem to make time for me. You have no idea how much it means." My voice quivered.

"That's what friends are for. And besides, who else could put up with me? Spa day soon?" she asked, securing a smile on my face to match hers. "Mani's, pedi's, lunch?"

"You got it," I managed through the tears.

And with that, she was gone. Alessia's departure was always difficult for me. She felt like my only link to the outside world. Greedy or not, I longed for a piece of that too. I knew I couldn't hold her hostage forever. I had to let her go. Standing with my back to the front door, I allowed myself to daydream, only briefly however, because I was soon interrupted by a loud wail. *Oh shit, Michael!*

Dear Diary,

   I know how very lucky I am to have my beautiful healthy baby and Jack, of course, but it would sure be nice to have some time for me again. Where did I go? I feel like I'm lost most of the time, and yet I'm still in this same house— my house doing pretty much the same thing and looking pretty much the same way. My hair is still neatly brushed, so I think I still look the same, although my hands, which were once soft and silky, are a little more chapped and ragged these days. And my clothes, well, my beautiful silk blouses and wrap dresses hang in my closet, calling me, begging me to come back to them... hmm... one day ... one day I will.

Later,
Me, Your Simple Girl

And it was from this moment on that I promised myself that I would always try to keep myself together. Make sure that I was always well-groomed and presentable. Even if on the inside I felt like I was going to fall apart, at the very least on the outside, I would look like I had it all together.

And so, one baby, two babies, three babies, no more, Alessia stood by me every baby step of the way. And for that I will be eternally grateful to her.

Somehow, I never did get around to answering her question asking me what I wanted. Not then anyways; instead, I just kept going through the motions of what stay-at-home mommies do best. They simply stay home.

~

Drin-n-g-g-g!

I roll onto my side and fix my eyes on the silver Tiffany clock resting on my night stand. Am I reading the clock accurately? Is it really 6:30 a.m.? *Whoa!* How long have I been lying here thinking about days long gone?

Okay, sleeping beauty, time to get up and face the world. It's morning, and what a glorious day it seems to be out there. Through the open window, I can hear the sweet canto of singing birds, making it feel like the current season is still smack-dab in the middle of summer, though I am only too aware that the familiar smell of the air wafting through the window clearly indicates that fall is imminent.

Either way, spring, summer, fall, or winter, I am going to make the best of this day and revel in the excitement of this new project that lies straight in front of me.

Chapter Seven

By the end of week one of back-to-school, life is anything but uninteresting. Just once I want to see what it will feel like to be bored. Really bored. I mean the sit-on-my-ass-and-flip-through-fashion-magazines-wondering-what-the-hell-to-do-next kind of bored. Suffice it to say, boredom is not a part of my vocabulary. *Frazzled, frantic, frenetic, overwhelmed*—these words depict me best. These are the ones that often describe my actions, my movements, my entire existence, but boredom?—not even once!

The kids seem to be back into the swing of things just fine. Michael is bubbling over with excitement since hockey season will soon be well underway. Jack had insisted on extra speed skating sessions this past summer to build Michael's endurance, and of course, Michael is now eager to show off all those hard-learned lessons. Dance classes have resumed once again for Nikki, and thus so has our additional mortgage payment. Because anyone with a child in competitive dance classes knows that the cost of seeing their budding ballerina twirl around on stage comes with an enormous price tag attached to it. Since she really is a natural-born dancer—graceful and swanlike in appearance, with the ability to shimmy her way across a stage with ease and overwhelming confidence, all of my angst about exorbitant costs seems to vanish once that vision became a reality yet again. I have to say that I admire Nikki's sassiness. If only she could understand how this will serve her well later on in life, like, say, when she is my age! She will get it one day, of this I am confident. And Ella, sweet Ella! If only I had a dollar every time Ella wanted to try a new extracurricular activity, I might not need to work at all. She is still trying to find her passion, because after all, when you're six-years-old, the world truly is your oyster!

"Piano?"

"No, Mommy, not piano. Drums?"

"Not likely, Ella. The clarinet?"

"Uh-uh. Hockey?"

"Really? Hockey, but you're a girl!" I protest. "Karate?" *Heck, a girl needs to defend herself.*

"No, Mommy. Skateboarding?"

"Skateboarding? What?"

So it should not have come as a surprise to me when on day four of grade one, *day four,* I receive my first of many "it's about your daughter, Ella," phone calls.

"Mrs. Bancari?" the voice inquires.

"This is she," I reply.

"Mrs. Bancari, this is Mrs. Mansor, the new principal at West Elm Public School."

Uh-oh. I like the old principal better already. She never called.

"There was a little incident earlier today that must be brought to your attention."

Oh boy! This isn't sounding so good.

"For no apparent reason, at least none that the on-duty teacher at lunchtime today could reasonably see or deduce for that matter, and quite unexplainably—*blah, blah, blah ..."*

Oh fuck, just get to the point, will you! What did Ella do, lady? Wait a minute? Oh shit! Was I just thinking this, or did I really say it?

"I'm sorry, what were you saying, Mrs. Mansor? I don't believe I heard you correctly. Who punched whom?" I question, making an attempt to decipher the gibberish she is regurgitating.

"Your daughter, Ella, for no apparent reason wound up and punched another child in the stomach. Apparently she was not instigated by the other child. She just did it right out of the blue! Of course, we've had to call in the parents of the victimized child."

"Of course," I muster. *Victimized! Ple-e-e-a-s-e! Ella is no more than forty pounds, soaking wet at that, who could she even injure?*

"Is she okay? I mean, the other child, is she all right?"

"Yes. She's going to be fine. She is just very upset, as you very well might imagine."

"Yes, of course. I'm terribly shocked and sorry, Mrs. Mansor, this is so unlike Ella. I-I, I'm not sure what would make Ella do such a thing," I stammer. "My husband and I do not condone such behaviour among our children. We will definitely sit down and speak with Ella tonight. Perhaps I should come and pick her up now. She must be feeling badly about what's happened." I don't know what else to say and feel that I am finally at a loss for words.

How could my sweet, little, itty-bitty Ella have hurt anyone? She can't stand it when I swat a housefly, never mind her thrashing another child. As it is, she is awfully small for her age, so unless she beat up some kid in kindergarten, from what I saw earlier this week there are not too many classmates that are much smaller than she.

I am mortified. What must Mrs. Mansor be thinking about Jack and me? That maybe we are inadequate parents who have no control over our children? That we don't know how to discipline our offspring?

What does a parent do in this situation? Quite frankly, I haven't got a clue. I have had no experience with a violent child before. Oh God! Is Ella considered a violent child now?

So at the risk of sounding repetitive, I ask again, "Shall I come and pick Ella up from school?"

"Absolutely not, Mrs. Bancari. Ella should not be rewarded for her behaviour by leaving school early."

Who said anything about a reward?

"She will be spending the remainder of the afternoon in my office, doing her schoolwork at my desk so I can monitor her behaviour and aggression, of course."

Aggression? Okay, lady, let's put things into perspective here, really. She is a six-year-old little girl, as cute as a button, and so she wound up and hit a kid who probably provoked her, but aggression is a little severe, don't you think? I can't help but envision Ella's slender and still summer-sun-kissed ankles fastened securely in iron shackles and chained up to some passé pressboard principal's desk. *Gasp—* not even real Canadian wood! Oh God, what if she's donning some ugly, faded orange, polyester romper? Not a vibrant and tangy tangerine colour, but some peachy, washed-out orange colour from the eighties. *E-w-w-w! My poor baby!*

I wonder what she is doing at this very moment. Have they asked her to draw a picture of what makes her happy? Have they called in a school psychologist, and are they hovering over her waiting for some demonic scribble to emerge from her crayons across a sheet of pristine, white, 8 ½" x 11" bond paper?

She'll show them! Knowing my Ella as I do, she is probably drawing a picture of trees and flowers, with a bright canary-yellow sun bursting from the top of the paper. Her sky! Okay, so maybe I'm being a little melodramatic here, maybe, just maybe. But I know my child, and she is anything but aggressive, for goodness sake! And besides, I didn't suggest picking her up early to take her out for ice cream and high-five her, all the while belting out "good job, kiddo."

That's it, my impression is firmly rooted. This new principal is a moronic fool!

On second thought, best to keep that little bit of insight all to myself for now.

~

I do my best to keep my focus on the file that lies spread open across my desk directly in front of me. Kip Rogers. Ah, yes, my young thirty-something-year-old single male client with slicked-back, black wavy hair, the brightest of aquamarine eyes, and the most charming of smiles that shows off his perfectly Zoom!- whitened teeth brilliantly. Mr. Suave came to me asking me to help him create a sexy single guy's condo in the sky. More like a love shack, if you ask me, since every time we are in the midst of a meeting, his BlackBerry insistently vibrates. From the look on his face, once he is deep in conversation, that's not the only thing that's vibrating! *Yuck!*

I am having a difficult time concentrating on Kip's love cave right now. Silver-grey moiré silk drapes or gauzy white billowy linen? This type of talk typically energizes me, fuelling my every notion, but for the time being, my tank feels as though it is running on empty. My thoughts have gone back to their default setting—Mommy mode—wondering what Ella is thinking and doing in this very instant.

I try to resist the temptation to call Jack at work and fill him in, but I am weakening rapidly, needing to offload some of my emotions on him. Typically I try to deal with the daily kids' stuff on my own, since most times it is a trivial matter, which to me falls under the job description of working-mother-from-home category. But this is different. This one is just too important, and I am just too upset. I can't wait until tonight. I need to discuss this with him ASAP.

I dial his office number first. Jack's perky receptionist, a.k.a. Ditzy Daisy, picks up on the second ring. Hey, now that's a switch!

"Co-o-per ... Ban-car-i ... and Ass-o-ciates ... how may I dir ..." she attempts to sing out. (*Note to self: Enough! Inform Jack it is time to inject this girl with a double shot of espresso in the mornings. This canto is painfully brutal to listen to at the best of times. And now, in a crisis, it feels even worse!*)

I cut her off. "Daisy! Hi, it's Katarina. Is Jack available, please?" The tone of my voice sounds urgent, yet still polite.

"Hi there yourself, Mrs. Bancari. How are you and the little Bancari children doing?"

Oh good God, she wants to make small talk, now, at a time like this! And by the way, how many times have I asked her to call me by my first name? "Mrs. Bancari" is way too formal for me. Not to mention that it makes me feel old, and today in particular, I am already feeling tired and worn-out and don't require any additional assistance from her.

Inhaling a deep breath, I reply cordially, "We're all doing fine, Daisy; thanks so much for asking." After all, it isn't the poor girl's fault I am feeling like a rabid dog needing to take a bite out of something. "Is Jack in by chance?"

"Well, let me see here." *Pause.* "His button says he's in, but you know Jack, he never moves his button." *Longer pause.*

I am so close to popping her button any second now!

Oh no! *It's me, isn't it?*

Maybe Mrs. Mansor is right. Maybe Ella is aggressive. Maybe she gets her aggression from me!

"Daisy," I plead firmly, "would you mind just checking if Jack is in or not? Please, this is rather important!" She made me do it. She made me lose my temper. It is all her fault!

Oh my God! Here we go again!

This is probably exactly what happened to my little Ella today. Some snot-nosed little kid probably egged her on, and she just came undone! Unravelled. It *is* my fault, damn it! My mother always tells me that the apple doesn't fall far from the tree. Maybe she is right. Or maybe, just maybe, Ella took a sip of my double-shot, no-sugar espresso this morning! Come to think of it, I asked Jack to make me a second one this morning. (My Jack is the world's best barista. Okay, so maybe all you have to do is just push a button on the Saeco machine, but still, that does take a little bit of work and some effort). In fact, my coffee did look rather short. I wonder if that little bugger took a quick sip while I wasn't looking. Maybe that's the reason she is all wound up at school today.

"Jack Bancari speaking." I guess he didn't forget to move his button after all.

"Jack, it's me. You're not going to believe what happened today!" I feel as though I am hyperventilating, but I don't care. Poor Jack is used to my implosions by now. So, detail by detail, I recount to Jack everything that Mrs. Mansor said to me, leaving no facet out, 'cause let's face it, in the end, it's the details that matter most. I wrap up my soliloquy with a deep sigh, followed by a desperate, "Jack, what are we going to do?"

"Kat," Jack speaks softly and calmly. This is always his way, thank goodness. He totally balances me out. "Is that the whole story?"

"Yes!" I cry.

"Did anything else happen?" He is obviously as upset as I am. *Duh!*

"No. I think that's all," I continue to bellow.

You won't believe what follows! You just cannot believe what follows! *Laughter!* Jack bursts out into a belly-filled, full-out, gut-wrenching laughter! In fact, I'm almost certain that he has even stopped breathing, if only momentarily. As he tries to catch his breath, all I can make out are a few barely audible words.

"Oh my God, oh my God, this is too funny!"

"No! It is not!" I clearly do not see the humour here.

" Kat, you should hear yourself right now." Jack is still laughing profusely.

Angry, hurt, and perhaps slightly embarrassed at my *minor overreaction to the situation*, but not exaggerated retelling of the horrifying event that has taken place, I protest, "Jack, I'm sorry, but I don't see how you can laugh about this. This is serious!"

"Kat, honey, listen, you're right, Ella should have known better. We tell her to use her words and never hit anyone, hands-off policy and all that stuff. And for hitting the kid, we'll punish her. But really, Kat, she's so small, and I've seen her try to punch Mikey in the leg, and as much as I hate to admit it, she throws a punch like a little girl, 'cause *she is a little girl*. I highly doubt that she could have really hurt this other kid. Think about it logically, please." Jack's throttled laughter has tapered off to a slight chuckle by now.

I know he is probably right, but I am still visibly upset.

"I promise you we will deal with Killer tonight."

"Jack!"

"Sorry, I couldn't resist. Relax, Kat, it'll all be fine. I'll see you tonight." And with that, Jack hangs up.

I, on the other hand, have to face the music and pick the kids up after school and deal with the scorned looks I am sure to receive from the principal and the parents of the "victim."

Killer is going to have to make a jailbreak from Mrs. Mansor's office in a few short hours, and this mama bear is going to have to be the one to spring her loose, like it or not!

Dear Diary,

Okay, so maybe I overreact just a little bit at times, but what parent doesn't when the well-being of his or her child is in question? I mean, we do everything to try and teach them right from wrong, good from bad, innocence from evil, and then you're faced with these kinds of issues. You try to replay all those talks in your mind, all those painstaking lectures you delivered, and wonder if you should have done it differently or worded your words another way because then the outcome might have been different. Okay, so I know this is little stuff, but it could have been big stuff, and maybe one day it will be big stuff. But for now, I guess it's really not the end of the world, right? And I'll deal with it just like I've dealt with other stuff and gotten over it, right? And just like I'll have to deal with more stuff later and somehow figure it out too. I always seem to.

Later,
Me, Your Simple Girl

~

"What do you mean you don't want to talk about it, Ella?" I ask. My voice is firm.

"Just what I said, I don't want to talk about it." Ella's lips are in a faultless pouting position, her thin arms firmly pressed across her body.

I have witnessed this stance far too many times. Her short legs are dangling down from the side of her bed while her feet never touch the ground. My eyes focus on her scraped knees. Are they fresh from today? No, they can't be. They look as though they have begun to scab over, most likely from some mishap that happened yesterday or the day before that. With Ella, you just never know. She is tough all right, so it's not as though she comes home crying to me with every scrape or every bruise she happens to successfully wear. I turn to face Jack. He is standing directly beside me, letting me do all the talking, clearly to no avail. He knows me well enough to know that my facial expression is to be interpreted as "you talk to her now," which he does.

"Ella," Jack's voice is terse but firm. I should remind him that this is our six-year-old daughter he is speaking to; he's not closing a business transaction. "Ella, we can do this the easy way or the hard way. I think you might want to do this the easy way. So let's try this again, shall we? Why did you punch your friend in the stomach?" Jack's persuasive tactics are clearly being lost on our child. Perhaps they work in the finance genre, but not in the child-rearing one.

Even I have to give it to her. Ella remains firm in her stance. "I told you—I don't wanna talk about it!" *Strike three and you're out, Jack!* Come to think of it, we both are. For now this inning is over, and we are clearly lagging behind Team Ella. So I decide to do what any reasonable parent does at this point: I put Ella on a time-out and march downstairs to broach the issue with Michael and Nikki, my moles where Ella is concerned. Maybe they can shed some light on what happened today.

Jack and I follow the frightening noise that is rising from below and make our way down to the dreaded basement. *What am I thinking?* I should know better than to interrupt them during a tense round of Rock Band. Too bad for them; this is serious. Their game will just have to wait. While I am at it, I should take the time and mention to them that "Living on a Prayer" actually has a little more pitch than they are offering up. Better yet, maybe I will wait and save that for a more appropriate time, when I actually feel like joining in and lending my artistic talents to them. Nikki's fingers slide off the toy guitar as she sees me stride through the door. Michael, drumsticks still in hand, takes no notice of our entrance and continues beating the pseudo percussion in front of him. Nikki throws him a look as if to say, "Are you stupid? They want to talk to us." Finally Michael clues in to her stare. The noise subsides, *thankfully*, and two blank faces gaze intently up at us.

"Are we in trouble?" Michael takes the lead.

"No, you're not in trouble," Jack responds.

"Did you talk to her?" Nikki asks.

I nod.

"What did she say, Mommy?" Nikki's tone is serious.

"Actually, nothing. She said absolutely nothing," I answer. The sound of frustration is evidently clear in the sound of my voice. "Did either of you notice anything, anything at all in the playground today?"

Michael shakes his head from side to side. Clearly he has no idea what could have provoked Ella to lash out at the other child. Like Jack, Michael finds the situation quite comical. Nikki, on the other hand, seems to share my overwhelming concern, or at the very least, pretends to—more than likely, the latter is in reality true. However, she too has no idea what would have made Ella strike her "friend."

Without warning, and still on a time-out by my account, Hurricane Ella seems to be entering the vicinity. It is the reverberation of the intense pounding down the stairs, one tread at a time, that suggests she might be approaching the area with a mighty force at any moment now.

And there she stands beneath the arched doorway. Had there been a celestial blue light above her, I would have sworn that here before me stood a considerably crushed but beautiful angel. Her usual, round, cherubic, porcelain face is now red and blotchy; salty tears have evidently made it that way. Her brown eyes typically dancing with zest are now replaced with a swollen and puffy pair. The only thing that has remained a constant is that they are still surrounded by a mass of tousled angelic hair spun with golden flecks, the only part of her that has remained unscathed by today's turn of events—thank goodness for that, at the very least. Clearly we are not prepared for the storm that is about to ensue. With her tummy concave ... no, make that convex ... concave ... no, make that convex again, Ella's rapid breathing suggests that she is about to become undone without a moment's notice.

"(hiccup) Do-o (hiccup) yo-u-u (hiccup) wan-n-t-t to know (hiccup) why-y-y I-I-I (hiccup) punched Raphaella? 'Cause she's a big fat meanie (hiccup), that's why. And she-she kept on calling me a midget, and I told her that I'm not a midget, that my mommy tells me that I'm big and strong, and-and she said that me and Mommy are both dumb then, 'cause I'm just a plain old *midget!*"

And with that, Ella burst into an ocean of rapidly flowing tears. Huge, raging tears full of all the pent-up emotion any six-year-old could possibly contain. Jack and I and the other kids stand motionless, not knowing what to do or what to say. Our stillness, however, is quickly broken by the floodgates of our hearts bursting open for Ella as we watch her sob uncontrollably. Nikki and I are the first to run towards her, embracing her from either side of her diminutive frame.

"Oh, sweetheart, it's okay." My voice serene, in an attempt to comfort her.

"You are big and strong!" Nikki adds convincingly.

While Nikki and I do our best to console Ella, I witness Jack and Michael huddled together deep in conversation. As Michael whispers into Jack's ear, I see what appears to be a grin growing on his face. Jack is making a valiant attempt to not burst into laughter at whatever information Michael is sharing with him. I can't imagine what is so funny at a time like this; I will probe him about that later. For now, Ella's frail heart requires some much-needed TLC.

~

With Ella finally settled in for the night and Michael and Nikki fast asleep, I rest my nightly read down on my lap and turn over to face Jack, who is trying to position his body just so for the peaceful few hours that hopefully lie ahead of him.

"Hey," I ask, "you never did tell me, what were you and Michael giggling about earlier?" I am exceptionally curious.

Jack's eyes immediately widen, imminent sleep immediately replaced with more laughter.

"That Raphaella girl that Ella apparently tortured today. Michael says she's as least twice as tall as Ella and is probably three times her weight. Michael says she's almost as big as he is. From what Mikey said, almost all of the girls in Ella's class are a lot bigger than her. I guess Scraper-Ella showed her today, huh?"

I rub my eyes. What a long day this has been. I have a hunch that this is just the beginning of what is going to be an incredibly interesting school year. And with that, I switch off my night-light and settle in for what I am hoping is going to be a night filled with sweet dreams. I could sure use some tonight.

Dear Diary,

Why is Ella so stubborn? Where does she get it from? Why didn't she just tell us what had happened when we first asked? Why on earth did the drama have to unravel just so? What made her think she had to be so brave with us and couldn't tell us the truth about what happened right away? Trying to problem solve on her own by punching this girl? I guess being teased finally got the best of her, I get that. I suppose she felt that her words were just falling on deaf ears with this girl. I hope she really understands that violence doesn't fix anything, it just makes things worse. And if this Raphaella kid is as big as Michael says she is, could Ella really have hurt her? I know, I know, she's just little, but still, violence is never the answer, I hope she understands that now. I suppose I'll just have to drill it into her a little more. And yes, I'm well aware this too shall pass ... but could you make it pass a little more quickly please? Yawn! 'Night ...

Later,
Me, Your Incredibly Tired Simple Girl

Chapter Eight

Monday morning. The first full week of school is about to begin for the kids, which means it's time for me to really get myself into gear and focus on my work.

The beauty of what I do, that is, being self-employed, is that I am my own keeper. I am my own boss. No clock to punch, no superior to report to, no weekly staff meetings listening to those colleagues who appear to make little sense and complain about trivial-type matters. On the flip side, there is no steady income (in fact, no income at all some months), no paid vacation days, no paid sick days when I feel like royal hell or when my kids have a cold, no mental health days, and the worst part, no one hanging over me making sure my work gets done when I just don't feel like doing it. Now some people may not think this last one is such a terrible thing. In fact, you might actually think this is a perk—a bonus—but let me tell you, it's not easy. I *am* the queen of procrastination! And the truth is that even I can only surf the Web, flip through tear sheets, scrub yet another toilet bowl, and push things around on my desk for so long—not necessarily in that order, of course. And I can't even begin to tell you how many times Nikki has strolled into my office only to find me pointlessly perusing Neiman Marcus.com for the latest fashion trends when I'm feeling "a little uninspired."

My only keeper is my client—that *guy* or *girl* who, too, is probably slacking off somewhere and sometime—who, too, is juggling a demanding schedule of his or her own so that is why they hire moi. Yes, moi. I am the one who is supposed to be full of inspiring ideas and creative thoughts; thus, the onus is on me to transform their square box, their four walls, into their sanctuary, their home, their office, their domicile address, their reprieve at the end of a long and exhausting day. Inevitably, I sometimes become their shrink, marriage councillor, babysitter, and all around go-to-girl schlepper. If this sounds like a complaint, let me clarify right here and now, it absolutely is not. I love my job, I adore my clients (most of them, that is), and I can't imagine doing anything else with my life.

With the kids finally off to school, it is time at last for me to sit at my desk, java in hand, and begin my work. *Hmm.* Who shall I start with? Kip? Sure, might as well try again; it didn't go so well the last time. I honestly feel that *Kipper*, my affectionate pet name for him, belongs among the beautiful people of Palm Beach and not among those of us living in the cosmopolitan city of Toronto. With his shiny ebony hair, permanent golden tan, pearly white teeth, and Lilly Pulitzer summer wardrobe (which he wears all year round), he is beyond doubt an authentic California golden-boy. For now, though, he is my golden-boy client, and I have no interest in letting go of him anytime soon. Kip has a slightly egotistical approach to just about every topic he broaches and with almost all people he encounters, but not in an unauthentic, snobbish kind of way. Kip is a finance guy—a Bay Street stockbroker in Toronto—which is the equivalent to New York City's Wall Street, but on a much smaller scale. He works hard, really hard, so if he is *slightly* pompous, I suppose he has just cause to be; he comes by his affluence honestly. He is the first to admit that he started out with very humble beginnings. Kip had very little for a very long period of time. Born and raised in a working-class family that could only provide the minimal necessities to him and his siblings has kept him honest. But he swore to himself that he would work hard and play hard and make something of his life. So he did, and he has. So what that he shares this little bit of trivia with almost all people who he meets along the way? I still adore Kip. At heart, I know that he is a decent man, and that's good enough for me. Yes, he is an it's-all-about-me kind of guy, but that is only on the surface. Deep down, if push comes to shove, Kip will be there in a pinch if you need him to be. In the meanwhile, I can deal with Kip and his overinflated ego. I have to admit, happily married and all, that Kip is easy on the eyes and has a great sense of humour on top of it all, which makes working with him enjoyable. It is definitely easy to get distracted at times by his charming ways and charismatic approach, but I know well enough to stay grounded where he is concerned. The only problem with Kip, if I have to find one fault in him, is that a one-hour meeting about furniture placement and breezy fabrics can easily turn into a long evening with yours truly playing Kip's designer/therapist. Ironic, isn't it? If you looked at Kip and didn't know him, you would think this guy had it all, and now months into this project, I realize that Kip is just a successful, good-looking guy searching for true friendships. See, this is exactly what I'm talking about. Here I am trying to figure out which fabrics are going to work best on his new white Roche Bobois tuxedo sofa, and I'm back into analyzing his life!

Floor plans? Where did I put them? In Kip's file? Of course not; that would have been too obvious. What's this pile here? *In Style* magazine, *Town & Country*, the telephone bill, a dentist bill (*what else is new?*), more school forms to fill in, oh look—Kip's floor plans—of course, why did I not think to look here first?

What a fantastic place Kip has found himself. A penthouse suite in one of the most sought-after buildings in downtown Toronto. Each room seems to be the perfect size—not too copious and not too diminutive, but just the ideal size to spread out the perfect balance of furnishings and still house friends among them without feeling overly crowded. The uncomplicated flow of each room connecting to the next makes it evident that whoever designed this space was so clearly aware of movement from one space to the next. And did I happen to mention the breathtaking view? Kip's apartment has such a fantastic view of the city. With so much natural light filtering through, he rarely has to switch on any artificial lighting—a designer's dream! Because of it, our lighting plan is entirely simple—some overhead illumination, but the majority of it is accent lighting by way of wall sconces, table lamps, and lots of candles. Kip made sure to inform me that he had envisioned his home full of candles just about everywhere. Need I say more? This guy is such a player (or just a romantic fool)! But who am I to judge?

Dear Diary,

Okay, so maybe I am judging, but just a little bit though. When I try to go for ambiance at home, you know what I get? "Mommy, why is it so dark in here?" "Mommy, I'm blind, I can't see!" Or ... the best is, "Mommy, whose birthday is it today?" Because, of course, candles of any shape or size equal a birthday, don't they? The more I light, the more the kids run around the house blowing them all out. Ella just runs around singing "Happy Birthday" to herself and making wishes at every stop along the way. Okay, so maybe it is sort of funny and cute when she does that—but only sort of. Once in a while, though, just once, I would love to be surrounded by that soft, tranquil glow of illuminated candles. You know what I'm talking about? The same thing I'm creating for Kip ... just once! Okay, so maybe I'm acting greedy, because who am I kidding? I want it more than just once; a few times would be fantastic. Is that asking for a lot?

Later,
Me, Your Simple Girl

I decide, and Kip agrees to position his sexy sofa against the wall of windows in his apartment. I have come to this decision after standing at great length with him in his living room one day, shortly after he has closed on the purchase of his love shack.

With arms wide open, Kip sings out to me, "So, Katarina, what do you think?" And not waiting for my reply (so I'm not entirely sure why he even bothered asking), "It's mine, darling, all mine!" Yes, it is.

I recall thinking to myself, oh brother, "darling?" And guess what, that's what Kip's been calling me ever since. "Darling"! And you want to know something funny? It's kind of grown on me. I'm his darling, and I have to admit that I sort of like it. So what that I've heard him on the telephone talking to others, and clearly I'm not his only darling. I can live with that reality.

With his sexy sofa safely situated (say that five times fast), I suggest to Kip that we pair it up with an equally sexy area rug below, "to ground the space," I suggest. Sure, the dark engineered plank floors are beautiful on their own and easy to clean (not that my confirmed bachelor is doing this himself), still, something supple and silky underfoot, an oasis for his pedicured toes to plunge into at the end of a tiresome day, that might be good, no? Boy wonder loves the idea, thinks that I am a genius for suggesting it. When I show him a tone-on-tone, iridescent, silver-grey silk area rug with an inlay pattern comprised of a luminous silk circular motif, Kip happily agrees—a perfect pairing for his sofa. So far, this is turning out to be pretty uncomplicated, and oh so swanky! I explain how the clean masculine lines of the sofa juxtapose the soft feminine curves of the rug's pattern. Thankfully Kip is sold on the rug. I can stop my sales pitch at any time. Now all I have to do is recommend fabrics for his window coverings. As much as he loves the unblemished view of the city, and being so high up privacy is hardly an issue, window coverings are still an essential element in my design expertise. Kip is easily sold on this idea at first. Vertical blinds are fine, he confirms. He will keep the windows bare most of the time anyways. Vertical blinds over my dead body!

"Kip, tell me something," I argue. "Your black Porsche has a leather interior, I assume?"

Staring at me as though I have two heads, Kip responds, "Of course, it does."

"Well then, tell me, do you think you would feel the same about your car if it was a sleek black Porsche with upholstered fabric seats?" Even I am completely aware of how dumb this question must sound to him. "Of course, you wouldn't. So it only makes sense that we dress your windows with a cool and luxurious fabric, a texture befitting its surroundings. Vertical blinds are not fitting at all!" I have no other choice but to appeal to his masculine side here. There is simply no other way with him.

Mission accomplished! A smirk begins to grow across boy wonder's face. I believe I made my point loud and clear.

"Show me some fabrics, darling, for my windows of course." He is enchanting.

And so, with ready samples in hand, off I go to perform what I do best, create.

Gauzy white linen? Beautiful. But too girly and sweet for my Kip.

Silver-coloured dupioni silk? Gorgeous, elegant, and classy, but perhaps a little too sophisticated for Kip's love nest.

Next! A sheer charcoal silk blend? *Hmm*. Maybe, just maybe, Kipper will go for this one. It's lavish, yet soft; a beautiful fabric to the touch; and super affordable. Now that is a bonus. Kip can still have a great view of the city with this fabric on his windows. There! I think I might have actually accomplished appealing to all of his senses. Not badly done, even if I do say so myself.

Next, Kip wants my advice on laying out his new kitchen. Thank goodness, kitchens are right up my alley. Growing up in an Italian family and being a designer has its advantages when it comes to functionally laying out a kitchen, since just about everything in my life revolves around food and food preparation. Fortunately I love designing and decorating kitchens almost as much as I love to cook and eat. Alessia still has trouble understanding my fascination with cooking, although she too grew up in an Italian household. A culinary chef she is not! I try to make her understand it is all part of the creative process. She thinks I am just plain old crazy.

The ringing of my telephone startles me out of my creative trance. With eyes still focused on my sketch pad, I pick up my portable phone.

"Katarina speaking." I turn on my professional voice, though a formal person I clearly am not.

"Alessia speaking," the voice on the other end rings back melodiously. "Whatcha doing, Kat, cleaning up poop or flambéing some tropical fruit compote thingy?" Alessia loves to tease me.

Grinning unassumingly, as though she can see me but plainly she cannot, I deliver my response wittingly. "Actually, I'm doing neither of those things, you domestaphobe. I am actually working on a client's file."

"Oh, you're playing the role of a big girl today!"

"Fuck you!" I offer with express amusement. Alessia knows I mean that in the most endearing of ways. We often taunt each other in this manner. Ladylike, definitely not! But since we have been best friends for what seems like forever now, we are fully aware when one is joking with the other and when one is not. Alessia and I have an incredible friendship, one that neither of us ever takes for granted. Although never jealous of each other (like a lot of our girlfriends growing up), we do often envy each other's life at certain times. One of the best things about our friendship, though, is that we do tell each other when we feel a pang of envy. Come to think of it, we tell each other almost everything. Alessia doesn't have a sister, only a brother, and frequently reminds me that I am the sister she forever longed to have.

"So, who's the client this time? Some rich, bored housewife?" she asks. I can hear her pause, just long enough to take a sip of her latte.

"Actually, no, not this time. Rich, hot guy this time," I respond.

I am almost certain that I have piqued her interest. Though "oh" is her only remark.

"Just *oh*, Lessi?"

"How rich? How hot? And single?" she questions.

Hmm. I pause before answering. She seems interested in *my* Kip. This is a good start, since Alessia has expressed very little interest in men since her tumultuous breakup with Marcello, focusing more on her work and even more on wayward retail therapy.

"Lives quite well, from what I can see. His place is totally posh and smart. Money doesn't seem to be an object. He's single and loving it from what I can tell. But I have this sneaking suspicion that he would love to have a certain someone to share his love nest with one day, though he won't admit to that very easily."

"Think I like this guy already."

"I don't know if he's your type, Lessi."

I realize only too well that I am sounding like an overbearing mother hen, but someone needs to be that way with Alessia. I have become quite protective of Alessia since her breakup with Marcello. Though most of the time she pretends to not be interested in ever having a serious relationship again, I know that that is exactly what she wants. And even though I know that Kip eventually wants to settle down, he is still too busy having fun, and the last thing I want is for Alessia to get hurt all over again.

"Kip's a great guy. A really nice guy, in fact, but I think he likes to play around still. I don't think he is looking for a serious relationship anytime soon."

"Who said I am?" Alessia's tone is defensive. BFF or not, I know when I have to bite my tongue, and this is one of those times. I could have reminded her that she had been very ready to settle down since she had only been weeks away from walking down the aisle with me by her side, but I decide now is clearly not the appropriate time to be bringing *that* up.

"Right, well … he's not the type of guy for you to even have drinks with. And besides, you've got plenty of other admirers lining up wanting to take you to dinner." I am hopelessly looking to sway the conversation towards some neutral territory.

"So, what else are you working on right now?" Alessia purposely changes the subject, something both of us do when we want to avoid an argument that is certain to ensue. Not a bad idea. She changes her tone right along with it, now speaking more delicately. She is being pensive. Shit! I can't help but feel that somehow we have managed to plunge into some deep water, and I feel that since I am the one who started the conversation, it is my duty to bring her safely back to shore. It is clear from the tone of her voice that Alessia has become lost in her thoughts now too. Since I had already filled her in on the Camilla news, she is current with what is going on in my life, so what is going on in hers?

Think, Kat, think! She's not saying something—something that our conversation has brought to the surface. What is it? Our conversation has obviously triggered some sort of memory—a Marcello memory? The silence is deafening. I can tell that Alessia just wants to keep me on the line, hear my voice, and not have to say much herself.

But why?

She needs to connect with someone she feels close to, someone who makes her feel safe, I suppose, and I have no doubt that someone is me. I should come right out and ask her, but that is not the way to approach her royal toughness. She won't tell until she is good and ready to—which quite possibly might be never.

"Can you do drinks and tapas tonight?" Alessia asks, her voice going up a couple of octaves. This is a positive sign.

I hesitate. I don't want to answer too quickly. "Less, I'm not sure. It's Monday." I am trying to be tender. "The girls have ballet, and Michael has ..." I stop mid-sentence. *You idiot!* The date! Today—what is it? September the eighth. Of course! This was supposed to be Alessia's wedding date. How could I have been so stupid to forget? I do some quick backpedaling. "You know what? I would love to go out tonight!" I am pouring it on thick. "Just the two of us. Like we used to do. Let me just check with Jack and make sure that he's going to be home tonight. Shouldn't be a problem, though."

"So, I'll see you later, then?" Alessia sounds vaguely cheerful.

"For sure!" Even though I am not sure at all. I press the "end" button on the telephone.

Now to call Jack. This is going to be a tough sell. Jack is faintly cynical when it comes to Alessia and her *issues*, Jack feeling like she has plenty of them—issues, that is. It's not as though he has a legitimate problem with my friendship with Alessia, but just that often she is her own worst enemy—ergo, the *issues*. Aren't we all though? Honestly? I have posed this question to Jack several times. Clearly he was never too interested in debating it with me. This is his observation of her, and there is little, if anything, I can do to alter it. We definitely have agreed to disagree on this point.

I dial Jack's cell number, half-hoping that he won't actually pick it up and I can leave a voice-mail message. It is so much easier to be firm with my intentions when there isn't an actual live and breathing human person on the other end. My heart seems to be beating fast. I am being foolish; after all, this is my husband that I am calling. Jack will completely understand even if he holds strong opinions about Alessia. He knows she is my best friend and I will always try and be supportive of her.

"Hello?" Jack's deep voice answers the call.

"Hi, honey. It's me. Are you having a good day so far?"

"Oh yeah, great." Sarcasm is ringing through loud and clear. "You know, the same old, same old. Clients are complaining about their investment returns. A lot of them seem unhappy. Same old stuff."

Perhaps my timing is not so good after all. "Well … um … I'm sorry you're not having a very good day, but I was just wondering if you would be home tonight … early, that is … and if it would be okay if I left you with the kids for a bit. See, Alessia called, and I think something's up with her. She asked if I could go out for drinks and dinner with her." *There!* I did it! I had asked. Actually I hadn't really asked, but I had said something to the effect of "Could you watch the kids so I can go out?" I sense the hesitation on the other end. "Jack, are you still there?"

"Yeah, I'm still here … sure, go if you want, but it is a Monday night. Doesn't Alessia realize you have kids and a family?"

Jack isn't altogether wrong, but he isn't the one on the receiving end of BFF 9-1-1 calls. So how on earth can he understand them or the importance of them? I suppose I can't really blame him much. Guys just don't deal with personal emergencies the way women do. If you really think about it, maybe that is not such a bad thing. For now, though, Alessia needs a friend. Not just any friend, but me, and I am not about to let her down. I understand that Jack is feeling a lot of pressure at work right now, so I am truly feeling a little, no, make that a lot, caught between my husband and my friend right now. If I try to explain Alessia's sadness to Jack, there's no way he will understand, and the truth is it is too exhausting to try and make him understand.

"Thanks for being a good sport about it, hon. I'll pick the kids up from school and have dinner ready for you guys, so you won't have to do too much with them."

"That's not the point, Kat." *Now who is being defensive?*

"I know that's not the point, Jack. But my friend needs me; you would be doing the same if it was one of the guys, and you know it."

"Yeah, I suppose you're right. I gotta go."

"Bye, honey."

It is too late. Jack has already hung up before even hearing my good-bye to him. For some strange reason, I am feeling defeated all over again.

Dear Diary,

So, what am I supposed to do? I understand Jack's frustration, really I do. We barely get time to do anything alone together anymore, and the kids are a handful for him, especially lately since he always seems to be on edge and they seem to be full of more energy at the end of the day. But Alessia's my friend. She needs someone to be with, and not just anyone, someone who gets her without her having to say anything at all. So how can I turn my back on her when I know she's upset about something? And besides, it's not just something small. This is big, really big. Her not-to-be wedding day! I can't leave her alone, not tonight anyways. I won't. I just won't. I hope I can make Jack understand eventually. Okay, I'd better get back to work now.

Later!
Me, Your Simple Girl

Chapter Nine

As I and my stiletto Jimmy Choo's click-clack our way through the parking lot at the kids' school, I can't help but feel as though I am some sort of a strange lone fish swimming in an enormous fish tank. All eyes are peeking in on me, curiously wondering, "What is this odd-looking creature before us?" Seriously, have all these yoga-pant mummies become so hypnotized by Lycra that they have forgotten what denim and heels look like? So maybe I am a little overdone for a mid-afternoon Monday in suburbia, but they have no idea where I've been or where I am going, for that matter.

Following my oh-so-brief conversation with Jack earlier this morning, I have managed to respond to my assortment of e-mails, find some kick-ass accessories on 1stdibs.com that even Kip can't say no to, engage in a lengthy phone conversation with Camilla about her New York City apartment (the true highlight of my day, I might add), manage to throw a couple of loads of laundry into the wash, dry and fold them, sweep the kitchen floor (could someone please tell me why it is that more food ends up on the floor than in the mouths of my children?), prepare tonight's meal of roasted chicken, potatoes, and salad, and get myself ready for my dinner date with Alessia! Whew! Am I tired? You bet your Gucci purse I am! But this is my life. I signed up for it, so complaining about it is hardly an option for me. And even if it was, nobody really wants to listen to my boring sob story; I've quickly learned that everyone else has their own. My saving grace is that I am re-e-eally good at multitasking. Not to mention the fact that I even feel that I look pretty good this afternoon, for Alessia's sake more than my own, so this seems to help my flippant attitude for the time being. You see, I stand firm by the motto, which I happened to learn early on in life, that when the going gets tough, the tough put on a little more lip gloss. And so I did precisely that today, and many other days before this for that matter.

Alessia and I have agreed to meet at one of her favourite restaurants in the city, close to her office. A pain in the neck for me to get to since I know that I will be sitting in rush-hour traffic to meet her on time, and Lord only knows what I could be doing rather than sitting in idle traffic for the next sixty minutes. *Whatever!* A girl's gotta do what a girl's gotta do. At the very least, I will look good while doing it, so that seems to make things appear brighter. My new, not-silver-and-not-gold Jimmy Choo slingbacks (they are, in fact, a silvery gold combination, fabulous), the ones with the peek-a-boo toe that are spectacular to look at, look pretty amazing on my size-six feet. In actual fact, a wise investment piece if you ask me 'cause the shoes can work with both silver and gold. *Ta-da!*

Okay, so the shoes are a little high—okay, make that a lot high—but since I am definitely vertically challenged (a.k.a. on the petite side of things … oh fuck it … I'm pretty short), stilettos serve me well in life. I decided on wearing jeans tonight. My new 7's are an awesome cut, just right for my curvy thighs. They actually make me look taller too, if that is at all possible, or is it the shoes? Oh, who cares anyways? And my new Milly peasant top? I love it! White silk with azalea and olive colours tie-dyed throughout—gorgeous! And who can resist my white patent leather Fendi Mama bag with its chain-link strap? What a classic keeper! See, I do practice what I preach. I tell my clients all the time, "You have to start with fantastic basics, and you'll never go wrong." Whether it's interior design or fashion design, the same principle holds true. The basics are always a sure bet, but can be considered boring if you don't add any funky accessories to them. Once you do, you will look positively fabulous! (Oh, and by the way, in case you're wondering, I never adhere to the no-white-after-Labour-Day rule—so restrictive)!

Once again, I take my place behind the chain-link fence. Keeping my eyes cast forward, I make sure to keep my gaze strictly focused on the visuals directly in front of me. If I don't, I am sure to catch the attention of some inquisitive parent wanting to know all about me. What is it about me that makes others feel like they need to ask so many questions? I can't figure it out for the life of me.

Okay, so you might think I'm being a wee bit paranoid, but I feel as though someone is staring me down. *Keep looking forward, don't look left or right, just straight ahead, thata girl.* Too late! Suddenly I can feel someone's breath on my neck in a kind of stalkerish way and it is creeping me out! A pair of hands reaches out and grabs hold of my left arm, jerking me back.

Startled, I turn.

"Look at you, Mrs. Bancari, always looking as though you've just stepped off a runway!"

Oh pleeease! It is Alicia Gould. Alicia is Maddie's mom, Nikki's friend—sort of.

Trying to deflect the overwhelming attention I am receiving from her is hardly entertaining for me, but I have to try. "Hi, Alicia. Last I checked, runway models were a whole lot taller and thinner than me," I joke.

"Come on, who are you kidding? You look great, and you know it! Were you at the spa today or something—you look so fresh?" Alicia asks. If I didn't know any better, I would think she is serious.

But I am more serious. *The spa? Yeah, I wish!* I gently manage to ease myself away from her grip, but am completely aware that my annoyance with her is written all over my face. I am sure that I am now wearing what Jack calls my what-the-fuck-are-you-talking-about face. My wrinkled-up cheeks and raised eyebrows give it all away.

"No, not today," I manage. Not today or any other day is what I really want to say, but know better since that would be the precursor to a longer conversation I do not care to have. "I was actually working today," is all I manage to utter.

"Come on—you were not!"

"Yes," I affirm, "I was." The after-school bell rings. I am quite literally saved by the bell this time. Thank you, God!

"Well, I don't really believe that you can look like that after working all day, but still, you look fantastic," Alicia bubbles over.

I am ready to throttle her. Searching across the playground for the kids, I offer Alicia a genuine thank-you. As usual, Nikki is the first of my children to come running towards the fence.

The truth is, I am genuinely flattered by Alicia's compliment, really I am, but it seems that she, along with the other members of the Yummy Mummy Club feel that I spend the better part of my day either at the gym (not their gym) or at a spa getting pampered, neither of which is remotely accurate. Any more than two hours of being primped, pampered, and poked is far too much relaxation for my high-strung body to handle. After a few failed half-day attempts at relaxation, I quickly realized that I don't know how to relax, at least not the conventional way. I figure I will have to find something else more suited to my character. (When I find it, I will be sure to let you know). The sheer fact that I have laid down on a massage table fantasizing about running into the streets clad only in my white terry robe and slippers, cell phone attached, makes me come to the quick conclusion that I am either adverse to quiet time or have an espresso addiction I am not prepared to sever ties with just yet. Infrequent mani's, pedi's, and the odd facial thrown in for good measure is about all I can handle.

"Mommy, you look pretty. Are you going to see a client tonight?" Ella inquires so sweetly on the drive back home.

"I'm going to meet Auntie Alessia for dinner."

"So who's going to watch us?" Michael's tone is one of concern.

"Daddy will, of course." Does that seem strange to Michael?

"But you never go out during the week, Come to think of it, you don't really go out at all at night, not without Daddy." Michael seems rather insistent on belabouring this point. I make a mental note to start going out more before Michael's view of motherhood becomes seriously warped. I attempt to make light of his concern in an attempt to ease the dense air, which is beginning to materialize into a cloudy haze.

"Actually, honey," I begin, "Auntie Alessia is a little upset about something right now and just needs a friend to talk to. That's all. And besides, I won't be home late."

"Will you be home to tuck us in?" Ella sounds upset, as though she already anticipates my reply is going to be in the negative. If I thought I was already tired by all that I had done today, I was now feeling completely and positively exhausted. The game of twenty questions with my children on my whereabouts this evening was not something I had prepared myself for.

"No, sweet pea, I don't think so, but I promise I will call you before you go to sleep." Ella seems satisfied with my answer. Thank goodness!

Finally home, the kids and I unload inside and immediately go about our after-school routine. The usual monotony of washing grimy hands, devouring predinner snacks, and textbooks laid out across the kitchen table has become such a norm I often wonder if every house on my street had the same appearance at this hour. A sea of textbooks all around, some tattered beyond the gently used phase, some new, some with large print, others bearing a small font for the more senior students.

"Mommy, can you do my bun?" Ella asks, all the while hanging onto my denim-clad leg.

Hurrying the girls up the stairs to get them changed into their ballet wear, I hold back and shout down to Michael, "No X-Box until your homework is done. Do you hear me?"

A barely audible "yeah, okay" is all I hear somewhere off in the distance. I am quite certain Michael thinks I am a world-class bitchy mom. Thankfully, I actually am not bothered by this. He will thank me one day.

With the girls prettily clad in ballerina-pink bodysuits and buns securely intact, I can't help but feel a pang of nostalgia yet again. How quickly the days seem to be passing with the kids. It seemed like only yesterday I was swimming in diapers and primary-coloured plastic toys and I couldn't wait to send them off to school. And here is Nikki now displaying exemplary leadership-like skills as she demonstrates to her little sister first position in ballet.

"Like this, Ella." Nikki poses, her feet turned slightly outward. Ella seems to have no interest in watching this display, preferring to concentrate on her dolls set in front of her, clothes on, clothes off.

"Mama?" Ella asks, never taking her eyes off the baby doll in front of her. Fastidiously fiddling with a dress she is buttoning up on her baby. "You'd never leave us, would you?"

Whoa! Where is this coming from? God, all I am doing is going out with a girlfriend, why the drama? I kneel down and take hold of Ella in my arms, hoping my embrace will make her feel safe. "Of course, I will never, ever leave you. Mommy will always be here for you, I promise." And I mean it.

Dear Diary,

> *Did I say or do something to make my children feel as though I would abandon them? Why would Ella ask such a thing? Where on earth did she get the idea that I might leave? Have I been working too much lately? Is that it? Have Jack and I been arguing too much? I don't really think we have. No more than any other couple with crazy-busy lives and school-age kids might. Is she scared, and this is how she is expressing her fear? I'd better keep an eye on this. Maybe spend some more one-on-one time with her, but it's so hard, there's only one of me and three of them. I'm outnumbered every time. I don't know where I'll find the time, but I'll*

make more of an effort to spend more time with Ella; I have to! Gotta go now, or I'll be late for Alessia!

Later,
Me, Your Simple and Really Exhausted Girl

~

Driving down the highway, I can't help but feel guilt ridden. An emotion I know I have no use for (like who does?), but one that unfortunately is imbedded into any dutifully abiding Italian female daughter. If our parents don't succeed at making us feel guilty for not visiting more often, not taking them to visit an ill aunt or uncle, not bringing the kids over enough, or the worst, not calling frequently enough, well then, our kids are more than prepared to pick up right where our parents have left off. Wait until my mother hears about my new client in New York. Oh, am I going to get an earful!

Driving with my windows down and letting the early September evening air warm my face and arms, I try to let nothing get in the way of how peaceful this is making me feel for the time being. Somehow Alessia is much better than I am at handling this guilt stuff. She is the one who informed me (told to her by her life coach) that guilt is a useless emotion. That it serves no purpose in our lives. That we should put guilt on our shoulders whenever it comes to visit and tell it to go and fuck itself. An entirely interesting approach. Alessia's coach obviously doesn't have an Italian mother somewhere in the background, or grandmother for that matter! Oh well, what the hell, it's worth a try anyways. What do I have to lose?

I raise my window a little, not wanting any of the guilt I am trying to brush away to catch a breezy tailwind and land right back on my freshly straightened hair. Do you have any idea how long it takes to straighten curly Italian hair? I clear my throat. I want to ensure that my words come out comprehensible and forceful. If I am going to do this, I have to give it everything I have. No point being a wimp about it. With all my womanly strength, I shout, *"Fuck you, guilt!"*

There. I did it. I giggle.

That felt kind of good. Childish, I suppose, but cathartic nonetheless. I have never really done anything quite so naughty before. Maybe I will perform an encore, just to send the message home loud and clear. I am ready to open my pink glossy Bobbi-Brown-clad Pale Pink lips once again when I notice the guy in this midnight-black sports car driving next to me staring and smiling. *Oops!*

Has he been there the whole time? Did he hear my stellar soliloquy?

I smile back. I turn my head swiftly in embarrassment and immediately press down on the button on my door to lift my window, making every attempt to separate his gaze from my stupidity, which has now flowed out of me like water from an annoying leaky faucet. He must think I'm quite the lunatic. Right about now, I feel like a world-class idiot. Wait until I get hold of Alessia and her life coach! Who is this person anyways? Didn't he warn her that by performing such egotistical actions, you will look like a complete ass in the process? Or did he figure we wouldn't really care?

Focus, Kat. Just focus. Just stare straight ahead, and Mr. GQ will speed up and forget about your psychotic episode. I pray he will in any event. Trying to distract myself from the idiotic actions I have just carried out, I turn up the radio, loud, and start to sing along with Madonna, whose voice is coming through the speakers. I am hardly about to miss my moment of belting out tunes alongside her. I cherish these moments. Come to think of it, maybe this is how I relax. Snippets of time here and there, where I can take a couple of minutes during the day and just be me. Not Katarina, the daughter. Not Katarina, the wife. Not Katarina, the mother, or God forbid the designer, but just Kat, the girl. I keep right on singing. Mr. GQ keeps right on staring—and laughing. Is he laughing with me or at me? I interpret his smile as laughing with me. I think he realizes how much fun I am having all by myself singing my heart out. I laugh too. This feels good, really good, and the simple fact that I am the sole source of entertainment for other motorists who too are stuck in this madness makes this an amusing drive.

It dawns on me that Alessia has only shared bits and pieces of wisdom that her life coach has bestowed upon her. I have to admit that I am a little intrigued, not knowing much about this new age way of thinking. If she is in the mood tonight, I will have to ask her what this is all about. What other kind of advice or wisdom has he shared that I might find worthwhile to know about? Alessia has this habit of being really good at steering the conversation away from herself when she isn't interested in sharing. But if all is coming up roses in her world, boy oh boy, she is a bundle of bursting energy just waiting to be released into the atmosphere. The conversations can last for what feels like an eternity. It is only a matter of time before I will find out for myself.

Dear Diary,

Hopefully Alessia won't be too sad tonight. I know that she really misses Marcello, and I sure hope that she will let me try and cheer her up because you and I both know that when she wants to stay in a funk, she won't let anybody in. I hope that her calling me to go out tonight is because she doesn't want to stay locked up in that miserable funk. Maybe tonight's the night she will open up more about what she is feeling; maybe she'll be able to be honest with me, not that I need to know everything, but maybe if she talks about it, she won't feel nearly as bad. And besides, if she can't be honest with me, her best friend, who can she be honest with? Her life coach? Yeah, I guess him, but I think she is still hiding behind something. She picks and chooses carefully what she'll share, but why with me too?

She knows I don't judge her, I've told her so. She has to believe me. Doesn't she? So seriously, why the secrecy?

Later,
Me, Your Simple Girl

Chapter Ten

❦

Some people might find walking into a restaurant all alone intimidating. I for one find it liberating. It allows me to scan my surroundings without any distractions or conversation buzzing around me. Quickly I am able to capture the vibe of what the place is all about, and this can help to solidify the tone of what the evening has in store. Call it the designer in me, but if the space pales in setting a stage that will knock my socks off, the food might as well be completely Zagat thrilling and still my interest will not be piqued. And yet if the restaurant makes a grand first impression and the food is quasi-palatable, chances are they will see me back again. Don't get me wrong: I absolutely appreciate good food, but a stunning surrounding can make even the simplest of foods resemble gourmet fare.

So far, the Crystal Flute has my vote as being entirely marvellous. Part urban warehouse, part Hollywood glamour, the Crystal Flute is an exquisite combination of Soho meets Philippe Starck. The interior walls consist of exposed reddish brown brick, most likely original to the building. The soaring ceiling seems to be primarily composed of bare steel pipes running in various directions. And the pièce de résistance? Hanging haphazardly throughout the restaurant dangle beautifully adorned, tiered crystal chandeliers, each one unique and each one comprised of twelve, maybe even fifteen arms, all completely adorned with crystal pendants.

And if that isn't eye candy enough, covering each of the fastidiously set tables are perfectly starched pristine linens the colour of freshly fallen snow. Amethyst-coloured water goblets rest on the tabletops anticipating the diners' elixir of preference. Silver-leaf-gilded ballroom chairs stand flawlessly in and around empty tables in expectation of the arrival of tonight's evening guests. All of this is set perfectly aglow against a soft panorama of luminous flickering of candles that warms the air. Randomly throughout the restaurant, an array of amethyst-coloured velveteen French chairs, representing different periods from Louis V all the way to Louis XV, are occupied by intriguing people equally as striking as the resting spots themselves.

To say that I am captivated by this venue is without a doubt an understatement. It is as though the walls themselves envelop the patrons with a sense of calm immediately upon crossing over the front threshold. Given the group of people gathered here as well, it appears as though this is the "it" spot for repose on a Monday night. Now I understand what people without children do to unwind during the weeknights. Sitting enjoying the company of friends in an intimate setting for a few hours appears to be the chosen activity. The simple fact that I don't do this very often sends a twinge of envy through my body now that I physically am here. My typical evening venues include cold hockey arenas or, more likely, a steamy dance studio. The most common, of course, is my very own kitchen space, preparing a meal for the following day or cleaning up after a usually eventful one. Ironically, though, I feel completely comfortable standing here, even though the Crystal Flute is as far away from the norm for me as Paris, the City of Lights, is.

I approach a black leather tufted hostess desk with a lustrous glass top. The under-mount lighting casts a glow on the visage of the attractive blonde standing across from me. Offering me a pleasant smile, she speaks with a sweet-sounding voice, "Good evening, miss. Do you have a reservation?"

"Good evening," I answer back. "I'm meeting a friend for dinner. Alessia Lamara?"

I wonder if Alessia has beaten me here. Alessia is a stickler for punctuality. Must be the attorney in her, since right from day one at the firm, she was advised that time is synonymous with money, therefore intended to be used judiciously. I used to be just as timely for appointments, before having children, that is, and before the days when I needed to do "just one more thing" before leaving the house, knowing that if I didn't, it would be still be there to greet me later on, only with more piled high on top.

The hostess points a freshly French-manicured finger towards the back of the restaurant, and I catch a glimpse of Alessia studiously perusing the menu. I figured she would beat me here.

"Follow me," the pretty hostess beams, already making her way.

Smiling, I concede, following her over to where Alessia sits contemplatively. I secretly hope that the menu is as appetizing as the restaurant itself appears delicious. I study the many faces of the various groups of people deep in conversation as I walk. Some appear to be groups of coworkers still dressed from their day at the office. Others appear to be husbands and wives out for an early evening meal. Some resemble lovers, escaping into the night for a quiet interlude. The rest appear to be friends, merely getting together for a night out, just because. Alessia looks up, meeting my gaze.

"Hi," I mouth in her direction as I approach.

She stands up. "Hi, gorgeous!"

Alessia and I exchange kisses on the cheek and a friendly embrace. I make sure to hold onto her a moment longer than normal, as if to say, "I know you don't want to talk about it, but I'm here for you if you do." We both sit down.

"I love the décor of this restaurant, it's beautiful," I comment with enthusiasm.

"I knew you would. I figured it was right up your glamorous alley."

Did I forget to mention that perched magnificently on each table sit elaborate, black-coloured, cut-glass candelabras? With their steady flickering of light in capricious patterns, the entire restaurant is set aglow in a fantastical, luminous, and magical way. Come to think of it, perhaps this is not the best choice of venues for Alessia to be tonight of all nights. The Crystal Flute reeks of noticeable romance.

A sultry and dark-haired twenty-something-year-old young man takes our drink order. Sparkling San Pellegrino to quench our thirst and two cosmos to settle our nerves seems like a good way to start the evening off.

Alessia is fidgety. Her eyes search aimlessly about the restaurant, not resting on anyone or anything in particular. I have an uneasy feeling that she is faintly fixating her glances at the couples who look engrossed in deep conversation. I decide the onus is on me to break the silence.

"So, how was work today?" I ask. "Working on anything interesting?" I dip my hand into the breadbasket that separates us, pulling out a warm and fluffy black-olive-encrusted roll.

"No, not really. Same old boring stuff." Alessia provides no elaboration or detail.

If we are going to be playing a game of Q & A for the rest of the evening, this is going to be one long night ahead of us. I can't allow this to continue. Reaching across the table, I grab hold of Alessia's hand and place mine atop it gently.

"Are you going to tell me what's really bugging you, or do I have to keep guessing all night long?"

Alessia raises an eyebrow, pretending to look surprised at my probing.

"I'm fine. Really I am." She does her best to sound convincing. The sheer fact that she also turns her head away from me—a habit of Alessia's that I am all too familiar with when she is trying to avoid conversation—makes me realize that tonight may not be the night she is going to open up about anything that is bothering her.

We continue to look over the dinner menu. Everything I read sounds positively mouthwatering. I finally decide on a warm goat salad accompanied by candied walnuts and cranberries to start and a breast of organic-fed duck with a port emulsion glaze. Alessia chooses seared sea scallops atop a baby arugula bed to begin her meal, followed by linguini in a fresh tomato with basil sauce with a lobster and crab ragout. Our dinner conversation circumvents our delectable menu selections: my children and the latest and greatest in fashion trends—this being our absolutely favourite mindless girl topic. Until, that is, Alessia decides to let down her heavily guarded wall and show me her vulnerable side.

"The firm hired a new lawyer last week. We've been working on a case together since he came on board."

"Oh-h." I'm cautious to not say much more *just yet*. I pretend to remain engrossed with my dinner plate. "This is so-o good. Want to try a bite?" I offer.

Alessia shakes her head from side to side. "No thanks, I'm good. Yeah, the new guy ... he seems pretty nice."

"Oh good," I say, remaining aloof. "You can never have too many nice lawyers around, can you?" I joke hastily. Curiosity is now killing this proverbial cat, but I continue to linger, holding out to see if Alessia offers more first.

Alessia tilts her head back as though she is building up to what she is going to tell me about her new coworker. "True, I suppose." She smiles. "Cass ... the new guy, is definitely sharp. He has a pretty fabulous sense of humour too, especially for a mergers and acquisition lawyer."

"Umm, good," I nod.

"He's re-e-eally hot too. Did I mention that?" Alessia is now blushing like a young schoolgirl, a look I have not seen her wear in a very long while. It suits her beautifully. "He asked me out for a drink. Do you think I should go?"

"*Hmm*, let me think." I am being purposely demure. "He's hot, you're both single, or at least I assume he is single or he wouldn't have asked you out, and you're asking me if you should go out for a drink with him? Are you kidding me, Less?" I am delighted. "Of course you're going to go, and I will make sure of it!" We both laugh. Suddenly our conversation takes on a different tone now, most of it surrounding Cass, the new guy at the office.

The spark that not that long ago vanished from her eyes, around the same time Marcello left, appears to be ignited again. The flame is neither burning bright nor is it soaring just yet, but nevertheless it is unmistakably present. I see it. Even our dessert of crème brûlée with an assortment of fresh berries tastes lighter and less sinful tonight. I think hopeful news simply has a way of doing that.

As we make our way out of the Crystal Flute into the dark night sky, the twinkling of the candles inside mixed with the twinkling of the stars outside sets the stage for the most romantic of nights—this sure would have been the perfect ending to a special anniversary dinner, had there been one tonight. This perfect night sky isn't lost, though. I don't believe that for a moment.

Maybe we will come back to the Crystal Flute some other time. Maybe it will be for a different kind of special celebration. For now, we are simply two friends just celebrating being ourselves, and there is something incredibly special about that.

Dear Diary,

I sure hope Alessia feels a little bit better after hanging out. I know she has a hard time talking about Marcello and how hurt and angry she still is over what he did to her, but sometimes I just wish she would scream and yell and finally get it off her chest. Who knows? She might actually feel better if she did. I wonder if sometimes she's afraid to share her feelings with me for fear that I won't or can't understand because I have Jack. I wish she would trust our friendship enough to know that I would neither judge her for letting her true emotions show nor would I minimize her pain over how he left her. Guess in the end, there's not much I can do but let her know that

I'm here for her and then leave the rest up to her. I do hope that she lets this new guy, Cass, have a chance. If he is interested in her, even in the slightest way, I hope Alessia lets herself find some happiness in their relationship, even if it's only a friendship. You can never have enough friends. And besides, you know what they say, sometimes friends can turn into lovers! Now wouldn't that be something? Nighty-night!

Later,
Me, Your Simply Very Tired Girl

Chapter Eleven

Week two of back-to-school. Thursday morning to be exact. The kids seem to be settling into their school routine nicely, and Jack and I seem to be running in perfect giant round circles around them.

With lunches made, knapsacks securely on, kisses circulated, and the first load of laundry of the day swirling around in the washer, it is time for me to settle in at my desk. How I cherish the aroma of this particular cup of coffee that I am about to enjoy! The cup I will finally drink now that the house is all to myself. So what, that it is my third cup of the morning? Third time's a charm, isn't that what they say? So is this cup of coffee. The fact that I will actually be drinking it steaming hot is the best part of all. No interruptions, no little people knocking into me, making me spill it as I try to get them out the door. This is the cup that, in fact, gets consumed while I sit at my exquisite Ralph Lauren Capiz shell desk. This is the cup I savour with each mouthful of the dark roasted blend liquid.

Even ponytails have all been securely fastened, though the lasting sound of the faint echo of Ella's voice still resonates in the distant background as she hollered out earlier, *"It's too loose, fix it, Mommy! No, it's too high … it's too low … make it tighter!"*

But luckily all of that has already been dealt with.

No more name-calling from the top of the stairs. *"Mom? Mommy? Can you come here please?"*

No listening to Jack reprimanding Michael yet again. *"Michael, get up! How many more times do I have to call you?"*

And my noisy outcry response. *"Jack, please stop screaming at him. Can't you wake him gently?"*

Jack detests when I chastise him about this part of the morning routine, making it complete with his eyes rolling at me behind my back. What Jack fails to realize is that I can always tell when he's mocking me and it doesn't bother me one bit. In fact, I find it rather comical.

Nope, none of that now since everyone has left. Vanished. Gone *bye-bye*.

I am all alone and loving it!

Which file should I start with this morning?—Kip? Naw! I'm still waiting for him to get back to me on my latest kitchen idea for him. Red lacquered free-floating shelves! Now that is sexy!

Camilla? Still waiting for her too to call me back and let me know when we, including her husband, can sit down and discuss their New York apartment. I am still pinching myself about this one. I am so excited!

How about Connor and Jonathan's place? This seems like a bright and colourful place to start this morning. Connor and Jonathan are life partners, as they so expressively put it. Connor is a dermatologist, while Jonathan has an exciting career in retail fashion.

Drawing back a long mouthful of pure heaven, I open the file, glancing up and down through some of my handwritten notes—the good old-fashioned way I still like to do things. I giggle to no one in particular, since I am the only one here. They call this work? *Ha-ha!* Work is what I was doing this morning right after the alarm clock sounded at 6:00 a.m. Work is what I was doing before sitting down at this desk. That's work! Of course, if you ask Jack, he will tell you *that* is Chinese torture most days. Do other parents with small children feel this way, or is it just us? Guess I will have to ask some when I find the time, but for now, Jonathan and Connor's condo is calling me.

The Carlyle Suite. How fitting that their suite model is named after the infamous classic New York City hotel, and how appropriately suited for the two men themselves.

Connor has seamlessly flawless skin. My guess is that he is in his mid-forties given his slightly greying hair, yet he is a handsomely distinguished-looking gentleman. He has a broad frame and carries it well. No matter what he wears at our meetings, it all seems to fit his body faultlessly. His hands appear graceful, something I always take pleasure in watching when exchanging niceties. In fact, his entire mannerism and way about him is unbelievably docile, an endearing trait for a physician.

Jonathan is a genius at ladies' retail fashion. I figure that his fashion suaveness influences the way Connor dresses—though I think Connor could make even a paper bag look great given his physical stature. Then again, you know what they say, behind every good man, there is another equally charming one at home laying out his Armani's and Dolce & Gabbana's. My guess is that Jonathan is probably close to forty-years-old himself. His skin is a luminous shade of a glowing olive tone; looking at him leads you to believe that the genetic gods were on his side when creating him. Mix it up with a little bit of Connor's western magic, and voilà, you have a recipe that would make even Martha Stewart crazy with jealousy. Jonathan does have one visible flaw, though it is only truly noticeable when he is laughing profusely. It is a small gap between his two front teeth. It isn't huge or anything like that, but it is unmistakably there. If you ask me, it only adds to his already boyish charm, making him even more adorable, if that is even possible.

Jonathan loves all things beautiful, and whenever I mention a particular colour or fabric, from floral chintz in peony pinks to silk charmeuse in buttercup yellow, Jonathan bubbles over with the most exuberant enthusiasm and bounces up and down in his seat, not unlike a child being offered a double scoop of ice cream with a rainbow of sprinkles floating on top. His hands clap together, most likely from the utter joy he is feeling, and he breaks out into song and with excitement shouts, "That's it, that's it! That's fantastic! That's exactly what I want!"

Of course, Jonathan's outbursts continuously result in sending me shrieking into fits of laughter as well—how could I not? Jonathan reminds me of my own children with his high-spirited fervour, only much taller and several skin tones darker.

The Carlyle Suite is situated on the eighteenth floor of a newish luxurious condo building right in the heart of downtown Toronto. At one thousand and six hundred square feet, it is hardly overly spacious, but a jewel box of a find with plenty of amenities. Connor and Jonathan came to me via Alessia—Jonathan being her personal shopper when time just doesn't permit Alessia to search pieces out solo or with yours truly. Prada, D&G, Theory, or Milly, Jonathan is the go-to man who can make it all happen. Never short on praise, the words, "*You. Look. Absolutely. Gorgeous!*" frequently manifest from his mouth. And I do believe that he, in fact, truly means it. He is the first to tell you that he calls it like he sees it. And if he doesn't see it, you'll know that too. One of these days, I may go on in and solicit Jonathan for his fashion advice, but for now I need to focus on his home sense.

My first meeting with my cheerful clients was something of an event; it will forever remain etched in my memory. Since Alessia had filled me in with details about them—too much information for my liking, if you know what I mean—I felt as though I already knew them fairly well, Jonathan at the very least. So my attempt at wearing a professional face at our initial meeting was no easy feat for me.

It was early last spring when I first went over to meet with them, mid-May on a Wednesday afternoon. I had been feeling pretty cheerful that day. The air was warm and had a sweet fragrance to it from all the freshly cut lawns outside, one of the benefits of living in the burbs. City living scents can best be summed up quite differently—hot dog smells, onion smells (courtesy of the hot dog carts and the hot dogs themselves), and a whole lot of whiffs of gasoline fumes. Suburban scents are definitely more palatable in my opinion. Anyways, like I was saying, on this particular day I felt like wearing white, and so I did. I am not one for following the old adage of white only after Victoria Day and never after Labour Day—I wear it whenever I feel like it, no matter what the season. And so I did that day—my gorgeous white Milly pantsuit that I had purchased on the fly on my last visit to New York City a couple of winters ago. Their new spring merchandise had just arrived on the shelves, and I was desperate for some vibrant spring energy, finding exactly what I was looking for on the racks of 5F at Bergdorf's. This was one of those unexpected trips Jack enjoyed surprising me with when we were barely treading water and needed a fast escape. I'm embarrassed to admit it, but I felt that way often when the kids were really little, and still do a lot of the times for that matter. Sadly these types of trips only happen once in a while. Only when we can get adequate babysitting and both of our schedules allow us to get away for a few days.

So like I was saying, on this particular day, the first day I met Connor and Jonathan, our meeting went something like this.

Bzzz. Bzzz. "Hello?" A deep masculine voice answered.

I leaned in, positioning my mouth closer to the speaker, and cleared my throat.

"Hi," I said in a confident voice. "It's Katarina. We have an appointment today. I'm the interior designer—Alessia's friend." I added this last bit in case the person on the other end was not Jonathan. I was hoping that the stranger would quickly recognize my voice or at the very least recognize my name and buzz me up. This talking-through-steel business was so impersonal.

A muffled voice answered back. "Of course, hon, we've been expecting you. We're so excited to finally meet you. Apartment 1804. I'll buzz you right up. Ciao, ciao!"

Ciao, ciao right back at you. This is going to be fun. I could already tell that much. The sound of the glass door clicking me through brought me back, since my mind had this uncanny habit of wandering. I pulled slightly on the handle and gently made my way through towards the elevators. Riding up to their suite, I took the opportunity to check myself over once in the smoky glass mirrored walls surrounding me. There was nothing worse than lipstick on your teeth to make a hideous first impression. I smiled, checking to make sure I was clear. Perfect. Stepping out of the elevator, I turned right, hoping that suite 1804 would present itself in front of me rather quickly.

Wow! If this was what the corridors looked like, what did the suites look like? I was completely love struck. You could easily tell that no cost had been spared in glamming this building up! The walls on this floor were clad in vivacious, fresh-printed wallpaper—the most fun I had ever seen in a public space. A concentrated pattern of oversize creamy-white and raspberry-pink flowers were set against a pale gold background. This felt so energizing and was such a refreshing change from plainly painted walls or the boring tone-on-tone striped wallpaper typical of a lot of condo buildings.

My sandals sank into the carpeting as I walked, feeling the fibres on my protruding pink toes. (*Thank goodness my pedi was fresh 'cause, let's be honest here, there is nothing worse than chipped toenails in open-toed shoes—ugh)!* The latticework pattern on the turquoise carpet looked absolutely scrumptious! I couldn't tell if it was silk velvet or mercerized cotton that I was feeling on my toesies, but either way, it felt absolutely lush! Looking around and making sure no one was visible near me, I bent down and ran my hands through the fibres. Divine! This truly felt like a little piece of heaven! If I were Connor or Jonathan, I would run up and down these hallways barefoot just for the fun of it!

Okay, there I was, Suite 1804. I knocked gently on the glossy ebony-coloured entry door, stood back, and inhaled a deep breath. Damn jitters!

Dear Diary,

Think they're going to like me? Maybe I'm not experienced enough for this whammy-glammy building. Maybe they're just meeting with me as a favour to Alessia for all the money she spends with Jonathan. He must make a healthy commission off of her. Maybe I should have worn something different, maybe something more classic, instead of looking like I belonged in Palm Springs or someplace else with freakin' palm trees. Shit! My power suit—the putty coloured blazer and pencil skirt ... maybe that would have been more appropriate than my lunching-with-the-ladies outfit. Now that's ironic, because when the heck do I ever lunch with the ladies? Actually when do I ever eat lunch at all? Although I have to admit, my outfit kind of complements this place if I really think about it. So, maybe I do fit in better than I think. If they only knew that a mere two hours ago, I was donning rubbing gloves and was elbow-deep inside the toilet bowl. Oh well, too late! I'm here now and can't change a thing. Just be yourself, kid, that's all you can do now. Gotta go; I hear footsteps!

Later!
Me, Your Simple Girl

The door swung open, presenting a bubbly, smiling face on the other side. What a gorgeous creature this man before me was!

"Oh my God, *you are* stunning!" the voice cried out. Precisely what I was thinking about him.

"Hi! Umm, are you talking to me?"

"Ahh ... *der*, of course I am, honey, is there anyone else there standing with you?" the handsome creature replied. This had to be Jonathan.

I laughed. If I was nervous before, I was certainly starting to feel more relaxed by the second, thanks to the handsome man standing in front of me. I looked to my right. "No, I guess not. In that case, thank you so much for the compliment." I extended my hand. "I'm Katarina. So nice to meet you, Jonathan."

Taking my hand, the animated man pulled me towards him in a rather manly embrace. "Hi, gorgeousness, you're right, I'm Jonathan ... Jonathan Weissman, and I am so-o-o happy to finally meet you. Please come inside and make yourself at home."

And so I did. First impression was a success!

Dear Diary,

A million thank-yous! I was so right in listening to my instincts and not wearing the boring power suit. Now that I'm here, that would have been way too businesslike for someone like Jonathan. Maybe I am way more intuitive than I give myself credit for. Well, let's see how the rest of the meeting goes.

Later!
Me, Your Really Excited Simple Girl

With the formalities out of the way, Jonathan, Connor, and I sat closely huddled together pouring over tear sheets, photos, and fabric samples that they had collected, obviously having done some homework prior to my arrival. This was actually a good thing. No, make that a *great* thing, since clients who know what they want are a designer's dream.

"I want Dorothy Draper chintz and stripes," Jonathan shouted out, sounding just like a child in a candy store pleading with his mother for another strip of wacky taffy.

I giggled. Connor placed his hand over Jonathan's in the most endearing of ways, and I have to admit that I felt a pang of envy for a second there. It was only heightened when Connor's soothing voice reassured his partner.

"Kat, whatever Jonathan wants for our home is completely fine with me. I completely trust his taste and your design sense. I just want him to be totally euphoric with it once everything is done."

Oh God! My heart be still. Did he just say that? Wait till I tell Jack this one! Forget envy! I was completely green with jealousy! Connor was a total dream. Jonathan was gushing over with happiness. But seriously, why wouldn't he be?

This couple was too good to be true. Were people really happy like this?

I needed to get hold of Lessi's life coach and find out—really fast! In the meantime, I felt like I needed to turn my head and give these lovebird clients of mine a moment of privacy. They are so-o-o sweet!

I had some work to do in here. Okay, so maybe not a lot of work, because it really didn't look so bad, but a bit more primping and dressing up would take it to a new and heightened level. It was a little devoid of colour and pattern, especially if Dorothy Draper was their muse and especially after walking through these hallways.

The condo had good bones, as we say in the business, and the layout was spacious enough. It boasted three bedrooms: a master suite, a guest room, and a third, smaller room that seemed quite empty in comparison to the rest of the rooms. The large living and dining area was surrounded by an expanse of windows overlooking the city. The kitchen, smallish, had a peninsula that overlooked the dining area. In my opinion, it was all fantastic, because you didn't seem to feel constrained or tight for space anywhere. The master bedroom had its own en suite, as did the small bedroom. I wondered why this bedroom had its own en suite and not the guest bedroom, already furnished and waiting for guests. I didn't question it aloud at this point. For now, I allowed them to continue with the tour. The powder room at the front of the suite was diminutive in size, a tiny jewel in my opinion, or at least it would be when I was done with it. The corridor leading into the home was long in nature, the longest part of the suite considering that all the other rooms appeared to be very square. It gave the apartment a feeling of grandeur. It even housed its own laundry facility and storage area, a bonus for anyone living in a high-rise building. The more I walked through this place, the more enamoured I became with it. I wonder how Jack, the kids, and I would fit in here.

"Give your head a shake, Kat." That's what Jack would have said if I had suggested that the five of us live in a smaller home.

"But why?" would be my obvious retort.

And then Jack would start in about how he is not going to raise his kids in the city, *blah, blah, blah.* And my argument would be, "But I love the city, Jack!" And on and on we would go back and forth. And eventually what started out as a joke—sort of—would turn into a full-blown argument. I would go to bed angry, and Jack would wonder what he had done wrong. On second thought, once again bringing up the topic of living in the city would not be a good idea after all.

Back to work. Why the hell did I have such a short attention span?

Jonathan and Connor's apartment … the bones were good … yes … right. Actually, after our meeting, I was well informed of the fact that my dynamic duo loved all of the finer things in life: trips, furniture, fabrics, and champagne. And thanks to Dr. Connor Shultz, they could afford those things too. Jonathan had no qualms about turning their modest home into quite the designer haven, and I loved the very fact that I would have a part in doing so with him. Since money didn't seem to be a problem here, I did wonder a little (okay, maybe a lot) why their apartment didn't resemble more of a home already. You know, the window coverings, the accessories, that sort of stuff. They spent their weekends browsing for things, or so they told me, but they just didn't seem to actually make many purchases. Since Jonathan was in the fashion business and had such a fantastic sense of style, it didn't really add up for me. I knew it was only a matter of time before Jonathan would offer up the information.

Seeing that Jonathan had mentioned Dorothy Draper chintz, I decided to run with it. Dorothy Draper was the most famous decorator in America from the 1930s until the 1960s. She was the doyenne of chintz and baroque interiors. She was the vision behind countless happy spaces from hotels to private residences. She was and still is such an inspiration to designers and decorators all over the world, including yours truly. I wanted to ensure I could deliver exactly what they asked of me. And so, as I set out fan deck after fan deck—greeny-blues, hazy-blues, creamy high gloss for trims, and bright botanical florals for chair upholstery and cushions, I could see that happiness was turning into exaltation on the faces of my new clients. It was clear that they were thrilled at my suggestions, and I was thrilled that they were thrilled.

Latticework on some hard finishes? Loved it!

Carrara marble countertops in the kitchen? Why not?

Prussian blue and corals and pink floral for accents? Absolutely stunning!

Celadon walls, oxford white trim in the powder room? Enormously essential!

And then, as if I hadn't been dazzled enough during this union here today, Jonathan belted out, "And how about pink and white stripes à la Beverly Hills Hotel for the nursery?"

I'm sure I stopped breathing. I know I did! Did he just say *nursery?*

Trying to keep a legitimate look of interest on my face and not appear shaken, I managed to somehow collect my composure long enough to pose the question, or statement, or both. "I'm sorry, Jonathan, could you repeat what you just said? I'm not sure that I heard you correctly." I didn't want to assume because, let's face it, even I know what happens when you assume. Looking like he had just let the cat out of the bag, Jonathan looked over at Connor for reassurance. When he provided it, an enormous grin sprang across Jonathan's face.

"I might as well just tell you now, Kat: Connor and I are trying to have a baby. So that very empty bedroom and en suite over there has been purposely kept that way until we hear news of the baby on its way."

His little faux pas was perfectly understandable given his excitement.

"Oh, okay!" was all I could manage to articulate.

For someone who usually had no problem with words, I was definitely at a loss right now. Not that this was such a big deal anyways. This was the twenty-first century after all. Lots of same-sex couples were having babies. Big whoop!

"Um ... well ... wow, guys. That's wonderful news. Children are such a blessing. I have three of my own, as you may already know, and there is really nothing more rewarding than being a parent." Okay, so maybe I was laying it on thick, but everything I was saying was true, even though at times I wondered what the hell I was thinking having more babies after Michael. So maybe I was trying to overcompensate and recover *just a little* for my look of bewilderment. I imagine they had seen through it, at least I think Connor had. Jonathan was too busy pulling out a Beverly Hills Hotel notepad from a gigantic file folder he had on the table. What the hell else did he have in there, a fucking rabbit?

"We have a surrogate mother. She will be carrying the baby for us. Biologically it will be Jonathan's baby since we used Jonathan's sperm to conceive," Connor informed me.

"TMI! TMI!" I wanted to scream out loud. I didn't need to know *all* of the details. One of my gifts, and in this particular moment my greatest curse, was that I am a very visual person, and so no matter what I read or what is told to me, I have this uncanny knack of always visualizing a scenario. I wish my gift would leave my brain right about now. *Leave! Be gone!* It didn't. It wouldn't.

So I did what I believed to be the right thing to do. I got up from my chair and gave both Jonathan and Connor congratulatory hugs. Connor went on to tell me in detail that they had hired a surrogate, a young and healthy woman who had done this before, and that with any luck, they would soon be announcing that she had successfully conceived. Of course, a healthy baby is all they wanted, but what fun it would be to have a baby girl. A pink nursery would be a must then. And what better a place to use as an inspiration for a pink nursery than the Beverly Hills Hotel?

And with that, as they say, the rest is history.

Dear Diary,

How severe was my look of shock when Jonathan told me they were trying to have a baby? Was I that obvious? Was my look of disbelief that evident? I didn't mean to be, but that was so not what I was expecting them to tell me. Not by a long shot! I am such an open-minded person and there is absolutely nothing wrong with same-sex couples having a baby, but they completely caught me off guard. I guess I just wasn't expecting this today. A pink nursery with the Beverly Hills Hotel as inspiration will be so much fun! This little girl or boy will be so lucky to have Connor and Jonathan as parents. Come to think of it, I think I might love to live here with them too!

Later,
Me, Your Tickled-Pink Simple Girl

Chapter Twelve

The ringing of my telephone startles me. My mind is somewhere else. So what else is new? Over and over again, my mind wanders away to dreamy distant places and frequently reminisces about events long gone by. Today is no exception.

I pick up the receiver, making sure to turn my voice back on to its professional frequency. "This is Katarina," I answer.

"Katarina dear, this is Camilla. How are you?"

"Oh hi, Camilla." My voice elevates an octave or so. "I'm fine, thank you. Is everything going as planned with the closing of the New York apartment?" My curiosity has gotten the best of me.

Camilla's voice is vaguely shaky. "Yes, dear, it is. That's why I'm calling you. Could we set up another meeting? I'd like to review the floor plans with you and discuss some of the changes I'd like to make to the space."

"Of course," I answer efficiently. My excitement surrounding this job has consumed most of my waking thoughts these days, though I know I have to act as though I am completely unaffected— like I have done this a hundred times before. "So I take it then that you and Shane have discussed some of the revisions you want to implement? He's fine with our meeting?"

Again, there seems to be some hesitation on Camilla's part. "Oh yes, of course, he's fine with everything."

The tone of her voice makes me wonder if everything is as fine as she would like me to believe. But who am I to question? "All right then." I open my day planner and check what I have scheduled for the following week. I suppose I could see them as early as tomorrow if they were available, although tomorrow being Friday is the day I typically try to keep free of client meetings, reserving it as my catching-up day for e-mails, phone calls, and—who am I kidding?—laundry and groceries. Given how very important this job is to me, I guess those things just might have to wait.

I will try plan A first and see how that goes before offering up plan B. "How does Monday morning at ten o'clock sound?" I pose.

I sense a touch of trepidation in Camilla's voice. "Not good. *Apparently* Shane has to be in Milan on Monday. I hate to ask this of you, but does tomorrow work at all? I realize it is such short notice, but he can make some time then if that works."

My intuition, along with the sound of Camilla's voice, makes me wonder if the short notice is bothering her more than it is bothering me right now. I'm getting the feeling that she is the type of woman who understands the importance of planning and, hence, the need for scheduling appointments in advance. I think I now understand the uneasiness in her voice. But the truth is, this is just as important to me as it is to her, so I am not about to say no. Laundry and groceries will have to wait. Not to mention that I am feeling slightly bad for Camilla. I can't pinpoint why exactly, but I want to reassure her that I, more than anybody, understand that sometimes things just come up. My valiant attempt at making the situation a positive one doesn't turn out as successful as I am hoping.

"Sure, I can make tomorrow work for me, Camilla. Does ten o'clock work for you and Shane?"

"Could we say nine o'clock, Katarina? Shane has to get to the office right after."

Whew! That isn't going to be easy to pull off, but I will have to make it work. I'm not sure how I will do that with having to drop the kids off at school first, but I will figure it out. I always do.

"Sure, Camilla, that's fine. I'll see you then."

"Thanks for your understanding, Katarina."

"Of course."

Click.

Dear Diary,

Give me the strength and endurance to make this project a huge success. I'm sensing that this woman has hired me specifically for a reason. Yeah, yeah, she heard I was good and that I do good work, but there's a lot more to this. I just feel it. The problem is, I don't know what IT is—yet. I guess I do sense a kinship of sorts here, like she's searching out for more than a designer, maybe someone who gets her, not just on a design level but more than that. Think I'm crazy? Maybe I'm overanalyzing the whole thing? It wouldn't be the first time, but I hear something, better yet I feel something. It's a vibe I'm getting from Camilla that I just can't put into words, just a sense, that's all. I know, I know, patience, right? I heard it said somewhere that infinite patience produces immediate results. I hope that's true ... nope, not working yet ... okay, so maybe the results aren't that immediate, but soon please!

Later,
Me, Your Not-So-Patient Simple Girl

My cell phone again! Good thing I love my personalized ringtone. The problem with these ringtones—for me, that is—is that I often get so caught up in singing the song that I take forever to answer the call, sometimes even losing the caller by the time

I pick it up. Oh shit, this one must be important. *Kids' School.* I wonder what this is all about.

"Katarina speaking." My voice is concise.

"Mrs. Bancari? This is Meredith, the school secretary from West Elm Public School."

My heart starts racing faster. Why does this have to happen every time the kids' school or a doctor's office calls me? Maybe it's just a sunshine call—they're calling because one of the kids did a good deed or something nice—it could happen!

"We have Nikki here in first aid."

"What? What happened?" Right now I am freaking out inside.

"Please don't panic, she's all right. Well, sort of, that is." Her voice trails off. Oh, that sounds really reassuring!

"What do you mean *'sort of all right'*? What's happened?"

"She was out playing with the other children at recess this morning and apparently fell and hurt her arm. She says it's not very sore; however, she does seem to be favouring that arm, so protocol says that we have to inform you."

"Is it bleeding? Is she crying?" I don't wait for the answer to the first question before posing the second one.

"No. No. It's not bleeding. The teacher on duty at the time of the incident didn't see it happen but said that some of the other children told her about it. As I said, she does seem to be favouring that arm and won't let anyone look at it."

I ask her to put Nikki on the telephone so I can hear her voice myself. A mother can always tell by the sound of her child's voice if she is telling the truth or not. I hear Meredith in the background as she hands the receiver over to Nikki, informing her that I want to speak to her.

"Mommy?" Nikki's small voice sounds like a soft whisper.

"Nikki, what happened? Does your arm hurt a lot?"

"Not a lot, Mommy, just a little." Now I know that she is lying. Nikki has an incredible tolerance for pain, more than most adults

I know. So the very fact that she is admitting that it hurts at all means that it is probably throbbing.

"Maddie and I were just doing some cartwheels, and I fell over."

I am not buying the entire story, but at this point, the entire story is irrelevant.

"Will you let your teacher have a look at your arm to see if it is really bruised, or do you want Mommy to come and pick you up?" With any other child, this would have been a rhetorical question, but with Nikki, who actually likes school, this question is the real thing.

"Maybe you should come and pick me up. I want to come home." Nikki's voice is quivering. I am positive she is crying gently now.

And so I do exactly that. I gather my handbag, find my sunglasses, and for once don't have to search high and low for my keys, since they are sitting directly on top of my bag, exactly where I had left them after I had dropped the kids off (thanks, big guy, I owe you for that), and head over to West Elm Public School for the second time today.

~

I try my hardest not to sprint across to the front door of the school, not an easy task for Ms. High-Strung. Over and over in my head, all I keep hearing is the sound of Nikki's small voice, the one reserved for when she is afraid of something or just plain sad. I am all-too-familiar with her happy voice, which is easy to detect most of the time; her excited voice, which rings out a lot of the time; her angry voice, which happens some of the time; and her frustrated-with-her-siblings voice, which these days seems to be an even constant. This one is definitely her frightened voice. As I reach out my hand to grab the handle of the front door and pull it towards me—hard—I lunge forward unexpectedly, almost crashing my entire body directly into the glass. *Ouch!* Damn security entrance—I had forgotten all about it. New to West Elm this year is this no-access security entrance. With recent incidences across the globe of crazed people entering into schools and randomly taking fire on innocent children, the school district took action and decided that it was in the best interests of the staff and students to implement a security system. School doors are no longer kept unlocked throughout the school day. The only access into the school now is by pressing down on a buzzer that hangs on the brick wall and waiting patiently for Meredith or her sidekick to grant you permission to enter.

It is unfortunate how scary our world has become. Children are now being taught at the beginning of each school year, lockdown and lockout procedures right after learning about snack routines and proper hygiene. They practice what to do and how to hide in the event of a harmful intruder gaining entry into their school. Teachers are being instructed on teaching little ones how to tuck themselves securely under their desks while they set about turning off lights, taking a head count of the children, and surreptitiously setting about shutting window blinds and covering sidelights on doors with construction paper already cut to size. Much as I will always maintain that we live in a beautiful world and in particular a beautiful country that is full of bounty and goodness, somewhere along the way, things got royally fucked up!

This is one of those moments when my usual wait time of two minutes or less feels like an eternity.

Click.

Access granted! Hurriedly I quickly stride in and head directly to the main office. Looking around, there is no sign of my little girl. However, I do spot a sweet, pigtailed little one, probably in junior kindergarten, with a timid look on her tiny face, which is perfectly proportioned to her teeny-tiny frame. Her backpack is securely on, with both shoulder straps squarely sitting on her back, though the significant weight of it makes it droop to one side. She is obviously waiting for a parent or caregiver to pick her up. An exceptionally tall boy is standing over in the corner, firmly holding a Ziploc bag full of ice cubes to his head. Given his height, my assumption is that he must be an eighth grader nursing a phys ed injury. God, that kid is tall! He must be at least six feet tall. Even with my four-inch pumps on, I feel small in comparison to this boy. What are parents feeding their kids these days? Oh, wait a sec! Who is that kid standing over there in the other corner? Another behemoth boy, only this one is holding his baggy on his hand. *Ah-ha!* Scratch out the phys ed injury theory. I get the picture now. Sucks to be them!

Standing impatiently in front of the secretary's ... oops, sorry, faux pas on my part, frontline staff is how they refer to themselves these days—I wait for Meredith to appear. Where the hell is she anyways? Come on, Meredith, what are you doing? Oh, here she comes from the staff lounge area, chewing voraciously all the while holding some sort of cookie or is it a square in her hand? Figures!

"Oh, hello there, Mrs. Bancari," Meredith blurts out between chews. "You caught me! Oh-h-h, nice look! You are always so put together."

I smile graciously. Okay, so I fake a smile graciously. *Whatever!*

"Thanks, Meredith." I remind myself to breathe. "Where is Nikki?" *You know, my kid, my child. The reason why you called me here in the first place,* I want to add, but don't.

"I'll go and get her. She's just in the first aid room."

And with that, Meredith is off again. Only this time she returns with my Nikki right by her side. I run around to the other side of the desk.

"Honey." I put my arms around Nikki.

She flinches when I touch her, all the while still holding onto her left arm with her right hand. I bend down so I am at Nikki's eye level. Lifting her chin, I look into her tear-stained eyes.

"Nikki," I speak quietly, "I want you to let go of your arm please." My intuition, the one I never used to trust because of often being told that I *overanalyze* things, is telling me now that Nikki is sporting more than just a bruise on her arm. I'll overanalyze, thanks very much!

Nikki starts to speak, her voice quivering. "I'm fine, Mommy, really I am. I just want to go home." The tears are now flowing steadily down her face.

Confirmed. She isn't fine by a long shot. I don't want to upset her anymore than she already is, so I stop probing. I put on a brave mommy smile and begin to wipe away her tears, reassuring her that everything is going to be just fine.

"Mommy just wants to see if there is a bruise on your arm, but if you don't want to show me right now, that's okay. Will you show me at home, though?" I ask patiently.

Nikki knows I am not going to leave this alone.

"O-o-kay, Mom-my. You can see-see it now if you really want, but be care-ful." Slowly Nikki eases away her right hand and lowers her arm.

"Oh-h-h-h!" Meredith gasps.

Thanks a fucking lot, Meredith!

Clearly, we are not going home. We are going directly to the emergency department. I am no doctor, but the obvious bow in Nikki's forearm suggests a broken arm to me. The bigger problem than the broken arm right now is that Nikki has a colossal dislike for doctors, so this is not going to be easy by any stretch of the imagination. I'm not even sure when her fear started or why, really. Nothing serious or major had ever happened to her, only regular immunization shots when she was a baby, and there was the tonsil operation when she was barely two-years-old, when the nurses and doctor tore her away from me screaming like a banshee, but surely she doesn't remember that, does she?

"Real-ly, Mom-my, it do-o-esn't hurt-t-t that much. Do we have to go to the hos-p-pital? I don't want to go to the hospital! Ple-e-ase, Mommy, no-o-o!"

Nikki is sobbing. Wailing, in fact. And how the hell does she know that I am taking her to the hospital, since I haven't even said anything to that effect?

Dear Diary,

Please give me the strength and courage to be brave enough for the both of us. I know Nikki is scared, but guess what, SO AM I! Scared shitless actually! Couldn't you have made me fall and break my arm instead, and not her? How do I reassure her that they are not going to hurt her anymore when I know for a fact that once they set that arm, it is going to hurt like hell? Do I lie to her? What on earth do I say to make her feel better when I'm completely freaking out inside right now? Where's the chapter about this part of parenting in that stupid handbook they were supposed to give me when I left the hospital with a new baby? Got you stumped now, don't I?

Later,
Me, Your Scared Simple Girl

I do my best to comfort Nikki, promising her that I will not leave her side for a minute if she agrees to let me take her to the hospital. Let's face it, either way we are going, but I at least want her to agree somewhat to going. She does sort of agree, because I sort of lie and promise her that the doctors will do their very best to not hurt her arm—which isn't a complete lie. A mother's got to do what a mother's got to do!

In Meredith's defence, she does try her best to comfort Nikki after her initial outburst, as does Mrs. Mansor, who by now has come scrambling out of her office to see what all the commotion is about. The three of us are pretty much in agreement that Nikki's arm is indeed most likely broken. Mrs. Mansor suggests calling an ambulance, which only sets Nikki's hysteria into full-speed motion all over again. I'm sweating by now, since my words of comfort seem to be falling on Nikki's deaf ears. I can't talk my way out of a paper bag right now, never mind convince Nikki that no doctor is going to further inflict pain on her.

Finally! The big guy upstairs must be taking pity on me because somehow he convinces my screaming kid to actually stop screaming and listen to me. I'm not so dumb after all. Nikki agrees that I can take her to the hospital, but no ambulance, as long as I promise to never leave her side. I promise. I even pinkie promise to get us out of there.

I carry Nikki to my car, securing her safely in the backseat and strapping her into her seat belt, all the while making sure to not even breathe on her arm because the slightest touch of it sends her into a shrieking frenzy.

I call Jack from my cell phone once we are en route to the hospital and fill him in on what is going on, including that he will now have to leave work early to pick Michael and Ella up from school. I'm certain that this turn of events will frustrate him since it will mean juggling his appointments—something with which I'm all too familiar.

Nikki softly asks me if she can speak to her daddy. I hand her the telephone carefully, ensuring that I don't whack her arm while still trying to keep my eyes on the road. This is not an easy feat for me. I can multitask like no other, but this is ridiculous! She listens while Jack speaks. He is obviously trying to cheer her up, and I am eternally thankful for that. He is either giving her the "be tough" pep talk or telling her something very funny. Either way, she giggles. Thank goodness! Whatever he said to her is working, for now.

At the emergency room, we wait and wait and wait some more. *Yes*, you don't need to be a brain surgeon to figure out my child's arm is severely broken. And *no*, nobody ever died of a broken arm, *so yes*, I realize we are not a priority and are therefore on the absolute bottom of the triage list, along with the splinters, sore tummies, and other non-life-threatening *emergencies*. In fact, we are so not a priority for the next eight hours while we continue to wait.

Bellyache after broken nose after vomiting toddler passes us by, each making their way through the swinging doors while Nikki and I still wait, shifting from one bum cheek to the other, never finding a comfortable position.

Finally, just around eleven o'clock, we are called through the steel swinging doors. Nikki fell asleep in my arms hours ago, exhaustion ultimately outweighing the pain she has been experiencing. Nikki is now looking very pale and frail as I put her down on the X-ray table. Poor baby, she has tried so hard to remain brave throughout this entire ordeal.

The X-rays confirm that Nikki's arm is, in fact, broken, in two places not just one. That's my girl! If you're going to do something, do it right and with gusto at the very least. She will require a long arm cast. "Quite a break," the orthopaedic surgeon tells me. "Nikki is quite a brave girl," he remarks. "How long was she at school with this broken arm and did not say anything?" "Four hours," I offer up. Not to mention, of course, the long hours we have spent waiting to see him. He's impressed. Visibly, I am not.

It is well after midnight before I am informed that Nikki's arm requires resetting. An operating room will not become available until at the very earliest four o'clock or five o'clock in the morning because, of course, this is not considered a life-threatening injury. "The one operating room available for these types of injuries is all booked up until then," Dr. Amazed informs me. "No point waiting," he tells me. "It's best to take her home, give her something for the pain, and let her rest."

She is exhausted, and so am I.

He will book an operating room for seven o'clock and reset it then. Since the damage has already been done and she has lasted this long with it, what's a few more hours?

So off we go into the night.

We leave. I am carrying my beautiful baby girl in my arms. I click-click down the sterile corridor stroking Nikki's hair, which has lost its lustre somewhere between the waiting room and the red exit sign. People stare at us as we pass by, most likely out of their sheer boredom too.

Once outside, I continue to nestle Nikki in my arms, her head resting on my shoulders as I pass through the still nighttime air. I look up to the sky. There isn't a cloud to be seen anywhere. The stillness of the night lends itself to peace, though being awake still at this hour is not something I had envisioned. I must admit, the serenity of the blackened sky actually sends a wave of calm over my fatigued body. Such a tranquil moment to recite a mother's prayer.

Dear Diary,

How strong my little girl has been today. I can't believe she lasted as long as she did with that broken arm. Wow, she's really a tough little cookie, isn't she? Don't know where she gets it from—ha-ha. She's so tired now. Please let her have a peaceful sleep tonight because I don't think tomorrow ... later this morning actually is going to be easy for her, or me for that matter. Why does such a little person have to suffer so much pain? Not fair if you think about it. Though I guess we're lucky, right? It's only a broken arm; it could have been worse ... a lot worse.

'Night,
Me, Your Really Tired Simple Girl

Chapter Thirteen

As I gently ease down on the brake pedal and move the gearshift into "park," it dawns on me just exactly how worn-out and absolutely famished I am. Nikki and I have spent the past several hours just sitting and waiting and waiting and sitting in that barren-looking, germ-infested holding pen. Let's face it, the appearance of a hospital emergency room is a cold and sterile place at the best of times, though I can't really think of a good time to be there in any event. But when you are relegated there not of your own free will but out of necessity, you realize how utterly helpless you are, particularly since you know that you are at the mercy of those frontline admission nurses. That's when it appears to be even more of a dreadful place than you had ever first imagined. Since they make you wait for what feels like forever when you are in there, the least they could do is make the place a little more comfy. Like paint the walls in a buttercup-yellow or Tiffany-blue colour and have some cosy armchairs to rest your weary body in—something with a bit of lumbar support would be nice. (Okay, so I'm really dreaming here, I know, but those stiff and cold tubular office armchairs with worn-out, black, grimy upholstery that who knows who has done God knows what to them and in them are so yuck! On second thought, I don't really want to know who did what in them). The thought of a hot shower is a much more pleasurable fantasy just now.

I notice that Jack has left the coach light on above the front door. I called him on our way home, letting him know what had ensued over the past few hours. Sure enough, as I carefully disengage Nikki's seat belt to take her out of the car, Jack is standing outside the front door ready to take over and release her from my arms and carry her still body the rest of the way to bed. As I carry her up the front walk and hand her off to Jack, we look at each another, forcing exhausted yet relieved smiles—the exchange of looks that only couples with children can understand and relate to. The what-are-you-gonna-do-kids-will-be-kids smiles.

Nikki stirs slightly as I discharge her into Jack's much stronger arms. Her left arm is safely secured in a temporary sling, to prevent it from moving around too much throughout the night; I look intently at her in amazement. I am well aware that children are resilient and strong and tough, but right here right now, she looks so small and so fragile to me, and let's face it, the kid has endured an enormous amount of pain over the past several hours. Her brilliant blonde hair, which typically cascades so neatly across her shoulders, is for the time being dishevelled every which way across her pale and tired complexion. I can't recall how many mornings I have watched her brush her locks so painstakingly smooth, like a young woman getting ready for her first date.

Gently Jack lays Nikki down on her bed, while I carefully undress her in an attempt to exchange her currently tired school clothes with fresh-scented baby pink floral pj's. I can't wait until I can do exactly the same thing.

~

I awaken the next morning not to the sound of the alarm clock letting me know that it is wake-up time, but to my inner clock—the more accurate one—the one that reminds me that today of all days is supposed to be the day that I have my oh-so-important meeting with Camilla and Shane. Damn! I will have to cancel that now, something I hate like hell to do. On the rare occasion that I have to cancel meetings, I always do so with great unease because I never want my clients to think that I am unreliable or not committed. And this being the project that I really want to make a lasting impression on has started out very unfavourably for me. But what choice do I have? I have to take Nikki back to the hospital and have her arm reset, followed by a cast, something that I am not looking forward to in the least. Jack has the daunting task of getting Michael and Ella ready for school without me and having to deal with all of their questions, which knowing Ella the way I do, there will be plenty of.

I tiptoe down the stairs so as to not wake Jack or the kids and make my way to my office. Turning on my computer, I wait rather impatiently for it to boot up. Why can't these things go any faster? Yet how did we handle last-minute cancellations in the "olden days," when we had no computers, no text messaging, and no BlackBerries? Back then, we would just have to wait until a reasonable time, at which point we could appropriately pick up a telephone and verbally call and cancel. Imagine that! Whatever happened to the personal way in which we communicated with people? Technology, though a lifesaver at times, often does little to enhance the personal niceties of life. Oh well, it is 5:45 a.m. and a not-so-personal e-mail is the best I can do for the time being. Personal niceties will just have to wait until a sensible time when the rest of the real world will be alert enough to be able to acknowledge one.

I have exactly sixty minutes to get myself and Nikki showered, dressed, and back into the car. Not an unrealistic amount of time for most people, if that's all that is really on my agenda, but I'm not most people and much to my detriment thrive on multitasking always—well, most of the time anyways. Truth is, I've become quite the multitasker over the years, regardless of whether I intended this to be the case or not, and it has just become a way of life for me. I know, I know, we all have free will, options, and choices, but sometimes we really don't. *Really, we don't!* Not if we put undue pressure on ourselves to try and be the best parent we can be and give our kids that head start in life that a lot of us strive for, while at the same time trying to live some sort of normal existence and have a life for ourselves. This is where the multitasking comes into play, so we juggle, reschedule, and finagle our way out of and into awkward situations. Because, let's face it, if we're not giving our all to our kids, clients, colleagues, and friends, or at the very least giving enough so they know we really do give a shit, who are we doing it all for?

I make my way back up the stairs, where I am greeted by a sleepy and not-yet-totally-awake Ella. She and her sleep animals must have had one great adventure overnight because she is looking rather rough around the edges this morning. The score: Ella, zero; sleep animals, one.

"Hi, Mama." Ella sounds chipper. Thank goodness! She is still rubbing sleep away from her drowsy eyes.

"Hi-ya to you too, sweetheart." Her good disposition always has an encouraging effect on my mood. I envelop my youngest child into my arms and hold her tightly. Breathing in, I wish this moment could last forever. I love the scent of Ella's hair and the feeling of her warm, rounded fingers against my back.

"Mama? How's Nikki?" Ella asks, concerned. "Did she really break her arm like Daddy said?"

I kiss the top of Ella's head. Her concern for her sister is heartwarming.

"She really did," I answer. "Mama has to take her back to get a cast put on this morning." I decide to skip the resetting part, figuring that she doesn't need to know all of the intricate details.

"Will it hurt Nikki, Mama?"

"I hope not."

"Will Nikki cry?"

"I'll do my best to make sure she doesn't cry."

"Will she have to stay at the hospital with the doctors?"

"No, honey, Mommy will bring Nikki right back home after the doctors put her cast on," I respond.

"Wait a minute, Mommy, I need to get something."

And with that, Ella loosens herself from my grip and runs straight into her bedroom. She returns promptly with Rosie, one of her many cherished sleep toys, and if I had to venture a guess, her favourite. Rosie is a shamrock-green velour mouse, extraordinarily well-loved, which is noticeable by her obvious tattered state of being. Pressing Rosie to her lips, Ella gives her a long drawn-out tender kiss and then proceeds to hug her tight before handing her over to me. If ever I was speechless, this is one of those times. Ella never before dared to part with any of her sleep toys, particularly Rosie.

"Nikki can play with Rosie, but just for today. She always makes me feel better when I feel scared. But she has to take good care of her and bring her back right after. Promise?"

"I promise."

What else is there left for me to say? I'm incredibly touched by Ella's affectionate gesture towards her sister. I'm not sure whether it is my lack of sleep, overwhelming concern for my child, or simply the emotions of the past twenty-four hours that has finally gotten the best of me. Either way, my eyes seem to flood with tears, and there is hopelessly little I can do to stop them.

Funny, isn't it? Camilla, Shane, and the project of my dreams don't seem nearly as momentous to me anymore.

Dear Diary,

I was so excited about today's meeting, and then real life happened and everything changed. Interesting how you can plan and schedule and organize, and then in a matter of minutes, everything you've so methodically planned out has to be completely recreated. I suppose Jack could take Nikki to the hospital to have her cast put on and I could take the kids to school and then make it to my meeting—late again, but I could get there—but that just doesn't feel like the right thing to do. To not be with Nikki while she's so frightened and wanting me there and putting my job first just doesn't sit right with me. I can't even imagine Jack taking her and me going to work. I couldn't even focus on it if I wanted to, and I guess maybe right now I don't want to. Yes, this is my dream project, but sometimes even our dreams have to get put on hold, don't they? I'm sure they will understand given what's happened, at least I hope they will. But if they don't ... well ... if they don't, there's little I can do to change that. I had to make a decision, and my decision is that my child comes first. That's never going to change. So whatever will be, will be ...

Later,
Me, Your Simple Girl

Thankfully just before lunchtime, Nikki and I are safely back at home. Who knew that securing a broken arm with a sturdy fibreglass cast could take so long? With her left arm firmly set into a hot-pink cast from mid-forearm to mid-fingers, she can cartwheel to her heart's desire, it isn't going to move. Quite frankly, though, I don't think Nikki's mind is on playing, given that she appears pretty much spent. Nikki is for the moment resting comfortably on the sofa, and so I take this as an opportunity to go into my office and attempt to focus on furniture plans and fabric samples—neither of which seem distinctly attractive to me for the time being.

Luckily I used the time while Nikki was in "surgery" to connect live with Camilla, explaining to her the sequence of events that had taken place since our telephone conference of yesterday and why I needed to cancel our appointment today. I suppose anyone without children might not have found my story entirely believable and might have thought that I was either: a) incredibly imaginative and fabricating a vivid anecdote, or b) one hell of a helicopter parent. I am neither. Fortunately for me, Camilla is more than sympathetic. However, she calls me back after she tells Shane and informs me he believes that if his wife is going to be spending all this money on a designer, surely I could make myself available to meet with him whenever necessary. "That's just how the business world works," according to Shane—jump when your client asks you to. It is becoming abundantly clear to me that I am definitely being employed by one of them, but am going to be compensated by the other. Since Camp Shane is the one who is going to be paying my fee, this seems to be a huge problem right about now. I have a lot of repenting to do if this man is ever going to take me seriously.

Dear Diary,

I know I did the right thing today—the right thing for my family, for my child, and for myself. But if I know I did the right thing, why am I feeling so guilty, and why am I giving this so much thought? It's as though I'm trying so hard to wear so many different hats all at the same time, and it seems that by doing so, someone is always feeling like they are getting the short end of the stick. And maybe someone is. And for that, I am sorry, but I can't do anymore or please anymore than I already am without completely coming undone. So I guess what I'm saying is that maybe it's time I trust my intuition, trust my feelings, and believe that what I am doing is the right thing. If I make a mistake, and I know I have, and will probably continue to do so, I guess I can only apologize and keep moving forward. Those that understand will believe in me; those that don't will have to set me free. It's a chance I have to take.

Later,
Me, Your Simple Girl

Chapter Fourteen

This is officially D-Day.

Today is the day that Shane and I are finally going to meet face-to-face. I can't put my finger on it, but there is something about this man that is making me feel moderately uneasy. I haven't even met him yet, and still he has this uncanny way of making me feel insecure about myself.

Camilla informed me that the offer to purchase on their New York City apartment has finally closed and that they are at long last the new owners. A Park Avenue pied-à-terre is all theirs, just waiting for an impressive makeover by none other than me.

But now I have this other problem—more like a predicament, if truth be told. I have this terrible habit of putting a face to a person before I even meet him or her. I visualize in my mind what he or she will look like purely based on the sound of his or her voice or whatever information I have gained about him or her. This time is no different. I imagine Shane as a tall, distinguished-looking man smartly dressed in a single-breasted, navy-blue, pinstripe suit. To complete his look, a milk-white, silk, pocket handkerchief is slightly peeking out of his jacket pocket, and of course, this is all to complement the perfectly starched white shirt. A shirt that is only befitting of French cuffs, not those diminutive white plastic buttons at the wrists. *Tacky!* The problem lies in the simple fact that if Shane looks nothing like the artistic image I have painted, I might (accidently of course) wear a stunned look on my face, and I just know that nothing good could come of that— particularly since he and I are already off to a shaky start.

Camilla and I are seated side by side on her very chic Barbara Barry cream-coloured sofa exchanging small talk when Shane enters the room. Fortunately for me, Shane looks almost exactly as I have pictured him. The only difference is that his suit is a charcoal pinstripe, not navy-blue pin—a minor detail in the grand scheme of things. I stand to greet him. Camilla introduces us. After some idle chitchat, Shane excuses himself and asks if he could have a moment alone with his wife. I nod obligingly (like I have a choice?) and watch as they move some ten feet away from me.

I can faintly hear Shane whisper to his wife, "She looks rather young. Are you sure she's qualified for this?"

"Yes, I'm sure, Shane. Just give her a chance. You haven't even listened to any of her ideas yet."

I glance over the room, pretending to fixate in and rest my eyes on an oversize piece of abstract art that hangs by the window. Dejectedly I have heard them and am now feeling more uncomfortable by the minute. Shane can't know that I'm intimated by him. I won't let him see that side of me.

Camilla makes her way back to the sofa. "Shane, Katarina and I were just about to start reviewing the floor plans. Why don't you join us?"

So he does. Along with the floor plans, they also present me with some current photos of the apartment. It isn't enormous, but decent in size by New York City standards—ten rooms in total, which include a vestibule, a living room, a kitchen, two bedrooms, three bathrooms, a library, and a dining room. I must admit that I am just as captivated as Shane is of his newest acquisition to his real estate portfolio.

"So let's try and preserve as much of the historical features as we can," I suggest, knowing from previous conversations with Camilla that Shane is quite involved in the arts and art preservation. It only makes sense to me then that he will want to restore as much of the historical allure of the apartment as he can.

"Well, that certainly makes sense," he says.

I continue, "If the existing hardwood flooring is in decent condition, we can keep it, just sand it and stain it. Why spend extra money if it isn't necessary?" Albeit faint, I do notice a quasi-smile coming across his face.

He leans in towards me. "What else could we preserve?" he asks.

"Well, those wonderful old mouldings, for one thing." I look at the photos again and ask, "And aren't those glass doorknobs from the 1940s?"

Camilla smiles and says, "Yes, I think they are, and I just love them."

"So do I!" I add enthusiastically.

I finally take a sip of water from the glass that Camilla had set down for me when I arrived. Excessive talking has made my mouth dry. We move on to discuss their preferences of periods, styles, fabrics, and furnishings.

At last, Shane says, "I think you'll do a fine job, Katarina." Then, looking only at me, he adds, "I want it beautiful, ladies, no, make that spectacular! A real showstopper!"

Camilla looks away, purposely, not making eye contact with either one of us.

"I absolutely agree, Shane. Together, you, Camilla, and I will create a home that you and she will feel utterly impressed with. A home that is entirely reflective of your tastes, but peaceful at the same time. I promise you that."

With that said, Shane and I carry on conversing about the apartment itself, the contractors who have already been put on notice by him, and our equal fondness of the city itself. Until, that is, he sweeps over to Camilla, kisses her swiftly, barely grazing her cheek, and makes a spectacular exit. Poof! Like magic, he disappears out the door.

Camilla turns to me and says, "Well, fortunately we both passed Shane's test."

"His test?" I ask.

"Yes, Katarina, Shane's test." She continues, "Shane is very particular. Particular about his appearance, his home, where we vacation, the friends we keep, and even the food we eat. He usually does all the hiring, not to mention firing, of any contractors or hired help. I asked him if for just this time, I could actually undertake this project without his constant interfering. I think I'm capable of handling such a task. I'm really not a complete idiot."

"Oh my goodness, of course not!" I offer in her defence.

"Do you have a bit more time to review the floor plans with me?"

"Absolutely! Nothing would please me more."

Camilla jumps right in. "As far as the second bedroom goes, let's just make it a neutral guest room for when our kids come to visit."

"For sure. Let's consider a serene hotel feel for this room. Since it already has that fantastic cornice plaster moulding that is heavily ornate, what I'm thinking might feel luxurious is if we incorporate warm whites and mix them with soft silver tones. We can accent with either a hint of robin's egg blue, or if you want it a little more exciting, maybe even lavender and plum tones for accents might work nicely too."

"Both sound equally striking. Let's think about it some more."

I know for a fact that Camilla and Shane will be spending a considerable amount of time in this apartment, so it makes perfect sense that what they want to create is a home away from home. Camilla wants a place for Shane and herself to unwind after he comes home from a long day at the office. It seems clear to me that Shane's intentions might be somewhat different. He wants a spectacular place to entertain in—a private residence all his own to impress others with. One thing is for sure, I definitely hope that he leaves the decorating to Camilla and me. Spectacular is one thing, over-the-top is completely different. And besides, he must have other, more pressing things to do. Like oversee his company affairs? All I know about Shane's business is that he is the CEO of some sort of manufacturing company that has affiliates all over the world. Given that he spends so much time abroad, and especially in New York City these days, he wants a place of his own when he is there—I can appreciate that. Hotel rooms must become old after a while, no matter how exquisite some of the ones in the Big Apple are.

Although Shane *says* he is handing this project off to Camilla and me, I know better. I've been around long enough to know how important it is to cc Shane on *all* correspondence. Every e-mail that goes out will be sent to him as well, and any decisions made will only be acted on after he is informed and has given written acceptance. One thing is for sure, I am not interested in holding the bag for extra, expensive furniture or fabric that Shane doesn't give his stamp of approval on.

I have to admit that there is a part of me that is feeling a little bit sorry for Camilla. Call it sisterhood, womanhood, or just plain camaraderie, but the more she speaks, the more I realize that she is just looking for a make-work project for herself. Since my first meeting with her and after some rather lengthy telephone conversations, I get the feeling that Camilla is insecure in her own way, not just about herself, but about her relationship with her husband. Barely a sentence has come out of her mouth that hasn't either begun or ended with the name Shane: "Shane this" or "Shane that." I learned the hard way a long time ago that in this business, you often become a marriage councillor of sorts when dealing with some couples. I figure this couple is no exception. Working with families, husbands and wives, husbands and husbands, I've all too often come across couples who have a completely different vision for their space. One wants contemporary and sleek (usually the husband), while the other lusts after tradition and tassels (usually the wife). It is part of my unwritten job description to remain neutral, let them hash it out, and only step in when absolutely necessary. The bottom line is I have to make it look extraordinary, mix and all.

And so we continue to sit together, Camilla and I, and continue to pour over the floor plans. I probe her about what her ideas for the space are, her vision and what she imagines it might look like when all is said and done. Simply by looking at her, I see that Camilla is the epitome of the quintessential Park Avenue elegant dame. Her personal aesthetic is classically chic and elegant. If I have to exaggerate this style for the apartment, so be it. Which, lucky for me, isn't such a difficult task—after all, I'm Italian, I can so-o-o do exaggeration! Camilla wants a space that is worthy of an era long gone by, where women wore diamonds and pearls for dinner and dressing like a lady was form, not effort. As per Shane's request, the apartment has to be conducive to enjoying cocktails either alone or with guests, daytime or nighttime.

"What about a classic, white and black checkerboard, marble tiled floor in the vestibule?" I suggest. "What with the wood panelling on the walls, we can really set the tone from the moment you walk through the front door."

Camilla loves the idea. I'm glad. What I love even more is that the vestibule to the apartment feels like a room, an actual room surrounded by three walls, not common at all with today's modern houses. With the right furniture pieces, lighting, and architectural detailing, what a grand entrance we can create! Do we want drama? If so, we can paint the walls a regal amethyst colour. Or do we want a clean, airy, metropolitan feel? This detail is still to be decided. For now, at the very least, we are headed in the right direction.

Moving forward into the interior of the apartment, we have the living area to consider. Not huge by suburban standards, but it boasts soaring ceilings and large, clear, double-hung windows with a spectacular view of the streetscape, a bonus if you think about it. Who wouldn't want to spend their time enjoying this particular view? A suburban, quaint feel smack-dab in the middle of the Upper East Side.

I am in love with this place!

In fact, the more Camilla and I discuss the structure of the apartment and all the possibilities, the more excited we both become about the project.

As you continue through the vestibule down the short corridor, you're greeted by double-entry doors directly in front of you. My thought is that we can paint out the doors in a glossy, high lacquered, black paint, allowing the existing glass doorknobs to sparkle like huge, oversize diamonds. So elegant and enticing you'll be dying to see what is behind the doors, but not so much so that you will become distracted and not focus on what is directly in front of you. The main living area, while long and narrow, can accommodate an array of diverse seating areas. We can create one with individual seating suitable for lazy nights and casual reading, while the other could be a formal space, conducive to entertaining. The room is large enough to fit in a dining table. The walls could be kept light, incorporating various tints of museum white, since they will become our canvas for the selection of art pieces Camilla and Shane still aren't aware they will be acquiring. Since Shane has made it quite clear that he is out to impress, I don't think he will object to my art acquisition suggestions here. Based on the floor plans, it seems as though I have a forty-eight-inch-wide space between some of the windows. A near perfect sight line as I make my way down the hallway—almost faultless. It is clear to me that the architect who designed this place so many years ago had been thinking along the same lines that I am right now.

How old could this building be? I wonder. Maybe from the 1930s or '40s is what I am suspecting. The Art Deco period was a time when just about everything in New York City was touched by glamour, or so it seemed. A liquor cabinet might be the right touch, just standing directly below the painting. *Yes!* That would be fantastic! Nothing tacky, of course. No scotch bottles in visible sight. Only beautifully cut crystal decanters and etched glasses calling out to greet you as you walk into the room. *"Hello, darling, how was your day? Can I pour you a drink?"* Tee-hee-hee! I can hear them talking now. That's precisely what they would say, if they could talk that is. All the while, the soft lyrics of Diana Krall or Ella Fitzgerald can be dimly heard in the background. Oh my God, I love this! My job, that is. The very fact that I am allowed unlimited mental creativity to paint out all sorts of scenarios in my mind gives me immense pleasure. My mind ... what a tool ... and how I love to observe it as it sets into motion. Not only do I have this ability to fabricate so many different scenarios, but I am allowed the mental freedom to play them all out as well.

I can't wait to pitch some of my ideas to Shane.

And so, what seems like only minutes passes by, and yet, glancing down at my watch, I notice that it, in fact, has been hours that have gone swiftly by. Camilla and I continue to exchange ideas about the apartment, tales about our children, and truths about life as "a mom."

It's time for me to go. I need to make my way back home and back to my office, where I can gather my thoughts into a proper written proposal presentable to Shane. Here is a man impressed by logical and well-thought-out ideas presented in an organized and comprehensive manner. If that's what Shane wants, then that is exactly what Shane is going to get.

Dear Diary,

Wow! Considering how nervous I was when I got here this morning, I think I even managed to impress myself today. If Shane and Camilla both like some of my ideas, I might have even succeeded at finding a common design thread between the two of them. Can you imagine, making both of them quasi-happy on my first attempt? And yet, the truth is, if they both do succeed in liking what I am suggesting, I think it will not only look fantastic but will be precisely the essence of what they are trying to capture. TBD.

Later,
Me, Your Elated Simple Girl

Chapter Fifteen

The days and weeks seem to be passing by ever so rapidly. Sultry summer days have become a sweet but distant memory and are replaced by brisk autumn ones. The leaves, having turned from a vibrant green shade to crimson red, are assembling their descent and cascading onto the ground, which appears more than ready to greet them. With the kids finally settled in at school again as though there had never even been a break in their routine, it is becoming more evident that Jack and I seldom exchange conversation that doesn't revolve around the dropping off or picking up of children.

Conversations of any great length seem to circumvent meals, hockey sticks, and the need for new ballet shoes. By day, my adult conversations consist of Italian marble and British textiles; but by night, my vocabulary is a menagerie of school-age gibberish mixed in together with a splash of juvenile lingo. Some days even I question what the heck I am doing and whose life I am, in fact, living. Am I pretending to be a designer when I am really "just a mom," or am I in fact kidding myself into believing that I can parent three overzealous children when in fact I revel in fluffy fabrics and overpriced designer deco?

I do know one thing with certainty. And that is that I will soon be travelling to New York City to visit Shane and Camilla's latest acquisition, and I can't wait.

Alessia called less than one hour ago to say she is on her way over this morning. She is *supposed* to be working from home today, though if she is on her way here, I can't see that she is getting much work done. Speak of the devil, there is the doorbell now.

"Come in, come in!" I yell as I run towards the door, flinging it wide open.

"Whoa, chic! Isn't it a little early to be already spiked out on espresso?" she asks, teasing me all the while.

"I'm going to New York, I'm going to New York," I break out into song, dancing around the hallway solely for Alessia's benefit since she and I are the only ones here. I stop swiftly. Grabbing Lessia's arm, I shout, "Oh my God, Less, what am I doing? What if I can't deliver what they're expecting? What if I fuck this up? Then what? I will look like a complete fool? Am I being insecure? What do you think?" I shouldn't really need Alessia to answer these questions. I know for a fact that my insecurities are definitely getting the best of me here, but unfortunately for me, there is little I can do to make it stop.

"You're exhausted, Kat, that's all," Alessia states flat-out, trying to comfort me.

"Do you really think that's all it is?" I question naively, like a young child looking up to her mother for guidance.

"Of course it is. You and Jack are forever running around from work to home to work again. You're overthinking all of this. You never find the time to just have fun and play around."

"Play?" I question.

"You know what I'm talking about Kat—just relaxing. Find the time to do something you love to do. I don't know, like going for a workout, going out with the girls, going on vacation with your best friend … *hint, hint* … that kind of stuff."

I roll my eyes at Alessia. We've had this conversation several times over the past few years. "You know that I would love nothing more than for the two of us to go on vacation alone, like we used to do when we were in university. But those days are long gone, my friend. You and I both know that only too well."

Alessia presses her lips together and nods her head. "Yeah, that's what you keep telling me. But one day you'll give in. I know you will." She looks down at her watch. "Sorry, but I've got to go. I just came to wish you luck in the Big Apple." And just like that, she is gone again.

Going on vacation with Alessia is completely out of the question. When we were younger and carefree, it was a possibility; it even happened. But that was long before marriage, kids, and a career. Maybe she does bring up a good point, though. Maybe I don't play enough in my life. Maybe I am taking life a little too seriously. I will have to give "*playing*" some thought. For now, I'd better get back to work, or playing—ever—will never happen.

Back to my party boy, Kip. He and I need to schedule a meeting very soon. I know full well that he is anxious to have his home completed and fabulously decorated before the holidays, which are imminent at this point. All throughout the city, holiday ads are working fervently to persuade shoppers to forget about the current season, though it has barely just begun, and focus on holiday spending in all of its infinite glory. I should call Kip like today, if I am going to be away in New York City for a few days. I need to ensure that he, as well as my other few clients, don't feel as though they are being neglected for what is now deemed to be my biggest job to date.

"Hey, Kip, it's me, Kat," I say in a cheery tone when I finally manage to get around to calling him. "How are things?"

"Hey yourself, darling, I'm great, never been better. Business is fan-tast-ic! So when are we going to get together again so we can finish up what we started?"

Oh brother! I am well aware that he is harmless, but I have to admit that I still get a little flustered every time Kip speaks to me in his flirtatious way. Knowing him the way that I do, I'm sure that he probably speaks to all women like this, but it never ceases to amaze me that every time he suggests we meet, it sounds more as though we are having a midday encounter rather than a designer/client meeting.

"That's actually the reason I was calling, Kip. I'm going to be going away for a few days next week and thought we could meet before that so we could discuss some of the ideas I pitched to you. You know, like window coverings, fabric, lighting for your space, that kind of stuff."

I was anxious to have as many details as possible finalized before I left.

"How about we meet at my office and then we can head over to this little French bistro up the street? The boeuf bourguignon is to die for!"

I know better than to agree to meet him this way. I have scheduled such meetings with him before. Kip is a friendly guy, and these types of meetings always prove futile in trying to get him to commit to anything. They seem to be more ego-boosting encounters for Kip and a reason for him to leave his office and be seen in a trendy eating spot. I have a funny feeling that Kip doesn't have a lot of close friends—confidants—who he can share important things with. As much as I am flattered to be held in this category—and truly I am flattered—I just don't have the time to stroke his ego right now. Decisions have to get made if we are going to get his home completed to the point where he is satisfied with it in time for his big Christmas gathering, and the only place we are going to make this happen is in the comfort of Kip's very own home. I have to get him to focus. He needs to see the fabrics in their element—held up against the windows directly in the rooms in question, or this will never work.

"Boeuf bourguignon sounds delicious, Kip, but I don't think it is going to work. You have to look at some samples in your own home. No other location is going to work. You know what I mean, Kip. You have to hold the fabrics up to windows, that kind of stuff." Even though I couldn't see him, I could envision Kip swivelling around in his chair and staring out into space through the vast windows that shed light into his office. Only when he begins to speak again do I know that he is resolute, focused, with his back pressed against the smooth leather of his chair and his palms flat on the desk surface.

"Got it, boss! How about Sunday morning at my place then?" Kip is back to business.

Sunday morning? *Sure, Kip, should I bring my entourage of kids with me in their jammies too? Maybe we could pop some Eggo waffles into the toaster while we go over fabrics—sticky little hands and all.* Kip obviously wasn't thinking before he spoke, because if he had been thinking, he would have known better than to suggest such an inappropriate meeting time. He is dumb. Not in a stupid guy kind of way, but in a single guy kind of way. The guy who has no idea what Sunday mornings are like in a house full of children. So I don't hold it against him. I just have to make him understand why that is clearly not going to happen.

"Kip, unfortunately that won't work for me. I have three kids. Sunday mornings are pretty busy around my house."

"Oh, right. Sorry, Kat, I forgot. Let's see then. How about Friday, say noonish, would that work better for you? I was planning on taking the afternoon off anyways."

I agree, all the while knowing that Friday is Halloween, a day just as important as Christmas, if not more so, if you're a kid. I had better be back in plenty of time to prepare for the evening's festivities, or I am certainly not going to be taking home the mommy-of-the-year trophy in my plastic jack-o-lantern.

~

"What do you mean you aren't coming to the Halloween dance on Friday? You promised!" Nikki is perched red-faced across from me as we sit for dinner. This is definitely going to be another case of indigestion for yours truly since I am once again attempting to justify my actions to my eight-year-old daughter.

"Nikki, I'm sorry!" I muster. "I have a meeting Friday afternoon that I just can't cancel. But I'm still going to come to the parade in the morning—that's just as important, isn't it?"

"No. Well, yes. Well, I don't know, but you promised you would be at the dance! All the other moms will be there. Maddie's mom, and Jessica's mom!" Nikki is sobbing uncontrollably.

I am trying to make her understand that *yes*, I did say I would be there, but that was before a client wanted to meet with me on the same day and at the same time. Never at a loss for words when it comes to discussing building materials and home décor, I now find myself at a complete loss for words.

"Shut up, stupid!" Michael interrupts Nikki's wails. "Mom has to work. Why are you trying to make her feel bad?"

And with that said, an all-out battle begins! Emotions are running rampant, hands are flailing, and tears are flowing like rapid streams following a springtime thaw. Nikki, being Nikki, is being relentless. Giving up on something she strongly believes in, like me going to her dance, is not something that is going to happen anytime soon. Not to mention that she also hates to lose an argument, but then again, so does Jack for that matter.

"Hey, guys, that's enough!" Jack has unmistakably lost his temper.

Jack immediately sends Nikki to her room, but not before she makes certain that I really understand how she feels, in case I have lost anything in the interpretation of the commotion that has ensued ... FYI, I haven't. So there she is, standing stoically facing me at the kitchen threshold, hands on her hips, tears still pouring down her already-streaked face. Her swollen eyes are barely noticeable any longer. The usual blue glint that typically radiates is clouded with all hope gone awry. Sobbing, she does her best to ensure that I hear her words loud and clear.

"I knew it! See! Just admit it! Your precious clients are more important than your family!"

Ouch! Double ouch!

Those words sting badly! Not that I think she cares too much whether I am feeling hurt by her words, because just as soon as the words have escaped her lips, Nikki is gone, leaving me sitting there speechless again for the second time in the same night.

Dear Diary,

Oh my God! She didn't just say all that, did she? I can't believe she would, could say all that to me. It's so not true. Yes, I love my work, and yes, it's true I adore my clients, and maybe, just maybe, I do coddle them a little too much sometimes, but never at the expense of my family. Never at the expense of my kids! She's just upset, right? She didn't mean anything she said, right? She's just a little girl upset because she wants her mommy to stick around school all day with her and her friends because it's going to be a big party. But I can't stay all day with her; that's just not possible. At the very least, I will be there for the parade. I'll watch her as she holds her cast up high and marches around the school. How many other mommies can say they will be doing that? How many other mommies will be there? I bet the Yummy Mummy Club will probably all be at the gym working out with their trainers and forgetting all about the stupid parade and stupid dance. They'll miss all of it and probably not even give it a second thought. On the one hand, Nikki tells me she loves that I am not like some of the other mummies and dress all fancy and go to work, unlike them, who hang around the school yard and gossip because they have nothing better with which to fill their days. And yet, out of the blue, she throws these tantrums. What's going on here? Please, can you tell me?

Later,
Me, Your Confused Simple Girl

Chapter Sixteen

The bright morning sunlight is pouring into our bedroom window. If I didn't know any better, I would have thought it was a warm summer's day and not a frosty autumn one. It is early November. The crisp air has a distinct chill to it, but we are still free of snow—at least for now, thank goodness, no small feat for those of us living in the great white north. We need to make the most of it while it lasts because before you know it, old man winter will be upon us, without much warning either. This is the thing about our Canadian climate that I invariably find intriguing. Today could be a semiwarmish day, hovering around the low double digits, and powie, tomorrow morning we could awaken to ten centimetres of snow and a thermometer hovering below zero degrees. For those of us having to dig our way out of our driveways, this is just the beginning of a season packed with a painfully inflicted workout regime. For the kids, it means days and weeks filled with rolling, aiming, and firing fluffy white snowballs at whoever is fated to cross their paths.

Later this same morning, Jack and I are sitting at the kitchen table sharing our Sunday morning coffee, a ritual I never seem to get tired of, and discussing our work schedules for the upcoming week. I will be leaving for New York City on Tuesday morning to meet with Camilla, Shane, and the contractors. Up until now, the project almost didn't even seem real to me, a concept more than a reality. But now, with my e-ticket printed and folded neatly into my Canadian passport, it is crystal clear all right.

I've been doing an enormous amount of thinking lately—some might call it soul-searching. Thinking back to Nikki and how upset she was pre-Halloween. Maybe Alessia is right. Maybe I don't know how to play. Resting my coffee cup down on our imperfectly dented and scratched kitchen table, a sign of a well-loved piece of furniture—at least that's what I tell my clients, so the same should hold true for me—I look over at Jack. His head is completely immersed in the sports section now, probably reading something about last night's hockey game.

"Why don't we tell the kids to get dressed and go for a family walk this morning?" I suggest.

"Like now?" Jack seems puzzled.

"Like now," I reply.

Why does my suggestion seem so bizarre to him? Okay, so maybe it is a little out of character for me to put forward something of the sort. Maybe because as sweet as it sounds, the prospect of having three kids get dressed and walk outside in the frosty cold air is no more than a recipe for disaster in my mind. At the very least, I should give it a try. You never know—I could be pleasantly surprised.

"I'll tidy up the house later. I think we could all use the fresh air. I know I could."

And that couldn't be more true.

~

With the kids bundled up in their fleece sweaters, mittens and hats securely on, and of course, the girls donning their ever-so-fashionable Ugg boots, off we go on our family stroll. The scent of the autumn air as it fills my nose is extraordinarily refreshing. My lungs seem to be in shock, since they are not used to such a calm pace or such a refreshing scent on a Sunday morning. It's as though they are asking,

"Lady, where's the Mr. Clean and bleach we've become so used to? What is this fragrance out here? Is this fresh air we smell?"

It's touching to see the kids laughing and giggling, prodding each other as they walk, then run, then stop, and for the first time in a long time, not push or shove each other when one gets too close. Jack and I lag behind, not saying too much but just observing the momentary state of joy of our children. Though he never mentions it, I suppose Jack understands what I am trying to accomplish. I am trying to find the balance. The balance so many of us search our whole adult lives for—the balance between working mom and stay-at-home mama. It's sort of like looking for Waldo in those kids' books, *Where's Waldo?* Just when you're so proud of yourself because you're certain that you have found him, you shift your gaze if only for a brief second. But that instant is all it takes to lose sight of him, because in that short moment of time when you were confident and therefore lifted your eyes, he either disappears or you become preoccupied with something else. All the same, he is gone, and disappointment reigns as you begin the search all over again.

Nikki lets Michael and Ella run ahead of her. In the morning sunlight, her long blonde hair shines even more brightly, similar to strands of shimmering threads of gold. If I could capture this moment and bottle it, I undoubtedly would. As I approach Nikki, she shifts her body towards me, lacing her tiny, wool-entrenched fingers into mine. Her rosy cheeks give way to an infectious smile.

"I decided to wait for you, Mama," she offers up to me.

I choke back some miniature tears that are in the process of forming. It never ceases to amaze me how one small sentence can deliver such an impact to my constantly melting heart.

Jack quickens his pace to catch up to Michael and Ella, who by now have managed to purposely fall into a neighbour's neat pile of crisp leaves, evidently ready to be bagged and taken away. Unfortunately for my neighbours, this is not to be today. They will be raking this pile all over again courtesy of my children.

Sorry! With Nikki's arm newly free of the cast that had taken up temporary residence, she is being more cautious than ever and desolately opting out of the childish play her siblings are taking part in.

And so we continue to walk like this for what seems like forever, yet at the same time simply feels like a fleeting moment in time. Nikki and I stroll in silence, hand in hand, her tiny fingers grasping hold of mine even tighter, as though letting go isn't even an option. We don't speak of the incident that led up to the Halloween dance. I know that her physical nearness to me is her way of apologizing. I give her hand a little squeeze and cast my eyes down on her. This is my way of saying, "You're forgiven. You always will be." We both look up at the brilliant sun. It seems to shine even brighter in this very moment. We both giggle a little. All is good again.

Dear Diary,

Is it possible to do everything and be everything to all the people who you care about? Is it possible to love your career, knowing that it defines a part of who you are, yet love your family with the same might, knowing that they too define a part of who you are? Can you really put yourself first without putting others second and appearing selfish? Where the hell are the answers that we are looking for when we're looking for them? Maybe there's some truth to what Alessia's life coach tells her. Maybe the answers we are looking for are right in front of us; we just can't see them clearly ... not just yet anyways.

Later,
Me, Your Simple Girl

~

By Monday evening I am packed and ready for my big meeting in New York City. My Louis Vuitton portfolio, a gift to myself fresh out of interior design school, at a time when I couldn't afford Louis

Vuitton (or any other name-brand designer for that matter), is packed with my handwritten notes, photos, and some fabric samples I have collected. Perhaps the samples are a little premature at this stage of the game, but experience prevails and experience has taught me that by offering clients something tangible to view and hold makes the end appear that much closer and not just some far-off date in time.

I am feeling confident that my meeting with Kip has gone well too—very well indeed, in fact. I have finally gotten him to commit to some of the ideas that we had earlier discussed, thank goodness for that. Concepts that now with samples in hand have become realities. Kip agrees that a sheer silk charcoal fabric that I had shown him and loved will be great for his place. Nothing too "frou-frou," he had said to me once, and this truly is not. Simple. Elegant. Sophisticated. That's what Kip wants, and that's what I have given him. Draping only to floor length, without being any longer or puddled under, on a simple, pleated, six-inch header and installed at ceiling height, the fabric is sheer enough to filter light through and yet still give Kip the privacy he requested. When I suggested installing a remote so that at the touch of a button the drapes would open and close, Kip hugged me, like I was some sort of genius. I'm sure I had told him that what I do is not rocket science! Still, he was over-the-moon at my stroke of so-called brilliance!

So far, most of the textures in Kip's space are sleek and cool to the touch and to the eye, just like its homeowner, and he likes it that way. Lighting is extremely important to Kip since Mr. Suave wants to ensure that only his best side shines forward at all given times. I recommend something a little edgy and modern, but full of antiquated charm and elegance. This comes by way of a pair of Versailles wall sconces by famed designer Bill Sofield. A mirrored back plate on the sconce allows for the light to reflect, and an antique gold clip at the top of it gives way to a luminous glow. Kip is enchanted. I am pleased. He thinks the sconces are fabulous. "That's because they are," I tell him. A pair of them flanking either side of a silver leaf console table will look spectacular. A second pair will flank the interesting abstract art piece that Kip is the proud new owner of. I hate to think what he paid for it since I am very familiar with the gallery it came from. Nonetheless, Kip said it spoke to him immediately when he laid his eyes upon it, which I, his designer, did advise him that it should. So the black-cherry, snowy-white, and midnight-black oil markings speak volumes to Kip. What does it all mean? To Kip, it probably suggests an incredibly fast sports car on an ominous dark and curvy road late at night. If my speed-demon client is happy with his art selection, I am elated too.

Kip's kitchen? More for show than anything else, since he barely cooks a meal at home, yet still essential. Its main function is for housing protein drinks, crystal goblets (what else?), and various serving platters. While Kip's galley-style kitchen isn't large, it works well with the rest of the space. While I usually recommend playing with various heights in a space to add visual interest if nothing else, Kip's home seems to be a lot more long and lean where furniture and cabinets are concerned. True to form, this is a clear indication of the homeowner, and this is precisely the way he likes it. My recommendation is to use an Italian kitchen manufacturer well versed with contemporary and modern flair; kitchens constructed with glossy finishes and nickel hardware. My recommendation for Kip is a glossy white finish highlighted with candy-apple-red, free-floating shelves. Along with a quartz countertop in a charcoal-grey finish and a backlit backsplash, and voilà, you have the makings of a space fit for my not-really-confirmed bachelor. Kip seems thrilled with his home and the progress we are making. He's just as excited as a child about to make his way through the front doors of FAO Schwarz for the very first time, totally in awe by the appearance of the soldiers standing guard at the entrance and eager to see what gloriousness awaits him once inside the doors.

Christmas is just around the corner, and Kip is looking forward to throwing his first party in his new home. I can't promise Kip all will be ready in time for Santa to come down his chimney (or via the elevator doors). "How about a New Year's Eve party instead?" I suggest. Now that was doable. No, my party boy was leaving the city for New Year's Eve, so a Christmas party it had to be. I promise Kip I will do my best, but Italian suppliers are not known to be the timeliest and working under pressure will only give them cause to delay the project even further. Kip is reasonable, thank God! He doesn't expect me to move mountains, small hills perhaps, but now that he can envision my concepts, like any other client who has the means to afford it, the money is burning a hole in his pocket, and he wants to put out the fire before it spreads.

~

By bedtime I am exhausted. One by one, I tuck the kids into bed, kissing each of them good-night. I am always in awe at how vulnerable and innocent they appear to me in the glow of the dim evening light. I know that my upcoming business trip isn't sitting well with any of them, so like any other doting mother, I promise them I will be back from my trip even before they have a chance to miss me.

"Hey, Ma." Michael's voice summons me back as I try to tiptoe across his bedroom floor, making my way finally to my own bed. I long for some rest.

"Yeah, honey?" I answer, wanting to respond to his query, but not wanting to engage in a full all-out conversation at this hour of the night.

I pick this time to ruffle Michael's mass of brunette hair, cut a little longer on top, "like the older boys" in his school. As much as Michael wants to be one of them, and often reminds me that as the eldest child of this family he isn't a kid any longer, my usual response is that he will always be my kid and I will always be his mama. I sit back down gently on the side of Michael's bed. He turns to face me. Even with his sleepy face, he manages to force his biggest big-boy smile. He speaks softly. Fatigue has taken over.

"I just want you to know how proud I am of you. I know you've worked really hard to get here, and working in New York has always been your dream."

If that isn't enough to bring me to tears again, I don't know what is. No matter how hard I fight to blink them away, they are growing larger and in more abundance. They have nowhere else to go but to form a steady stream down my already blazing-hot cheek. I'm certain a few of them land on Michael, forming a small but shallow pool of water before I have the chance to wipe them away.

"Gee, Mommy, I didn't mean to make you cry," Michael proffers in his tired slumber.

My lips part in an attempt to construct an audible sentence, but nothing seems to come out. I make another attempt, this time caressing my little boy's face. It is apparent that he is trying to act so grown-up, so strong, just like his father. Only he isn't Jack. He is merely a miniature version, still unscathed by the sometimes tough decisions we grown-ups are forced to make. The truth is, I have never been away from Michael, Jack, or the girls for more than just a few hours. So as much as they are apprehensive about my going away, I am even more nervous.

"It's okay, honey," I offer. "Thanks for understanding why I need to do this … and, Michael," I add, "thanks for being proud of me. It means a lot to me to hear you say that."

Michael simply smiles. "Mommy, you go and get 'em in New York. I'll help Dad take care of the girls."

Listening to Michael's innocent voice warms my heart. His eyes are shining back at me. I kiss him, again, reiterating how much I love him. I attempt to leave his room for a second time tonight. Closing the door partially behind me, I stand outside of Michael's room for a few moments. I can hear him breathing, slowly, gently. I know that once and for all, he is finally succumbing to sleep.

Dear Diary,

If parenting isn't the toughest job in the world, then I really don't know what is! All those talks with Michael, all the times I thought my words had fallen upon the playful ears of a

little kid who only processed them as "wha ...
wha ... wha," like in one of those Charlie Brown
comic strips. He heard them! He's heard every
single one of them! Now I'm the one standing
here feeling as though I just got a brave send-
off from my parents as I journey into the big,
beautiful world. Talk about role reversal! Thank
you for sending me Michael and allowing me
to be his mother. Come to think of it, thank you
for sending me Nikki and Ella too, for as much
as I thought I was here to teach them about
life and love, I really think they are the ones
teaching me something! Huh! That's interesting,
isn't it? Maybe I should let them in on this little
secret—who knows? Maybe they already know it.
All the times I really thought I sucked at being
a parent, I was actually being tested, wasn't I?
To see if I'd stick it out or just give up? Right! How
could I give up? And let them down? No way. Not
a chance. I'm going to New York. I'll show my
kids that I can do both—be their mom and be
a great creator. In a way, maybe they're both the
same thing ... maybe I should just stop trying so
hard to figure it all out and get some sleep.

Later,
Me, Your Exhausted Simple Girl

Chapter Seventeen

Standing all alone at the airport terminal, I do a quick scan of the events that have led up to my arrival here. All I could manage to do was toss and turn all of last night, mostly due to the anticipation of this trip. I suppose I was also a little anxious knowing that I would be gone for four days and that Jack and the kids would have to fend for themselves without me. I don't see anything good coming out of that, and yet I have to do this—go, that is. I awoke early enough to take my leisurely time getting myself ready this morning. What a decadent feeling that was! Getting prepared for the day that lay ahead of me without the sound of voices arguing, without anyone opening my steamy shower door and posing questions as I watch water drip all over the floor, without being interrupted causing me frustration that in turn would force me to toss my makeup back inside my vanity drawer and simply make-do with whatever I had managed to apply. It was early enough that I even had plenty of time to put a pot of coffee on and early enough to still pack the kids' lunches so it was one less thing that Jack would have to contend with today.

Speaking of Jack, he must have sensed my anxiety this morning, because not long after the last coffee bean had been ground and the percolation process had begun, he made his appearance in the kitchen.

"Did I wake you?" I ask apologetically.

"No, not you," Jack smirks, "it was that dolphin that must have escaped from the zoo and was flip-flopping all over our bed all night long that woke me. You should have been there; she was flipping and flopping and kicking me the entire night. She woke me up, not you, honey."

"*Ha-ha.* Sorry."

Jack comes towards me, entwining his arms around my waist in a comforting gesture. "The kids and I will be fine, Kat. You just go and impress your clients the way I know you can. Stop second-guessing yourself and just do what you do best, nothing more and nothing less."

See, this is precisely the problem. I'm not entirely too sure what it is that I do best anymore. And so, standing here in front of the American Airlines agent at YYZ on this morning, I am doing what I think is nothing significant at all—by myself no less—and this is entirely new for me, not to mention enormously weird.

On the flip side, I am relieved that Camilla and Shane decided to fly to New York a few days ahead of me. The plane ride, albeit a short flight, will give me time to review my notes and just collect my thoughts, which is something I feel I am in desperate need of. For the next four days, until Friday afternoon, I will be "on," so to speak, so I need to ensure that I am ready for this.

My Louis Vuitton Neverfull shoulder bag begins to vibrate courtesy of my ringing cell phone. Digging deep down into it and pushing aside sunglasses ... hand wipes ... eyedrops ... and *eww*, what is that ... *nice*, a *gently used* tissue à la Ella, no doubt, I finally find my metallic pink link to the rest of the world. Flipping it open, I read the words "Text Message" across the screen.

I press the "Read" button.

Go get 'em, diva girl!
Lessi xoxo
☺ is my only reply.

Dropping the phone back into my bag, I wonder who on earth ever came up with the name Neverfull Bag. Personally speaking, mine is always full. Overflowing in fact, and mostly jam-packed full of stuff that I seldom have any use for, but it is there, just in case. Well, besides the snotty tissue, most everything else could potentially be useful.

That's it, I've decided. I will rename my bag the Always Full Bag. This is without a doubt a more appropriate name for it. Whatever were those designers over at Louis Vuitton thinking? Must have been a man who named the bag! The contents of my Always Full are an ongoing joke among Jack and the kids. Laugh as they might, on any given road trip, whether it is to the grocery store, hockey tournament, or dance recital, whenever any one of them looks inside my bag for something they urgently need, chances are it is there.

~

Landing at LaGuardia a short seventy-five minutes later, I am standing amongst the crowd of other passengers at Carousel D. It appears that most of us are impatiently waiting for our luggage so we can finally set off on our business trip (for some) or vacation (likely for the others). It is at times like this that I wonder what it must feel like to travel lightly—say, with just a carry-on roll-away or something of similar size. I watch in envy as a young, blonde, bohemian-dressed girl strolls right past me with her roll-away following obediently behind her. Her hemp-like, colourful, Bob Marley pouch is slung across her waist, and her long, tie-dyed skirt gently grazes the ground as she sashays past. I am utterly amazed by the ease with which she saunters by me.

What is that scent that she is wearing?

Rose, bergamot, and orange linger in the air after she is no longer in clear sight. *Hmm*, pretty good taste in fragrances. Her hippy-like appearance is obviously just a guise for her obvious feminine preference in fragrances.

I direct my attention back to the still-empty carousel. The good news is that I am only waiting for one, very large, thirty-inch suitcase. The bad news is that I am waiting for one, very large and heavy, thirty-inch suitcase. Between my Always Full shoulder bag and my portfolio, which holds not only Camilla's file but also my portable laptop, I'm positive that I have everything covered. Fortunately my hot-pink Heys is large enough to house my array of jackets, skirts, trousers, jeans, and an excess of toiletries ... just in case. And, of course, I never leave home without my way-too-many pairs of shoes!

I am pretty impressed with myself. The fact that I was able to get everything to fit in one piece of luggage in the first place is a fait accompli in my opinion. Still, I am glad neither Camilla nor Shane is present to witness the way in which I travel. To be honest, it is a *little* embarrassing. How many times have I told myself that I really should streamline my packing, get it under control, and only take essential things with me, and still I have not managed to master the fine art of packing quite yet. I think I am finally coming to terms with the fact that this is just how I travel. I like to have extra items of clothing with me, just in case, because let's face it, you never know how you're going to feel on a given morning and what if you don't like what you packed, then what? You have to wear something you're not in the mood for? Not likely, 'cause that's a terrible way to start off your day and a sure way to make the rest of it unpleasant.

Clunk!

Finally! The sight and sound of luggage dropping one by one through the rubber sweep of the carousel. I stand and watch as suitcase after suitcase goes round and round. *Gee*, people are really boring with their luggage since most everything making its way down appears to be dreary black canvas. *Honestly, how drab!* I usually don't have the time to take notice of such pettiness since most of my visits to airports include Jack and the kids—also known as airport entertainment for all other passengers who are present. See, it usually goes something like this: Jack, being the stronger and much taller of the two of us, is the one standing amongst the other passengers waiting impatiently at the carousel, while I do my best to amuse my very restless and bored children, who by this point of the trip, resemble escaped wild monkeys from a local zoo. Ella and Michael are characteristically on the loose taking turns riding on freed luggage buggies, while the zoo keeper, Nikki, stands by, shouting at them in what typically are failed attempts at rounding up her chimps.

The most entertaining scenarios, for those who are not witness to this free diversion from the everlasting carousel roundabout, are for those interested in being my privy audience and watching as I sprint through the arrivals with Ella, desperately searching for a washroom because *"Mama, I have to pee right now!"* So, par for the course, Michael is usually left standing with Nikki and our carry-ons (which to most other travellers typically resemble a month's worth of belongings), and I frantically take flight in search of a stick figure decal that resembles the female anatomy, while Ella's small feet attempt to keep pace with mine.

But now I am standing here alone, serenely, with no crazy childhood maladies or immediate needs to distract my attention. Just me, myself, and I.

Plonk!

There it is. My hot-pink Heys, or at least I think it is mine. Looking around at the group of people waiting here alongside me, I doubt that anyone else among them might claim ownership of a pink suitcase. Most of them don't strike me as the pink type, but you just never know. I wait until the pink piece of hard plastic makes its way towards where I am standing. I carefully lean over so as to not catch the green frill of my jacket on the rather dirty conveyer belt and manage to read the luggage tag.

Knew it! Mine!

I heave it off the conveyer belt as forcefully as I can, attempting to maintain my composure given the obvious fact that I am immensely vertically challenged and my Heys looks as though it is almost as tall as I am.

There! I've got it! And thankfully both of us are still standing. All I need to do now is to wait in a taxi queue for a ride, and I will be heading off uptown.

~

Sitting comfortably in the back of a New York City yellow taxicab, I try to relax as we weave our way through Manhattan. OMG, how I love the sound of that! *MAN-HAT-TAN!* It even has a nice sound to it as it rolls off my tongue.

I gaze out the window, observing the groups of people as we make our way into the city. I think I'm beginning to realize, or at the very least understand better, what a large part of my fascination with this city is. It's the diversity of the people. The way they dress; their hair, long on some and almost nonexistent on others. Some wear it bleached and others colourful, but it doesn't seem to matter to most of the passersby since everyone just keeps right on walking and doing their own thing. Some people talk on cell phones, while others scuffle past drinking their Starbucks, and still others bop their heads from side to side as their earphones sit perched snugly in their ears.

This city is so very colourful, and I love colour! All colours, in fact. Sure, I am more partial to some colours, like peony pink, celadon green, and turquoise blue, but it's the diversity of the colour surrounding me and the fact that for most people it goes unnoticed that I find to be amazing. No judgment, no stares or glares or scowls, just people going about doing their own thing. Perhaps this is one of the reasons I've always been fascinated with interior design too. It's just a part of my DNA—who I am. I didn't choose it; it chose me. I love guiding people in making their spaces their own. Helping people, not any people, but my clients, people I have come to care about, create spaces that give them meaning and purpose. Spaces that reflect who they are and what they're all about and what they need to surround themselves with to be happy. Bringing colour into their worlds that might otherwise lack colour. This is what I do. This is what I was born to do. And since so far all of them have been so very different, it's the coolest, neatest thing being able to stand by and observe as each project takes shape, a different shape from the last one, and if all goes well will probably achieve a different shape from the next one. And who says that you have to have a "label" for the shape? Who says it has to be square or round or octagonal? It can be "squarish" or "round-ish" or "octagonal-ish." Right? Of course, it can. I've made it my motto to never label my clients or their spaces as traditional or modern or Art Deco. Of course, often there is more of a sense of one particular style over another and many do steer in one specific direction, but that doesn't mean we're limited to that style or period. Since the Upper East Side does exude elements of the Art Deco period as well as a great deal of classicism, I want to make sure that my judgement isn't clouded or biased when I walk into Camilla and Shane's new apartment.

My taxi pulls up outside of the Hôtel Plaza Athénée, a European boutique hotel. Exquisite! As I step out of the car, I can't help but feel overwhelmed by a sense of peace and calmness as I stand in its presence. Is it the simply groomed round topiaries standing erect inside uncomplicated concrete pots, or is it the red awnings with effortless gold lettering overhanging the windows that lend a European charm to the street? I'm not certain just yet. But one thing I know for sure, I will figure it out by the time I leave. And besides, it's not even that important right now because I have finally arrived.

Dear Diary,

Wow, I'm here, really here on my own ... sort of. I've always wanted this. I've been waiting my whole life for this moment. An opportunity to get here, in New York City, not just to do the touristy thing and visit the Statue of Liberty and the Empire State Building, but to perform a job. This isn't just any project, though. This project is a huge opportunity for me to show people what I've got, but more importantly how I can share it with others. It almost seems too easy. Like it just landed on my lap, and maybe I didn't work hard enough to get here. Like it was too simple—like this place—this hotel, I mean. On the outside, it gives the appearance of being so sophisticated and so uncomplicated, but is it just as simple on the inside? I bet there will be so much more to take in. So much detail to absorb. I have to wonder if I am still talking about the same thing. Because all of a sudden, I'm not sure if I'm still talking about this hotel anymore or if maybe I'm talking about something else, like myself instead. Maybe in a way, we're pretty much the same. What I mean is, often we put on this façade of being so composed and so typical on the outside, but it's the interior details—that is where true beauty and diversity really lie. So well thought-out, methodically so, and your only hope is that someone is savvy enough to catch all of the little details, the innuendos that make up that whole classic exterior. Funny, until I got here, I was really nervous and scared about a job in the Big Apple, like only the big designers get to work here. And now I realize that I have just as much right to be here and so much to offer too. Maybe it's because creativity and imagination are so welcomed here, so embraced in this city, that I am not as scared anymore. Maybe that's why I feel like I can breathe easier now that I'm here. Deep down, I know the kids and Jack will be fine without me. I think it's about time for me to lay my doubts to rest and let my imagination finally soar.

Later,
Me, Your Excited Simple Girl

Safely inside my room, I sit on the edge of my bed. My coat is still draped over my body as I sit motionless, embracing the stillness of the moment. I feel as though I have at last arrived, not just physically but emotionally too. Arrived at a place and point in my life where I am ready to take on this new challenge. I am ready to face my fears—including my weaknesses. Nothing monumental or explosive took place getting here. It wasn't preceded by fireworks or pomp and ceremony. It is simply an accumulation of lots and lots of baby steps that, if I look back at them now individually, they don't seem like a whole lot of anything, but if I look at it them as strung together, as a sequence of moments in life, they take on a unique shape. A shape that forms a real life story.

My life story.

I have to savour this moment because I don't know how long it will last.

This is definitely real.

I know I will have to call Camilla and let her know I'm here—just not yet.

Chapter Eighteen

Having changed my clothes and freshened up, I have time for a quick stroll around the hotel before my meeting with Camilla and Shane. As my heels click away on the lobby's glistening marble floor, my eyes shift from left to right soaking in the ornate gold finishes and rich jewel-toned colours that envelop the space. My body tingles from head to toe as though I am being caressed by a warm sea of rich and luxurious finishes. As my excitement mounts for what still lays ahead of me, I make every attempt to try and focus on the pleasures I am privy to right here and now. Since I haven't actually seen Camilla and Shane's apartment as yet, except via photographs, I need to remain unbiased, being cautious to not project the grandeur or beauty of this hotel onto their space. In the meantime, my mind is festooned with ideas, brimming over with colours and finishes, fabrics and materials. I can't wait to actually set foot inside to see if what I have envisioned can in fact be brought to fruition.

Once I am seated comfortably inside yellow taxicab number two for the day, I head over to the address that I scribbled down inside my day planner under today's date. In an age of BlackBerries and iPhones, I still pen most everything down—addresses, telephone numbers, and memos—the good old-fashioned way. Call me crazy (or technophobic), as no doubt many have, it is my way of doing things, and it works well for me. The idea of typing into a little machine makes me quite nervous if you must know. See, I'm not idiotic enough to believe that technology is foolproof. And since I am a woman with intense purpose right now, should technology fail me in this instant (like I have seen happen to plenty of others plenty of times), my address in question isn't going to be held hostage on some little piece of defunct technology.

We agreed to meet at 2:00 p.m. outside the apartment building. Looking down at my watch as the taxi comes to a grinding halt, I realize I have a few minutes to spare. This is intentional on my part, since I want to absorb the exterior of the building and the surrounding neighbourhood first, by myself and without any distractions or interruptions. Fortunately for me, it is pretty much what I was expecting—an old limestone building with symmetrical windows on either side of a grand front entrance. Breathing in the cool afternoon air, my lungs feel as though they are bubbling over with a newborn energy. If nothing else, being outside makes me appreciate the importance of spending time with nature and how something so basic and free for the taking can be so beneficial to my well-being. Maybe I could aim for some early morning walks when I get back home? It is something to think about at the very least.

One thing is for sure: I may not know a lot about this city, but I know enough to know that the air I am breathing in this neighbourhood reeks of Manhattan wealth. The street boulevards are pristinely manicured. Blades of neatly manicured thick grass are trimmed with exact precision, and rows of mature, bright green, leafy maple trees stand in perfect unison. From where I am standing setting my sights down the boulevard, not a tree branch or leaf appears to be out of place. I can see why Shane wants to be a part of this neatly orchestrated neighbourhood. He, too, is a man of impeccable and harmonious order and sophistication. So far he seems to fit right into place.

Before long, Camilla and Shane are in sight, immediately morphing me back into being Katarina the interior designer.

Making our way up the elevator to the fifth floor, I once again am under the distinct impression that Shane is sizing me up. Is he trying to figure out if I can step up to the plate, or is he wondering if I will crumble now that I am physically here? One thing is for sure, there is no way in hell that I am going to allow that to happen; I am not going to give any indication that I am the slightest bit nervous. I try to be nonchalant about observing Shane and Camilla since here too there appears to be some tension in the elevator air. This tension, more than the butterflies that are fluttering around in my stomach, makes me feel considerably unsettled. Trust me; this is neither paranoia nor anxiety. It is very real apparent tension. Where Camilla is usually chatty and to some extent lively when we meet alone, in the company of her husband she becomes slightly reserved and moderately introverted.

I focus my attention on the elevator's interior. The dark mahogany panelling, with its wide, scalloped-cornice mouldings and vintage mirrors, adds to the already luxurious appearance of the rest of this building. This is definitely the prelude to Shane's Manhattan world.

"This is just the beginning," Shane says. "Wait until you see my place."

Oh-oh! Camilla shoots Shane a wounded look. *His place?* Shane takes no notice of her injured visage; instead, he is self-absorbed in adjusting the brilliant gold cuff links on his white shirt. I offer her a reassuring smile. Camilla's face reads of anguish. I just hope that my imagination is not creating a scenario that doesn't really exist except in my mind. *But on the off chance that this is some kind of bachelor pad for Shane, what on earth are Camilla and I doing here?*

Not usually one to judge a book by its cover, I do exactly that upon setting foot inside the front door to their apartment. To say that I am awestruck is an understatement. Even with the renovation well underway, construction dust flying haphazardly throughout and workmen doing their thing, I can already see the shape this place is taking, and it reads like a fairy tale in the making! I take some time to walk around the space and get a feel for it. I want to ensure that I am not fast-forwarding to the end of this story before reading the pages in between one by one. Not even the photos I saw back home paid adequate homage to this place. The real thing is so much more fantastic.

The vestibule is, in fact, a room of its own, full walls and all. So what better place to start than here? If I can create a grand entrance of sorts right from the minute you set foot inside the front door, this will surely set the tone for what the rest of the apartment will feel like. The walls are already panelled in a classic white panelling, so I suggest having the ceiling barrel vaulted and adding a detailed cornice moulding, which will give the illusion of even more drama and grandeur. Shane and Camilla love the idea, and fortunately the contractor agreed that logistically speaking it could still in fact be done. The contractors are hard at work on this part of the space today. Even I have to admit it was a great idea and a well-thought-out plan. Now that I can actually see it being executed, it looks as spectacular as it sounds. After walking through the apartment, I am pretty confident that some of my inspirations and the samples I have brought with me today will lend a new life to this place without giving up any of its antiquarian feel.

I lay out my materials on the makeshift table that the contractors have set out. I have become very familiar with this type of setup and all of the dust and debris that go along with it. This is all part of my job and doesn't bother me in the slightest bit, perhaps because I understand that before a home can be all sparkly and glamorous (the end result that I especially adore), we have no alternative but to progress in a steady manner in this direction. I find this type of progression somewhat scary and exciting at the same time. That sense of the unknown is what always keeps me coming back and pushes me forward. It's like I just have to keep on going, no matter what.

Several hours and a great deal of discussion later, plenty of decisions have been made. Marble tiles have been chosen for the vestibule from the samples that had been delivered here earlier in the day. We agree to sand and stain the existing oak plank floors in the main hallway and principle rooms in an ebony-coloured stain that will act to enhance the black marble tile we are going to use. The galley kitchen, small by suburban standards, isn't going to prevent me from giving it the stylish makeover it deserves and can masterfully handle. Frequently I am told that, though I might be small, I am certainly mighty, almost too mighty for my frame, and so my intention is for this kitchen to portray this identical resemblance. It is going to be a jewel box of a space if I have anything to say about it, and luckily I do. Though my concept might be a tad bit too racy for most people, Shane and Camilla aren't most people, so if I am going to take an opportunity to suggest such a concept, this is the time to do it. It is now or never. I choose now. It seems like the better and gutsier of the two options.

"Now with respect to the kitchen, I want it to not only look magnificent but also be entirely functional as well, so I thought that while we're in town we could visit the Clive Christian showroom and have a look at some of their kitchen displays. I believe you'll be pleased with what you see there." *You'd be crazy not to since the showroom is drop-dead gorgeous and you can't help but fall in love with all of their vignettes.* "Their cabinets are exquisite, one-of-a-kind craftsmanship you won't find anywhere else. I assure you of that." I pull out an empty cardboard box of cocoa. Not any box of cocoa, but a container of cocoa that I had purchased a few years back at the Parisian patisserie Ladurée. Both Camilla and Shane are looking at me with perplexed faces. I can see they aren't sure where I am going with this. I am beginning to feel a little bit nervous, hoping that my eclectic approach won't be viewed as off the deep end or too eccentric. I continue, cautious to speak slowly and clearly, aware that when I get too excited about a concept or a new idea, I can get carried away talking quickly and leaving out important details that could turn my pitch into a big, fat flop.

"I want to create a grand over-the-top space for you, but not so much that you won't feel comfortable in it," I continue.

Shane maintains his puzzled expression. "I'm sorry, Katarina, I don't think I'm following you here. What does that container of cocoa in your hands have to do with anything?"

Duh! I am such an idiot! How stupid of me. I had left out the most important part of my kitchen concept.

"Of course," I say stridently, expressing deep embarrassment while still making a valiant attempt to make light of my omission. "The purpose of the container is that I thought we could paint out the cabinets in this shade of Ladurée celadon green. It's a green with grey undertones to it. It's so subtle and yet such a classic tone of green. We can incorporate the gold by using gold leaf or ormolu inlay into the cabinet mouldings. What do you both think?" I hold my breath and wait for what I am praying is a positive reaction.

"A green kitchen? That's your idea? You want to paint our kitchen cabinets green?" Shane's voice gives me the impression he isn't feeling what I am feeling. In fact, he doesn't seem impressed with my proposal at all. Oh boy, I am starting to feel completely foolish for even suggesting this. But I can't take it back now, so I have to keep going with my concept, hoping and praying that he might understand the rationale behind my idea.

"Not just any green, Shane, Ladurée green!" I repeat jubilantly, as if I had just announced some sort of earth-shattering revelation that he is supposed to understand. He obviously does not. Okay, maybe earth-shattering is a bit of an overexaggeration, but it is one hell of a fantastic idea. If he could just follow my train of thought for a minute, he might just understand where I am going with this.

"Katarina, I'm not sure how to phrase this without offending your stylistic capabilities; however, green cabinets are not my idea of classic and subtle. In fact, the entire suggestion sounds rather awful to me if I can be quite honest."

Shane runs a tense hand through his wavy locks. His facial expression appears a bit terse. I am not feeling that my future in this job is looking bright for the moment. I had hoped that Shane would be a tad bit more open-minded and would have at least given my idea some consideration before rejecting it the way he is. This is not what I had expected one bit.

Thankfully Camilla rises to the occasion first and beats me to my defence.

"I don't completely dislike the idea, Shane. Maybe we should at the very least consider it." Camilla trumps her husband's dismissal of my concept. *Wow, now that takes guts on her part.* Shane is clearly not impressed with either one of us for the time being. He looks annoyed—really annoyed, as though a vein on the side of his tanned head might explode. Gross!

I go on to explain the infamy of the Ladurée pastry shop in Paris. How it is well-known for delicious cakes and pastries, but gained infamy thanks to its world-famous macaroon—a small, round cookie made of meringue and almonds, with a ganache-filled centre. My idea is to incorporate the celadon-green colour of the Ladurée brand with the exquisite millwork of Clive Christian. Since I have already witnessed this similar colour on their cabinets, I am already familiar with how marvellous it looks. The sparse touches of gold on the mouldings will only add to the already elegant millwork. All in all, I could offer them a kitchen of fine craftsmanship that would withstand the test of time. The result, if he would entertain my concept, will be breathtaking to say the least. Could he at least think about my idea before rejecting it completely?

"I actually think it sounds lovely. Very unique and lovely. At the very least, let's go and have a look at the showroom, shall we?" Camilla says with hopeful enthusiasm. Thank goodness she is at least behaving open-mindedly; now if only her husband could. "After all, darling, what difference do the kitchen cabinets make to you? It's not as though you will be spending much time in there now, will you?"

Shane raises a brow. Is it Camilla's comment or the thought that he might have to actually go along with an idea he is hardly impressed with that rouses his irritability?

Irritated or not, moments later we are off to the Clive Christian showroom, and I am feeling nothing short of relieved. Once they see what I have seen, they will agree to my concept—they just have to!

Dear Diary,

How is it that a great concept has now become a bargaining tool in the throes of a marital mishap? I do believe that Shane will love my kitchen idea when all is said and done; he just has to keep an open mind about it. But will he keep an open mind? The bigger question, though, and more important one right now is, does Camilla really like the idea, or is she just appeasing me to stick it to her husband? Not that it's any of my business, but I don't want to be caught in the crossfire of a marriage in trouble and I think that there might be some big trouble brewing here. I can't ask 'cause that would be nosy, so what do I do? Pretend as though I'm not noticing any jabs between them? Impossible, since you can't help but notice that something is completely wrong here. But since I work for both of them so technically they are both my clients, do I please one while pissing off the other? Or maybe it would be better if I just came up with another idea for the kitchen? But the thing is, I really do believe this is a damn good concept. This style of kitchen would flow beautifully in their apartment, so I won't take it back because then I would be going against everything I believe in. Maybe I should just stick to my ideas, stand back, and wait and see what happens. Who knows, maybe once Shane steps inside the showroom, he will love the idea as much as I do.

Later,
Me, Your Simple Girl

Chapter Nineteen

I cannot tell a lie—I am thoroughly enjoying the tranquility of my hotel room. Finally all alone, I gently unbutton my coat and toss it carefully on the edge of the bed. I'll hang it up later. My tired feet are aching—I've been standing for the past few hours on four-inch Jimmy Choo's. I think I read somewhere in a magazine interview once long ago that Tamara Melon claimed her shoes were made for the everyday woman ... wait, on second thought, maybe it was me who made that claim, not her—once—when I was trying to justify to Jack why I had so many pairs of shoes. Oh well, whatever, can't worry about that now. Rubbing my feet one small toe at a time, I am so relieved that I am at long last barefoot and alone. Many a night Jack and I sit watching TV—usually the late-night news—long after the kids have been read to, kissed good-night, and tucked into their beds, and he is the one in charge of rubbing my tender toes. I seldom have to ask (which is such a bonus); it is just a given. It is as natural as a child taking his mother's hand as they walk through a park. In this case, Jack is usually sitting at one end of the sofa, and I generally lie at the other end, my head propped up against a downy pillow while my feet rest securely in his lap. No pleading or probing is necessary. Jack habitually begins with the baby toe on my left foot and works his way across, one by one. Then it is on to my right foot. Jack loves to tease me about the size, or lack thereof, of my feet. He argues that the only reason I even paint my toenails is so that I can locate my feet. Lucky for him they are as small as they are, since I don't think he would be too fond of oversize feet sprawled across his lap. My pedicurist frequently reminds me that I have one of the prettiest pairs of feet she has ever worked on. I remind her that this is due to the meticulous attention she pays to them. Either way, I miss that now, Jack rubbing my feet, that is. Sure, I am enjoying the stillness of the moment, the quiet that prevails—who wouldn't?—but with no more client conversation for the time being, my thoughts revert back to home. It is evening. Dinnertime. I wonder how things are going on the home front, so I call.

"Hello?" a boyish voice answers. It belongs to Michael.

"Hi, baby," I reply, tears welling up in my eyes even though my face is aglow with an enormous smile as I hear my son's distant voice. "What are you doing?"

"Oh, hey, Mom. Nothing really. Just helping Dad with dinner. How's your meeting going?" Michael asks. I can hear the faint clattering of dishes in the background. Jack is unmistakably hard at work.

"Great baby, really good," I answer, not bothering to share with Michael that in the midst of "great" and "really good," I am in the company of clients who at the moment are barely speaking to each other. I don't bother sharing this information with my son because he can't possibly understand it. He is a child, and this is above his level of comprehension, as it should be. And if he could understand it, he probably would not care. And quite frankly, why should he? I also purposely leave out the details of the cab ride back to the hotel, the one where Camilla rode alone with me only to cry—no, make that sob profusely—the entire way back as she brought me up to speed on the fact that she has become very suspicious lately that her husband is having an affair. In her view, this New York City apartment is nothing more than a make-work project for her so she will be less focused on Shane's frolicking ways. I for one can hardly believe that she shared all of this information with me, so

I am still trying to process the information myself. Things aren't going exactly how I had anticipated they would, so "great" and "good" will just have to do for the time being.

"Michael, could I speak to Daddy please?"

"Sure, Ma. Love you."

"Love you too."

Fortunately, the sound of Jack's voice temporarily grounds me somewhat. I manage to fill him in on my arrival details: "yes, fine"; cab ride: "noneventful"; hotel: "beautiful"; clients: "you're not going to fucking believe this, Jack!"

"Come on, Kat, you're kidding, right?" Jack's voice takes on a note of disbelief.

"Uh, no, Jack, I'm quite serious. And like I was saying, so there we were at the Clive Christian showroom—and I could tell that there was so much tension between them—you know what I mean, Jack—little jabs here and there with each other, but I just figured it was more of a power struggle between the two of them because I thought he didn't want to give in on my colour suggestion for the kitchen cabinets and she really liked it. But clearly I was *wrong*! It had nothing to do with Ladurée green. It had everything to do with this woman, Candy!"

"Candy?" Jack queries.

"Candy," I repeat, at the risk of sounding like a parrot.

Pause. Longer pause. "Jack? What's wrong?" I ask, because from the length of his pause, I am astute enough to realize that he is assessing something.

"Kat, this whole thing … this situation, it just seems really weird to me. It doesn't sound so good and not very professional of this guy who is *supposed* to be this great businessman. I know you were really excited about working in New York and all, but maybe you should just back out of this project and come home. Don't get caught up in all the b-s going on there."

What? What is Jack saying? I mean, consciously I know what he is saying. Obviously, the words he just said make perfect audible sense to me, but why? Why would I back out? Why would he even suggest that I consider quitting? After all, this has nothing to do with me at all. It is my turn to wait out a long pause now. Think about what I want to say and how I am going to respond to him without sounding all defensive.

"Jack, I can't quit." My voice is sullen. "What I mean is, I won't quit. My ideas, my concepts for this place are good, really good, and they both really like me—well, I know the wife likes me, and I think the husband likes me, sort of—anyways, that's not the point. The point is, so what if Ladurée green wasn't his first choice, maybe not even his second choice ... but that doesn't matter anyways." Even I realize that I am no longer making any sense.

"Kat, we can go back to New York City another time. We'll take the kids in the spring if you want ... for a long weekend. You can even take the girls to that stupid doll store they talk about, and Mikey and I will walk around and wait for you guys to shop and do girl stuff and ..."

"Jack, please stop!" I'm flabbergasted ... shocked ... taken aback, and I guess just fucking angry at what he is implying. "First of all, that '*stupid doll store*' is not stupid in the eyes of our daughters, if you must know, and secondly, this isn't about me coming to New York to go shopping in Gucci or even to see the Statue of Liberty for that matter. It's about a vision, Jack. It is about my vision of creating a home for someone in this city. Don't you get that?"

"Kat, from where I'm standing, all I get is that these people are going through something, something serious, and I don't want you, my wife, who I know means well, to get caught in the middle of it."

"I won't get caught in the middle of it. I'm just going to do what I was hired to do, decorate a space for them. That's it. Please don't make this bigger than it really is. You know what? Just forget that I even said anything about it. Look, I'm tired. I'll call you guys back later to say good-night." I'm not lying. I really am very tired. And I am especially too tired to be arguing with Jack about Camilla and Shane and their marital mishaps. And besides, what project goes on without its fair share of problems? I mean, seriously, every job runs into a little obstacle here and there, so what? You deal with it and move on.

I switch off my cell phone and sit back down on the bed, revisiting the events of the day in my mind. Everything seems to feel like a big mishmash swirling around: right from my arrival to New York City, standing amidst complete strangers in the airport, to meeting Camilla and Shane outside their apartment building. Even staying in this fabulous hotel seems rather surreal to me just about now. The one thing that does feel really real to me is the rumbling of my stomach. It reminds me that I have hardly eaten anything at all today. Usually by this time of the night, I have already fed the kids their after-school snack, my portion of it consisting of whatever they have decided to leave on their plates. Okay, so maybe it's not the healthiest or smartest way to eat, but I'm anything but a breakfast or lunch person, so my predinner snack is typically my first partial meal of the day, my only sustenance until I actually sit down to a proper dinner at the table once Jack comes home from work.

Dinner with Camilla and Shane is officially off. She called my room professing a headache. I must admit, I am feeling somewhat relieved about this, not that she has a headache, poor thing, but let's face it, dinner with the two of them tonight would be anything but palatable given the current state of affairs. In a nutshell, I am dining solo this evening.

I decide to change into something more comfortable (okay, so maybe this sounds a tad bit cliché-like, even I must admit, but let me just tell you that my something-more-comfortable consists of a great pair of jeans, stiletto boots, and a cashmere sweater). Tonight I will take a walk down towards Rockefeller Center. I can find a dinner spot somewhere along my route and feed my hungry body, which is not letting up. New York City certainly does not lack in the fine-restaurant department. And besides, the Christmas tree has already been set up at Rockefeller Center, and I am dying to see it. The tree is a spectacular display in my opinion, and apparently others feel the same way since it attracts hundreds of thousands of spectators year after year. I have only had the opportunity of witnessing it on television, and each and every time I do, I am completely awestruck at the pure majestic size of it. I'm amazed at how something as simple as a Christmas tree always manages to somehow put a giant smile on my face. This time is going to be different, though. This time will be better than ever. This time I am actually going to see it live and in person. And for this, I am about as excited as a kid in a candy store, if not more so.

For the record, I'm not one of those crazy women who obsesses about Christmas. Yes, I love it, but I don't go crazy decorating my house from top to bottom with holly and mistletoe and holiday decorations scattered throughout every room of the house. In fact, you won't even find garland on my staircase. Sure, it looks pretty enough in all the magazines, but I'm not fooled by pretty pictures. It's completely not practical for everyday life in my chaotic home. I do often wonder what the garland on those glossy pages must look like after a couple of days of real-life interaction. Tastefully and simply I go about decorating my house. Hosting small intimate gatherings with friends and taking advantage of the season as a perfect time to share some appetizing food and fine wines with friends is truly what the season is about for me, in any event. And, of course, the holidays wouldn't be complete without running out to the malls to purchase some great things I know that the kids and Jack will like. But let's be honest here, this part would be so much more enjoyable if I didn't have to circle the mall parking lot for thirty minutes to just find a parking spot, and I could really do without the crazy-long lineups at the stores to pay for just one small item. But even I forget all about that once I am back in the sanctity of my home surrounded by the sight of sparkly and colourful Christmas wrap. My favourite part of all, the part I take the greatest pleasure in, is walking through the brisk cold air to show the kids the nativity scene at a nearby local church. (Ella and I still get a chuckle out of the Cabbage Patch "Baby Jesus" we saw resting peacefully in the manger last year).

But now, standing alongside the crowds of people in Rockefeller Center, I am in sheer awe over this giant presence erected before me. This tree must be at least thirty feet tall. Thousands of tiny white lights encircle it with accurate precision from top to bottom. They sparkle so brightly in the faint night sky that the entire surrounding area is illuminated with a magical light. The sound of laughter can be clearly heard all around, and I am beginning to feel like a small child once again. Much like when my parents would take me to see the lavishly decorated Christmas windows in a downtown Toronto department store when I was a little girl. I can still remember that affectionate feeling that surrounded me as I stood on my tiptoes in wonderment at the scene that I was witness to.

And although I am encircled by what are literally thousands of strangers, I scarcely feel alone. The truth is that I am feeling a vast sense of peace wash over me as I just stand here and gaze about, not really alone at all. The mood amongst the crowd is a festive and jovial one. Christmas carols play in the background, setting the tone for the laughter and joyfulness that is being shared in the foreground. Excited children bounce about, shifting from one foot to the other while they impatiently wait until it is their turn to lace up their ice skates and take a whirl around the magnificent tree that stands soaring in the centre of it all. Tonight's air has a distinctive chill to it, causing me to tug gently at the black cashmere scarf that is faultlessly knotted around my neck. I realize just how imminent winter now is. As a child growing up, my friends and I would joke that we knew it was wintertime when we could see our breath when our mouths were open—and you can definitely see your breath tonight. For a brief moment, a wave of nostalgia washes over me. I mean I am happy, elated in fact, to finally be here in this city again, working this time, and I am happy to be standing here doing exactly what I am doing, which is people watching, but I am definitely missing something—or somebody. And that somebody is more than one body. It is four bodies actually. It's Jack and the kids. They aren't here with me to share all of this. They're not here to share in the realization of my dream, and I miss them right now, more than I ever imagined I would.

Dear Diary,

How can I be so happy one minute and yet so sad the next? I'm finally here, where I want to be, doing everything I dreamed of doing, and yet I still don't feel completely happy, the way I thought I was going to. I miss my family. Yes, I'm here living out my dream and for that I am so lucky, and yes, having a "fun" job like mine is fantastic and wearing designer clothes sometimes is definitely a huge luxury that I am entirely grateful for, so why is it that just standing here and gazing at this silly Christmas tree is what really makes me the happiest ... on the inside, that is? Maybe it's not so silly. Maybe all of the fabulous clothes and shoes and bags, the fabrics and trims I play with all day, maybe all of those things are who I am on the outside, but they sure don't define who I am on the inside. On the inside, I think I'm still like a little kid finding splendour in the simple things—like the twinkling lights on this Christmas tree. I find real happiness in doing stupid, mundane things like just roasting a chicken for dinner for Jack and the kids or making cupcakes with colourful sprinkles for their birthdays. What's wrong with me? Chanel purses; Gucci shoes; Clive Christian cabinets, and Pierre Frey fabrics, that's what I'm supposed to be about, isn't it? Isn't that what people who look at me tell me they see? So why does that evergreen tree, or is it a blue spruce—?I don't even know—whatever kind of tree it is, why is that making me such a sap right now wishing I could be right back in my kitchen, when all along I insisted I wanted, no, make that needed, to be right here? Maybe Jack was right. Maybe he's been right all along, I am really complicated. Actually I think he said "fucked

up and complicated," wanting one thing one
minute and something completely different the
next. Maybe I really am "all that" and "so fancy,"
just like Nikki always says. Or maybe that's just
what people on the outside looking in want to
believe that I am all about. Maybe they don't
want to believe that I can roast a chicken and
bake cupcakes—at the same time too, and be
happy about it—and still be all giddy over twinkly
lights. Could it be that if they knew I really loved
those things just as much as the material stuff,
then they couldn't judge me as much for being
"all that"? If only they realized that I'm so much
more, and it's the so-much-more that they don't
want to see or believe! Is this really it? Is that
why the Yummy Mummies want to believe I take
two hours to get myself together in the morning,
and is that why Alessia likes to make fun of me
for cleaning up poop and making baby food?
Maybe that's what she would rather be doing
instead of trying big legal cases. Maybe she too
would rather trade in her Manolo's some days
for a Swiffer mop? Maybe, just maybe, I'm not as
confused as I thought I was. And maybe, just
maybe, I needed to stop doing all of it for even
a minute so I could finally attempt to figure it
all out. Maybe the minute I took to just stop and
stare at the twinkly lights was all that I needed
to make sense of my crazy life.

Later,
Me, Your Enlightened Simple Girl

Chapter Twenty

I wake up early the next morning, my head swimming with an array of ideas and elaborate details. Not just straightforward ideas, but ideas that can turn something ordinary into something extraordinary. Details that had kept me from getting any rest at all during the nighttime hours, and details that I know can make an enormous difference between a client being just pleased and a client acknowledging that I have truly captured their very essence. See, in my opinion, that's what distinguishes a good designer from a great designer—one that wants to walk away from a project having made a positive, lasting impression. And it's among this group that I want to be an elite member. Designers in this group don't leave their own personal stamp or markings on a space, but rather infuse the space with their clients' own personalities—capture who they are and surround their environment with what the client wants to be surrounded with. What I need to do first, though, is to unload these thoughts into basic black and white print. I scurry to search the desk in my room for a pen and paper before all these pertinent details are lost forever. Could it have been that just being still last night, if only for a short period of time, gave my mind a chance to open itself up even wider and allow thoughts to flow freely without inhibitions? Could that episode of inner solitude and quiet have provided me with the answers to the questions I had asked so many times before and never gotten a response to? And if so, could an instant like that have made so many things that were so muddled all of a sudden become abundantly crystal-clear now? And if the answers to all of these questions are in fact yes, what should I do differently now, here today, because of it?

I plan on meeting Camilla and Shane at the Clive Christian showroom again this morning, since our meeting yesterday came to an abrupt end. We hardly got past the threshold yesterday, spending minimal time there, when our tour came to a sudden but final finale. It only makes perfectly logical sense that we go back again this morning and continue what we started. Shane is now at least considering my kitchen concept, though he's not completely convinced it is a viable one just yet. I for one am grateful that I have at least come this far with him. I want so much to share my new ideas with them about their apartment, but this time I won't allow myself to get dragged into their emotional battle, not even for a second. I will remain completely resolute and unbiased. Their issues belong to them and them alone. I am feeling rather strongly about my kitchen concept, and when I feel strongly about an idea, an idea that I am sure not only sounds great in theory but could be just as spectacular in practice, I try to maintain my determination and follow through with it; at least I fervently attempt to have my clients understand my approach. If they absolutely hate the idea, then fine, I will concede and squash it, but if there is even a slight glimmer of hope that they might consider it, I want to secure that they understand exactly what I have in mind. I wish I could say I have always followed this approach, but that would be a lie. It has only been very recently that I have finally allowed myself the courtesy of standing firm in my design beliefs.

I took on this project with both Shane and Camilla as my clients, and I want both of them to be equally impressed. Taking sides with either one of them could prove potentially dangerous to my career, and I have come way too far to let that happen.

~

Standing here again, admiring the walnut panelling on the kitchen display in front of me, I become lost in the patterns that the intricate grains of wood have formed. They circle round and round in formation and appear to be never ending. It's as though I am being absorbed into them ever so slowly. I don't even notice Shane standing beside me until he starts to speak to me.

"About yesterday, Katarina ... I'd like to apologize on behalf of my wife and myself. Camilla was upset about something, and I've been extremely preoccupied with work lately and haven't spent much time at home with her, so she was feeling ..."

I cut him off. "Shane ... Shane," I repeat, "really, it's perfectly okay, fine actually. There really is no need for you to apologize. Unfortunately these sorts of things are all too common in my business. Renovations are very stressful on a marriage." *And so are affairs.* I shift my bag to the other shoulder. "And in your case, it's even more difficult given that we're trying to do most of this from afar, so frankly, I completely understand the stress you're both feeling. Really, I do."

"Well, then, I thank you for your understanding. Shall we continue with our little tour?" Shane asks.

I shift my gaze from Shane to Camilla, putting on a cheerful smile. She looks back at me, smiling weakly, at best.

We continue to walk through the showroom examining the displays before us. Although I have been here before, I am nonetheless captivated by the displays before me. Henry, the associate dedicated to us for our visit today, walks us through various vignettes with such grace and charm, directing our attention to the minute details in the millwork. He is both unbelievably informative and delightful as a guide. Opening drawers, pointing out the fine dovetail detailing, showing us drawer inserts, and taunting us with intricate mouldings, glass inserts, and ormolu inlay, Henry is a natural-born salesman. When I mention to him what I have in mind for my clients, he smiles, apparently smitten with my suggestion. Grinning like a schoolboy who has just experienced his first stolen kiss, he suggests we follow him.

And so, like swooning teenagers, we do as told and follow in his quick steps. We trail Henry up the black iron circular staircase and down past the short corridor that lies ahead. Henry swings open a set of heavy double doors, and to our amazement, what we witness behind the doors is truly a masterpiece if ever there was one. There, spread out before us, before our very eyes, is the most magnificent kitchen display in none other than Ladurée green! Camilla gasps. I beam. Shane remains silent, his index finger slightly curled under his chin. If I were a betting girl, I think it would be fair to say that I might have just won the man over!

~

Three very long hours later, Camilla and I are sitting across from one another sipping sparkling water out of crystal water goblets at no other than BG Restaurant in Bergdorf Goodman. For ladies who lunch, this is definitely the "it" spot to lunch at. For me, this is the ultimate in luxury, especially so early in the day. For another thing, any small-fish designer like moi in the vast designer sea loves nothing more than to observe the creativity of other designers, not just in books but firsthand as well. Since I am all too familiar with Kelly Wearstler and her work, being a huge fan and follower of all she creates, sitting inside one of her significantly designed restaurants is an enormous pleasure for me.

The neoclassical mood of the dining room is amazing. The sunflower-yellow leather egg-shaped chairs are invigorating. This is truly a taste of characteristically classic New York City interior design in all of its splendour, and I can't get enough of it.

Camilla gently lowers her menu and places it on the table in front of her. "I'm glad he agreed to the kitchen after all. I think it will look lovely, dear." After the high of the past three hours, she now looks defeated.

"I'm certain of that, Camilla. It will be beautiful! Not to mention how it will flow harmoniously with the rest of the apartment. Camilla, it's going to look spectacular. I really believe that you and Shane will be overwhelmingly pleased with the finished product once it is in your home." I feel so good about this decision we have made today and am incredibly relieved that she agrees.

"He only conceded so I would become too engrossed in the apartment to think about his philandering, you know."

Don't get sucked in! Don't get sucked in! DON'T GET SUCKED IN! I know I am becoming engulfed in some very deep waters—a territory I have absolutely no desire to be in. Clearly anyone else's matrimonial territory is not a place I have any business being in, and yet, since I really like Camilla and feel sorry for her, what could it hurt to engage in a little bit of female conversation if this is what she is after? Besides, just looking at her crushed demeanour, even I know it is too late for me now. Tears are forming in her eyes. *Shit!* Other peoples' tears always get the best of me—why do I have to be such a sucker? I place a comforting hand over hers, hoping this might help console her.

My voice is soft yet firm. "Camilla? Are you sure? Are you really sure? Maybe the two of you are just going through a difficult time; it happens with people. I see it often enough with clients when they are renovating a home. Renovations are so-o-o stressful!" I emphasize this last point.

Camilla half-laughs and half-cries. She wipes away gently at the tears she had desperately attempted to keep at bay. Blowing her nose delicately, with one of several tissues that I have offered to her over the course of the past few minutes, she proceeds to hold onto one securely in her left hand, while my right hand still shields hers. She seems awfully fragile, and I want so desperately to pacify her.

She gazes up at me, her face deep with sorrow. "No, Katarina, I wish I had it all wrong, but I don't. After so many years of this going on, you know what the signs are."

Really? What are the signs? I admit I am a little curious but realize that right now is not the appropriate time to inquire about this. So instead I ask, "Have you confronted him? In private, I mean?"

"Of course, I have, dear, but he tells me that I'm crazy. He denies any wrongdoing whatsoever. Tells me I am fabricating stories, going through a midlife crisis. That I have no proof."

"Do you have any proof?"

"Yes. Well ... no. Well, not concrete proof like from a private investigator or anything of that sort, but I know what I've seen and heard and that's enough for me. I'd have to be a complete idiot to not recognize the signs that are so blatantly obvious."

Our conversation is interrupted by a very pretty, blue-eyed, blonde young woman asking us if we are ready to order.

Camilla doesn't even glance at the menu. Evidently she's been here before. "I'll have the lobster salad." She barely makes eye contact with the pretty young waitress.

"I'll have the same." I smile. Lobster salad sounds yummy. Even during moments of despair, a person has to eat. "What will you do?" I ask ever so curiously. Camilla stares right at me, cocking her head slightly to the right, rubbing her brow as though she has been struck with a horrific migraine headache. She forces a slight smile.

"What will I do?" she repeats. "Nothing, I suppose. That's what I've done all these years. Why would I do something different now?"

This is definitely not the response I am expecting. *Wait a minute. Wait a freakin' minute!* She's the one who brought up the conversation in the first place; I certainly didn't. And now she's telling me that she's not going to be doing anything about this at all. *I don't get it!*

"So what are your thoughts on the master bedroom and bath?" Camilla asks me, completely switching topics on me again and forcing me right back into my role as designer and not therapist.

Whoa! I am having a hard time keeping up with this woman today. I am so not used to this. This job of mine can really take its toll on me sometimes! I know I'm a pro at multitasking, but seriously, give me a break here! I clear my throat, as though by doing so, I can pull together my thoughts more precisely. "Your bedroom? Yes … well … I have been giving it some thought. New York City is so hustle and bustle all the time that I was thinking that a serene bedroom space for you in this city would be ideal. What I am proposing is that we maintain the colour green here. With its association to the natural elements of the outdoors, we can utilize it to our advantage indoors and can transfer your bedroom into a paradise of sorts. A tranquil mint-green colour in the room for the fabrics is what I am suggesting. What I'm thinking is that the window coverings can resemble a lady's evening gown. Imagine a mint-green pastel chiffon dress, so gauzy and soft, glamorous yet ethereal, all at the same time. Perhaps a sage-green silk tufted pouf in the room as well as sitting on top of a silk or wool area rug. It would make for an intimate and cozy space without being too frou-frou or over-the-top. What do you think?" I hold my breath.

Taking a sip of her sparkling water and staring upwards to no one or anything in particular, Camilla sighs deeply. What seems like several minutes pass before she utters a word.

"Whatever you say, dear, is fine with me. I'm certain *you* won't disappoint me."

Dear Diary,

So is this what happens? Is that what it all really boils down to? You suspect your significant other of having an affair, approach him, and then when he denies it, you just do nothing about it, like "a good wife" and keep on going? Um … I'm just a little confused here. Could you please help me out? It's like Camilla knows something, and Shane knows that Camilla knows, and I now know that Camilla knows and I'm still here picking cabinets and fabrics and furniture as if nothing has changed. Wait a second! So whose bedroom is it anyways? 'Cause now I'm not so sure. Is it her bedroom or his bedroom or their bedroom? She's quite obviously upset, as she has every right to be. and so here I am, the one she unloads it all to and then in the midst of it all, she decides to change topics on me. And like a yo-yo, I am supposed to follow. Does she just need a sounding board, is that it? Did she realize maybe that once she started talking about it, that it was too much for her to handle and she couldn't keep on going any longer? So what then? Just keep busy, keep smiling, keep moving, and don't face your fears, is that what she's doing now? One thing I do know for sure is that she obviously felt comfortable enough to talk to me about it, but why did she stop then? Was it fear of saying too much to a stranger, or fear of saying too much to herself and then feeling like she has to do something about it when she is well aware that she is not prepared to? Okay, so I ask a lot of questions, I know, I know, but could you give me some answers please? Even one would be a great start. And so what am I supposed to do now? Just keep doing my job and design their place? Bring the vision to life and then step back? I suppose in theory that's not such a bad idea, since that is what has been asked of me so that's what I should do, right? Hello, is anyone listening to me?

Later,
Me, Your Simple and Really Confused Girl

Chapter Twenty-One

It is bittersweet knowing that our delectable lunch in the most delicious of settings has come to a close. In this time together, Camilla and I have shared stories of our favourite treasures and much-loved noteworthy interiors. We have exchanged affectionate family memories, causing us to burst out laughing one minute while leaving Camilla to feel nostalgic yet cautiously hopeful about her future with Shane at other moments. She has not completely recovered from the candid revelations she openly shared with me when we first sat down, and though she might have felt the need to share at the outset of our lunch date, common sense tells me that her greater need now is for some undisturbed solitude. I respect that, knowing that if it was me in her shoes, I might be just as confused about which road to travel. We agree to part ways for the remainder of the afternoon—maybe do a little private shopping at Bergdorf's, she chides, hoping that her interjectory humour might lift her solemn spirits. Quite frankly I think that is a wonderful idea myself since Christmas is right around the corner and all of the stores are decorated in their holiday finery. There's nothing like a bit of festive sparkle to rouse the senses. I am convinced that several of the stores are calling out my name too, taunting me. This year the holiday decorating theme seems to revolve around old-world Hollywood glamour, and what better place to take it all in but Bergdorf Goodman?

Walking into Bergdorf's a few hours earlier, I had taken notice of all of the ornamentation, but now standing here by myself, I can actually observe the small nuances more intimately. How pretty everything is. Elegant and stylish, but not overdone; this is how I have always summed up New York City. In a class of its own, forever sophisticated and polished, but never ostentatious or untouchable. Crystal chandeliers sparkle brightly overhead throughout the department store. Faux black mink fur throws (at least I think they are faux, but after all, this is Bergdorf's so who knows? They might actually be real) are slung over white lacquered framed bergère chairs. Throughout the store, the most vibrant red amaryllis flowers that I have ever seen stand high in enormous crystal flowerpots on gleaming glass countertops. The faint whiff of Christmas lingers throughout the entire department store courtesy of a combination of orange-, cinnamon-, ginger-, and nutmeg-scented candles burning all around as well. Perhaps this is part of my attraction here. A part of this city is all yours for the taking; all you have to do is ask, or spend in this case, because *ouch!* things are so-o-o pricey around this place!

5F, my favourite floor (maybe it is my favourite because it is the most affordable to me), ladies' contemporary fashions, and how gorgeous are these clothes? *Hmm, I wonder, what is Milly showing this season? Oh, and there's D&G! Focus, Kat, one designer at a time.*

Milly first. Chocolate-brown chunky-knit sweaters, how cozy over a pair of jeans and stiletto boots? Ohh, what's this? A lilac silk chemise? Gorgeous! With that plum wool pencil skirt over there, okay, that is so-o-o going to be mine. I have to try this on. Subconsciously I can hear Alessia coaxing me on. She would have told me I was crazy not to try almost everything on if she had been here with me. I miss not having her here shopping with me. We are a shopping tag team. Though neither one of us needs much coaxing in the purchasing department, we're never short of having fun in the most trivial of ways while enjoying some retail therapy at the same time.

A really attractive and—holy shit—unbelievably tall sales associate approaches me. "Can I help you, miss?" she asks ever so harmoniously.

Talk about an effortless sale. Fantastic manners and being sensible enough to call me *miss*, when clearly I am old enough to be her mother. I can already smell her fat commission cheque courtesy of the damage I am going to do in this department today.

"I'm just trying to find my size," I smile, being just as cordial.

"Let me help you," she offers, glancing me over. "You're so tiny. You must be a size zero."

I'm genuinely flattered. "A two, actually."

The pretty salesgirl, already in the midst of fervently pushing hangers from one side of the rack to the other, hands over some garments she has vigilantly selected for me.

Once I am safely inside a beautifully carpeted change room, I begin to undress, cooing over the items I have hanging before me. I feel a little mischievous, though, since over the course of events that have led to my getting here, I have today already eaten lunch (sitting down grown-up style, no less) and am now trying on pretty new clothes, all in the same afternoon! This is really new for me. I could get used to this, but I know better. I need to remind myself that this is still a working trip, not pleasure. Skipping off a couple of hours to *play* is okay, but not something I can afford to be doing often.

I am trying as hard as I can to turn off the wheels that are churning inside my head—the ones that I have single-handedly and successfully trained to burst my very own bubble anytime an exquisitely round and fluffy one attempts to form. I have a funny feeling that I am about to successfully sabotage my modest diversion from work. And for what reason? I'm not doing anything wrong. I'm not lying to my boss about my whereabouts, and I'm certainly not billing my clients for my shopping excursion. Since we have already worked out a payment schedule, I have already allocated my time for consulting and sourcing, and this isn't part of it. So what am I feeling bad about? Even I'm not quite sure. Could it be Jack and the kids? That they're home and I'm here? No. I'm just being silly, that's all. At least that's what my brain keeps trying to tell my heart. Jack and the kids are perfectly fine without me. In fact, they are probably having more fun without my being there, since Jack isn't nearly as strict as I am about the "small stuff." Stuff like the kids having a bath before bed or eating *all* of their vegetables at dinner. I'm sure he has everything under control. So what that after-school pickup and activities, not to mention feeding the kids in between, might be a little hectic for him? He can handle it; after all, it's just for a few days. I do it every other day, and I seem to manage. And besides, he handles millions of dollars of people's money every single day at work, so what's a few meals to prepare, some ponytails to tie, homework and art assignments to work on, and pizza lunches to serve? Indisputably these insignificant things can't possibly be any more demanding to deal with than what he does. *Oops*—did I forget to mention to Jack that it was my turn to hand out pizza this week to Michael's class? I wonder if I should call him and ask him if he could take my place, though I doubt he will be interested. On second thought, I'd do best to leave this one alone; there will be plenty of other mummies present. Something tells me that Jack may not be too keen on distributing cardboard-like pizza to squirrely fifth graders.

Oh-h-h, I do love this lilac blouse! And the skirt too looks so cute, if I do say so myself! Where's the price tag on this thing? I search frantically for it. Before I really express too much affection for it, I need to know how much this dose of flimsy "amour" is going to be costing. Looking down, I feel my way around the back of the skirt, groping in search of the price tag, which of course is discreetly tucked inside the garment. This is my first indication that this garment is going to cost me. *Whoa!* Am I reading this right? Does this tag really say four hundred and ninety-five dollars? Now I understand why they so prudently had it hidden away. Why does beauty have to come with such an exorbitant cost attached to it? This outfit really does look stunning on me (not that I'm trying to brag or anything like that); being in interior design, I have an eye for what looks good and what doesn't. Even I don't need the pretty young thing to coo at me (*but thanks anyways, sweetie*). But the real question is can I in fact justify the cost of this outfit? I weigh the pros and cons in my mind. In the pros column is the fact that I can get lots of wear out of this skirt, pair it with a black turtleneck and my black stiletto boots. I can wear the blouse with the skirt or any pair of jeans in my closet and really dress it down. On the con side ... well, there are no cons, except for the cost of the thing, that is. The fact still remains that these are investment pieces. Classics. Timeless pieces. I will have them forever and ever, and I can wear them for just as long. In fact, I can even pass them down to Nikki and Ella; that way, they can own vintage because of my savvy shopping expertise. Okay, done! That's enough convincing for me. These two are going to be mine. All mine! Who am I kidding? I was well aware of that fact before I even crossed the threshold of this cubicle. I had no intention of leaving Bergdorf's empty-handed today. None at all!

~

Making my way back onto Fifth Avenue feels somewhat surreal. On the one hand, I am perfectly aware of the fact that I am really here in New York City standing at the corner of Fifty-Eighth and Fifth, but how the heck did I really get here?

Here? Here being this place in my life?

I decide to call home—a lucid reminder of my reality. It is now 4:45 p.m., and if all is going as scheduled, Jack should be well on his way driving the girls to their dance class. Hopefully he will answer his cell phone, a clear indication that all is proceeding smoothly on the home front. Thankfully, he picks up on the third ring.

"Hi, honey, how are you guys doing?" I ask in a most cheerful voice, I'm sure in part due to the plain fact that shopping always puts me in a glorious mood.

"We're great. Are things any better there?" Jack asks. He too tries to sound chirpy, though there is an underlying note in his voice that rings of fatigue.

"Absolutely! They loved my kitchen concept after all, Jack. Things are looking so much more positive here."

"That's great to hear, honey. I'm really happy for you. I know how important this is to you."

You're not kidding. I fill Jack in with small tidbits of information—minute details. Given what happened yesterday, I know better today than to recount too much of what is going on. And besides, too much detail doesn't interest Jack (too much drama in my world, he maintains), and at times even I have to admit that Jack might be right.

In the background I can hear the kids' voices arguing over who is going to talk to me next. Ella wins. *Like there's a shock!*

"Mama? When are you going to come home? I miss you!" Ella cries out in her sweetest little girl voice ever.

Great, just great! Straight to my heartstrings, yet again. Though Ella hasn't intentionally set out to play me like a violin (I don't believe she has quite learned the trickery of that just yet—at least I hope not), she sure has it perfected. The elation of my big girl purchase has just fallen to the wayside at the sound of my little girl's voice. I do my best to put on a brave front, probably more for my sake than for hers.

"Ella, sweetheart, Mommy will be home in two more sleeps—just two!" Ella's reference to time is still best counted in sleeps.

"You promise?"

"Of course, I promise. In the meantime, tell me what you would like me to bring you back. Mommy is going to a huge toy store now, which I'm sure will be full of pretty dollies." I often wonder why as parents we refer to ourselves in the third person when talking to our young children. Still, I am just as guilty of it as anybody else. Ella's moment of mommy nostalgia immediately passes at the mention of a "toy store" and "dollies," all wrapped up into one neat and wonderful sentence. She doesn't miss a beat.

"I don't want a dolly, Mommy. I want a puppy," she states emphatically.

Uh, hello! I am talking dollies, not puppies. Clearly the child has misunderstood me. I'll try this again.

"A toy puppy, right, Ella? You want me to look for a stuffed puppy instead of a dolly?" Though the question might sound silly to anyone overhearing me, I feel obliged to probe my child for clarification. I want nothing left to interpretation here.

"No, I want a real puppy. You're so silly, Mommy!"

I let out a nervous giggle, not sure if she is really serious or not, but this time I don't ask for further clarification because I really don't think I want to hear the truth from her any longer. I am now the one who can't handle the truth. I'm not about to buy her a real puppy. Not now or ever quite frankly. Though I'll just keep that to myself for now. There is no sense upsetting the child.

"Ella, puppies are so much work, honey. We don't have time to take care of a puppy dog right now. How about I get you a beautiful, soft, cuddly toy puppy instead?" That should do the trick.

Oh God, *no!* Not again! I am positive that Ella's sobs resonate all across Fifth Avenue.

"But all I want is a P-P-UPP-E-E!"

And the earsplitting screaming has begun yet again. A cacophony of voices rings in behind Ella's shrills. Most likely all of the kids are now taking part. Jack's voice, being the strongest and the loudest, overpowers them all, so the only thing I can make out clearly is him bellowing, *"Give me that phone!"*

What ensues is an eerie silence. Very scary from where I am standing.

But it isn't Jack's voice that I hear next at all. A softer, younger voice appears on the line. "Mom?"

"Yes, Michael?"

"She's fine."

"Really?" I ask, completely unconvinced. What I am convinced of is that either: a) Jack has muzzled my youngest child, or b) one of the other kids has tossed her from the vehicle's window. Neither scenario is good.

"Really, she's fine."

"She doesn't sound fine to me. In fact, I don't hear her at all now, Michael. That re-e-e-ally worries me more."

"Well, she is ... fine, that is. Just bring her back a stupid stuffed dog. Really, Mom."

Another voice. "Mommy?"

"Yes, Nikki?"

"How's your trip going, Mama? Did you buy any pretty clothes yet?"

I ogle down at my parcel, which at this point is being firmly held inside my sweaty palm. My latest acquisitions to my wardrobe, vintage or not someday, neatly folded and wrapped all snug and secure, are a complete oxymoron to the mess that has just unfolded on the other side of my pink communication device.

"No, not yet," I lie.

More screaming. Again. In a weird kind of way, I am momentarily relieved. At the very least, Ella is: a) still in the vehicle and b) not gagged and bound. Ella sounds somewhat like a wounded animal this time.

Dear God, how can such a small person make such a hideous sound?

"*Shut up, stupid! I can't hear Mommy!*" Nikki's voice sounds guttural, like a military command.

Jack yells at Nikki.

Ella cries louder.

Maybe I should just hit the "end" button on my phone and pretend that the line has gone dead. Or I can tell them that I was mugged because the muggers wanted my pretty pink phone. This is New York City, after all—doesn't everyone have to worry about getting mugged here? *Not!*

Okay, so both of those ideas are poor cop-outs. Very immature of me, especially since I am the parent here, but good Lord, either of those scenarios seems far more appealing to me than continuing to listen to this. I'm not sure whether to laugh or cry right now. Laugh at the severe episode that has unfolded and my unbelievably creative (and immature) way of wanting to handle it, or cry because I am not there to lend a hand to my unfortunate husband whom I have left to his own devices to handle it all.

My voice remains composed. "Nikki, please don't call your sister stupid. In fact, please don't call anyone stupid. You know I don't like you using that word. It's not nice." I must say that I am impressed with myself. Where is my good sense coming from all of a sudden? I never deal with these sorts of things in such an unruffled and rational manner. In fact, I'm the one who usually ends up screaming the loudest by the time all is said and done, and the kids are the ones who typically by this time have made peace with each other and are left wondering "What is she freaking out about?"

Nikki, being Nikki, won't let it go.

"Mom, she is still going on about a dog. Just ignore her. We already told her you're not bringing her back a dog. You and Daddy are too busy for a dog. She just won't listen, so I'm not listening to her anymore either." The voice of reason has spoken. I swear Nikki is an adult stuck in a little girl's body. "So, Mama, let's try this again. How is your trip going, and what do you mean you haven't bought anything?"

"Nikki, darling, Mommy is here to work, not to go shopping for myself. I'll try to get in a little time to shop before I come home."

Okay, so I lie again. So what? I'm not hurting anyone. This is merely a little white lie to appease my child. The ones we parents tell from time to time for the sake of damage control. Can you imagine what Jack might be thinking if he knew I had had time to shop for moi while the animals are in his care and behaving so badly?

Aggh! I shudder to think.

"Could you put Ella back on?" I ask, almost regretting what I am about to get myself into.

I can hear Ella sniffling in the background, trying with all her might to catch her breath.

"H-h-hel-l-l-o?"

The tears have welled up in the corner of my eyes again. *Great!* I have got to do something about forming a backbone where these kids of mine are concerned.

I can just imagine, though, my little Ella strapped into her booster seat and sandwiched in between Michael and Nikki, neither one of which is much comfort to her now in her moment of distress. Their favourite road-trip pastime is to thrust Ella's seat back and forth between them, only to annoy my youngest child. Though I have done my utmost best to secure her seat firmly into the seat belt, it still has plenty of slack and has this uncanny way of sliding around on the leather backseat. When Michael and Nikki really want to annoy her (more than she already is), this is what they partake in. After all, what's the point of having a little sister if you can't completely crawl under her porcelain skin?

"Ella, why are you crying still?"

"Because."

"Because why?"

"Because I want you to come home, and I want Nikki to stop being bossy, and I want you to bring me a *puppy!*"

Dear Diary,

Oh boy, here I go again. When I'm home, I want to be at work; and when I'm at work, I want to be at home. Right now I'm not sure where I really want to be or what I want to be doing for that matter! Actually on second thought, maybe I do know what I want. I want Ella to stop crying, like NOW! I would love to be the good mother and buy her a puppy, really I would, but who would be taking care of it? Me! Moi! That's who, and that is not going to happen, not in this lifetime it isn't. Who would be walking it? Me. Who would be pooping and scooping? Me.

Like I haven't scooped enough poop with three kids! And why the fuck am I still giving this one ounce of thought or remorse when I already said no? That would mean that I might actually be considering the puppy, and I am not! But see, here's the problem. I know exactly how the rest of this night is going to play out. Jack is going to drop the girls off at dance class, and Ella will still have tears all down her dewy face. He will have no clue how to comfort her because he just doesn't. He'll tell her to "get over it," but she's only six-years-old; she doesn't know how to "get over it." Adults don't know how to "get over it" most of the time, so how could a little kid know? Now I think I know why God created mothers! We know how to better handle stuff like this. I'm not saying we're perfect or pros at handling teary situations, but we are definitely better than fathers are at it. So why then am I feeling so guilty? Who the hell created this guilt thing anyways—it's for the birds! Think I'll try both the stuffed-dog route and the dolly. What have I got to lose?

Later,
Me, Your Mixed-Up Simple Girl

Chapter Twenty-Two

"*Ladies and gentlemen, this is your captain speaking. Our flying time today will be approximately ninety minutes to the gate at Pearson International Airport. Conditions are clear, and I anticipate a pleasant flight. Should you require anything during this short flight to Toronto, our in-flight crew would be more than happy to assist you. Please sit back and enjoy your flight.*"

Home. I am finally going home. Nothing seems more gloriously satisfying to me than the sound of that simple, squat, monosyllabic word. Four fundamental letters of the alphabet on their own are just basic, undemanding letters, but strung together comprise such a significant place on earth. Not just any place, but the one place in this world that makes the most sense to a whole lot of people, and right at this moment, makes a whole lot of sense to me.

My trip to the Big Apple has been anything but uneventful. I had absolutely no qualms about coming here and doing what I had to do. But nothing—and I do mean *nothing*—beats the feeling of finally going home. Notwithstanding the dramatic highlights of the trip, I have to admit that my first international project went better than I could have ever anticipated (minus the one minor hiccup of the philandering husband, but besides that trivial detail, the renovation itself is moving along without any major incidents—as far as renovations are concerned, that is).

Fascinating how only four short days (or long, depending on how you look at it) away from the craziness of my home existence has given me such a different perspective of my ordinary life. Wait a second, did I just say that? Did I just call my life *"ordinary,"* as in boring or uninteresting? Well, if it is, I think I am perfectly okay with being boring. Come to think of it, maybe my boring life treads on relative normalcy. Maybe I've been wrong all along. Maybe my home life is *"normal,"* as far as anything can be normal. Maybe it's my career that's gone a little wonky and has become laden with peculiar events.

I'm definitely confident about one thing, though. And that's that Shane and Camilla's Park Avenue apartment is going to look incredible when all is said and done! The three of us together were able to make so many concrete decisions on this trip that I know for a fact that any doubts that Shane had about me or my lack of experience have unquestionably vanished now. And for that, I am eternally grateful.

Our stunning Clive Christian kitchen—rather, *their* stunning Clive Christian kitchen—is on order. Dimensions have been checked and double-checked (and triple-checked by tomorrow afternoon). Ladurée green is a go! The marble tiles for the kitchen flooring have arrived and on time, no less, which in the design industry is almost unheard of. One thing is certain: the design gods were watching over me on this one. Shane and Camilla loved my suggestion of a carpet-like pattern on the kitchen floor using the tile. My proposal to them was to run the white marble underneath the cabinets and then create a black marble border or carpet-type frame on the floor directly in front of the cabinets outlining the entire kitchen space. We'll complete it with a checkerboard pattern on the inside. Our space isn't big, but that is no reason why it still can't look dazzling. Shane loved the idea. Thinks it will look amazing. I couldn't agree with him more.

When I suggested Italian mosaic glass tile for the powder room in a caramel, topaz, and gold combination, Shane was in total favour of it. When I suggested using it on the walls of the powder room as well as the ceiling, totally giving it an over-the-top Donatella Versace look, he went for that too. Am I surprised? Well, maybe a little, I guess. Surprised or not, he seems to be right on board with lots of my ideas now. Ultimately a happy client makes for a happy designer, and I am oh-so-happy on many accounts. With the apartment transformation well underway and Christmas fast approaching, we agreed that I would make another site visit in the new year.

For the time being, I am eager to get home and see Jack and the kids. I am missing them just as much as I know they are missing me. Maybe it's true what they say. Maybe absence does make the heart grow fonder.

I can't wait to see the looks on Nikki's and Ella's faces when I show them their American Girl dolls. Whoever invented this doll concept is clearly a marketing genius. The all-American girl in countless unique shapes and skin tones. A blue-eyed blonde for Nikki and a light brunette with brown eyes for Ella. My one bit of remorse? That they hadn't been there with me to witness that fantastic store firsthand. Who would have thought that anyone could fill four floors of a rather spacious location with just one doll and all sorts of doll paraphernalia? Clothes, shoes, party dresses, musical instruments, camping gear, sports equipment, and of course, what else, an infirmary for when your dolly has a boo-boo. Even I have to admit that this place is a haven for any doll-loving child. Cooler still will be the day when I finally bring them to see all of this for themselves. As for Michael, his gift is safely stowed in my overstuffed suitcase. A three-thousand-piece LEGO set. Mr. Construction Man is going to recreate the Eiffel Tower. Hopefully that will keep his hands busy long enough so he will have little time and energy left over to beat up his sisters.

This is Friday night. Fridays are our only night of the week without scheduled activities for the kids—thank goodness! Years ago, Jack and I designated Fridays as family night. If we stay in, dinner frequently consists of homemade pizza, followed by a movie and popcorn. If we choose to brave the elements and go out for the night, we often frequent our favourite local Italian restaurant, just as good as home, even by my scrupulous standards. I am hoping for dinner in tonight; home-cooked by none other than Jack this time would be so nice since I have had my fill of eating out in restaurants this week. The truth is, though I have been lucky enough to dine at some of New York City's most famous and fabulous restaurants, nothing would be more comforting than a home-cooked meal tonight.

I was fortunate enough to dine at the Four Seasons Restaurant while I was in Manhattan. With its elegant interiors and phenomenal food, it was a gastronomically tantalizing dining experience. As for Buddakan, *oh yeah*—if it was good enough for the cast of *Sex and the City*, it was most definitely good enough for me! But for right now, I could sure go for something really simple, like pasta pomodoro and a glass of Amarone.

My blue chariot, also known as my airline taxi service, courtesy of my imported driver Singh, pulls up onto my darkened driveway at last. Home, sweet home!

"That will be fifty-five dollars and seventy-five cents, madam," Singh announces. I hand him three twenties and bolt from the backseat. He can keep the change. I want to race inside as quickly as possible. He attempts to carry my luggage to the front door for me. Nice touch, Singh, but no thanks, I can take it from here.

Please leave. Like *now*!

I really want to get inside.

He insists.

So do I.

I win!

Inserting my key into the lock, I carefully push down on the satin nickel latch, unlocking the door ever so gently. I want to surprise the kids.

Ella is the first to notice my entrance. I swear that kid can smell my presence anywhere. Little Miss Up-to-No-Good appears to be on her way to the kitchen when she stops dead in her tracks, her mouth agape at the sight of me.

"*Mommy! Mommy's home!*" And into my arms she runs. Nikki, Michael, and Jack follow quickly behind the heels of my mini-troublemaker.

They waste no time. The questions start to fly in my direction.

"How was your trip?"

"What did you bring us?"

"Is New York City really big?"

"Did you get mugged?"

"Did your clients get divorced?"

I avoid all questions, diverting them with mommy hugs instead, which by now are flowing aplenty. Laughter rings out throughout the walls of my house, and gifts are distributed to all.

I am back where I belong. My home is complete once again.

Dear Diary,

Could it be that I think I'm finally starting to understand this? "This," meaning my life. I'm not sure why it has taken me so long, but it has. It seems that anyone can have a house, but not everyone has a home. Helping people with the design of their homes is what I do. It's probably about one of the only things I know how to do really well—at least I think I do it pretty well. But that's only just the beginning of the story. My part in all of it is really so small. The rest of it, the most important part of all of this, lies in the artful hands of the homeowners—the people who live in that house. Once I've done my part, it's completely up to them to create the rest of the story, which if you ask me is the best and most fascinating part. It's up to them to create a warm and loving space. A safe place to go to anytime of the day or night. A sacred place to wake up in, and a soft place to land at the end of a long and tiring day. A place where the people within those walls can share things—all sorts of things. Things like laughter, lots of laughter; sometimes tears; tons of joy; plenty of delicious food; great stories; but above all, everlasting memories.

Later,
Me, Your Very Tired and Resolute Simple Girl

Chapter Twenty-Three

Christmas is fast approaching, only two weeks away, and the kids are excitedly anticipating Santa's arrival. I'm standing just looking out the library window on this particular morning after the kids are safely at school and Jack well on his way to the office. More than ever, the library is my favourite room in the entire house. This is the one room in the house where I can escape, where nothing is expected of me, although monumentally a lot does take place in here. No cooking or baking happens in this room. No laces are tied in here, and no arithmetic problems ever get solved in my much-desired sanctuary. However, this is the one space where guaranteed pleasure is always a constant … just because. Though it is never enforced and it is not obligatory, it simply happens.

Pleasure comes by way of reading mostly, not just me alone, but the kids and Jack too. My choice of reading material is by and large interior design magazines, beautifully illustrated coffee table books that once I become engrossed, I could spend countless numbers of hours absorbing (if only time would actually permit me to)—or the latest picks from Amazon, which regularly show up at my front door ready for me to dive into. Jack and I are known to share the odd cocktail or two in this room as well. If I were a betting girl, I would bet that most of my real work does in fact begin and end in this room. I am lucky enough to have a home office with a desk, laptop computer, fabric samples hanging throughout (mostly on the backs of chairs—and more chairs), furniture catalogues aplenty, but most of my thoughts, creative processes, concepts, and ideas are routinely brought to life and nurtured among these four library walls—and habitually while I gaze out this very same window as I am doing this morning.

The past few weeks since returning from New York City have been a blur. Camilla and Shane, while pleased with the majority of decisions made on-site, are now having second thoughts with respect to fabrics we have chosen for the master bedroom. Or should I say Shane is having second thoughts?

"It's too green. It's too feminine," he tells me. "Perhaps you can tell Camilla you've had a change of heart, Kat, and want the vibe in the space to feel a little sexy." Shane springs this on me while I am in the midst of driving to pick Ella up from school. I am in no mood for this.

Fuck!

Here we go with the green thing again. I should have never picked up the phone. *How ironic,* I think to myself, *that someone so enamoured with money would dislike the colour green. Furthermore, the whole room is not green, dumb-ass!*

The fabric for the window coverings has already been ordered— several yards of it, in fact—as has a rather expensive Scalamandré sage-coloured dupioni silk, to be used for an ottoman that Camilla has her sights set on and thought would make a lovely addition to her bedroom. I have no intentions of being left holding the proverbial bag, or bolt in this case—a bolt that consists of twenty-five yards of seafoam-green silk—just days before Christmas. Now that would put a huge ding into my Christmas budget! Not to mention what the hell would I do with all that silk anyways? So now I'm left with no choice but to put out a fire that, although I didn't start it, I'm now left to my own devices and have to extinguish—all because I picked up my phone.

See, this is what in fact happened this morning. All was going good. It was another run-of-the-mill day, which for me means no major crisis with either clients or children, and that's a huge bonus, so I'll take it. Since I had promised Kip that I would ensure his condo would be party-worthy for the holidays, I took the liberty today to search out table linens and tableware for him. Kip being Kip had little time or inclination to source such things out on his own, so I, his designer, and now party planner extraordinaire, piped up and offered my services.

"Sure, Kip, I would love to help you with all of the details for your cocktail party." Kip, of course, was ecstatic. Jack was not.

"You're a designer, not a party planner. He needs a wife and not mine."

Jack wasn't altogether wrong, but I am a pleaser and saying no to my clients isn't easy for me, especially when what I am helping with is something I thoroughly enjoy. So I set out to fulfill a client request, which I was all too happy to do. An ordinary day didn't last too long, though, because then my life would have seemed unpleasantly boring, which I have come to realize it is anything but. So I'm standing serenely examining crystal wine glasses, holding one glass up, then another, the light catching the many facets, giving life to a luminous sparkle. I resemble a young bride trying to decide between Rosenthal or Baccarat. In case you're wondering, this bride favours the Baccarat. Anyways, like I was saying, all the while I'm standing there like some indecisive, spoiled bride-to-be, I am deep in conversation on my cell phone with Alessia. She is filling me in on the details of her latest date with Cass. Things seem to be looking quite positive in the romance department.

"Come on!" I cry out, a little too loudly. The scrunched-up face of the other and possibly real bride-to-be standing not so far away from me with what appears to be her mummy in tow makes me realize that maybe I am being a tad bit loud. Both of them glare at me with turned-up noses. Oh well, too bad for them. I didn't tell them they had to listen. And besides, this conversation is rather enlightening. Even more illuminating than the brilliant clear glass all around me. And anyways, shouldn't Bridezilla be more caught up in her stupid registry than listening to my telephone conversation? *Love on the rocks already, babe? Oh just wait, the best is yet to come—but you didn't hear it from me!*

"I swear, Kat! It was amazing. I was just sitting there listening to him. I swear I was in a trance, and then out of the blue, he just pulled my hand across the table and started kissing my fingers softly one by one. And here I thought we were going to be talking shop all night." Alessia's tone of voice is completely giddy, like a schoolgirl. I can't help but feel vaguely envious since who has time for that kind of romance anymore? By the same token, I am completely joyful for her. If anyone deserves happily ever after, she most definitely does, and Cass seems to be the perfect guy.

"So what did you do?" I am ever so curious, still twirling a Baccarat stem between my fingers. Wow, this wine glass is really spectacular. I wonder if it could survive an entire meal in my house.

"What did I do? What could I do? I was speechless. But get this! So there we are staring into each other's eyes, and then Cass gets up—rather coyly, I might add—and starts to walk around to my side of the table, while he's still holding my fingers and I can smell his cologne, which I swear, Kat, made me want to pounce on him because he smelled so good and then ..." *Beep.*

"Oh shit! Less, wait, there's another call coming through." Checking the caller ID on the display screen, I quickly notice it reads *Kids' School.* "Less, it's the kids' school calling on the other line. Let me call you right back, okay?"

"Okay, but hurry. I'm just getting to the best part."

Click.

"Hello, this is Katarina speaking."

"Mrs. Bancari?"

"Yes?"

"This is Ms. Tromini from West Elm Public School." The ominous Madame X is on the line. What does she want?

"I'm calling about Ella."

"What happened?" I panic.

"Ella is fine. There's no need to sound alarmed, but there was a little incident today involving her." Her voice sounds morose.

"What kind of *incident?*" My heart is racing. I set the glass down, not as gently as I would have liked based on the reverberating clanking sound it makes. Lucky for me, I didn't break it. On second thought, good thing it isn't coming home with me. It would never survive under my care, or lack thereof. Just the same, I had suddenly lost complete interest in crystal.

"Well, you see ... I was in the middle of teaching a math lesson when Ella raised her hand asking to go to the washroom."

"Yes?" This story is already taking way too long to tell; my blood is rapidly percolating, like one of those coffeepots where you can tell the coffee is starting to brew in the little glass knobby-thing on the lid. I have a bad feeling I know where this conversation is going, and I do not like it one tiny iota.

"Well ... it was a rather longish lesson and quite important too, I might add here, and so I asked Ella if she could wait until I was done teaching it. She said she could, and so I had no reason to believe that she couldn't, so I continued ... with the lesson, that is."

It is time to take this story into my own hands and fast-forward to the ending. So I do. "And so what happened, Ms. Tromini?" If I don't calm down quickly, there is the slightest possibility that I might say something extremely unladylike in my now-heated temperament.

"Yes, well. I'm getting to that part. After I had finished teaching, I allowed her to go to the washroom. She seemed to be taking quite a bit of time to return, so I sent Ms. Parker to go and find her."

"So, where was she, Ms. Tromini, and who the hell is Ms. Parker? Are you not Ella's teacher?" I snap. I know I am being rude, but quite honestly I don't care. Pacing around the crystal department, I notice Bridezilla and her mother shooting me dirty looks all over again. If she knows what's good for her, she should keep her distance because Mama Bear is about to pounce and if there is any cold porridge sitting in a bowl somewhere in plain sight of us, she will likely be wearing it very soon. When my baby bears' well-being is in question, this Mama Bear becomes one ugly beast!

"Mrs. Bancari, there is no need for profanities, please. Ms. Parker is our student teacher. Anyways she found Ella in the girls' washroom. She's fine. However ... however, she was quite upset and apparently was drying her pants under the hand dryer. Mrs. Bancari, if I had thought she couldn't wait, I would have let her go earlier. Really I would have."

My mouth is hanging wide open. I am speechless—not something that happens very often to my overactive Italian jaws, though lately it seems to be happening more and more frequently. More often than I can count.

I begin to walk briskly towards the exit sign and out of the store. I make a mad dash in none other than my very high-heeled suede Stuart Weitzman boots, while my winter white Mongolian fur-collared wool car coat flies up behind me as I dash down the escalator through the clothing aisles and race along the moving sidewalk to the parking lot. I'm convinced other shoppers are questioning the number of items I have stashed beneath my getaway ensemble. I too might be thinking the same thought if I had been witnessing this spectacle of anyone other than me, but right now I am hardly concerned with what this looks like.

Completely out of breath, I still manage to shout into the phone, "Ms. Tromini, where is Ella now?"

"She's in the office. She's quite upset, and I think it would be a good idea if you could pick her up. Perhaps take her home early." Her voice sounds slightly remorseful, but only slightly. By the time I am done with her, she will be the one wishing she had wet herself and not Ella!

"Well, of course, I'm on my way to pick her up. I wouldn't expect that after wetting herself, she would want to sit in class for the remainder of the day! Would you, Ms. Tromini?" I shout in my are-you-fucking-stupid? voice.

If Ms. Tromini can't tell by the tone of my voice that I am positively furious, then she is truly an imbecile. Short of telling her as much, it is pretty clear that I am less than impressed with her. What is she thinking, preventing a six-year-old from using the washroom? Anyone who is a parent or knows the slightest thing about children knows that little kids wait until the very last possible minute to go and then they make a speedy beeline for the toilet.

"I'm terribly sorry about this incident, Mrs. Bancari. I had no clue that Ella needed to go that badly." Evidently the woman is a mind reader since quite accurately she is sensitive to the fact that I am blaming her for this one. Then again, if she was so smart and could read *my* mind, why was she not able to read Ella's when she had asked to be excused in the first place?

In the back of my head, Jack's recurring speech to me when I become upset or *overreact* (in his opinion only, of course) resonates: be calm, relax, don't freak out, she was just doing her job. *Yeah okay, Jack. Well, guess what? I'm just doing mine.*

Calmness is for the birds. I feel more like a scorned cobra.

"Ms. Tromini, let's get something clear here, shall we? Ella is six years old, thus making her a child. As I'm sure you're well aware, children at this age don't have exceptional bladder control since they are still quite little, so perhaps from this point going forward, if Ella asks you to be excused, it's because she really has to go *pee!*" My voice is loud.

There is no doubt in my mind that this woman thinks that I am absolutely, positively, certifiably crazy! And for once, even I might have to agree with her. I hang up without so much as a good-bye. I know. I'm being rude, right? I don't care. I am not interested in a courteous conversation. Jack would have reprimanded me, telling me that I hadn't handled this appropriately or professionally. For the first time in a long time, I don't care what Jack or anyone else thinks. I don't feel like handling things in a professional manner. Right now I am just plainly and simply a mom. I have to advocate on behalf of my child, who is still too young to do it for herself. So

I am doing what I think needs to be done. And if I am making a colossal mistake, so be it. I'm well aware of the fact that it is still early in the school year and being at odds with Ella's teacher won't serve her well, (Even in my rage, I'm smart enough to realize this). I will just have to deal with all of that later. Jack can't understand how embarrassing this type of scenario can be for a little girl. Little boys are different; they laugh most everything off, including this kind of stuff, but little girls can be downright mean and nasty and the last thing I want is for Ella to feel self-conscious about this. It's hard enough being a kid nowadays without giving your schoolmates a discomforting situation to dangle over your head like a flimsy carrot.

Over and over, all I can think about the entire time as I race across the highway again is how mortified Ella must be feeling. I imagine her standing there all alone, making a wild attempt to hide the evidence on her small pair of Gap denim jeans. I wonder how many times she has pressed down on that metal button of the dryer. Her long ponytail, neatly coiffed when she left the house this morning, must be completely dishevelled by the swirling of hot air caused by her current mission, not an easy one at her age.

And this is when Shane calls, complaining about too much green. Since I am so distracted and upset about Ella, I pick up my phone without even casting a glance at the call display screen. Now who is the dumb-ass?

"I understand your apprehension, Shane, since often clients do have some second thoughts after making an important decision, particularly about such an important space. But if you recall, we did wait until you and Camilla mulled this one over before I went ahead and ordered the fabric. You both agreed to it." *So what's changed?* "Think of the window coverings as a beautiful evening gown, flowing and elegant, all the while being ethereal with a hint of mystery. Makes for an intriguing room, don't you think?" *Pause.* "Shane? Are you still there?" *What is that? Is that a voice I am hearing in the background? Is that a female voice I hear?*

"Is Camilla there with you?" I innocently ask.

"No. No, she's not here. I'm calling from the office. That was nothing!" he snaps. *Nothing?* It doesn't sound like nothing to me.

"I'll tell you what, Shane. Since this is obviously not sitting well with you, if both you and Camilla are having second thoughts, then we should sit down and readdress the direction of the master bedroom. Why don't the three of us meet first thing tomorrow morning, and we can brainstorm? I'll come up with some new concepts in the interim." *Like I really have time to do this!* "Something more sexy—I believe that's what you said." *Definitely a transgression from the elegant and classic New York feel we had discussed.*

"Let me give it some more thought; I'll get back to you." *Click.* Shane's voice is tense.

If that wasn't Camilla's voice I heard in the background, then whose voice was it? Maybe Camilla's suspicions are justified. Maybe she is right. Maybe she's been right all along. Is Shane having a little fun on the side? Oh well, too bad for Candy, or whoever the mystery woman is, that green isn't her colour; it isn't her bedroom and it's not her decision to make, so from where I am standing, it appears to me that green is a probable go! Something tells me that Shane won't be inquiring any further about colour selections. Given Camilla's suspicions and the fact that he wants to keep her busy, he'd be rather foolish to get involved with any more fabric or furniture decisions. In the end, I don't think he really cares much whether we select Biedermeier or Baroque, Art Deco or Contemporary. Shane just wants it to look marvellously decorated. End of story!

If anything positive has come out of Shane's phone call, it is that it has temporarily distracted me from thinking about Ella and what has happened in school today. The bad thing is that now that Camilla's suspicions have been pretty much confirmed to me, I will have a hard time remaining neutral in my discussions with them, something that is essential in my line of work. One thing I know for sure: whether I feel protective of Camilla or not, unless it involves trinkets or tassels, I had better keep my opinions to myself.

Look, I'm no fool, I am well aware of the fact that I should not have let Ella's slight childhood incident interfere with my work today. After all, she is a little girl, and these types of things are sure to happen, especially now that she is in school all day. If I really think about it objectively, maybe Shane does have a genuine concern here, and he deserves my undivided attention. After all, it is my responsibility to address his concerns, whether I am upset about real life getting in the way or not. At least, this is what the *professional girl* in me is telling me. But maybe this is the real problem. Maybe I'm not the professional girl I'd like to think I am.

I speed up to the school parking directly in front of the front entrance doors, disregarding the sign that reads *Bus Entry Only*. What can I say? I'm a bit of a deviant. It is still only 2:15 p.m., and the afternoon buses won't be here for a while yet. After waiting for the standard protocol of being permitted entry, I promptly make my way through the steel double-entry doors and head towards the main office. I attempt to acknowledge Meredith by looking directly at her, but my focus is fixated on the head I spot from the corner of my eye. Ella.

"Mommy?" I hear a smallish voice call towards me. I dart over to her and bend down to kiss her damp forehead, sweaty from the laborious activity she has been forced to undertake. Brushing away some loose strands that have haphazardly slipped out of her ponytail and lie across her freckled nose, I offer her a much-needed warm smile.

"Want to go home and have a bubble bath?" I ask, all the while caressing her cheek.

Ella nods.

And so, hand in hand, we walk out of the office and out the front doors I had entered merely minutes ago. We don't talk about the incident. There is no need to. Ella needs her soft place to land, no questions asked and no discussion required. At this very moment, I realize that I am her soft place, not because I have to be but because I want to be.

Dear Diary,

All I want to do is take Ella in my arms and hold her tight, but I don't want to embarrass her anymore than she already has been. She seems so fragile right now, so tender and sweet, looking to me for reassurance that she's okay. I'm just glad that I was able to come and pick her up. What about those kids whose mommies can't leave work and come running when life throws them a curveball? My heart goes out to those children and those mommies, because it's moments like this that children need their mommies the most—to let them know that it's okay, they've done nothing wrong. When they feel scared and embarrassed or don't know how to deal with a situation, these are the times when we have to give them our unconditional love and support. Comfort them and assure them that they've done nothing to worsen the situation. That this is all part of growing up, and nobody said growing up would be easy or without surprises. As for Shane and Camilla and even Kip's party decorations, all will have to wait for now. Real life has come calling once again, and I won't ignore the call.

Later,
Me, Your Simple Girl

Chapter Twenty-Four

Thank goodness my frenzied work schedule is at last quieting down, or so it appears to be in any event. That isn't to say that suddenly my days and nights are laden with hours of free time to lull unreservedly in pigtails and flannel jammies while munching on bonbons. Oh no! It simply means that I can redirect some of my attention to some of the other things that I have singlehandedly deemed essential during this hectic holiday season.

Since the countdown to Santa's arrival is sweetly lingering in the frosty air overhead, I need to don yet another warm and, of course, trendy hat. This one will disguise me as the lady in red—no, not the sultry songstress type—the jolly, white, wiry-haired, round-belly type. And for the record, this Mrs. Claus has a whole lot to do still, with no elves to count on for assistance. I still need to purchase some last-minute gifts, including one for Ms. Tromini, much as she isn't on my "nice" list, to say the very least. She is most definitely at the top of my naughty one, her name spelled out in big, red, uppercase letters, lest I forget, which I'm not likely to! Jack suggested that given the spirit of the season, perhaps I should be more forgiving, have a change of heart, and do some reshuffling of names. Move Ms. Tromini over to the nice list for Ella's sake, he had suggested. It is still only December, and the school year is not even halfway finished. So, maybe, just maybe, he isn't altogether wrong *this time*, which doesn't mean I think he is right, just more levelheaded than me, that's all. I take my crimson Sharpie and squiggle a curly line directly through Ms. Tromini's name—grudgingly so, I might add.

By day my hours are filled with school plays and concerts— there seem to be so many of them. Do teachers not focus on reading and writing during the month of December? It must take them weeks to prepare the kids for these types of assemblies. At the end of each and every one, I partake in the exchange of the usual niceties with the other parents: "So cute," "Yes, they were darling," "Oh how these teachers put so much work into these performances"—and then when I think the coast is clear, I make my quick escape out the back door and return safely to the sanctity of my own home, where I continue to attend to the task of gift wrapping, which seems never ending and is now relegated to intermittent spurts of time while the kids are in school. And if by night I too am not having sweet dreams with visions of sugarplum fairies dancing in my head, it is only because Jack and I are out at friends' or neighbours' gatherings, which are currently in full swing all around us. Neighbours call inviting us to join them for a festive drink—"just one," of course—though typically one turns into two, which then proceeds to turn into a night of all-out laughter and cheer.

And though it wasn't easy, I'm proud to announce that I did manage to pull together Kip's condo in time for his December 20 soirée. It was nothing short of a miracle, I might add, but I did it. As much as I had decided on a streamlined and sleek feel to his Christmas décor, it still required a little bit of layering mixed together with a whole lot of sparkle, which in essence equalled a considerable amount of work on my part. If I had to attest to a Christmas décor adage, it would be that I am hardly a designer who decorates for the holidays since my design philosophy has always been that you decorate your home to suit your lifestyle three hundred and sixty-five days a year and don't overindulge on holiday decorations just for one season. And besides, how depressing it all seems when you have to undo all that you did in the first place. Not to mention the painstaking hours it takes to primp it all up. Instead, my method consists of a few tasteful seasonal items, usually in the form of fresh flowers, natural greens, or potted plants alongside bowls and containers filled with decorative holiday ornaments. In Kip's case, once he fixed his eyes on the sparkle of the Baccarat wine glasses I had finally managed to purchase and a stunning Lalique bowl, magnificent all on its own with its simple detailing, more dazzle is what he requested, and so that's what I gave him.

~

"What about organza cocktail napkins in silver?" I suggest early one morning on yet another telephone call to Kip. This man is all about the details.

"Sounds expensive," he retorts.

I let out a quiet sigh. Good thing he can't see me. I definitely hope he can't sense my frustration either. "Sounds expensive, but they're not." I'm quick with my comeback, knowing full well that Kip admires this quality in me. I smirk to no one in particular since I have no audience members present.

"And the new Lalique bowl I purchased for you, we can fill it up with silver-wrapped chocolates and have them spill over. It will look so chic and is not costly to do."

"Hmm, don't know about that either. Sounds sort of girly, but I'll trust you."

That sounds encouraging!

"We can hang black feather wreaths on wide black velvet ribbon from the mirrors in the hallway and living room, and on your front door we can hang a larger version of it with an even wider red velvet ribbon instead. Simple, but elegant. What do you think?" My fingers and toes are crossed at this point. My vision is starting to fade, and my ideas are beginning to run low—perhaps this is a case of burnout. If so, I am in big trouble!

"Sounds a little kinky, Kat." Kip seems amused. I presume he is the one smirking this time. *Oh brother!* Even after all these years,

I still have to be so careful in my suggestions and choice of words, especially to a single male on the other end of the telephone.

"I'll get everything set up for you, Kip. All you need to do is hire the caterer. You can handle that, right?"

"Kitty-Kat, I can handle a lot of things; just say the word."

Oh ple-eass-e!

Fortunately I have gotten used to this kind of humour from Kip, though I sometimes wonder whether, if I took the bait, he would reel me in. It hardly matters, though, since I am not at all interested in anything more than a professional relationship with Kip. If nothing else, he is very amusing. The one thing I do try to impress Kip with, though, is the work that I do for him. Luckily for Kip (and me), he loves his new kitchen (it actually arrived without any delays) and the industrial look of it. Since he seldom prepares a meal for himself, it is more the wow factor than anything else that pleases him. One thing is for certain: the caterers will have a comfortable space to work in. I know I would sure love it if I had the opportunity to work in that space.

"Of course, you and Mr. Kitty-Kat will be at the party, won't you?" Kip's voice suddenly sounds childlike.

What do you know? Kip does a 180-degree turn on me and becomes serious. This so-o-o freaks me out! I wasn't really expecting an invitation from him. I wonder what Jack might say. He isn't keen on attending parties that my clients host, preferring not to mix business with pleasure. I, on the other hand, love attending such events. Kip, being Kip, is a harmless and social kind of guy just looking for friends, and as luck would have it, I had made his short list. He enjoys being the centre of attention, and the more people, animals, and inanimate objects present, the merrier. So maybe he is a little egotistical, but he means no harm by it. And since I am the assistant party planner for this occasion, it is only logical that I should attend, isn't it? And besides, this might be just the place to search out some new hip clients for the upcoming year.

"Gee, Kip, thanks for the invitation. I'll have to check with my husband to make sure he hasn't committed us to anything else. Could I get back to you?"

"You do that, Kitty-Kat, but tell hubby that I need my favourite designing girl there. After all, I want to show you off to all my friends."

I giggle. "Sure, Kip, I'll let Jack know."

~

Party day is a busy one. Whew—that's an understatement! My day planner looks something like this:

9:30 a.m. – Set up @ Kip's house

1:00 p.m. – Christmas assembly @ kids' school

2:15 p.m. – Blow-dry and polish change

3:30 p.m. – Pick up kids

6:00 p.m. – Pick up babysitter

7:30 p.m. – Christmas Cocktail Party at Kip's

Starbucks' espressos might have been strong enough pre-6:00 p.m., but after that, who can blame me for looking forward to a really dirty martini at Kip's place later tonight?

~

God, could you please tell me why the hell I am always running? I apologize. I said "hell"—wrong choice of words for you, sorry, big guy! This is my second time making my way through the parking lot at the kids' school today. Okay, why the heck (*there, that's better*) am I always five minutes fashionably late for everything? Maybe Nikki is right. Maybe I am always trying to do too much. But what am I doing that is so special or different? I'm purely doing the day-to-day stuff—the stuff that has to get done. She'll understand one day.

Pulling open the front doors of the school, I race inside. Everything about my movements is eerily feeling like déjà-vu. If I'm smart, I'll keep my eyes pinned to the floor and hightail my ass to the auditorium so as to avoid any and all distractions, particularly of the human kind. The Yummy Mummies are sure to be seated by now, no less than in the front row. They thrive on these types of events where they can sit and do absolutely nothing but simply be audience members. If they have managed to do any toning or firming since the beginning of the school year, this will be the one day where they will shed their yoga pants for painted-on jeans and black leather thigh-high boots. This also means that they are never tardy for these types of events, since this is their time to shine, showing off all of their intense gym training to watchful admirers.

The concert is sure to be eminently underway. Good thing, because God, my feet are sore! My toes feel like ground-up sausage meat stuffed inside a leathery casing in these knee-high wedge boots. Though I must admit they look damn good, I seriously doubt that Prada is intended to be worn the way I wear it. There are shoes and boots that you run in and shoes and boots that you sit and look pretty in; I'm pretty sure that these fall into the latter category. Nike would have been the ideal choice for today—yeah, okay, like that's going to happen— the only Nikes I ever wear are for the infrequent tennis lessons I participate in now and again, when I attempt to take time out and *play*. Though I can't remember when I did that last.

The auditorium is dark save for a few stage lights that are brilliantly shining and the bright exit sign that is erected high above, radiating a hazy reddish light. Thank you, God, it hasn't started yet. I haven't missed a thing except for the preshow shenanigans and the scurrying of teachers and students alike preparing for the stage, neither of which is essential to observe. I look all around me. Well, looky looky! Front row, just the way I called it. Piper and Alicia are standing talking to each other so closely I am sure one has spit on the other given what appears to be a gravely intense discussion. Hopefully they will be too engrossed in their banter to even notice me.

It obviously isn't my lucky day. *Shit, they see me!*

"Kat, over here!" Alicia shrieks like I am some long-lost friend she hasn't seen in like forever.

I pretend to be caught off guard, as if I have no idea they have been there all along.

"Hi!" I mouth back only in gesture, trying to inch my way discreetly to the back of the auditorium, where I might watch the concert in peace while drinking my third latte of the day; this is midday after all, and this latte is my liquid form of lunch.

Alicia is on to me. Her eyes become wide as she motions with a perfectly French-manicured index finger to an empty seat beside her. Had they in fact been thoughtful enough to save me a seat? Great! Just swell! I should be more appreciative and not the bitch I know I am being, but if the entire Christmas concert is going to be a Q and A, I would much rather sit alone like a wallflower at a grade-seven dance waiting impatiently for a cute boy to muster up the courage to ask me to dance.

Sheepishly, I make my way over to them. *Slowly. Very slowly.* Any more slowly, and I will be crawling backwards.

"Well, well, well … look at you, Mrs. Bancari, in your fluffy white coat and your perfectly coiffed hair!"

I smile graciously. I figure this is better than the alternative, which is to tell Alicia to go and fuck herself. *Not very Christmas spiritlike of me, is it?*

"It comes with the territory of being a designing girl. Kat is always done up to the nines, you should know that by now," Piper pipes up with her two cents' worth. "I can barely get my yoga pants on before I have to run out the door to drop the kids off, and here you show up all dolled up all the time."

All dolled up, that's a joke! I haven't washed my hair in five days. Suffice it to say, I barely managed to allocate all of about five minutes this morning to brushing it out, running a straightening iron through my bangs, and clipping them back. Thank goodness I have a hair appointment scheduled right after this, because there is no way I am going to Kip's party looking like the rag doll I am feeling like. What I don't bothering sharing with Piper is that the "shine" she is admiring is grease. Why burst her bubble?

My thoughts are interrupted by the sound of jingling bells coming from behind the stage curtain. The crowd of chatty parents, grandparents, and younger siblings quickly become silenced. The stage lights dim. Jingling bells ring louder, encouraging a round of applause from the audience.

The show has begun.

~

Once the carols have been sung, the birth of Baby Jesus imitated by a rather young Mary and Joseph, and jolly old Saint Nick himself has ho, ho, ho-ed, the crowd does a tween-like serenade of "'Twas the Night Before Christmas" to close the show, bringing this year's Christmas performance to a merry and joyful end.

"And to all a good night. Ho, ho, ho, Merry Christmas, everybody!"

Applause. More applause, and then a much-deserved standing ovation cheer.

The curtains close one final time. I stand up and stretch out my arms and legs, my face still brimming with a deep-set smile I have worn since the beginning of the concert. It never ceases to amaze me how much time and effort truly does go into putting this type of production together. It's no wonder that the teachers have to start preparing the children weeks in advance.

Ella is the first of my children to find me among the crowd of doting family members.

"Hi, Mama!" Ella flings her arms around my waist.

"Hi, sweetheart!" I hug her tightly. "You were the cutest elf I have ever seen," I proclaim cheerfully. Out of nowhere, Nikki appears from behind me, her entourage of girlfriends in tow. I free up one arm so I can stroke the side of her face, as if to say, "A job well done." "You girls all sang beautifully."

Eight-year-old girls adore being praised, and I feel it is my parental duty to bestow it upon all of them, even though I am the parent to only one. They all blush. Just as quickly, however, they all scurry off again, still in group formation. Something else (probably a group of eight-year-old boys) has captured their attention. Ella still clings to me for dear life. She relishes having me stay at school with her, especially since the pee-pee incident. My presence here is just a little bit of extra security for her.

The auditorium lights are still dim, but I make a desperate attempt to pan the room searching for Michael. He had been one of the readers during the assembly. A more grown-up role had been given to him, unlike his younger sisters. I spot him standing near the stage with his friends Josh and Zach. Their teacher, Mrs. Worthwright, is reciting some sort of instructions to them, or at least so it appears, because the boys are staring blankly at her with what seems like their deer-in-the-headlights look, faces aglow.

Michael must have felt my stare because he looks over in my direction and offers me his infamous "hey Ma" head nod—a sign of acknowledgement. Michael has mastered this gesture in his first three months of grade five. I learned straightaway that the nod signifies, "I'm too cool to come over and let you kiss me and embarrass me in front of my friends, but I recognize that you're here, and by the way, thanks for coming." I let it go and don't make a fuss. Michael is trying to spread his wings and exert his independence. I have to give him credit for that much. I know he'll be back one day. So until then, I can wait.

Unleashing Ella's grip, I bend down to her level and envelop her in my arms. Ella loves to bury her round, freckled face into the long, curly fur of my coat collar.

"Ella, Mommy has to go now," I say calmly as I stroke the back of her silky hair.

She gazes up at me. "Two more minutes, Mommy?" She immediately buries her head again.

It's these very types of *two more minutes* that make me perpetually late for just about everything, but these *two more minutes* are something that I simply cannot surrender. Sometimes I wish I could bottle them and save them for later, when free time might be more plentiful; but the reality is that who knows what the future has in store for any one of us, so I believe the wise thing to do is to revel in this for now. Tardiness notwithstanding, I just won't give this up.

So, what might appear to someone on the outside looking in as insignificant childish episodes are actually incredibly monumental moments for both Ella and me. This is her first Christmas concert at school. It's her first performance in front of such a large audience that doesn't just consist of family members, but in essence strangers to her; having me here to cheer her on, just like I had done with Michael and Nikki so many times before, is all the assurance she needs. This is the icing on the cake, or in this case, the sprinkles on the Christmas sugar cookies. I must admit I feel a little twinge of melancholy for all the little ones standing here who don't have their mommies or daddies present to share this with. My guess is that some of them feel a little envious of their friends who do have family present in the crowd, watching them and praising them on their performance after the fact. I take notice of some of Ella's playmates gazing over at her, probably hungry for a hug from their mommies too. I'm so glad I'm here and present, crazy day notwithstanding.

~

While I'm getting ready for Kip's party, Nikki sits on my bed studying me attentively, her barely-there pink toes dangling off the side. She watches me admiringly. This is an all-too-frequent scenario: my getting ready for an evening out and Nikki observing my every movement. I often wonder what goes through her head while this practice goes on.

"Need some help, Mama?" Nikki asks. I have just wiggled into my black, knee-length D&G feathery cocktail dress.

"Sure, honey. Could you zip me up?"

Nikki loves being helpful; it makes her feel all grown up.

"Sure!" Nikki hops off the edge of the bed enthusiastically and skips over towards me. I can feel her delicate fingers on my back, causing a warm shiver to be sent up my spine. With a gentle zip, my dress is securely fastened. I thank her by placing a tender kiss on her forehead.

"You look pretty, Mama."

"Thank you, angel, I feel pretty," I say. I actually do feel pretty. My basic little black dress (you know, the one every woman should have in her wardrobe) isn't quite so basic; it's a little more edgy courtesy of my favourite Italian dynamic design duo and their kitschy detailing, an element I love to incorporate when dressing up. My pearl and crystal combination bracelet cuff is the highlight of my outfit, though, and I purposely keep all my other jewellery simple since one magnificent piece of jewellery is enough to make a lasting impression with one single outfit.

I guess you can say that I often dress my clients' space in precisely the same way, opting to keep it simple but elegant at the same time, purposely limiting the "pop" to just one single piece. Other times, though, and depending on who the client is, I may opt for several focal points, ensuring that the entire space is a panoramic mirage of never-ending interest, making you thirsty to go back for more. Kip's apartment is dressed somewhere in between the single "wow" and the "never-ending wow."

Jack saunters into our bedroom. Nikki turns to face him, her eyes dancing from the pre-party preparations that she adores being a part of, even though she usually isn't a party participant—not just yet, in any event.

"Daddy, doesn't Mama look pretty?" Nikki poses it as a question, though it comes across more like a statement.

Jack smiles, scooping Nikki up into his arms. "You and Mommy both look pretty," Jack sings to her.

Now that is music to Nikki's tender ears! She doesn't need to leave the house to attend a party. Her party is already well underway.

Dear Diary,

Interesting how we can buy our children the latest and greatest of toys and gadgets, spoil them with pint-size designer clothes, enrol them in private schools, ski lessons, and dance lessons, but what they want the most, what they crave the most, and what they probably will remember the most is just spending idle, boring, mundane time with us, just doing nothing special, which is probably why it in fact is so special. I often wonder if all the running around here and there is really necessary, or would they rather have more fun just being acknowledged ... just BEING with us! It's so simple really and so easy to give them what they need the most, costing us nothing but our time. Yet how many of us actually do enough of that? Is it really that much easier and faster to part with our dollars to entertain them without giving them of ourselves? Well, that seems to be a different story most of the time. We live a world so consumed with consumption, but we never seem satiated. When the heck do we become satisfied? We can't continuously consume without giving back, can we? And the giving back, well, if we don't give back to the people we love the most, then who do we give back to? Sure, I admit it, I'm a little tired tonight ... okay, a lot tired actually, but I'm so glad I made the time to go to the kids' Christmas concert today. Imagine if I had missed that! In the short run, it might not seem like such a big deal, but I know it would be in the long run. So yeah, I run ... a lot ... and I do feel tired ... a lot ... but I have to make the time for the things that are important to me, and for that, it's worth being exhausted!

Later, I have a party to get to!
Moi, Your Simple Girl

Chapter Twenty-Five

As luck would have it, the party gods are on duty this evening filling the sky with a radiant full moon, the glow of which casts a miraculous spell not just outside of Kip's building but inside his apartment as well. The interior brilliance is further highlighted courtesy of the copious numbers of twinkling candles strewn about setting the scene as a magical winter wonderland. Ambient lights have been placed on dimmers, and the sound of smooth jazz music lulls delicately in the background. It is apparent that Kip is at ease, not to mention highly experienced, in his role of remarkable host extraordinaire, dancing his way across the apartment like a young Fred Astaire. He is all too seasoned with forming introductions, acquainting friends with colleagues, and working his schoolboy charm on all of us in his presence.

Even I feel rather accomplished standing here. Kip's home looks spectacular—magazine worthy, if I do say so myself. Jack and I barely have time to meander across the living room when a waiter takes to our side offering us a glass of bubbly champagne. I accept graciously. While a dirty martini it is not, it will work superbly to transport me into a tranquil state, which I am in desperate need of. Jack declines, opting for a glass of red wine instead, which is brought to him without delay.

Jack's brow rises. "Quite the place, hon, you did a really nice job."

Jack is not flowery with his compliment. This is quite plainly Jack's way of acknowledging what I do. I know he means well. Ask him what he really likes about the space, what stands out to him, and chances are he more than likely can't tell you. He just thinks that it looks nice, and for Jack that is good enough. His interest in interior design goes only so far as how excited I get when working on a job. Translation: he otherwise has very little interest in it. It just isn't his thing. But it is my thing, and because of this, he tries respectfully to make the best of these situations.

I smile. "You really don't want to be here, do you?"

Jack doesn't miss a beat. "I never said that, Kat. It's just ... well, you know, furniture, art, and all that stuff, it just isn't my thing. It's your thing. Me, I like other stuff."

"Jack, maybe some of these people like other stuff too. Could you just make a concerted effort at conversing with some of them? Please? It might not be so bad," I add. I'm not angry with Jack, but I know him well enough to know that taken out of his element, he becomes uneasy and relaxing in this type of environment might prove difficult for him. No different than for me these days, the past few weeks have proven to be completely exhausting for Jack, with long days at the office and even longer nights at home, so getting out, mingling, and having a good time making idle conversation with complete strangers comes about only with some concerted effort.

Leave it to Kip to notice some slight uneasiness in our attitude because within moments he is attached to Jack's hip, chatting him up about his business, stock prices, and other financial jargon, which quite frankly is way out of my element. Lucky for me that Jack and I complement each other so well. This might be why our relationship works well most of the time. We recognize what our limitations are with the other and accept it as much as a person humanly can.

I take this opportunity as my cue to work the room. It is one thing to design a space and take it all in from a creator's perspective, but it's quite another to examine it from the perspective of a guest, which I now happen to be.

An intimate group of three has gathered around a glossy macassar wood sideboard that stands in front of a high wall, a wall that leads to the private rooms in Kip's apartment. I stand back observing them for a short while, not wanting to appear as though I am eavesdropping, which I'm most definitely not. I enjoy people watching, particularly when it is in this kind of setting; observing the way they interact with each other and how they move within the space is fascinating to me. The sheer fact that they are admiring the art and the light sconces gives me reason to smile too. The tall, blond, athletic guy with the boyish face smiles back at me.

"Hi, I'm Jeremy, I'm Kip's personal trainer." Jeremy holds out his hand for me to shake, so I do. "We were just admiring these lights."

I nod as if to concur. I can't help but feel proud. I picked them out. They're by Bill Sofield, an incredibly creative interior designer whose work I so much admire. The sconces are exquisite pieces of art all on their own.

"They are beautiful, aren't they? The light shines through them beautifully picking up the reflection from outside. It's magical, really."

Jeremy and his friends stare at me in bewilderment.

"I'm Kat, Katarina Bancari," I offer up. "I'm the interior designer Kip's been working with."

Jeremy breaks out into laughter. "Of course! I should've realized. You're the infamous Kat that Kip has been talking about. We've heard so much about you."

And so with the proverbial ice broken, an hour-long conversation ensues between me and my newfound acquaintances: Jeremy, his life partner Hector, a hunky Mexican artist, and their friend AnnaLisa, a dog breeder.

~

By the time the party is winding down, or should I say, by the time Jack and I are ready to make our exit (since clearly the party is still in full swing; we are the ones winding down), we have learned a great deal about downtown urban-chic single men and women—much more information than we can possibly process in one night. Life for some of them is definitely about living carefree and soaring high up above the clouds. While Jack and I spend endless hours consuming ourselves with whose turn it is to carpool, the cost of braces times three kids, and how much money we need to save for university educations, my engaging new companions come home from work in time to shower and change before heading out for a fabulous night on the town. Weekends for them seem to consist of a leisurely awakening, followed by carefree hours where time is truly their very own to savour. Heading out to the latest trendy bar on a Saturday night, not before attending the toniest art exhibit in town first, while a reality for them sounds more like a fantasy to me. Don't get me wrong; I find this group to be a lively and interesting bunch—brilliant and engaging, vivacious and worldly, but sadly I cannot relate to their world anymore than they can relate to mine.

So how on earth did our conversation steer to a topic that I swore I would never consider, succumb to, or give even the slightest regard of interest to? Is it the joy of the festive season, or is it in fact one too many glasses of Laurent-Perrier? Whichever it is, all I know for certain is that somehow in all of this, somewhere between mention of mod interiors and a dialogue about Miami Beach ultra white interiors, I have agreed to not only consider, succumb to, and give more than a slight regard of interest to, but I have fallen into a hypnotic trance under AnnaLisa's guise for her passion and chosen career path. I have fallen head over heels in love with and agreed to purchase a real, live, and breathing, not to mention untrained, puppy dog! A Yorkshire Terrier puppy dog.

Not a real dog, as Jack will tell you, since real dogs are big and husky, but I on this starry and snowy night agree to purchase a purse dog! What are we thinking? Okay, so maybe it's not a *"we"* thing, it's a *"me"* thing. So what am *I* thinking? Me, *the Simple Girl?* The girl who has sworn off dogs *forever!*

A dog! A real dog! Breathing and with four legs and a tail! I have always maintained *"no dog"* like forever, and I meant it, and I mean it, or at least I thought I did. Seriously, I have no time to take care of a dog. I can barely handle the three kids. Why did I agree to look at those photos?

Why didn't I politely excuse myself and keep working the room? There were other interesting people there. Other people I could have lived vicariously through for a few minutes. Why did I stay? I should have known better than to look at AnnaLisa's iPhone with those damn, adorable doggie pictures.

Imagine, carrying pictures of your poochies around on your iPhone! Then again, I've seen more bizarre things on those phones, so why not your puppies, if that's how you make a living. If I really think about it rationally, it is unbelievably smart thinking on her part. AnnaLisa is a wise businesswoman appealing to the emotional senses of others. Other crazy and sappy people like yours truly. And I on this spellbound night have fallen for it, hook, line, and sinker!

~

Who can sleep? Lying in bed, I do nothing but toss and turn. No, it isn't the champagne, though I almost wish it were, since a hangover does eventually pass—but what have I done? What have I agreed to? I really hate to go back on my word, but I can't go through with this. Who am I kidding? I've never owned a dog before. I haven't even owned goldfish, like ever. I don't know the first thing about taking care of a pet, and one thing is for certain, I don't have either the time or the inclination to learn.

"Jack? Jack? Are you awake?" I sit up, propping myself up on one elbow while resting my tense body above Jack's unresponsive body. Even through the shadowy night air, I can see Jack's chest moving up and down as he sleeps. Sleep? How can he sleep so soundly at a time like this, while I am having convulsions over a pooch I don't even own—yet? "Jack!" My voice squeals in desperation.

Jack's body immediately responds to my cajoling as I shake him repeatedly trying to rouse him.

"Wha … what? What's wrong? Is it one of the kids?"

"No! The kids are all asleep! Jack, I *can't* sleep. Maybe we said yes too quickly to AnnaLisa."

Jack rubs his eyes like a small child might, still in a state of slumber. "What are you talking about Kat? Who's AnnaLisa?"

"Oh my God, Jack! That woman! That woman at Kip's party with the dogs! Remember, the dog breeder?" Is he really so clueless? How could he have forgotten so quickly? Jack looks confused and furious at the same time. Even in the darkness of the night, I can tell that much.

Jack's voice sounds perturbed. "You woke me up in the middle of the night for this? I thought one of the kids was sick or something. And secondly, *we* didn't agree to anything. You did after looking at those stupid pictures of those stupid little dogs that look more like furry rats if you ask me!"

I can't believe this! I am already freaking out enough on my own, and Jack is trying to pin this entire thing on me, and me alone. I ignore his accusations that this is just my doing, preferring to refer to it as a "*we*" thing.

"What are we going to do, Jack? We can't go ahead with this, we just can't!"

I am certain that Jack's reply was premeditated right from the onset of my rousing him. "Go to sleep, Kat, and just forget about it. The damage has been done now. How hard can it be anyways? You just feed the stupid thing and give it some water. Let it go outside once in a while to poop. But do me a favour, next time *we* agree to a dog, make it a real one, not a little yappy thing."

And with that, a sleepy and cranky Jack kisses me abruptly on the cheek, and rolling over onto his side, cocoons his body between the sheets, disregarding my minor and still ongoing meltdown. And so while I sit up and brood over my hasty decision to become a mother of sorts again, my Jack fades back into a blissful and dreamy sleep, leaving me to commiserate all on my own.

Dear Diary,

How hard can it really be to own a dog? I mean, lots of people own dogs, so it can't be such a big deal, can it? I'm the mother of three kids and manage to take care of them pretty well, at least most of the time anyways. A little teeny dog has got to be easier than that, doesn't it? And just think how surprised the kids are going to be when they unwrap their family Christmas present and find a box with the puppy's picture! Now, who's going to win the prize for mommy of the year? I' m just being silly. I'm just tired and overreacting right now, that's all. After all, there are five of us and one of him—how much work can a dog really be? Okay, okay. I should just turn off the light and go to sleep now and forget all about this silliness. Everything is going to be just fine ... I know it will be.

Nighty-Night,
Me, Your Simple Girl

When I wake up in the morning, I don't feel any better about my decision made in haste. Sure, the picture of the puppy was incredibly endearing, with black and tan fur and teeny, round, brown eyes—how could anyone resist him? As much as he resembles a stuffed animal, like the ones you see in toy shops, he isn't a toy. He is real. Really real! He requires walking and feeding and trips to the vet and the inevitable house-training. I have potty trained three kids, hating every minute of it, and now I am going to have to do it all over again, with an animal this time!

No way! Not this girl! I *cannot* go through with this! This is too much, even for me! I need to call AnnaLisa and tell her that we changed our minds!

I search all around my bedroom. Where's the damn phone? Is it possible in a house with five cordless telephones that I can't ever find one in a moment of desperation and panic? What on earth do the kids do with them? And who the hell do they need to talk to on the telephone anyways? Stomping into my closet, I reach in to flick on the light switch, searching to get my pink Juicy Couture velvet housecoat. *Oh shit!* What did I just knock over? Rubbing the sleep from my weary eyes, I look down and find one of the missing telephones. Oops—guess it wasn't the kids after all.

I had written AnnaLisa's telephone number on a piece of paper. Rummaging through my gold chain-link purse, I pull it out, along with most everything else in there—keys, lip gloss, cell phone, and breath mints. The clanking sound of the contents of my purse have made a little too much noise, startling Jack out of his sleep.

"Kat, what are you doing?" Jack sounds annoyed.

"I'm calling AnnaLisa and telling her we made a terrible mistake and after discussing it we've realized we cannot buy one of her puppies."

Jack sits up. It seems that *now* he is ready to discuss my change of heart. I am feeling a strange sense of déjà-vu again—as though we have been here many times before. He pats a spot on the crumpled sheet beside him. "Come here and sit down."

Like an obedient child, I do as told. I look down and begin to nervously twirl the belt of my robe between my clammy fingers. I can't even look at Jack in the eyes because, in some weird way, I am feeling rather childish. "What is it?" I even sound childish.

Jack smiles demurely. "First of all, you can't call AnnaLisa yet. It's 7:30 in the morning, and you're the first one to say that it is rude to call people before 9:00 a.m. unless it's an emergency."

I'll give him that much. I do say that, hating it when people call me early in the morning just to say "hi," as though they don't have the rest of the day to offer niceties.

"But this is different," I argue. This is a quasi-emergency.

"No, it's not," Jack disputes.

"Fine, I'll call her at 9:00 a.m. sharp." I'm determined.

Jack continues his lecture, disregarding what I have obviously just said. "Secondly, we told her we were going to buy one of her puppies, and we will. You're freaking out over nothing."

"This isn't nothing, Jack. We're so busy already between work and the kids—where are we going to fit in taking care of a dog too?" My concerns are valid; even Jack has to admit I am being relatively rational this time.

"I'll help you. We'll do it together. Truthfully I would have preferred a real dog and not a yappy little thing, but maybe this is a good place to start. And besides, he's so small that even when he pees on the floor, how big of a mess will it actually be?" Jack clearly isn't helping my already jittery nerves, finding humour in my angst.

"He's really going to have accidents on the floor, isn't he, Jack?" I panic.

Jack smiles, nodding his head in accord. "And on the carpets too."

"Jack!"

I know that Jack is right. Of course, the dog is going to have accidents. That's why they call it puppy training. *Duh!* House-training is not going to be easy. Potty training the kids was hardly a walk in the park, but I did it. I got through it. Grudgingly, I might add. But that didn't stop me from having more kids after Michael, so why should it stop me from getting a dog for my children? Something they will most certainly love. Something that will become part of our family. I know I am overreacting. That happens to me sometimes when I make a quick decision without thinking through all the implications first. But then when I actually go back and assess it all judiciously, I realize that I was right all along. This is just one of those times. It has to be. I can do this. The kids are going to be over the moon. I can't wait to see their reactions.

~

"Where are you going, Mommy?" Nikki asks, brushing up against me as I carefully apply my usual Bobbi Brown Pale Pink lipstick to my overly red lips—overly red because I have been biting on them all morning due to my anxious state of emotions.

"Oh," I muster with a half-opened mouth, "Daddy and I just have some errands to run, some stuff to buy—just boring stuff like that." I turn around to face Nikki, cupping her delicate chin into my hands. "Auntie Alessia will be coming over to stay with you guys while we're gone."

Nikki has a puzzled look on her face. With a raised brow, she asks, "Since when does Daddy go shopping with you, Mommy? Daddy hates to shop."

Smart kid! Nikki isn't entirely wrong. In fact, she is completely right. Jack detests shopping as much as I detest Sunday afternoon football. There is no appeal for me in watching 250-pound men pounce on one another while a roaring crowd cheers them on. I just don't see the point of it. An unnecessary form of activity and a ridiculous sport is what I think. Jack says the exact same thing about the sport of shopping. So I guess you could say we're even.

I can't very well tell Nikki that what Jack and I are going shopping for is probably the most desired gift under any child's tree this year. At least for one child I know it is. The other two want it just as badly only they are more reserved in their requests, figuring it is wiser to ask for the gifts that they are more likely to receive, relegating the highly unlikely ones to the bottom of their lists.

Does anyone care what I want for Christmas? 'Cause if anyone is asking, I could use a brand-new Louis Vuitton purse. Monogram, of course—my preferred pattern of them all. No, instead I am about to spend a small fortune on a furry little creature and all the paraphernalia that goes along with him. I should really have my head examined!

What is that noise? Not again! From downstairs I hear a cacophony of screaming voices. What on earth is going on down there? I shout down to Jack, asking him what is happening, only adding to the already elevated noise frequency in the house. Since he doesn't respond, I figure he can't even hear me over the screeching voices of Michael and Ella. Not five minutes have passed when out of the corner of my mirror, I see Alessia's face materialize, a teary-faced Ella in her arms. Alessia and I embrace as best we can with my small child in tow.

"What's going on?" I ask, to neither one of them in particular but hoping I might get a straight answer from one of them.

They look at each as if to say, "Who is going to answer the question?"

Alessia speaks first. I figured she would. "Oh, it was nothing really. Just a little scuffle about who was going to answer the door, that's all. Michael beat Ella to greet me, and she got a little upset. But guess who gets to be with Auntie Alessia now!" Alessia's voice goes up an octave, tickling Ella's side and sending her into a fit of childish laughter.

Another major war diverted.

"So where on earth is your mommy going, girls?" Alessia asks in a teasing, rhetorical, I-know-something-you-don't kind of way.

I shoot her a look as if to say, "I'm going to kill you if you spoil the surprise!" She knows precisely where Jack and I are going. I called her this morning after Jack managed to calm me down so I could fill her in on the details. Alessia almost dropped the receiver to the ground when I told her what we were up to. She laughed hysterically.

"Are you kidding, Kat? You? A dog? Now I know you've completely lost all of your senses. While you're at it, do you have a new minivan on order, and maybe you've started wearing Birkenstocks with sweat socks too!"

Alessia evidently thought she was being funny. I suppose in a smallish way she was, since this is completely out of character for me given how I swore I would never change my mind on this dog issue and here I am doing exactly what I said I would never do. But I'm not going to give her the satisfaction of telling her how I had freaked out after agreeing to this. She is already having an enormous laugh at my expense, not that I can blame her or anything.

"Shut up, Less!" I snapped on the telephone earlier. "Maybe it won't be so bad. Maybe a dog will calm me down too, make me more …"

"What? Make you more one with nature? Since when did you become the Mother Earth type, Kat? You, with all the fancy designer clothes and shoes; you, with the perfect hair and nails; you, with more La Mer products on your bathroom counter than at the department store? Come on, every time I see you, it's like you've just stepped out of the shower smelling all perfume-like, *all* the time, and you are going to walk a little dog with your stilettos and like what, pick up dog shit? Tell me, did they come out with Gucci doggie bags, and you want to try them out or something? Is that what this is all about? Oh, wait, let me guess, are you going to be carrying him around in a Louis Vuitton doggie purse à la Jessica Simpson? Of course!"

I let Alessia ramble on until I figured she was done mocking me. "Are you finished yet?" I asked, rolling my eyes at Alessia, as if she could see me telepathically or something. "I think I get your point."

"Do you? Do you really? 'Cause I've gotta wonder if you really do! Kat, you know I'm right with this one. You are SO-O-O not a doggie girl! Who are you trying to fool, Miss New York City Glamorous Mummy?"

So maybe this is a little out of character for me, I admit it. But I really have no clue why Alessia is making such a big fuss out of nothing. I mean lots of people who like designer shoes and bags own dogs. Have a dog as part of their family. Some even have two dogs, and a cat and goldfish, so why not me? Can't I change my mind about something? Have a change of heart?

Dear Diary,

I'm a big girl and a smart girl, so I think I can handle a silly dog! My business is finally blossoming, and the kids are adjusting to school just fine. In fact, a puppy might be just the thing our family needs to connect us again. Jack and I both seem to be working such long hours, and we're running in different directions all the time with the kids. Maybe a dog will make us regroup, unite as a family again somehow. And besides, the kids are a bit older now, old enough to handle the responsibility of a pet, I think. We have so much stuff to be grateful for, so why not learn how to take care of a living and breathing creature? Every dog owner I know tells me how their Charlie or Rambo or Lola has added so much to their lives. Perhaps it will do the same for us. I think a puppy will be good for us. Fantastic actually! I can't wait to see the looks on their faces Christmas morning. This is going to be the best Christmas ever! Just you wait and see!

Later,
Me, Your Simply Elated Girl

Chapter Twenty-Six

Christmas morning! What a Christmas this is going to be! I suppose if I had the actual live puppy dog to hand over to the kids, I would definitely be a contender ... no, make that the first-place winner of the mommy-of-the-year award because really, what better present could there be for a kid than this? At least Jack and I have picked out and paid for our little furry boy, but for now, a photo of him is the best I can give them.

It is barely 5:30 a.m. as I tiptoe quietly down the stairs. I don't want to wake the kids or Jack out of their peaceful sleep on the off chance that visions of sugarplums are still dancing around in their heads. I for one have been roused from my glorious visions of Louis Vuittonland by the rude disruption of my chirping alarm clock letting me know that it is time to put my mommy gears into drive.

As I put a pot of coffee on and lay out a tray equipped with cups, breakfast plates, and homemade cookies, I can't help but feel troubled over Alessia's words to me when I filled her in with the details of our little—on second thought, make that big—surprise for the kids.

Who do I think I am? I am more of a New York City glammy mummy type, not the type who walks the dog while taking her kids to the park. I admit it, I hate taking the kids to the park, but what

I dislike more is those little stones that cushion the playground. I hardly ever take the kids there, in fact, because of them. Does that make me a bad mom? And besides, I know that Alessia didn't mean any harm with her comment; we've been friends forever and ever, always being truthful with one another—maybe a little too honest at times—perhaps this was just one of those times. When your honesty can really hurt someone you care about, quite possibly that's when a little white lie may not be such a bad thing after all.

But what if Alessia is right? What if she really does know me better than I know myself? Is that a possibility? *Naw!* That's unfeasible even for me to comprehend. It has to be. Nobody knows me better than me. Not even Jack, who has known me for what feels like forever now, knows me better than I know myself. Not even my mother knows me that well, and she gave birth to me for God's sake! Not even she knows me anymore. Since my life is so much busier than hers ever was, she can't even begin to understand me.

I have this day—Christmas Day—all planned out and orchestrated like the most melodic of sad love songs, only this one is going to have a happy ending. Each event is going to flow flawlessly into the next with such ease and grace. My plan is brilliant, and the kids have no clue whatsoever about the dog!

As the coffee brews, I plug in the tree lights, the ones that Jack is in charge of arranging year after year. Similar to a conductor in charge of his orchestra members, he must position each one with care, or the sound (or in the case of our tree, the sight) will be off ever so slightly. The trimming of the tree always follows the lead of the conductor, who stands methodically before it ensuring its faultlessness. Once his wand is thrust downward, he is completely confident that he is prepared to take us through the lines of the melody as fluidly as possible. Watching the lights now as they twinkle in the stillness of the morning glow sends a shiver up my spine. For the time being, everything seems so absolutely perfect. How can anything get better than this? I find it remarkable that I, the one who is privy to so many splendid textiles, fine furniture pieces, and the most exquisite crystal accessories available in the retail market, am standing here solely in my pyjamas and sweat socks marvelling in the magnificence of these uncomplicated strings of sparkling white lights.

The sound of footsteps nearing brings my attention back to the present moment, since I am drifting off to my perfect place where time, I truly believe, might actually stand still.

Jack appears shadowlike in the soft shimmer of the Christmas lights. "Merry Christmas, honey," he says, his lips lightly touching mine.

"Merry Christmas to you too." My response is affectionate as I am still in a trancelike state, not wanting to come out of the spell I have been put under by the magic of the vision before me.

As we stand there just enjoying the stillness of it all, a loud voice seems to shout from the rooftops (actually, if you must know the truth, it is in fact a shrill coming from Ella's bedroom), "Merry Christmas, family!" And with that, the echo of silence has been entirely broken, only to be replaced by something far more sweeter sounding.

~

Christmas carols echo harmoniously throughout the house. The kids are engulfed under a sea of colourful wrapping paper, sparkly bows, and sateen ribbons in a rainbow of colours. Ella has already torn open copious amounts of American Girl packaging, courtesy of Santa's last trip to the Big Apple. Michael, with his new earphones tightly fitted into his ears, seems oblivious to the rest of us as he pretends to play air drums; and Nikki, well, Nikki is trying to maintain order and conduct amongst all of us, where clearly none is to be had. I stand leaning in the doorway, sipping my cup of coffee as if all is normal. Which, I suppose, it in fact is, for our home at least.

Jack glances over in my direction as if to ask, "Now?" I nod delicately in agreement. Right on cue, Jack reaches behind the tree for the lone box that remains still neatly wrapped in cerulean-blue and gold polka-dotted wrapping, a shiny gold bow perched loftily on top.

"Wait a sec! What's this?" Jack pretends to be perplexed over the contents of this remaining exclusive package that he holds between his arms.

"Daddy," Nikki cries out, "you know what it is! You're just teasing us!" Nikki is all smiles at Jack's silly antics.

"Me?" Jack's voice sounds shocked.

I interject from where I am standing, pretending to be just as baffled, "What does the tag say, honey?"

Jack holds the box slightly away from his face, as though he is having difficulty reading the tag. "To Michael, Nikki, and Ella. Love, Santa."

I play along. "Another gift from Santa!" I exclaim. "You guys sure got spoiled by Santa Claus this year."

"Oh, Mama, what pretty paper the elves used for this box." Ella's eyes are as enormous as the polka dots on the paper itself and just as sparkly too. I am rather delighted that she likes the wrapping, though she is going to be over the moon once she realizes the meaning of the contents.

"Pretty paper, dumb-head? Who do you think wra ..."

I give Michael that look as if to say, "If you spoil the whole Santa thing for her and blow my cover, I will put you over my knee." Michael is smart enough to decode my look and wise enough to renege on what he was about to articulate.

"Of course, the elves use pretty Christmas wrap, Ella. Do you know any elves that use anything but?" I annunciate my words oh so clearly, the way I usually do when I'm trying to make a point, which, of course, I am now.

"Is someone going to open this?" Jack asks curiously.

"I will, Daddy!" Nikki offers in her sweetest of tones. Jack hands her the box. Nikki examines the box tentatively, further heightening the excitement of what could be inside of it. Slowly, being ever so careful to not tear the wrapping, Nikki gently lifts the elongated pieces of clear scotch tape that hold the paper taut.

"Just rip it open, Nik!" Michael shouts out. "The elves have loads of wrapping paper. We don't need to save it." The boy child smirks at me, perceptive enough to know that I will do anything to preserve Ella's innocent belief in the jolly old bearded man himself. Jack punches him lightly on the arm, male bonding, I presume.

With all the paper off, Ella and Michael can't resist getting their hands on the box too. Michael lifts the lid off. Ella pulls out the generic brown carrier bag (sorry, no Louis Vuitton carrier this time).

Ella looks confused. "Why did Santa give us a purse?" she asks innocently, her nose twisted with curiosity. "Maybe Santa made a mistake and it's for you, Mommy." Ella holds out the carrier for me to take hold of, her face laden with disappointment.

Jack and I giggle. Michael and Nikki look intently at each other incredulously. They are knowledgeable enough about this kind of special purse but seem to be dumbfounded, not quite believing that Jack and I might have actually gone through with it.

"I don't think Santa made a mistake." Jack winks over at me. "Why don't you open it and see what's inside? That might help," Jack suggests to Ella, who still seems just as confused as ever.

Shaking the carrier bag midair, out tumble a menagerie of puppy chew toys, a cozy blanket, and a blue and brown polka-dot dog leash and harness set. AnnaLisa had also been thoughtful enough to give us a snapshot of the puppy we had chosen, so the kids could "ooh" and "ahh" over him until such time as we could actually bring him home. Nikki is the first to take notice of the photo. I had expected no less from my very inquisitive and astute child. With her mouth hanging wide open, she looks over at me in disbelief, not knowing whether to laugh or cry.

"Really, Mommy? This is for real?" Nikki is reserved in her excitement on the off chance that Jack and I are playing some cruel joke on them. I smile and nod my head.

My poor Ella! Her six-year-old brain can't quite process the pieces that have been loosely strung together.

"Thank you, Mommy. Thank you, Daddy!" Nikki runs to each of us, arms wide open.

"Don't thank us; thank Santa," I remark, wondering how long I can keep this façade up.

Nikki bends down to show Ella the photo, all the while explaining to her what all of this means. "See, Ella?" She points to the big brown eyes staring up from the photograph.

"Oh-h-h! He's so cute!" Ella cries in excitement.

"Ella, do you really get it? This is our puppy, and all this stuff, the bag, the toys, they're all for this puppy in this picture." Nikki is thrilled. It is as though she is playing a game of *Clue*. Only this time the who-done-it isn't the butler in the drawing room, but the overzealous mommy at the glitzy party.

Michael stands up and makes his way over to Jack. Maintaining his enthusiasm, he asks somewhat reluctantly, "Are you sure about this? Like really sure?"

"We had nothing to do with this, buddy. I mean, you guys asked Santa for a dog, and he brought this to you, not Mommy and me."

No, of course not, 'cause this mommy swore she wouldn't cave in, but I did! Sucker!

"See, Michael! I told you! I told you that Santa Claus is real! I told you! I told you he would bring us a puppy if I asked nicely!" And to no one in particular, Ella shouts up into the air, "Thank you, Santa!"

Michael looks directly at me, mouthing barely audible words so his sisters do not take notice of him, but ensuring that I do, "And thank you, Mrs. Claus."

Dear Diary,

Could you send me a container so I can bottle this moment right here, right now, please? This moment of absolute peace and joy among these four walls we call our home. Honestly, look around, could it be any more the proverbial Bing

Crosby Christmas right now? Carols are playing, my children's laughter is ringing throughout the house, Jack and I are watching them in thorough amazement as we drink HOT coffee and see them actually get along with each other for once. Wow, this is nice! At the risk of sounding like some teenage kid, this is so-o-o cool! No one is screaming or fighting, no tears are flowing like a river, and no one is bolting out the door late for an appointment or to a kids' activity. We're all just here, just being a family. A normal family! A family that is just living. A family that is just being present in this very moment of sheer contentment and joy. But hold on a minute here, if you don't send me a bottle so I can save this, preserve this memory for later, will it happen again? I mean, can it? Don't take this away from me, please, because when will it ever come back? These feelings, the smiles and laughter, it's all real, really real, but don't tell me that it's all because of a little puppy. It can't be just that, can it? Because if I had known things were going to be like this, I would have bought one for them years ago. It has to be more than this; it just has to be!

Merry Christmas!
Me, Your Simple Girl

Chapter Twenty-Seven

I should have my head examined! Lobotomized is more like it, because clearly there has been a malfunction somewhere up there that requires thorough examination, if not extermination!

Life with this dog is anything but peaceful. In fact, peaceful does not even enter the realm of emotions that I would entertain to describe this miniature fluffy monster. What happened to dog being man's best friend? What happened to unconditional love when you get home ... *blah, blah, blah?* What happened to the serene tranquil moments you are supposed to share with your newfound companion? Because from where I'm standing, my pooch has done nothing but add giant-size problems to my otherwise already frenzied life! How is it that a three-pound pup can cause such havoc and create the workload of a ginormous Saint Bernard? Giving birth to another baby would have been easier than this. Okay, so maybe I'm exaggerating a tad wee bit here (drama is my middle name), but honestly, I'm pooped—no pun intended!

Let me enlighten you with some of the fine points so you can understand what I am going on about. When Jack and I first met our pooch, he was a mere eight weeks old. AnnaLisa explained that she typically allows her puppies to leave her at twelve weeks of age, which suited Jack and me perfectly fine. It would give the kids and us all a chance to get used to the fact that we were beyond doubt going to be welcoming this little ball of fur into our home and into our family. In the interim, we could visit him on a weekly basis. So far, so good.

Once back at home, in the comforts of our serene existence, we all took turns carefully studying his photo, hoping that by scrutinizing it for some time, a name for the pup would mysteriously jump off the image. That never happened, so we took turns going around the room in an attempt to come up with something suitable—a name that would appropriately represent our hound.

Here are some of the contenders: Blackie—no. He isn't all black, and AnnaLisa did say most of his black hair would change to a silvery-grey colour during his first year.

Ella's choice was Spot. *Naw!* Too common.

Nikki suggested Coco.

"May I remind you he is a boy?" Jack interjected.

Michael's pick was Rambo. Though it was endearing, I do have a problem naming a then-two-pound dog Rambo. Michael's argument was that Rambo would grow up to an adult size of a whopping seven pounds. This bit of trivia did nothing to sway me towards his preferred name selection. And besides, Rambo seemed a little harsh and awfully powerful for this *docile* little guy.

"Jack, what do you like?"

"Yeah, Daddy, what do you think we should call him?" Nikki inquires with her usual enthusiasm.

Jack raises his eyes from his computer screen scowling a false disturbance, something he does when he is about to approach a topic with sarcasm. "How about Lucky? Because in looking at my credit card statement, it seems to me he sure is the luckiest dog out there! Look at all this stuff we have for him. I mean really, Kat, is all this paraphernalia necessary? Let's see: a bed, blankets, a set of dishes, toys—we didn't buy this much junk when Michael was born!"

"Oh gee, thanks a lot, I feel loved!" Michael adds in a humorous voice, knowing full well from the hundreds of baby photos we have of him that he never went without the necessities or even the nonessentials of life, not as an infant and certainly not now as a young boy. I nudge Michael.

"You had everything you needed, honey, then and now, and you know it. Furthermore, Daddy knows it too. It's just that some things don't change, and he hated shopping then just as much as he hates it still today. If he doesn't remember buying anything for you, it's because he never did the buying, I did." I offer Jack a smile. He knows I am accurate with my recollection.

"I was too busy working to pay for those things. Looks like I'll be doing the same thing again, only this time it's not for our kids, it's for a dog!"

Touché, Jack! Thank goodness he is only half-serious. The quasi-smile he is sporting on his weary face suggests he isn't gravely upset.

"Oh, Daddy, but he's so-o-o cute! How could you be so angry?" Ella asks adoringly. Leave it to my love child to have her father eating out of her petite hands. Peace, love, and happiness, that's all Ella requires to be content in her life. Since Christmas Day, which was almost four weeks ago now, Ella has studied the photo of the puppy for what seems like hours on end each and every day. I think she truly believes that Jack is angry about all the items that were purchased in preparation of the dog's homecoming. Her young mind being too pure still, Ella does not understand the fine art of sarcasm just yet. With time, she too will comprehend it.

"I've got the perfect name," I suggest. "How about Louis? I gave up a new Louis Vuitton handbag for him."

"*Oh brother, Mom! You would* come up with that." Michael rolls his eyes in jest. "And besides, I thought Santa brought him to us, Mom." Michael smiles, knowing I have just slipped up badly.

Ella looks puzzled. Jack smirks, most likely wondering how I am ever going to talk my way out of this one. Quite frankly, I wonder the exact same thing. Careful not to make eye contact with either Michael or Jack, I look over at Nikki, hoping she might jump in at anytime now and rescue me, as she characteristically does, especially where her younger sister is concerned. The look in her eyes seems encouraging. They twinkle fiercely as if they are saying, "You can do it, Mommy. You can fix this one. I know you can."

I clear my throat, looking down at my fingernails and fidgeting with my wedding band. I begin, "What I meant to say was, I ... I called up Santa on that 1-800-Santa Claus hotline we have and told him how much you all wanted a puppy. Santa said he was fresh out of puppies but had some beautiful Louis Vuitton Monogram handbags ready to deliver to the good mommies out there. And while they may not be the same as a Yorkie puppy their subtle chocolate and tan colouring resembled a Yorkie, sort of, and would that do? Well, I told Santa that although that sounded lovely ... really lovely ... and I was so glad that he was considering me for one of those handbags, I knew that my children desperately wanted a real live puppy, so if there was anything he could do, anything at all, like maybe swap that stunning new Louis bag with another family that was going to receive a puppy, well, I knew my children would be forever grateful."

There!

Did she buy it?

I take a breath and look up, hoping that I have sold my story to someone in the room—that someone in particular being Ella. She is far too young and far too innocent to have her vision of Santa shattered by none other than me! Jack and Michael simply stare at me with stunned faces. If I am reading the expressions on their faces correctly, they are either: a) telepathically attempting to communicate to me, "Are you for real? This is your way out of this one?" or b) forcing themselves to contain their emotions, which in this case, amounts to holding back wholehearted fits of laughter. Fortunately for me, and Ella, they opt for c) none of the above. They say and do nothing, which is a welcome change.

Nikki, sweet Nikki, comes to my aid yet again. God bless her! Running over to me and encircling me with her fragile, thin arms, she breaks into song, "I think Louis is a super name, Mommy! Daddy, Michael, what do you think?"

"Whatever," Michael concedes, apparently still in complete shock over my fable.

"I love it!" Ella shouts with exuberance.

"Whatever makes you guys happy!" Jack adds.

And so, then and there it was decided. Louis it is.

~

It is a mere two excruciatingly long weeks after Louis's arrival, and I collapse into bed, defeated with complete exhaustion.

"Jack, I can't do this anymore. I mean, yeah, he's cute and all, but I've cleaned up more pee-pee and picked up more poop than even I could have ever imagined. He's so little, he barely eats, so how on earth can he shit so much?" I cry. I am feeling hopeless.

Jack laughs. Sitting up and turning to me, he does his best to comfort me. This feels like yet another case of déjà-vu all over again. "Kat, it's going to take some time. AnnaLisa told us it would. Didn't she tell you it was going to be just like having a new baby in the house? Would you send a baby back? You know you can't send him back. You and I both know you won't do that. And besides, what would you tell the kids? They would be heartbroken. Would you tell Ella that Santa wanted him back now so he could give him to the other family and give you back your rightful purse?"

Hmm, I never thought of it that way. "Yes!" I yell out. *I could do that, couldn't I? Even Santa has a right to change his mind on stuff, doesn't he? Oh God, I've lost my marbles!* "I want the Louis Vuitton purse. Me! Really I do!"

"No, you don't. You just think you do. That's just material stuff anyways. A dog, well, a dog is love … and …" Jack's sarcasm is not fooling me for one second.

"No, it's not! And even if it is, I don't care! I'm a materialistic person, Jack!

"But you're not!" Jack chides, pretending to be shocked at my confession.

"But I am! I want the purse! Give me the purse! It doesn't pee on the floor, the leather … oh it has such an intoxicating fragrance to it, and I will never have to feed it or clean poop off its fur again."

"Hair," Jack corrects me.

"What?"

"Hair, a Yorkie has hair, not fur. Remember, that's what you told me when you were trying to sell me on it."

"Jack!" I scream out, "I don't care! *I don't care!* Fur, hair, it doesn't make any difference. I can't do this anymore. I admit it, I'm weak, I made a mistake, okay? *I want my life back!*" I partially cry and partially laugh, burying my face into my pillow, hoping it might muffle my sounds and not wake the kids. I am reduced to a theatrical overexaggerating drama queen by virtue of a teeny tiny animal that I agreed to bring into my home in the first place.

How the hell did I ever get myself into this mess?

Jack seems puzzled. "This is your life," he says very matter-of-factly.

"No, it's not!" I shout out again.

Now I am the one who is perplexed. Am I speaking a different language than Jack? Why is it that husbands do not, cannot understand their wives? Just because we say we want something it doesn't mean in actual fact we do. *Duh!*

"My other life, Jack. The life where I get up in the mornings, run around and get the kids ready for school, go to work making things pretty for people, and come home and run around like a crazy person again—without a dog to attend to! That's the life I am talking about. Not this …"

Wait a minute. What is that noise? No, please God, not again. Oh come on, give me a break, P-L-E-A-S-E. I beg of you!

There it goes again. That sound. Crying. Louis is whimpering. He has to stop soon and go to sleep; he just has to.

But he's not stopping. He is still crying. And now, for the love of God, so am I.

Dear Diary,

This will get easier, right? I'll eventually be able to sleep through the night again, won't I? Like seriously, I want to love him with all my heart, but how can I love something that requires so much work? Yes, he's adorable, and no, I wouldn't give back any of my kids, but this is different. I didn't give birth to him. He's just a dog, for crying out loud! If he could just sleep through the night, then so could I, and I might not feel so miserable and hate him so much. In just a few short hours, I have to get up and go to work, and I'm not sure either one of us can survive the next few hours. So please, could you help me out, just this once? I won't ask again, really I won't ... Okay, so maybe I will, but I can't keep going like this, or I will crumble to pieces and tomorrow, well, tomorrow, my clients, you know the ones, Camilla and Shane, the ones who handed me my dream job, they're expecting big ideas, and I'm not feeling anything but total defeat right now.

Later, but not too much later,
Me, Your Simple Girl

Chapter Twenty-Eight

Days are suddenly turning into weeks. A new year is upon us, and time seems to be moving swiftly, a little too quickly for my liking. Camilla and Shane are eager to get back to New York City to move forward with the apartment renovations. Truthfully so am I. Domestic life has taken its toll on me, and I am ready for glitz and glamour to be resurrected back into my life once more. Real? False? I don't care which form it takes. If it allows me to be content, even if temporarily, and gives me reason to believe that there is still hope, then I'll take it. Hope that this is just a transitory period of my life and that there is so much more waiting on the other side after all of this subsides. There is no way that my life could have been reduced to the trials and tribulations of daily domesticity all over again by simply getting a dog, yet it feels as though it has. I know for a fact that I did not sign up for this. Okay, so maybe in a roundabout way I did, because I did agree to Louis, but I didn't agree to the chaos that came along with him. Had I known it was going to be like this, I would have never let my guard down. But I did, and the rest, as they say, is history. What seems to matter most now is that I pull myself together—and promptly, because I am beginning to feel like someone else. I don't know who that person is, but the one thing I do know for sure is that she and I are not getting along so well.

For the time being, the drama in my clients' lives does not seem to compare with the drama that has been created inside my very own four walls. How was I supposed to know that Louis would bolt for the door at precisely the same time as I was closing it? This *minor* incident resulted in Louis's paw being struck by a heavy, swinging, steel door. A wounded doggie paw can only signify one thing as I'm racing out the door, already late. It means that pretty soon I might as well kiss my dream job bye-bye because now *a little late* is going to be the understatement of the year. And how exactly am I going to explain this one without sounding like a complete idiot or a fantastic storyteller?

My yelping three-pound dog means one thing and one thing only—an emergency trip to the vet. And as my bad luck should have it, this emergency vet appointment equals an astronomical bill, namely, to the tune of $830.58. Though on the bright side—if there is a bright side—my very small puppy is donning the latest silicone fashion accessory over his pint-size head due to his scraped paw, so if nothing else, he looks even more adorable and stuffed-animal-like. Even after a further cost of $67.89 for antibiotics for Louis, all we ended up with was a furious Jack, sad children, and a guilt-stricken me.

It has become abundantly clear to me lately that my career is getting in the way of my home life. A much wiser person from the outside looking in might think that, in fact, it is the other way around. Either way, I have no idea which direction to run to any longer. The one thing I am perfectly clear about is that something has to give. A balance has to be found or at the very least searched for, or I am going to have a nervous breakdown. And honestly that isn't a real feasible option for me given *how much shit I still have to do!*

~

"What do you mean you had to cancel your appointment because of Louis?" Alessia sounds puzzled.

I needed to call someone and vent, or at least have someone take pity on me. On second thought, perhaps Alessia was not the ideal candidate for this position, but I am weak and in this moment of weakness, who else can I call if not my best friend? I sit cradling Louis in my arms, uncomfortably I might add, since his plastic cone head is getting in the way of a peaceful encounter between the two of us. I want to hear a sympathetic voice—I *need* to hear a sympathetic voice—because, let's face it, between my role as Louis's nursemaid and his new headgear, he is covered from all angles, but I'm not.

"He got caught in the door, Less. What was I supposed to do?" I cry in frustration.

"Leave him in his doghouse and go off to your sensational job! Kat, you've really lost your mind. You need to see a shrink!" *Tell me something I don't already know.*

"I couldn't do that," I say, gazing down at Louis. I am stroking his back, trying to make him more restful and ease my guilt at the same time. Since I am the one who inflicted pain on the poor animal, the least I can do is try and make him feel snug now. Finally after many attempts, Louis finds a comfortable position and at last falls asleep in my arms.

"Kat, may I remind you that you have finally landed the client of your dreams, and you have now cancelled an important meeting because of your stupid dog? Are you crazy? You just can't do that. Do you realize how much damage you've just done?"

I take a slight offence to Alessia's reference to Louis as *stupid*. Evidently she knows nothing about the intelligence of my puppy. We have already been working on the command "sit" with him, which I might add, he follows ... sometimes ... okay, just once, but that's a positive start. I decide to share this wealth of knowledge with Alessia, though why, even I'm not sure. Approval perhaps?

All I succeed in accomplishing is to provoke her into a rendition of her infamous lawyerish laugh, the snicker that is one part "Are you a fucking moron" with two parts "I cannot believe we are having this useless conversation."

"Kat, he's not one of your kids, hon, he's a dog! A dog! Remember, a four-legged animal? God, you've gone mad!"

I figure now is as good a time as any to end this conversation, realizing that it is pointless to try and defend my actions to Alessia. I do value her opinion most of the time, but now it is just starting to plainly get on my already frayed nerves.

Louis continues to sleep on my lap, stirring every so often and then adjusting himself to a new and more restful position. I am just as sleep deprived as he is, wishing that I could be the one lulled to sleep. I look down. My fingernails are uneven and jagged due to the constant wiping up of the floor. I need a manicure desperately. I can't remember the last time I allowed my hands to look so sheepish, always claiming the importance of well-groomed fingers, especially in my job, where I frequently make use of my hands to show items to clients, mostly expensive fabrics that are par for the course. My mental state of mind is somewhat tattered today given all the activity that has ensued. Maybe a soothing cup of camomile tea might help, though if I attempt to move, Louis might wake up too. Forget it, I'll brew some tea later; for now an apology e-mail to Shane and Camilla might be more valuable. If nothing else, it will make me feel a little more at ease; and with any luck, it will work to do the same for them.

Hi, Camilla,

Sorry for the short notice on cancelling our appointment today. As I mentioned to you, a family medical emergency arose, and I had to attend to it immediately. I realize Shane is quite anxious to move forward, but please feel reassured, so am I. Could you kindly let me know when he is available next and I will accommodate his schedule accordingly.

With kindest regards,
Katarina

Okay, so maybe I am telling a little white lie. It's not as though there is no truth to it at all. It was a medical emergency, and it most definitely needed attending to immediately. I mean, you should have heard the poor little guy howling. So what that it is my dog and not a human person? I don't have to share that. Some things are sacred.

So maybe Louis is starting to grow on me. So what? He's still a ginormous pain in the ass. But he's my ginormous pain in the ass. So why then didn't I just offer the truth to Camilla? I do believe she would be very understanding; of that I have no doubt. But Shane, well, Shane is another story. Mr. Corporate Mentality Man would have never comprehended why I did what I did; he would have thought I was just as extreme as Alessia does. So, I have no choice but to tell a modest fib—just a little white lie—and nobody gets hurt, so really then, what's the biggie?

> Dear Diary,
>   So the thing is, I lied to my clients today, something I promised myself I would never do. But see, real life got in the way—my real life, that is—and I couldn't just ignore it. Well, I suppose I could have, but I wouldn't do that, so I had to make a choice, and I chose to not tell the complete and whole truth. Sure, my career, my clients, this particular project mean the world to me, but where do you draw the line between focusing on your dream and allowing everything else to take a backseat? And besides, the dream job is still there; I just had to put it on hold for a little while today, that's all. It will still be there tomorrow. It's still there now. And Louis, well, I took him in, so I guess he's my responsibility now too. Not like I didn't know that before, but I'm starting to understand a pet owner's mentality better now, and how they can fall in love with their pets, because I think I have too, or at least I am starting to. My little guy is totally dependent on me for his care, and I wasn't going to let him down today. I couldn't, I just wouldn't. So what?

*Let the Shanes and Alessias of the world think
that I'm crazy; people are going to think what
they want to think anyways. I can't do anything
about that. I know what I have to do and what
is important to me, and I was not going to leave
this house today ignoring my first responsibility.
I'll make it up to my clients, I always do.*

*Later,
Me, Your Simple Girl*

~

Days have passed, and at long last, I make it out to meet with Shane and Camilla. Though I am only too aware that Shane is less than impressed with me, again, I maintain my stance of not allowing him to intimidate me, though he certainly tries.

"We'll need to get back to New York to see what progress is being made in the apartment." Shane speaks to me with such an authoritative voice, you would have thought I was a child being reprimanded for misbehaviour. I believe that he is questioning how committed I actually am to his project.

"Of course, I will work my schedule around it. I promised you I would fly over with you as often as needed, and that hasn't changed." I make sure to keep my tone even and not sound defensive. *Seriously, Shane, meetings get postponed all the time. And besides, I'm not performing brain surgery here. Who said I was at your beck and call anyways? So please stop power tripping just because you feel as though you can boss me around.*

"Right ... well then ... I've got to get to the office." Shane speaks matter-of-factly as he eyes the large gold wristwatch on his arm—no doubt an expensive Rolex or Cartier. I have never gotten close enough to him to figure out which one it actually is, though the bulky watch face itself is a clear indication that this guy is serious when it comes to time.

As Shane gathers his belongings before making his exit, Camilla sits reasonably still on the sofa, continuing to sip her coffee while gazing attentively right through the room. I interpret this as habit more than genuine interest. I, on the other hand, rifle through my file that I have now extracted from my portfolio, pulling out photos of furnishings I want to consider with Camilla. Concepts for different looks for the living and dining spaces, which I anticipate with hope that she will express interest in.

At last, with Shane's departure, Camilla seems to breathe a genuine sigh of relief. Let's face it, so do I. "Camilla," I begin, my tone contrite, "I do want to once again apologize for cancelling on such short notice ..."

Camilla interjects midsentence, "Really, dear, no apology is necessary, I completely understand. These things happen. It's just a part of life."

"Camilla, I didn't mean to insult him by disregarding his time by any means." I am well aware that I sound defensive.

"Of course not, dear. Don't give it another thought."

I know she's right. Fortunately I manage to get us back on track almost immediately. We pick up the pieces and continue to discuss the apartment once again.

"So I've been thinking, Camilla, rather than a standard matte finish on the walls, why don't we incorporate something different? Something that is more lustrous to the touch and more brilliant to the eye. How would you feel about something like that?" I ask.

"What are you suggesting, Kat?"

"What if we use a glossy paint finish on all the walls in the apartment? Not too shiny," I add, "but enough sheen so that we catch some light reflection off the walls and onto the furnishings? The whole thing will sparkle ever so faintly. Believe me, it won't be garish, but I do think the walls will look glowing, with a soft patina to them. We can have the painters try it on one wall first—so you can have a look and ensure that you like it."

Camilla smiles in my direction. This is the first smile I have seen on her face since my arrival almost an hour ago. "I think that sounds quite striking, Katarina," is all she says.

We continue to make conversation, albeit it seems somewhat strained. I take the opportunity now to broach my concept for the library, since I know she is an avid reader, hoping I might release some excitement here.

"Now for the library," I continue with fervour. "I am so excited about this space because I know how much you love to read, so I want this room to completely engage you whenever you set foot inside it. You told me once that particularly in the evenings or when you are alone that you enjoy relaxing and reading in a comfy space. But I want you to cherish this space daytime and nighttime, so what I am thinking is to use deep eggplant-coloured velvet upholstery on a tuxedo-style sofa. It will be unbelievably elegant but not too feminine." (I know this is one of Shane's strict requirements). "Built-in bookshelves in Antique Yew Lustre, courtesy of Clive Christian again, can act to enhance the space with a rich, warm feel. I want you to feel completely cocooned inside this room, Camilla." (A feeling I know will placate her when her husband fails to).

"It all sounds marvellous. Really, it does," is all she can rally. I want to believe her but don't. I am more of the opinion that she really has no interest if the cabinets are yew or pine any longer. Though physically Camilla might be present, emotionally she is a million miles away. No matter how hard I try, talk of lustre paint finishes and velvety fabrics does relatively little to engage her enough to be mentally present.

"And, of course, together we can look for just the right accessories, if you'd like, that is. I saw some gorgeous Kelly Wearstler pieces when we were in New York. Interesting accessories in metal finishes, just the right accents for your place, though of course you will have to agree, but I think you just might. We can take a look when we go back." I feel very enthusiastic, though I wish I can say the same for Camilla, who clearly is not feeling my bravado.

"Camilla, are you all right?" I question. "You seem rather quiet. If you don't like my ideas, you can just say so and I can make some other recommendations, maybe more traditional pieces like blue and white porcelain china or Wedgewood, something different?"

Camilla stares right through me. *Oh no, I think she is about to break down yet again.* But she doesn't. She stops herself. She just sighs intensely and murmurs, "Of course, dear. Nothing is wrong, I'm fine."

~

Driving home, vivid images of our meeting keep popping up inside my head. Poor Camilla. What should be so much fun, so enjoyable for her, doesn't appear to be shaping up that way at all. This is not how it is supposed to be.

My thoughts are interrupted by the ringing of my cell phone. My call display screen tells me it is Connor—thank goodness! I haven't heard from him or Jonathan in weeks. And to make matters worse, my umpteen telephone calls and voice-mail messages to them have gone unreturned, making me positively inquisitive as to what is going on. It seems as though everything has just been left in limbo, and I haven't the faintest idea why. Last we spoke, they seemed positively elated with the progress we had been making on dressing up their condo, and with the baby's arrival imminent, I would have thought that they would be more eager to have things finalized by now. Not to mention that I have already spent countless numbers of hours sourcing furniture and fabrics and spending time with the electrician ensuring that fixtures are hung in precisely the exact locations we discussed. I cross my fingers, hoping that he is calling for a status report on arrival dates of pieces that have been ordered.

My concepts for their apartment are turning out to be exciting, with a look that will be fun and fresh, just as exuberant as the homeowners themselves. Flowers and fauna, bold patterns and soft textures, it is truly going to be such a happy space by the time we are finished with it. I am so keen to share some of my recent finds for the nursery. I located the most perfect coral-pink area rug, with black princess crowns embossed on it. What a gem! Okay, so the price tag that goes along with it is a little hefty, but I am hoping that they will be receptive to it given how much they are anticipating the arrival of this baby and want her nursery to be as perfect as perfect can be. Jonathan is going to be elated when I show him the photo of it—I am positive! I can always count on Jonathan for his energetic enthusiasm. But I have to admit that time is really beginning to be of the essence now, or I may be disappointing them and may not be able to deliver items in time for the baby's arrival. If I'm not mistaken, the baby is due to arrive in approximately ten weeks, not a long time when you're trying to get the whole house in tip-top condition. Fortunately the electrician has already installed the most luminous crystal chandelier in the baby's room. And get this, the pièce de résistance is a Louis XVI-style bergère chair in soft baby-pink crushed velvet, which sits in one corner of the room with—are you ready for this?—an identical one in a miniature version for the princess baby! It will be there and ready to welcome the baby home when she arrives! Do you believe it? This nursery is going to be a princess paradise for this much-loved baby girl, and I for one couldn't be happier for them since they have been anticipating this moment for what feels like an exceptionally long time!

"Katarina, this is Connor." His voice sounds sombre.

"Connor, is everything okay?" I put on my cheeriest voice, hoping it might coax him out of his mood.

"Have you ordered everything for the nursery already?"

"Gosh, yes! It's all under control, Connor. There is nothing for you and Jonathan to worry about. It should all be arriving soon, and once it all does …"

"Can you cancel it? Cancel everything? All of it?"

"What? What are you talking about, Connor? Why do you want me to cancel it? What's happened?"

"The baby's gone, Kat."

What? Connor and Jonathan are not the type to jump into anything without checking and double-checking all the details first, so that anything could go wrong with something as significant as this is utterly unfathomable to me.

"Connor ... I'm sorry ... I don't understand. What do you mean 'gone'?"

It sounds as though Connor is doing his best to fight back tears. He chooses his words to me carefully. "The baby had to be delivered by emergency C-section yesterday. There were complications ... she was stillborn. Our baby is gone. She's not coming home." Connor is beside himself with anguish.

Dear God, please tell me this is not happening! What do I say? What do I say that doesn't minimize what he's just shared with me?

How could something so terrible happen to two such wonderful people? Two people that I know for a fact will actually make the most wonderful of parents? If anyone is deserving to raise a child, these two people are it. This is so not fair.

I pull my car over to the side of the road. I have to. Tears have flooded my eyes, making it next to impossible for me to see the road clearly. I try to regain my composure, unsuccessfully, since now the tears are flowing freely and there is no way for me to stop them.

Connor goes on to explain to me that it was just one of those fluky things. Everything had been going so well throughout the pregnancy, uneventful in fact, but recently their surrogate had been feeling a bit "off." At yesterday's doctor's visit, a heartbeat was no longer detected. The baby had to be delivered since she was only weeks from being due.

"Kat, she was beautiful." Connor's voice is filled with melancholy.

My voice is laden with sorrow. "I believe she was." I cannot hide my sadness.

"She had the most angelic face you've ever seen. Her face was so round and sweet. And her skin was the softest baby skin you could have ever touched. My baby ..." Connor is beside himself with anguish. All my attempts to pacify him are to no avail. I feel so hopeless for myself, but mostly for Connor, completely aware that nothing I can possibly say or do can lessen his pain.

Through my tears I ask, "How is Jonathan?"
"Inconsolable" is all Connor tells me. There is nothing in this
world that he wanted more than a child of his own, and for now
his dream has been bitterly taken away from him.

Dear Diary,

*Could you tell me why bad things have to
happen to good people? Jonathan and Connor
were so excited about this baby—their baby.
Finally they were going to have the family they
so desired and deserved to have, and yet it just
wasn't meant to be for them. It just seems so
unfair to me. I know that I am supposed to believe
that everything in life happens for a reason, but
honestly right now I can't think of one good
reason at all for this to be happening. And if you
can, maybe you could share it with me, because
I would like to know, just so I can understand
this better. Who knows, perhaps with time, we'll
understand ... maybe in time, Jonathan and
Connor will be able to come to terms with this
and make peace with it, and maybe, just maybe,
with time the overwhelming hurt and pain they
are feeling right now will go away. But for now,
two unbelievably good people are grieving the
greatest loss a parent can suffer, and that really
sucks! If somehow, someway, you could ease their
pain, I would really appreciate it.*

*Later,
Me, Your Simple Girl*

I manage to drive slowly and carefully the rest of the way home.
As a parent, I know how much I worship and cherish my children
and how wanted each one of them had been.

I unlock my front door, fully aware of just how abundantly
privileged I am to be walking into a space filled with people and

things that have such special importance to me. People who cannot be replaced, and things associated with these people that are laden with cherished memories—things that only mean something because of the people who I am able to share them with. Otherwise, those things, they mean nothing. Nothing at all.

Chapter Twenty-Nine

Winter is upon us with a vengeance. So much for the *Farmer's Almanac*, which claimed it was going to be a mild one. While the billowing snow gives off the appearance of being fluffy and tranquil as it cascades to the frozen ground, I know better than to be fooled by this calming façade. The deep-freeze temperatures we've been experiencing lately do nothing more than contribute significantly to the accumulation of the powdery white substance.

"Why do I have to wear all of this stuff? It makes me too hot!" Ella proclaims as I wrestle her into her winter apparel one frigid morning. I do my best to ignore her fidgeting and focus on just getting her dressed, fully aware that if I give in to her now, I will never get her out the door, making us our usual fashionably late.

"You have to wear all of these clothes so you can stay warm and dry while you play outside in the snow and have lots and lots of fun," I explain as I secure her hat onto her head, the final piece of apparel before setting her on her way.

"Let's go, Ella, or we're going to be late for the bus!" Nikki shouts in her usual distinctive manner. Nikki is a stickler for punctuality.

Michael brushes past me, making a beeline for the door in the hopes that I am too caught up with Ella to take notice of him. I am distracted, but not enough so that I am oblivious to him. I manage to stop him dead in his tracks. When I grab hold of the back of his jacket, he comes to an immediate and abrupt halt.

"What?" He sounds puzzled.

"*What?*" I repeat, questioning his question. "Where are your boots, Michael? Where is your hat? It's awfully cold outside."

"I have my gloves on, Mom, I'll be fine."

"No, you won't, Michael. You'll get your feet all wet and your head will get cold, and then you'll wind up sick. So may I suggest you hurry up and get on some more clothing quickly?"

"But I am dressed," he retaliates.

"Not to my standards, you're not."

"You worry too much!" Michael professes.

"Move it, Michael!"

"Aggh! You guys are so frustrating!" Nikki is at her wits' end. "Hurry up!"

Michael stomps away, only to return moments later wearing his winter hat and winter boots, no more and no less than I asked for. Snow pants would have been a bonus in my books, but since I hadn't mentioned them before, it was too late for me to do so now without an all-out war taking place.

The kids are off! Another morning ritual concluded with relatively little catastrophe.

I make the short journey down the hallway to my office and sit down in front of my computer screen. One by one, I watch as each new e-mail pops up onto my screen. Louis has dutifully followed me into my office and is now rolled up in a tight round ball snuggling comfortably at my feet. I can't help but smile down at him. It wasn't that long ago that I was positive he was going right back to AnnaLisa, and now today as I stare down at him, I realize just how much joy he has brought to our family.

Hmm, an e-mail from Alessia sent late last night. I wonder what that is all about, since she very well knows that I hardly ever turn on my computer late into the evening. I click on it, figuring nothing like the present moment to find out.

Hi, Kat,

OMG!

Call me as soon as you read this!

I have great news to tell you!

Less

xo

Knowing Alessia the way that I do, I bet that Cass—a.k.a. Mr. Wonderful—has done something even more wonderful, if that is at all possible since up until now he has been a complete gem—a precious gem she still keeps at arm's length. *I don't get it!* My guess is that she is afraid of becoming too attached to him, so she won't let herself fall under his spell. But I'm not about to give her advice in the love department, since God only knows that if I do try and say something, she will bite my head off! I grab hold of the telephone and dial her cell number.

She answers on the first ring—a sign that her cell phone has been glued to her waiting for my call. Alessia very seldom shares her cell number with anyone, especially clients, since those who do have the number have no qualms about calling day or night, quite literally, I might add. And even more infrequently will she dare to answer her cell phone during work hours, should it ring, since every minute of her day needs to be accountable for in accordance with the firm. Any business calls have to get to her via the company receptionist.

"So do tell, please!" I ask in a playful voice, opting out of the usual niceties.

"You are not going to believe this, Kat! You are not going to believe what happened last night!" I haven't heard Alessia this enthusiastic about anything in a very long time.

"So then tell me, please. I'm dying to know!"

"You are talking to the newest associate partner at *Brownstein, Roberts and Associates!*"

Alessia is ecstatic. She has every right to be. If anybody deserves being made an associate partner, she is definitely the person. Ever since her breakup from Marcello, she has put so much vigour into her work. In fact, she does very little else but work. Until lately, that is. It's only been very recently that I have seen Alessia happier, moderately more content, since she has started dating Cass. But still she maintains some reservations, and most definitely never lets her guard down, ever! Though Alessia has always been dedicated to her work, after her breakup, she jumped in with both feet first and has seldom looked back. I figured it would only be a matter of time before the firm would have to recognize the insane number of hours she has billed over the past sixteen months. I'm just thankful the time has finally arrived.

I congratulate her profusely. "We need to celebrate! Are you up for dinner on Friday night?" I offer, thrilled with her news.

"I have a better idea," Alessia responds.

What can be better than a good meal and a fabulous bottle of wine?

"Come and look at a house with me."

At first, I think Alessia is joking. Evidently she isn't. I have always known her to be a little impulsive, but now with her new position and healthy bonus under her wing (or in her wallet), she is obviously ready to spend. And who better to help her?

"Are you sure about this, Less? Maybe you should wait a bit, let the new job settle in first?" I don't want to seem like a downer or anything like that, but I think it might be a good idea to be mildly cautious and wait until the bonus cheques have cleared the bank first.

"Okay, right, thanks for the lecture, Miss Goody-Two-Shoes, I hear you. But forget it ... so ... are you going to come with me, or am I going solo?

"Less, of course I will come with you. All I was trying to say was ..."

"I know what you were trying to say, but I'm not listening to you. And besides, you promised me you would decorate my place when I finally got one, and now it looks like I might finally be getting it. So please, just shut up and be happy for me, and come and see this house since this could be the one!"

"And I am happy for you, Less, it's just that maybe ..."

"Maybe what?" Alessia sounds irritated.

I retract my thoughts. I have to believe that she knows what she is doing.

"Maybe nothing. Of course, I'll come with you!" I say immediately. And I mean it. Friday night it is, and I can't wait.

After our conversation, I continue to check my e-mails.

Amazon—delete; no more new books for the time being. I still have a whole pile of unread ones from my last order.

Dell—software update—delete.

Neiman Marcus—del ... no, on second thought, leave that one. I'll open it later.

Shane. *Oh-oh.* I'd better read this one.

> Hello, Katarina,
>
> Things seem to be moving quite nicely on the New York apartment. A trip over for a couple of days is appropriate at this time.
>
> Would late next week work, say Thursday or Friday? Please advise my assistant as soon as possible so that she can make the appropriate arrangements.
>
> Regards,
>
> Shane Saunders, CEO-SWS International Corporation

I sigh deeply. I suppose next week will work. With everything at a standstill with Jonathan and Connor, and Kip's apartment almost completed, save for some minor accessories here and there, my workload seems to be manageable for the time being.

I call Jack.

"Think you can handle the fort if I go away for a couple of days next week?" I ask, wholly aware of what Jack's response will be.

"Of course."

"I'll only be gone one night. Back before the weekend even starts."

"Hey, what's wrong? You don't seem very excited about going. What gives?"

He's right. I don't feel very eager this time around. Not like the last time, and certainly I'm not feeling the excitement I had been feeling when the idea of working in the Big Apple was simply my dream, not a reality.

"I don't know, Jack, maybe the novelty's worn off. It seemed so much more thrilling and fun when things were good, but now my clients are at odds with one another and I told you about my other big job. That couple is just so sad right now that what I do just doesn't seem so important. I guess it all just seems so irrelevant in the grand scheme of life. It's just stuff, Jack—what I do is just create rooms full of stuff for people."

Whoa! Did I just say all that? More importantly, do I actually mean it?

"But that's what they hire you to do, Kat, and you're great at it. You're just sad for your clients because that's who you are. You're a touchy-feely person with a big heart, and that's what makes you special."

"I understand what you're saying, Jack, but it just doesn't seem as important anymore when so many unpleasant things are happening to them."

"Maybe you're just beginning to realize that all of that *stuff* on its own doesn't mean all that much after all."

I think about what Jack says for a few seconds. "Yeah. Maybe," I say. But I already knew that. The only difference now is that for the first time, I am working on projects that are faced with real challenges—major life challenges, not plumbing issues or oops, the-sofa-is-too-big-for-the-room issues, but real life, real people challenges. Not even French silk or all the plush velvet in the world can fix these problems.

"Tell you what," Jack continues, "since you're going to be going to New York anyways and the weekend follows, why don't I fly down with the kids and meet you there? We can all stay the weekend."

I'm stunned. Am I hearing him correctly? "You want to come to New York and bring the kids and walk and shop and do all that stuff that you absolutely detest doing? In the dead of winter on top of it all? Are you feeling all right, Jack?"

"Well maybe not shop ... do I have to shop? And it's going to be too bloody cold to walk outside for any length of time, but I'm sure there'll be plenty of other things we can do together. And besides, you're always reading that Louise book to the girls and they seem so impressed with the Plaw-w-w-za Hotel, maybe now might be the right time to show it to them firsthand."

I have to giggle. "It's not Louise, Jack, it's Eloise—*Eloise at the Plaza*."

"Whatever. You know what I'm talking about. So what do you think? Should we come and meet you there on Friday night and make a family weekend out of it?"

I'm entirely taken aback by Jack's extraordinarily sweet gesture. He is trying so hard to make me feel better. This is one offer I am simply not going to refuse.

~

Jack decides to surprise the kids at dinnertime with the news of our mini-holiday getaway.

"New York? Really, Mommy? We get to come with you?" Nikki is in awe. Even at her tender young age, she is already beginning to understand and appreciate my fascination with the city that never sleeps.

"And we really get to live with Eloise, Mama?" Ella asks in amazement.

I giggle at her innocence. "Well, we won't get to live with Eloise, honey, but we will be staying at the same hotel Eloise lived in."

"Will we get to see her?"

"Well, sort of. You know that Eloise isn't a real person, right? She is make-believe—a character in a book—but we will be able to have tea like Eloise does in the story and see the room that Eloise slept in."

This is more than sufficient information to thrill Ella. She is giddy with joy that she is actually going to be staying at the Plaza. And quite frankly, so am I.

Jack glances over at Michael, who continues to shuffle food around on his plate, deciding to not eat much of it. Somehow I don't imagine that Eloise is nearly as enchanting to a ten-year-old boy as she is to his younger sisters.

"So, Mikey, tea with a bunch of dolls sounds like fun, doesn't it?" Jack is wearing a coy look on his face—the look he wears when he is up to something.

"Yeah, that sounds just great, Dad. It's gonna be a lot of fun. I can't wait." Michael's tone chimes suspiciously of sarcasm. I do know one thing where Michael is concerned: though not amused about spending an afternoon with copious numbers of dolls, he would never ruin the excitement for his sisters by complaining. Michael is a caring brother in that regard.

"Anyways, you're not going to believe what happened today. So there I am on the Internet, just surfing different sites, and somehow I manage to get onto this website that sells hockey tickets. So I poke around in there for a while, and can you believe it? This page pops up and says something about a Rangers game at Madison Square Garden next Saturday afternoon—the day we actually happen to be in New York. What are the chances?"

Yeah, right, what are the chances? I smile at Jack. I understand exactly where he is going with this.

Michael stares right up at Jack while at the same time trying to contain his excitement on the off chance his surmising might be wrong. "Really, Dad? There is?"

"But then I thought, naw, Mikey will probably want to stay with his sisters and go and have tea or check out the cute little girls in that pretty doll store. I figured you probably weren't going to be interested in going to see a hockey game—besides, we can do that here at home. In New York City, we're going to do touristy stuff like ..."

Michael's face has gone from elated to sullen in a matter of seconds.

"Enough, Jack," I cry out. "Stop teasing him."

Jack smiles at Michael. "Buddy, of course, I ordered us a couple of hockey tickets. Do you think I'd make you sit through a tea party with dolls, or whatever it is they are going to be doing? Not a chance."

Michael's face changes from solemn to elation. He is beaming from ear to ear with happiness. "Thanks, Dad, that's so cool! Wait till I tell the guys!"

The sound of children in our kitchen has suddenly become loud and uncontainable once again, but this time around, I don't mind the noise even a slight bit. A wide smile comes across my face. I look over at Jack before saying a word. I don't want the kids to hear me. But there is very little chance of that happening since they are in their glory laughing and shouting and are paying absolutely no attention to us.

"Thank you for being so thoughtful," I say.

Steadily this trip is shaping up to be an extraordinarily pleasurable one after all. It is no longer going to be solely a business trip, but a chance to spend time with my family in a location I can't imagine sharing with anyone else. Because, let's face it, there's no point in going to incredibly fabulous places if you can't enjoy them with the people you care about the most.

Dear Diary,

This is what it's all about, isn't it? Moments like this. Life is all about these teeny tiny moments in time. When I string them all together, this is what makes up what my life is all about. Imagine, then, how much we miss out on when we don't seize those moments. When we forget about them, or pay little attention to them, thinking that they're unimportant when in fact they actually shape who we really are. Moments with our family, moments with our kids, moments with our friends and colleagues—this is what makes for a great life. Even moments with our clients—the good and the bad ones, that's all we truly have. All of these fragments of time and all of these events—the happy and the sad ones—this is what makes each and every one of our lives unique and sacred, isn't it? All we can do is try our best to make these moments special and memorable. When times aren't so good—and sometimes they're not—we have to do our best to try to get through them the greatest way we know how. Maybe that's when we ask for help, talk about what's troubling us with the people we care about. The important thing is that however we choose to deal with our issues, what we need to keep in mind is that we have to focus on getting through it and pushing forward. Always push forward; never look back. Maybe that's the secret, then? Could I have discovered something here?

Later,
Me, Your Simple Girl

Chapter Thirty

I am back in New York City yet again.

Only this time is different. This time my presence here doesn't seem nearly as momentous. My meeting with Shane and Camilla is equally as important as the last time, if not more so, since we are finalizing the installation of hard surfaces and this time around need to discuss the finishing touches for their space. It's often these very details that can make or break a project.

The excitement all around me in the streets still lingers, and the buzz of the city is still omnipresent. The city that never sleeps is fully awake and entirely rocking, but still something feels completely different this time around. No matter how I try to dissect the equation, no matter how many various ways I attempt to examine it, the common denominator always comes back to me.

I am different. I am looking at my role here in this city and my position in this job from a completely different perspective this time around. And for the very first time in my adult life, I think I'm perfectly okay with it.

~

I give a gentle knock on the apartment door, protocol if truth be told, since I don't wait for anyone on the other side to answer it and permit my entry. I ease the door open carefully, since I never know who could be standing there, like say, a contractor on a ladder and oops, I accidently knock him over! It's not as though that has ever happened to me or anything like that, but I'm just saying, it could happen!

"Hello?" I call out to no one in particular.

"In here!" a familiar voice shouts back to me. It belongs to Camilla, and it sounds as though it is coming from somewhere near the vicinity of the kitchen.

As I make my way towards her, I take notice of the progress I encounter along the way. The marble tiles have been laid down in the vestibule, and they look fabulous. They lend a characteristically classic and stately presence to the entrance and set a formal tone immediately once you set foot inside the front door. The neoclassical cornice moulding, while ornate and over-the-top, makes such a bold statement, performing the exact function we had intended it to. Tall baseboards with an uncomplicated profile have been installed throughout, and the painting of the apartment appears nearly complete, casting a faint glow throughout. From what I can see through the heavy construction paper taped to the hardwood floors, they too have been refinished to a smooth and satin sheen. Even with construction dust and debris circumventing all around, I can still see that everything is coming together brilliantly and, more importantly, as intended. Now this is what I call characteristic New York City glamour in all of its brilliance! I am satisfied, to say the least, with what I have laid eyes on so far, hoping and praying that my clients are equally as thrilled.

Please tell me that the rest of this place is just as fantastic! I approach the entryway to the kitchen and come to a sudden halt. My eyes do a little dance from one side of the kitchen to the other. *Oh my God! Oh my God! Oh my God!* This space, this room is breathtaking! I almost can't believe just how beautiful it in fact looks now that it is real and here. Was I really the one at the helm of all of this? Was I the one who had the vision for this, trusting myself enough and believing in my ideas enough that I pushed myself hard to present those ideas to my clients? I was, damn it! Though I had some doubts along the way (okay, who am I kidding, I had a whole lot of doubts), I knew that if Shane and Camilla just trusted and believed in me that the end result would be one of utter beauty and pure satisfaction. And this room is exactly that!

Camilla and Shane are standing side by side. Camilla turns to me first.

"Hi!" My excitement is uncontrollable. My voice sounds more like a schoolgirl than a professional working woman. "So, what do you guys think?"

The expression on Shane's face, or better yet, lack of expression tells me nothing. My heart is racing. I detest trying to guess at what this type of benign expression connotes. I want so much to assume that he is just as delighted as I am, but I'm plainly aware that doing so could prove to be a big mistake. I need to know if he loves the look as much as I do or if he abhors it, in which case I am in immense trouble. Either way for the time being, I am in my own state of glory, stroking each cabinet door, caressing each crystal doorknob as I move throughout the space with such ease. For a brief moment, I am enraptured in such a state of visual ecstasy that I don't even care who is with me. Unfortunately the moment doesn't last long, because Shane clears his throat about to speak, reminding me exactly whose company I am in.

Am I seeing what I think I'm seeing? A slow but modest smile seems to be in the making on Shane's face.

"You're right, Katarina, I was sceptical. I was sceptical of you, of your ideas, and of your experience, or perhaps lack thereof. I won't lie about that, but you've proven me wrong. What you've done here, your vision for this space, is really incredible. This is exactly the timeless elegance that I was after. You've captured here precisely what I had in mind, and I would have never thought of this on my own. I think my wife will agree."

Well, what do you know?

The kitchen is beautiful beyond belief. Clive Christian definitely knows how to finish their millwork. Not a detail is amiss. This is the most elegant galley-style kitchen I have ever set my eyes on. What it might be lacking in size, it unquestionably makes up for in elegance, and I'll take that on any given day. One very ornate crystal pendant light fixture hanging down the centre of the galley will enhance this look luminously. I'd better make a note of that.

I want to see more. Pensively I walk back into the corridor. Kneeling down, I carefully pull up a corner of the construction paper so I can take a closer look at the hardwood floors. Fantastic! Stained in a dark ebony finish, each of the wide wood planks has soaked in the stain in its own unique way. No two boards appear to be the same. This is precisely the magnificence of old wooden floors. A sense of history can be captured in your very own home. It reflects a harmonious balance between the old and the new. Everything is faultless without being overly perfect.

Now that most of the hard finishes are nearly complete, we can begin working on the soft finishes. The decorating process can begin. This is the part of the project where as a designer, you can truly tell a story about your homeowners.

Camilla places her hand on the back of my arm. She smiles shyly at me. I offer the same back. She seems content. She appears to be peaceful in a melancholic sort of way, if that makes any sense. It does to me. I suppose I understand what she is feeling. Quite possibly it's because I am feeling the same way too.

"We're so pleased with how it's all coming together, Kat. We couldn't have asked for anything better. It takes a lot to impress Shane, and I know for a fact that he is thoroughly amazed."

I know that I should be elated with Camilla's praise and Shane's ultimate acceptance of me. And yet now that I seem to have it, where are the fireworks? In my mind, I was expecting fanfare in this moment while the jubilant sound of trumpets played in exaltation in the background, but now that it is here, they are nowhere to be heard. More importantly I don't feel any differently about myself now than I did when I walked in here only moments ago. Of course, I'm happy, content that they are pleased, but that's all. The looks on their faces are worth more than a thousand words of praise, and that is good enough for me.

I make my way through the rest of the apartment. Each room appears equally as remarkable. All these months of planning, concept generating, and reciting a common prayer for the end result to be what my homeowners were expecting has paid off.

Finding the appropriate furniture and accessories is next, so I know that I'm not totally in the clear just yet. Given my shopping options in this city, though, I'm positive that somewhere between ABC Carpet & Home, Ralph Lauren Home, Baker, and so many fabulous others, I will find just the right pieces that suit them and above all satisfy them.

~

One black tuxedo sofa and two crystal chandeliers later, we are off to an excellent start. Shane extends his good-byes to us, his BlackBerry never ceasing to beep and sing the entire time we are perusing our way through Ralph Lauren Home.

"I'll see you back in Toronto, Kat. Thank you for flying in. Darling, I'll see you later at the hotel." Shane's lips barely graze Camilla's cheek since she has turned her face slightly, purposefully avoiding contact. I try to pretend that I haven't noticed. Shane jumps into a cab he so effortlessly hails, while I simply stand there and watch it as it speeds away. Camilla never once glances in his direction.

"I don't want to keep you from your family, Katarina. How exhilarating your weekend sounds."

Camilla does appear to be genuinely happy for me. I had mentioned my plans to her earlier while making idle conversation as we took a brief pause from design chatter. I must admit that I am impatiently anticipating the weekend, with some mild trepidation since I'm unsure what it has in store for Jack, the kids, and me.

"Actually, you're not keeping me from anything," I try to reassure her. "Their flight isn't due to land for a couple of hours still. Want to walk for a bit? It is really lovely out here." The grey morning sky of earlier has parted way, with a beautiful, midday, golden sun shining bright enough that its rays warm us as we walk, helping to take the cold edge off the slight wind that still persists. We walk in silence, Camilla and I. I feel that the appropriate thing to say in this moment is nothing at all, so I don't. It's clear to me that just being by her side is comforting to her, so conversation seems scarcely appropriate. Now that I think about it, there truly isn't anything that needs to be said that can't wait anyways.

Camilla slips her arm through mine, never turning her head and merely keeping her eyes fixated at the sidewalk directly in front of her, her pace never changing speed. She continues to walk slowly and steadily, one immaculate Gucci boot in front of the next. She begins to speak, her voice ever so quiet.

"I have proof now, you know." She speaks so calmly that I'm uncertain if she is speaking to me at all or just thinking out loud. Either way, we continue to walk. I don't know how to respond to this, or even if I should.

"You do?" is all I manage to offer. Perhaps benign, but the only thing I deem appropriate to utter.

"I hired a private investigator. It didn't take long at all for him to report back to me with what I already suspected. I just wanted concrete proof."

"What are you going to do now that you have proof?"

"For now, I'll keep on doing what I've been doing. We'll finish the apartment here. Keep moving forward as though nothing has changed. For now, anyways." Camilla's voice trails off.

Although it might appear that Camilla is speaking aloud to me since I am standing right beside her, it sounds like more of a monologue. Her arm is still safely linked through mine. I place my free hand over it, protecting it gently from the wind, which has now picked up speed. We continue to walk. Words still don't seem essential, because even I know that there is nothing I can say right now that can make her pain go away.

Dear Diary,

My heart really does ache for this woman. It appears as though she has just become a shell of a person, with nothing inside of her left to give or wanting to take. It's as though she feels or loves nothing. And yet I have to believe it is only temporary, since I know for a fact that there is plenty inside of her. I've seen it. I've heard it. She has lots of substance within her—to say and to give. I know it because over the past few months, I've gotten to know her and have had intelligent conversations with her. Things will improve for her with time. I really do believe that. Camilla loves life too much to let this get the best of her forever. I hope she believes in herself just as much as I do. I know I have to continue to work with her and Shane as though nothing has changed, and I will because for me nothing has changed where this project is concerned. But for me personally, well, that's a different story. One very important thing has changed, and that is my knowledge and perception of reality. I suppose there is no good reason why bad things happen to good people. They just do, and I have to accept that. It's really quite that simple.

Later,
Me, Your Simple Girl.

~

"*Mommy!*" Ella's voice resonates through the gilded lobby of the Plaza hotel.

"*Ella!*" I sing back. My elation in seeing my little girl in this setting makes this instant a momentous one. As she runs into my arms, I embrace her in the tightest hug I can manage without crushing her diminutive figure. Oh how I love the scent of her freshly washed hair! As I kiss her head profusely, like my Italian grandmother used to do to me when I was a little girl, Ella bursts into a chorus of giggles. Each and every time I do this, I elicit the very same response from her. The rest of the gang hangs back a little, letting us savour this mommy-and-me moment. We are all aware that Ella is a force to be reckoned with when she is on the hunt for her mama, and this appears to be one of those times.

"See, stupie, I told you she would be here!" Nikki has obviously lost her patience with her little sister, who I can imagine has probably been pacing the grand hallways of the Plaw-w-w-za in a frenzied search for me.

If the Plaza patrons thought Eloise was a precocious child to deal with, and she is fictitious, they are unquestionably going to be in for a rather grand treat with Ella. The expression on Jack's face suggests that he lost his patience some time ago, like probably yesterday, right after I pulled out of the driveway in my bright yellow taxicab. Michael—sweet Michael, true to form, has been oblivious to all since his iPod earphones sit snugly in his warm ears. This is his way of sheltering himself from any childish lamenting on his sister's part. Jack and I exchange a warm kiss. I smile my "I'll-deal-with-her-now" smile, the one I'm certain makes him inhale an exhausted but ultimate sigh of relief. Jack is probably the most patient man I know, like, say, in the whole entire world. He can deal with economic downturns, clients' ear-piercing hollers regarding minor investment losses, even my dramatic tantrums (*on occasion, of course*)—all are handled with virtual grace, but for whatever reason unbeknownst to me, a shrieking six-year-old, *our* shrieking six-year-old daughter, can send him unswervingly over the edge in a millisecond.

"Has she been crying the whole time I've been gone?" I ask.

"Yup!" Jack, Michael, and Nikki answer in unison. Interesting how iPod boy heard me this time!

"I just missed you, Mommy, that's all. They were all so mean to me, especially Daddy!" Ella doesn't miss a beat to tell all, her big brown eyes staring intensely at me. In case I miss anything in her voice, her eyes do the explaining for her.

"I missed you too, honey, but see, now you're with Mommy again," I speak reassuringly.

Ella sees me all right; in fact, she is hanging on to me for dear life, and I am certain that she isn't letting go of me anytime soon. She remains glued to my side all the way to the elevators and the entire ride up to the nineteenth floor.

"Whoa! This place is pretty cool," Michael beams. His earphones are now dangling around his neck in New York City-ish fashion.

"*Cool*, Michael? The Plaza is not *cool*. The Plaza hotel is BE-A-U-TIFUL!" Nikki offers in her most grown-up voice. She looks to me for encouragement. I grin, but remain silent. Nikki smiles back but immediately shifts her attention back to the elevator doors, clearly anticipating their parting of ways. Her smug expression informs me that she is oh so proud of her visible maturity.

I chuckle. This is exactly what I was expecting and exactly what I had been missing—the glorious sounds of my children's voices bantering back and forth. Even the charm and elegance of *the Plaza* doesn't prevent my kids from just being themselves. And why should it? Where is it written that charm and elegance should be reserved for a particular type or class of person? Charm, elegance, grace—it's all there for any one of us to share in if we are at all inclined to. Anyone of us who is interested in experiencing the finer things in life can and should if we want to. It is available for all of us whenever and however we want it waiting when we're ready to accept it into our lives. It appears as though my family is all set now.

I follow Nikki as she walks across the suite that will be ours to share and enjoy for the next forty-eight hours. I can see that she is taking it all in. She is absorbing the old-world ambience that surrounds us. Heavily gilded ornate night tables with marble tops made me awestruck when I first set my eyes on them. To an eight-year-old, their beauty must be immeasurably indescribable.

The en suite bathroom is a classically charismatic space. It is decorated with a mosaic marble floor and floral inlay, while the white marble mosaic shower walls and the overall aesthetic is irrevocably breathtaking. Serious brass plumbing fixtures and door handles suggest old-school prosperity and power to any adult. To Nikki, they speak of the fanciest surroundings she has ever laid her eyes on. She feels like a princess in a palace. She runs her hands across every surface she passes, every finish and every fluffy white towel in sight.

"Mommy, this is so-o-o prett-i-ful." Nikki enunciates every letter as she speaks, never taking her eyes off all that she is visually absorbing. "Do you get to look at these pretty things every time you come to New York?" Nikki asks.

I chuckle. "Not all the time, honey. And not every hotel in the city is this fancy. Daddy and I just wanted you to see where Eloise lived and let you live like she did for a couple of days. But I want you to remember, Nikki, Eloise is just a book and movie character, she was made up in someone's mind. Do you understand that?"

"But do people really live here, Mommy?"

"Yes, some do. They have private apartments in the Plaza that people really live in."

"Wow, Mommy, they must be really rich!" It is hard not to smile at Nikki's bewilderment with this hotel. But I am curious as to what her definition of "rich" is.

I bend down so as to make eye contact with her. I don't want my words to come across as a lecture, but I do want her to comprehend what I am about to say as best she can. "Nikki, what do you think 'rich' means?" I ask.

This seems like an easy question to her, not understanding yet the full intent of my probing. "Having lots and lots of money to buy anything you want and live in a palace like this." Nikki is particularly proud of her answer.

"Well, I suppose that is one way of looking at it." I add, "But there's so much more to being rich or wealthy. It isn't just about money, you know. 'Rich' is also about being healthy and being happy inside of yourself. It's about having a family and having friends that you can share things with. It's about being able to help other people or give to them the things they may not have. Not just stuff or material goods, but things from our minds—maybe advice, ideas, give them emotional support when people are sad and scared or even unsure about something. It's about sharing in fun times with the people who mean the most to us. Like going to the movies, taking a walk in the park, or even taking your family to a beautiful place for a few days to have fun together."

"Or having ice cream with Maddie?"

"Yes, especially having ice cream with Maddie." I laugh. "You can have all the money in the world, but if you're lonely or sick or don't have any friends to have ice cream with, what good is it to you then?"

Nikki thinks about this for a moment before responding. "Not so good, I guess."

"No, it's not so good, angel. So you see then, Nikki, Daddy and I brought you here to enjoy this place and see Eloise's home. Even though we may not be able to live here, we sure are lucky enough to visit. But more than that, Nikki, our family is rich in so many other different ways that have nothing to do with money. Do you understand?" I hope she does, and I hope that this is a good enough explanation for her, for the time being at least.

Nikki puts her arms around my neck. "I understand, Mommy. Thank you for bringing us all here. This hotel is really, really pretty, but we're even richer because we can all go home together after we leave here."

Mission accomplished! This is going to be a fantastic New York City weekend!

~

Tea with Eloise is a huge success! How could it not be when you're a rambunctious little girl in a fabulous hotel playing dress up with an equally precocious fictitious character? Nikki and Ella are living out a dream any little girly girl can only dream of. I'm not sure who is having more fun, them or me just watching them. Just as quickly as dresses and shoes are put on their dolls, they are quickly stripped down again with such enthusiasm, only to don completely new and interesting attire. The giggles are endless—a far cry from the quiet of my walk with Camilla. In an odd way, I am feeling somewhat guilty about having such juvenile fun with my daughters when I am well aware that my newfound friend is going through such emotional pain.

Walking back through the hotel corridors and up the smooth, flowing escalator, the looks on the girls' faces say it all. With their dolls properly coiffed and securely in hand, they now have plenty more Kodak moments for the pages of their scrapbooks. These are the photos that will secure these memories for a lifetime.

~

Later that night, with the five of us back together again, we celebrate our evening in the city that never sleeps with a festive dinner back at the Plaza.

"Mom, you should have been on that subway with us. It was so cool, wasn't it, Dad?"

"It sure was, Mikey." Jack smirks at Michael's retelling of the day's events.

"There were all these people and so many different trains on all these different tracks. It was like a maze. But Dad figured it all out."

Cool is also the buzz word Michael uses to describe the hockey game he and Jack went to, their walk through Little Italy, and well, just about everything else they did today. And I have to say that it is so "cool" for me to see Michael so joyfully engaged.

"So, Michael," I ask, "was this trip more fun than you thought it was going to be?"

"Oh yeah, Mom! Way more fun!" Michael's enthusiasm is electric. "New York City is such a cool place! Dad and I saw so many cool buildings while we were out walking today."

I bet they did. "Think you might want to come back again one day?" I ask, deliberately, since I think I already know exactly what his answer is going to be.

And with confirmation that he will be returning to the Big Apple one day soon, by ten o'clock that night in a *cool* city that apparently never sleeps, Jack and I tucked our tired kids into bed one by one. We feel reassured that this trip, our first trip to New York City with our kids, is only the beginning of more *cool* trips to come.

Dear Diary,

What a fantastic end to a trip that I wasn't so sure of. Goes to show you that as much as you might think you can predict how something is going to end or how the events of something will play out, you in fact have no idea what the end result is going to be. I was so worried about Shane and what his reaction to the apartment was going to be. And as much I was hoping he was going to be impressed, I could have never expected that he was going to be as impressed as he was about me and my work. I guess the problem is that often we think we know how something is going to turn out based on past experiences or events, but the truth is every situation takes on a time and momentum all of its own. And as far as the kids and Jack are concerned, well, where do I even begin? My kids taught me something today, something undeniably valuable about just being present and just spending time with your family, just because. Instead of me teaching them something, it looks like they taught me something invaluable. It goes to show you that you're never too old to learn. It looks like this trip was incredibly significant after all.

Later,
Me, Your Simple Girl

Chapter Thirty-One

Back at home and back to routine. Though routine can frequently be thought of as being mundane and boring, from time to time the very presence of it in my life can also be enormously comforting. Alessia has texted me a bigillion times since my return. While Jack and the kids and I were away in New York City, she was busy setting up appointments with the realtor for the two of us to view several houses upon my return. I'm back now, in body and in mind, and she being the relentless girl she is isn't about to waste any more precious time.

"Why don't I just meet you at the house, Less?" I ask her on the Tuesday morning after my return. Alessia is going on about something, what I'm not completely sure of, since I'm only half-listening. I have my eyes pinned onto vivre.com sourcing some wonderful and unique accessories for Camilla's place.

"Sorry, what were you saying, Lessi? Louis is scratching at the door; he needs to go out." I'm not telling a fib—he really is.

"Are you not sick and tired of that pooch of yours yet?"

"Sick of him?" I repeat into the receiver as I bend over to gently nudge Louis out the door. *This toilet-training thing isn't going so bad after all.* "I adore him, most of the time. With the exception, of course, of when I caught him chewing my new Stuart Weitzman black pumps. You know the ones. I think you were with me when

I bought them," I add, finding some humour in it now—after the fact, but definitely not at the time.

"Yes, I remember exactly which ones! Good thing it wasn't a Louboutin."

"I don't own any Louboutin's, Less, that's you!" I say jokingly.

"Yeah, right, well, if you trade in your pup, you can get yourself a pair with all that money you'll get back," Alessia states—I think in jest, though I'm not entirely sure.

Louis is once again scratching at the door, only this time to come back inside. He has finished his doggy business and is all set to join me back in my office.

"Wait a minute, Less. *Good boy, Louis, you pee-peed! Good boy!*" I hold out a treat for him to take.

"Kat, what the hell has come over you? You're praising a freakin' dog for taking a whiz! P-L-E-E-A-S-E!"

I giggle quietly to myself. I am now cradling Louis in my arms like I used to do with the kids when they were babies. Good thing Alessia can't see me, or she would really think I have lost all sense of sanity.

"It's called positive reinforcement, Alessia. This way he knows that when he pees outside and not on the carpet that he'll get a reward."

"I just don't understand you anymore, Kat. I never thought I would see the day when you would get a dog and *enjoy it!*"

"Actually, Less, Louis is a ton of work, I'll admit it, but he brings so much love and joy to our family. I would have never believed it myself if I wasn't living it. You really should try it once you find a place."

"Ahh, me … no, thanks, I'll pass."

"Suit yourself, but you don't know what you're missing."

"Right. So back to my house. There's this one I really want you to see. The pictures look pretty good. Does tomorrow at noon work for you?"

"Even if it doesn't, I will make it work. Send me the directions, and I'll meet you there."

~

By the end of the weekend, Alessia has submitted an offer to purchase a fabulous row townhouse, and the offer has been accepted by the vendors. I am so happy for her. The house does need a bit of work—aesthetic work mostly—but that is nothing Alessia and I can't handle, with the assistance of a few contractors and Cass. Fortunately (for Alessia) he is still in the picture. And though he is an attorney by day, Mr. Wonderful likes to tinker with his power tools by night. He has offered to help Alessia bring the house up to her standards, though she is resisting his offers. I tell her to stop being such a hard-ass; she can be so stubborn sometimes, which makes Cass and me totally nuts. I give the guy credit, he is very patient with Alessia, more patient than I am being with her these days. And to make matters better, the guy is not only smart, smooth, and handy, but totally gorgeous and absolutely head-over-heels mad over Miss I-Am-Going-to-Shield-Myself. I can hardly understand his patience with her sometimes. Whether she wants to hear it or not (and I know she doesn't), I remind her now on a regular basis that if she doesn't let her guard down soon, just a little bit, she might very well lose a great guy, and then she'll be sorry.

~

"I want a pink house. No, make that a pink palace!" Alessia announces at dinner on Sunday night. We invited her to join us in a celebratory dinner in her honour, now that she too is becoming a homeowner. Jack looks at her with his are-you-for-real? look. The one typically reserved for me when I hurl out one-liners that catch him totally off guard. Believe me, I have seen this look enough times to know it when it's being cast, only this time I'm glad it isn't directed at me for a change.

"Jack, why are you looking at me like that?" Alessia asks, knowing full well why he is looking at her the way he is. Evidently she's become familiar with Jack's expressive features too.

"A *pink palace?* Alessia, what the hell is that?" Jack questions honestly.

It is my time to interject before this conversation takes an immediate turn downhill. "We'll infuse the house with various elements of pinks and fuchsia, even magenta accents, to show a flirty and feminine side without it being over-the-top girly." *That should be enough to convince her. Shit, even I'm sold.*

"Yes! That's exactly what I want. But I do want it over-the-top, Kat. It's my house, and I can have over-the-top if I want to. I'm so-o-o excited! I can't wait until I take possession of it. I can't wait to spend lots of time with you working on it," Alessia announces.

"Easy there, sister. How much time are you talking about exactly?" Jack quickly asks.

Oh boy, leave it to Jack and Alessia to get into it about who is going to monopolize my time and when. If I didn't know any better, I would say that Jack is a little envious of our relationship, but who could blame him? Put two ultra-feminine women best friends together, and things can spin out of control very rapidly.

Come to think of it, I can't wait to get started either!

Dear Diary,
Thank you for bringing us together so many years ago. I can tell she is really happy about her new place, and I want to be the one to help her make it the home she wants it to be. Good friends ... you know the ones, the ones who last forever, the ones that last a lifetime ... well, they are hard to come by. I know that some people are never touched by anyone like this their entire lives. I'm so lucky to have been, and I never want to lose that with her. So she's a bit crazy at times, but then again, so am I. Our craziness never hurt anyone. We just have innocent fun with it. If a pink palace is what she wants, then a pink palace is what she is going to get!

Later,
Moi, Your Simple Girl

~

Winter is at long last giving way to spring, and Alessia's house is evolving into the pink palace that she requested. She has been the rightful owner now for five weeks. While not too many structural changes have been necessary, between the hired contractors and Mr. Wonderful, lots of aesthetic improvements are well underway. Worn-out carpeting has been removed and replaced with hardwood floors, walls have been stripped of lifeless colours only to be replaced with a fresh, bright palette of energy, and luminous bathroom tiles have been installed in the powder room, creating a bedazzling and alluring private space.

While the spring air still has a slight chill to it, a brand-new, glorious season is unmistakably upon us. The brightness of the sky persisting overhead, in combination with vibrant and fresh colours springing up all around us outdoors, serves to heighten the pops of colours we are infusing inside of Alessia's house. What a perfect home Alessia has become the proud owner of. Perfect for her, that is.

"Oh, come on, Less, even you must admit that he's fabulous. Seriously, what more can the guy do to try and win you over?" I propose on one of our now frequent sourcing excursions. I'm hoping that the newfound vigour of the season will give way to renewed hope and faith restored within Alessia's heart. I leave it alone for the time being and say no more. I make-believe to be more interested in the sofa I'm examining as I wait for her to respond.

"Well, we have been spending a lot of time together these days. Who knows? Maybe he is the one," she says with some trepidation in her voice.

Well, that's a switch! She shrugs her Burberry-clad shoulders. "I don't know. He's been so helpful with the house, and every time I mention hiring someone else to do something, he insists that he wants to do it."

"So, what's the problem with that?"

Alessia hesitates before answering. "Maybe I'm scared, Kat."

"Of what?"

"I don't know, falling too hard, getting hurt all over again. Everything about this relationship is just going too perfect right now. And you and I both know that nothing this good can last forever."

I turn to face Alessia. "What? What are you talking about?"

"I'm scared that he might leave me after I've completely fallen for him. That once we get too comfortable, he'll decide I'm too bossy or too pushy, too fat or work too much."

Alessia seems on the verge of tears. She blinks, maintaining her focus away from me.

"Less ... hey, look at me," I say, motherly. "That was then; this is now. Marcello is not the same person Cass is. You're not the same person anymore either. You can't be so afraid to love again. Okay, be cautious, I agree with that, but don't shut Cass out. He is trying really hard to be your friend, more than your friend. Don't close your heart off to him, because you'll never know what could be if you don't try."

Alessia doesn't say anything. She continues looking away, then down, and then finally directly at me. Easing her hands free from mine— I had taken hold of them in case she thought about bolting—she wipes her eyes. I pretend to not notice, though we both know that I have. The tears are real. Authentic tears of confusion—wanting to open her heart but so fearful of the unknown. I get this, plain and simple.

Alessia is quick to change the topic, something she does when the conversation gets a little too intense for her and she isn't ready to let the floodgates open up entirely. Wiping her eyes and clearing her throat, she gets all businesslike on me again. "So, this sofa you've been busy staring at, what do you think of it?"

I take her lead. For now, it is best to leave well enough alone. "Look at it, Less. I mean, it's gorgeous! It's so-o-o you! The tufting, the white velvet, it's so-o-o girly. We can throw some pink pillows on it for you, baby pink mixed with fuchsia or even violet or black velvet, spectacular in your living room. *What do you think?*" I ask in excitement.

She is coming around. A soft pinky glow is beginning to appear on her face again. The same glow I have become used to seeing when Alessia is feeling blissful about something.

"It is nice," Alessia says as she runs her hand across the rolled arm of the sofa.

"Nice?" I squeal, questioning her choice of words. "It's fantastic! It's totally you, my diva girlfriend, and you know it!"

Alessia throws herself down, sinking immediately into the soft billowy fabric. She lets her hands caress the fabric on either side of her. "Who am I kidding? It's fucking gorgeous!" Alessia exclaims. She is back! Thank goodness!

I clap my hands with juvenile exuberance. "Yeah, you've come to life again!"

"I want it. Let's buy it!" Alessia pats the cushion as if to say, "The deal is done."

I sit down beside her, wanting to make sure she is really okay, not just spewing words to get me off her case. I look directly into her eyes. "Less, you're doing great. Time will heal your heart. You and I both know it will."

She maintains her gaze at me too. Smirking, she shouts out, "Let's keep shopping!"

And so we do. We browse and shop for the remainder of the afternoon. Velvet square cushions in peony pink are our first purchase for the new sofa—a perfect pairing. I can already picture Alessia in her coral Juicy Couture velvet jogging suit stretched out watching *Sex and the City* reruns, or according to her, reviewing legal briefs. Either way, it is a terrific start to dressing her living room and her new beginning.

My eyes move onward to a round, glass bevelled coffee table with a brass, twig-like base. Not a piece I would have initially considered for the space, but seeing it here now, I can't take my eyes off of it. Obviously neither can Alessia, because it too becomes one of her purchases on this day.

Hours and many credit card charges later, Alessia and I plunk ourselves down in her car, tired but exhilarated with all that we have accomplished on our shopping extravaganza. Turning to face me, Alessia seems undisturbed, the first time in a very long time. "I know I don't say it often, Kat, but thanks."

"For what?" I question.

"Today. Coming with me to look at all of this stuff ..."

"Buying," I correct, jovially.

She laughs. "You're right, buying all of this stuff. Being my friend, trying to help me feel better when all I really want to do is run and hide and cry. Thanks for leaving the kids with Jack and spending so much time with me when I know that they want your attention too. I guess I just want to say thanks for being in my life."

I am thoroughly touched by her gentle words.

"You're so very welcome," I reply. "And besides, don't thank me too much just yet—you haven't seen my invoice!" I add playfully.

She gives me a mild shove on my arm. And with that, we both break into our typical schoolgirl laughter, even though at our age, we are anything but that.

And so we drive off, together, with Alessia quite literally in the driver's seat. Laughing and singing; talking about the great pieces we purchased today and how we are going to position it all into her house. As soon as Alessia's car comes to a screeching halt outside of my house, my motherly instincts kick right back in.

"You're nuts!" I shout, half-laughing, half-serious. "This is a family neighbourhood. You can't drive like that in the burbs!"

"Gosh, you're right! Sorry, Kat, but it sure felt good!"

"You're crazy!"

"But fun—oh my gosh—what's he doing here?"

"Who?" I ask.

"That car, in your driveway, that's Cass's car."

I look over. "Oh." I shrug curiously, my brows raised. I have no idea why Cass would be at my house. I didn't even know that Cass was familiar with where I lived. It's not as though Alessia brings him by when she comes to visit, opting to keep their relationship more at arm's length. I must admit my curiosity is piqued now.

"Well, there's only one way to find out, isn't there?" I gesture as I jump out of the car.

I aim for the front door quickly, while Alessia takes her sweet time, evidently not sure what to make of this. Not that I can blame her. It's not as though Cass and Jack are the best of friends or anything like that. Sure, they've met a couple of times over at Alessia's new house, but it's not as if they have formed a tight friendship in that time—like women do. We're completely different. We can meet one minute and be exchanging telephone numbers and e-mail addresses the next. Say we'll get together for coffee and actually do it, but guys, they just aren't like that.

"Mommy! Auntie Lessia!" Ella, our solo welcoming committee, has arrived at the front entrance to greet us.

"Hi, sweet pea! Where's Daddy?" I ask, rather interested at this point since there is no sign of either Jack or Cass anywhere in the background.

Ella doesn't get a chance to answer since I immediately hear the back door closing and the sound of hearty laughter making its way through the house. Both men stand at the kitchen door, partially empty wine glasses in hand. They look just as surprised to see us as we do to see them.

"Hey there, shoppers, you're home?" Jack rings out.

"Hi, yourself." I look past Jack and give a faint wave. "Hi, Cass, nice to see you too." I smile.

"Cass, what are you doing here?" Leave it to Alessia to choose not to use her verbal filter and cut straight to the chase.

Cass doesn't get an opportunity to answer since Jack takes it upon himself to answer for him.

"Less, my doing completely. I called Cass and asked him if he could come over and give me a hand to hang the new TV we bought for the basement. Since I was going to be home all day anyways, I figured it would be a good day to do some stuff around here. We just finished a little while ago. I figured you would be getting home around dinnertime, so I invited Cass to stay and have dinner with us. I hope that's okay."

I glance at Alessia, hoping beyond hope that she is in fact pleased with Jack's invitation. I for one most certainly am.

"The more the merrier," I announce playfully.

"I don't mind at all, Jack. In fact, that was really kind of you," Alessia adds. And her ear-to-ear smile tells me she is telling the honest-to-goodness truth.

And so, Jack and I and our kids, Alessia and Mr. Wonderful, and Louis the dog, all sit down to a Saturday evening dinner in the suburbs. Though it isn't accompanied with French champagne or Russian caviar, it is complete with home-cooked food, first-class friends, the sounds of children's laughter, and the playful barking of a spoiled, five-pound pooch. It is the utmost enchantment this designer girl could ask for.

Dear Diary,

What a fantastic end to a fantastic day! I mean, how lucky can I be to have shared this day with my best friend and the night with all the people who I care about? Sure, Alessia and I don't always see eye to eye on things, and at times we argue over trivial issues, but who else can you really do that with one minute and then forget all about it the next? I know Alessia's been through a lot in the past year, and I know that she has been on an emotional roller-coaster ride, but I'm convinced that with time, her heart will mend. And it will take a lot of time probably. I'm not foolish enough to think that it will happen right away, but that's okay 'cause there's no time limit to this stuff, is there? And besides, if friends don't stick by friends during the hard times, how can we learn to appreciate the good times? See, just like today, it was a bit of both, and our friendship is that much better for it! I know we can endure anything—we already have.

Later,
Me, Your Simple Girl

Chapter Thirty-Two

The days and weeks are flying by so quickly. In part because my daytime hours seem to be filled with the kids, their school projects, and the common line of, "Oops, Mommy, I forgot my lunch; could you bring it please?" This happens to be code for, "Mommy, I just wanted to know that you were home and close by, just because." Did I mention that in between all of this, I am supposed to be working? *Damn that work thing again. It does seem to get in the way some days.*

Louis is another story. Louis is a full-time job all by himself. He's in and then he's out, in, out, in and out. *Fucking dog!* But I love him to pieces and wouldn't trade him in for the world—or even a real Louis Vuitton handbag.

Connor and Jonathan have called with what I deem to be fabulous news. Though their pain is still very real and very present, they are going to make another attempt at bringing a baby home. Could I go over and discuss the nursery with them again? Wild horses couldn't keep me away!

As for Camilla and Shane, their Park Avenue apartment looks magnificent. One more trip over, and I think my work there might actually be finished, once and for all.

Alessia … well, let's just say that Alessia provides me with almost hourly updates on the progress that she and Cass are making. She still wants to take things slowly, she tells me, but for the time being, she is letting Cass spoil her with his affection. Now that is music to my ears.

"I think he could very well be the one," she offers.

Like I didn't already know that was coming.

As for her house, it is at last her haven. The white and gold Bisazza mosaic tiled powder room is a hidden gem. I'm so glad I discovered it!

~

"Mommy, it looks just like the bathroom at the Plaza!" Nikki burst out one beautiful Saturday morning while we are spending some time at Alessia's home putting the finishing touches on her now-lived-in space. Nikki is so proud of herself. Alessia explodes into laughter at Nikki's innocent remark.

Sweeping Nikki up into her arms, she adds, "You really are your mother's daughter, aren't you?" And with that she plants an affectionate kiss on Nikki's forehead. Nikki mirrors Alessia's laughter.

We continue to sip our morning coffee at Alessia's kitchen table. The white marble top is a perfect juxtaposition to Alessia's industrial-meets-traditional kitchen design. Now if only I could teach her how to cook!

I can't take all of the credit here actually since most of it is compliments of the previous owners, who had already undertaken an enormous kitchen renovation complete with stainless steel appliances, Carrara marble countertops, and floating stainless steel shelving for glassware. The circa 1920's crystal chandelier we found on 1stdibs.com sparkles like an enormous diamond ring. It dangles over the kitchen table demanding attention. From where we are sitting we can see Ella as she lies sprawled across the turquoise and chocolate woven wool carpet in the living room. Not pink, but just as tremendous, covering the walnut floors superbly and lying safely beneath the sofa and coffee table we purchased. The

Philippe Starck end tables complete the whimsical look we were after, capturing both the elegant and whimsical sides of Alessia.

The drapery, oh the drapery, is impressive. Extra-long full panels of pleated snow-white velvet hook across polished silver rods. To this day, I still can't believe we were able to score such a find, but we did and the result is more alluring than I could even have imagined. This home is a blissful heaven on earth for any girly girl, and no one is more worthy of this little piece of divinity in their life than my BFF.

"Auntie Lessi, do you think Cass will like all these pink pillows?" Ella questions, her nose scrunched up in wonderment, all the while transfixed on the dolly she is changing for the fifth time this morning.

"Well, sweetie, I'm not sure, but this is my house, so I guess if he wants to come and see me, he'll have to be okay with it." Alessia's speech sounds well thought out to me. I wonder who she is trying to convince more, Ella or herself.

Nikki and I cast each other a reassuring look. I for one am convinced that Alessia longs for nothing more than for Cass to make their relationship more permanent. Her apprehension in surrendering her heart to him is what is holding this relationship back from moving to the next level. I think she would gladly give up her pink palace to accommodate her macho man. Okay, maybe not surrender entirely, but at the very least, I believe she would be willing to make some allowances, and for Alessia that is huge. Truth is, I have firsthand information that Cass is completely smitten with Alessia. No major reno will be necessary in this department. If only she would relax a little more and let her guard ease up, she might actually begin to believe it herself. I think it's only a matter of time before this happens. For now, Cass continues to romance her slowly.

~

Though visiting Alessia in her new home gives me the notion of having spent a glorious period of time in a magnificent adult dollhouse, nothing is better than the feeling of coming back to my very own home.

I utter very few words during my evening dinner preparations tonight, going about them in much the same way as I usually do. Vegetables are being chopped, steaks are marinating, and an artisanal green salad is waiting to be tossed. The grey winter skies that have lingered over our heads the past few months have left us and are now but a faint, distant memory. They have made way for longer sun-drenched days and warmer evening nights.

Jack stands close by observing me, *the mother species*, in my natural habitat, according to Ella. Maybe she's right. Maybe this is my natural habitat. Pouring two glasses of Shiraz, Jack offers one to me. "To us, and to our family."

Jack is a man of few words, but always seems to choose the right ones at the appropriate time. We clink glasses. Taking a sip, the liquid soothes my throat as it goes down, sending a shiver throughout my tired body. I continue what I am doing; I chop, slice, and wipe as I go along. Maybe I'll make some chocolate soufflé for dessert. The kids always get a kick out of inspecting it so fluffy and light when first pulled from the hot oven. It never ceases to amaze me the awe that fills them at the first glimpse of it once done, as if I have created something so truly incredible.

"How do you do that, Mommy?" It never fails. One of them always asks this question.

For now, I watch as they toss a ball back and forth to each other in the backyard. Michael leads the group, instructing them on who should stand where.

"There."

"No, stop!"

"That's good."

Nikki flinches every time the ball comes near her. "You're doing that on purpose, Michael. Stop it! Don't hurt me!"

Ella. Oh, Ella! Her jacket is off again as she rolls around on the grass.

"Get up, Ella! You're going to get dirty! Mommy's going to be really mad if you stain your clothes!" Nikki shouts as the older and wiser sister.

And Louis? Well, Louis stands in the midst of it all, barking his newfound big-boy bark. *Now what's he doing? Silly dog!* He is running back and forth, back and forth, back and forth. Ahh … the thrill of the chase! His stubby little tail wags all the while. This must be what poochie paradise feels like. He appears to be elated over his first spring in his new home, and so are the rest of us, I might add.

For now, Camilla and Shane's Manhattan pied-à-terre is a fait accompli. It was definitely worth all the work, all the sleepless nights wondering if I could really live up to their expectations of a designer. I only wish the end product could have made their lives happier, but I don't believe that it has.

While my first New York City job might not have been the "perfect" job the way I had envisioned it was going to be, with happily ever after, it sure did come neatly packaged with its fair share of excitement and challenges.

And so with one client relationship less than ideal, another is hanging onto a glimmer of newfound light. Maybe that old cliché is right. Just because one door closes, that doesn't mean plenty more windows won't open up. I truly believe that I will have the chance one day to bring to life a special nursery for a very special baby. I'm so thankful Connor and Jonathan have decided to hang onto their dream and firmly believe that it will come true.

"What are you thinking about?" Jack interrupts my daydreaming. "Going online to Bergdorf's and getting those new summer sandals you've been eyeing?"

I laugh. Many a night Jack catches me online—"just browsing"—rather than working, though each and every time I claim emphatically that that is what I am doing. Everyone needs a little break now and again, don't they?

"No, don't think so, not tonight anyways, the shoes can wait," I say, never taking my eyes off what I am privy to outside in my very own backyard.

Jack seems surprised. He changes the subject. "You want to do something special tonight, to celebrate the completion of that big project?"

I turn to face Jack, and then look back to the window again, shaking my head. He doesn't get it. It's not his fault. He can't get it; he's not a mom.

"I already am doing something special tonight."

Dear Diary,

The truth is, I have made a difference in someone's life. Actually three little someones, to be exact. Three little someones who call out, "Mama, Mommy, Mom" (even "Mother," when they're really mad at me for something I've apparently done). So, baking cupcakes for yet another birthday party may not be so glamorous. Field trips to an Indian aboriginal festival while riding on a yellow school bus sans shocks and listening to twenty-five first graders singing "The Wheels on the Bus" for the umpteenth time isn't nearly as alluring as lunching at BG with the ladies and drinking vodka martinis, nor is spending weekends driving to yet another hotel with the hockey team in below-twenty-degree weather. Even worse, though, might be cheesy Niagara Falls hotel rooms (they really could use a face-lift; I should leave my business card the next time I'm there) with hundreds of screaming tiny dancers. There is something to be said about attempting to apply false eyelashes on squirmy six- and eight-year-olds at six o'clock in the morning while any type of caffeine beverage has yet to penetrate my veins. This is most certainly a far cry from selecting fabrics in silence at a soothing Pierre Frey showroom. But the truth is, this is my life, a real life, and it's not very glamorous most of the time. Believe me, I periodically wonder what the hell I am doing! But you know what? I do know what I am doing, and I wouldn't trade it in for the world. Who knows? Maybe one day I'll go back to Manhattan a little more frequently, and maybe Jack and the kids will come too, maybe, just maybe ...

Later,
Me, Your Simple Girl

The End ... for now ...